EARLY REVIEWS

"An astonishing reimagining of the life of Eugene Marais, *The Farther Shore* is as intellectually daring as it is lushly immersive. Seth Fleisher renders history with a decadent richness—each page steeped in atmosphere, obsession, and unease—while excavating the dangerous fictions of race and the seductive machinery of rising fascism. What emerges is not just a portrait of a man, but a mirror held up to our own moment: a world still grappling with identity as both inheritance and invention."

—Jamie Ford, NYT bestselling author of *Hotel on the Corner of Bitter and Sweet*

"In a rich and visceral style akin to Abraham Verghese's *Cutting for Stone*, this novel asks profound questions about memory and instinct in a cross-continental tale of father and son that is deeply moving and unforgettable. Set mostly in South Africa in the early decades of the 1900s—with that new nation recently ravaged by British concentration camps and twisting toward the ugliest of human beliefs—*The Farther Shore* tells of Eugene Marais, a real-life doctor and lawyer whose passion was furthering Darwin's work, and his son, Charles, whom Eugene abandoned after his beloved wife died in childbirth. Charles teaches ancient Buddhist texts at Harvard in the 1930s, when the university is embracing Nazi fascism and researching a mode of social control based on the misuse of Eugene's studies."

—Janet Benton, author of *Lilli de Jong*

I08781 95

"In this achingly relevant debut novel, Seth Fleisher achieves great magic by embodying continents and centuries. Recalling aspects of *The English Patient* and *A Gentleman in Moscow*, this rich exploration introduces a cast of fascinating, complex mortals whose voices are accurate not just to history but to the longings of their flawed hearts."

—Edie Meidav, author of *Dogs of Cuba* and *Crawl Space*

The Farther Shore

The Farther Shore

BY

Seth Fleisher

GREEN CITY
BOOKS

This is a work of fiction. While certain characters, places, and events are based on or inspired by historical figures and real occurrences, the narrative, dialogue, interior lives, and many details are products of the author's imagination and should not be taken as historically accurate. Any resemblance to actual living persons, other than the historical figures who inform the work, is coincidental and unintended.

Library of Congress cataloging data has been applied for.

ISBN 9781963101249

First edition 2026
Printed in the United States of America
Book design by Isaac Peterson

Green City Books
Bend, Oregon
Distributed by Publishers Group West
www.greencitybooks.com

GREEN CITY BOOKS

10 9 8 7 6 5 4 3 2 1

For Terri and Richard,
who taught me to write, and to read,
and to raise a child.

"Let go of the past, let go of the future, let go of the present and cross over to the farther shore . . ."

—Dhammapada

Preface

One morning in 1936, a vivid bursting morning on a farm eighteen miles west of Pretoria, South Africa, I was awakened by a flock of weaver birds and the shrill report of a gun.

Maybe I'd always known that this piece of my story would end with the pull of a trigger. How, though, in the aftermath, could I not think of other futures—worlds where I'd run seconds faster, where I hadn't paused at the edge of the field, disoriented by the light? *What if?*

If I had started a moment sooner, if I hadn't stopped to catch my breath, I might have salvaged a life. I might have saved my father.

September 1935, Cambridge, Massachusetts

What Charles will remember of the day's early moments is the blur of feet and legs, the mechanical flow of bodies along the Yard's interlacing pathways, from one brick-red building to the next. Harvard's every-morning march. After five years here, he still envies the ease with which these young men—these Americans—bend straight into their futures.

Charles's shoes tick-tock against the pavement. From the gate at Massachusetts Avenue, he takes the footpath that skirts Wigglesworth, then edges alongside Widener Library and Emerson Hall toward the towering spire of Memorial Church. In his pocket is an invitation from the university's president, James Bryant Conant.

The day thrums with possibility. It's a fine September morning, polished and fresh. Thin-trunked trees rise up on all sides, each papery leaf a tiny explosion of color. Charles has the urge to absorb all of it: the filmy sun and the blizzard of mourning doves, red and blue bicycles whizzing past, legions of coveralled gardeners, swatches of lawn watered so munificently that the grass springs up like fur, the fleeting earthy scent of azaleas, a young couple's discreet kiss. Memorial Fence, a massive structure of brick and ironwork, rings the entire Yard, and today Charles feels as if he is being held in the arms of a giant. As if Harvard itself has become his personal guardian.

Just outside the fence, poverty runs as deep as the Atlantic. Every day he exits the Yard—in his passable suit, with his modest Harvard salary—to find barefoot children begging for bread, sun-scorched men in ragged trousers queuing for a bowl of soup, the sick languishing outside cramped hospitals. Sometimes, late at night, he tries to imagine the collective pain of change and loss and death—of every individual heartbreak—not only in Cambridge or even the United States, but across the planet, and he wonders how the world can contain so much suffering.

As he strides through Harvard Yard, though, such thoughts are subsumed by this brilliant day. His loneliness dissipates in the crowd. For forty years, he's been floating, rootless. He grew up without parents or siblings, tended only by an aunt who has faded from his life. He's had friendships, of course, a handful of romances, but none strong enough to keep him from drifting across continents: from Africa to Europe to North America. Yet, here is the sun warming his face. The breeze ruffles his coat. It's taken four decades and three continents to realize that he can will himself content. He is an assistant professor at Harvard, tenure at last on the near horizon. All his life he's waited for this. A chance to plant roots, to establish himself permanently in a place he can call home.

"Marais, don't tell me you've returned for another year of torture." Frank Williams charges over the grass, a grin smeared across his pale face. He shakes Charles's hand enthusiastically and hikes his trousers back above his hips. Williams is his closest friend on faculty, a fellow member of the Indic Philology Department.

"As they say in Afrikaans," Charles replies, "'*Die môrestond het goud in die mond.*'"

"Translation, please?"

Charles hasn't thought of this saying in years. "The morning has gold in the mouth. A bit like your early bird who catches worms, I suppose."

Williams nudges his spectacles back over his nose. "Well, aren't we jolly and will o' the wisp today?"

"Look at this place. Who would ever want to leave?"

"I don't know what's got into you," Williams says, "but I like it. Don't take this wrong, but you've always struck me as a sort of . . . stray."

Charles turns the word silently on his tongue. *A stray*. Is that how they think of him?

Williams proudly traces his academic lineage through a long line of Orientalists who refused to let the perfected, imagined India of classical texts become fouled by reality. The trick, Williams has suggested, is never to travel to the Indian subcontinent, never taste Indian food, and never interact with an actual person of Indian descent. A few years ago, Williams decoded a short esoteric passage in the Rig Veda, an acrostic whose initial characters spell the equivalent of the word for *PISS* if you looked at them in just the right way. The PISS poem has brought him a degree of fame among certain circles in American and British universities. Very small circles.

Charles's own ambition is subtler, a quiet urge that he keeps balled up inside him. He doesn't crave fame. If he did, he'd never have specialized in Pāli, which his colleagues view as a quaint, simplified dialect of Sanskrit. They consider his work a footnote to their more important academic endeavors. But Charles thrills to the long-forgotten texts he studies. At times it feels as if he is exhuming—preserving—whole civilizations. He can almost hear the voices of the scribes whose work he translates, whispers from crenellated palm leaves: *Hey, Charles, look over here. Don't let them forget us. We're no less alive than you will have been.*

"Well," says Williams, "I suppose I'll see you at the department meeting in a few minutes." The breeze whips up his hair like a flap of leather.

"You're not coming to the memorial at the church?" Charles assumed all of his colleagues would be there.

"The church? Marais, do I look like a man who has suddenly found religion?"

"For the service, I mean—it's some sort of event to honor alumni veterans."

"Haven't heard a peep about it."

"Hmmm. I figured everyone would be going. The invitation said attendance is compulsory."

"No one else mentioned a memorial. But I'll look forward to hearing all about it," Williams says with a wry wink, "if you still have a pulse when it's over." He hikes his trousers back up again and shuffles away.

From a dormitory window, a radio broadcast infiltrates the air. Charles continues up the path toward Memorial Church, his mind humming. He is the department's only junior faculty member. Why did he receive an invitation if Williams didn't?

A small group has congregated in front of the church, half a dozen undergraduates clustered off the side of the path by the trunk of an elm. Two boys speak in undertones. They shake their heads in his direction.

Charles tacks past, continuing toward the church's staircase.

In the recesses of his mind, he hears a throat clear, a wet thwack, a soft spattering. He stops at the bottom of the steps and spins around. A gob of yellow saliva glimmers on his shoulder, dripping slowly down his coat sleeve.

Charles searches the young faces but recognizes none of them. "What the hell do you think you're doing?"

In the tower overhead, church bells collide. A trio of dissonant notes clashes, dissolves, then clangs again. Nine times the bells ring. The service is starting. His composure has vanished. Someone needs to discipline these kids. But there's no time now. He dashes into Thayer Hall and cleans himself off, then hurries up the stone staircase.

On the other side of the double doors, in the front two pews of the chapel, fifteen men sit shoulder to shoulder, their gray hair cut with uniform closeness across the backs of their white necks. The rest of the hall is empty. James Bryant Conant, president of the university, looms like a lion before them in the chancel.

Charles pads down the right-side aisle as quietly as he can, but half a dozen heads swivel toward him. He recognizes the men immediately, scions of the Academy. Nobel Prize winners in chemistry, medicine, literature. Americans, French, Austrians, all of them far more accomplished than he is. There is not one from his country. Not one from his continent.

He whispers an apology and tucks into the end of the second pew next to an ancient classicist with a handlebar mustache that seems to defy gravity. The group is smaller than he expected. He pulls the envelope from his pocket. It's addressed, he notices only now, to *Eugene Charles Gerard Marais, Assistant Professor, Department of Aryan Language Studies*. An odd mistake. The name of his department is Indic Philology. He peels open the envelope and slides out the thick ivory card once more. "Your attendance is required at Memorial Church for an intimate ceremony honoring fallen alumni who honorably served their country during the Great War. Tuesday, the seventeenth of September, nineteen hundred and thirty-five, at nine o'clock in the morning. By invitation only. Your most humble servant, James Bryant Conant, President, Harvard University." Emblazoned at the top of the card is Conant's seal with its swirling coat of arms.

Conant clears his throat to speak. He is a chemist by training, a thin, wiry man whose presence occupies the entire front of the chapel. His deep voice echoes against the vaulted ceiling.

"Several years ago, we dedicated this church as a memorial to the three hundred and seventy-three alumni of Harvard University who died fighting for this country in the Great War. Their names are inscribed for eternity on the walls of the Memorial Room beneath this bell tower. Sadly, the names of four other alumni who died in that tragic war have gone absent from these walls. Until today. On this solemn occasion we extend our condolences to the German consul as we pay tribute to our fallen German brothers." Conant nods to a hulking man in a black top hat at the far end of the first pew. "Harvard has not forgotten her sons who under reverse circumstances gave their lives for their country—that is, for Germany."

The consul, a tall, beefy man, rises to his feet, coat buttons barely able to contain his torso.

Charles tries to fit his head around these words. Germany just passed its Nuremberg Laws. The news is everywhere. Jews are stripped of their citizenship; they can no longer marry Germans. Yet, Conant has invited the consul here. It seems a strange signal to send, honoring Germans who fought against the United States.

"A most gracious sentiment," says the consul. "May our two nations never again be separated by conflicting ideology."

Charles shifts uncomfortably in his seat. *America and Germany?*

The consul reads aloud four names from a plaque honoring the dead alumni—Daur, Delbruck, Peters, Schneider. Then he props a wreath of pine branches beneath the plaque and kneels there, paying his respects to the deceased. When he turns to the congregants, his hands are clasped. His eyes look moist.

The top of the wreath, Charles can see now, is crowned with a small metal diadem, barely an inch or two in height. It takes a moment before he recognizes the emblem for what it is. When he does, he nearly falls out of his seat.

Right here, at the pulpit in Memorial Church, in the center of Harvard Yard, the oldest and most prestigious university in the spacious-skyed, purple-mountained, fruited-plained United States of America, is a hand-forged, blazing silver swastika.

Somewhere behind him, a fan's blades whir. Charles glances from face to face. Several of his colleagues have closed their eyes. Gruber, the octogenarian chair of Philosophy, seems to be praying. Has no one else noticed?

Conant shakes the consul's hand and sets a rose next to the wreath. "We shall never forget these fine young men."

In response to some invisible signal, the audience rises—even Gruber—and begins filing past. The consul doles out stems from an armful of cut flowers. Each man deposits a rose by the wreath. Charles takes a place in the aisle at the end of the line.

Some of the brightest minds in the modern world are here. Why was he asked to join them?

He stares for a moment at the wreath. *Su-asti-ka*. The word comes from Sanskrit, "that which is good." Every Hindu household, temple, and school has the emblem painted across its doors. For millennia across the ancient world, it was the mark of auspiciousness. But the Germans have turned it, almost overnight, into a symbol of bigotry, as if brute force could erase thousands of years of history. They've been obsessing over India's "Aryanism." They seem to believe if they can establish themselves as descendants of ancient Indo-European language speakers, they'll somehow bolster their claims to membership in a master race. But the āryans of ancient India weren't a race at all. They were a hodgepodge of people who called themselves "noble ones" simply because they worshipped Indra and performed Vedic sacrifices.

Charles glances again at his colleagues, wondering what they think. Is no one else concerned? The elderly classicist and his pet mustache have already reached the plaque. Charles hurries to follow. He stops next to the consul. The man smiles a meaty smile and hands him a yellow rose, a single thorn protruding from the stem. Charles walks the few remaining steps to the wreath. He watches his fingers uncurl. The rose seems to hang for a moment, suspended between heaven and earth. Then it falls, a tiny corpse, and comes to rest at the top of the pile.

After the service, visiting professors from the University of Heidelberg gather in the rear of the chapel. They introduce themselves and Charles does his best to make small talk. Still, he itches to break away. Just as he finds an opening to excuse himself, he notices the president approaching from across the room with long, brisk strides. Charles halts, straightens his back, extends his hand. "Sir, Eugene Charles—"

"Marais!" says Conant warmly. "Of course. Wonderful people, the French. Not so hygienically minded, but a lovely disposition, a fiery intellect, and such a cultural heritage: music, art, literature, philosophy. Incredible to think what's come out of that nation. But you were, in fact, born in South Africa."

Conant knows who he is then. Half a dozen generations ago, his father's side of the family sailed from France. They settled on the Cape along with the Dutch Huguenots.

"Ja, that's right," Charles says, conscious of the South African accent he still hasn't lost after all these years—the *ja* of affirmation, the way he swallows his Rs in the back of his throat. His origins seem now to blare from his body.

"It's a fine corner of the world to have civilized. Marvelous work you've done down there."

"I can't take all the credit myself," Charles says.

Conant briefly smiles. "I mean your people, of course—they have something to be proud of." His gaunt face is radiant. "I'll tell you, Marais, we're most grateful for your support of Harvard-Germany relations. It was important that we have representation from like-minded individuals today. Helps us send the right signal."

"It's nothing, sir," Charles says as casually as he can. "We do what's required of us, for the good of Harvard." But the words sour in his mouth.

"I'm glad to know you feel that way," Conant says *sotto voce*. He moves in closer, and Charles can smell the man's breakfast on his breath—black coffee and herring. "You'll be pleased then to hear about our progress in retaining individuals who share our same values. Our faculty is on track to become completely *Judenfrei* within a few years. It's one huge and thrilling step forward. Proof that we moderns are not the terminus of the evolutionary process. We are its progenitors."

A string of sweat begins trickling down Charles's spine.

"You know the threat better than anyone," says Conant. "It's humbling to think of the trials your people have faced in southern Africa. Faced and overcome. I'm impressed by your heritage,

Marais, and by your family pedigree. How inspiring to think that your own father is, in fact, one of the fathers of Afrikaans literature, that he helped forge the very language of your country, and in doing so, helped build an enduring white nation amid a sea of blackness."

Charles feels thrown off balance, shocked that Conant has even heard of his father. "We were never terribly close." This, the understatement of the century.

"What a pity. Such a fascinating man. I've become captivated by his scientific studies. His work merits far more attention than it has received."

"You know his research?" What interest could Conant possibly have in baboons and termites?

"Of course. Several years ago he wrote our faculty seeking funding for his work. That was ultimately impossible, but some of our Dutch-speaking colleagues recently decided to translate his articles to English. It turns out your father is an inspiration. Which is precisely why I invited you here today. I'd like you to do us a favor, Charles." Behind his round wire glasses, Conant's eyes shine a severe cobalt blue. "We're starting up a committee of sorts—I trust you can keep this confidential for now—to advocate, discreetly, for the rights of the superior races. We'll hold the committee's first meeting later this year. I'd like you to participate."

"I'm afraid I'm thick with university commitments right now," Charles manages to say. "My tenure review is coming up soon . . ."

"Indeed it is." Conant gives Charles a significant look. "All the more reason why we'd like you to join the committee as soon as it's operational. You have a remarkable career ahead of you, Charles."

He tries to swallow. "I appreciate that. I'll be sure to give it some thought."

Conant beams. "Excellent. Don't think *too* long though. We intend to move quickly." Charles takes Conant's outstretched hand, unable to contain the trembling in his own.

Thus have I heard.

July 1895, Pretoria, South African Republic

Eugene Nielen Marais dipped the nib of his pen in ink and started again on the speech. The floor of the study was littered with crumpled debris from a dozen previous attempts.

In the next room, Lettie lay battling in labor. His mother was attending to her, or rather, guarding the bedroom to prevent Marais from entering, perhaps to prove that she was still of some use in her advancing age. Marais hadn't been able to concentrate long enough to craft more than a sentence or two. The same five words kept echoing through his head: *the baby will come tonight.*

Outside, he could hear the Apies River thrum and crash against the bank. The swath of grass between the house and the water had turned silver with frost. Fog rolled across the winter sky, painting the moon first blue, then indigo, and casting shadows over the sprawling garden. As a boy, Marais had imagined strangers lurking behind garden hedges, errant animals from the bushveld forcing their way through windows. He'd feared most for his mother—the possibility that she might die before he did.

It was past midnight already. Nine hours until the ceremony, and Marais had written next to nothing. Only twenty-four years old, he was set to speak at the inauguration of President Kruger's long-awaited railway project, a line that linked Pretoria with Delagoa Bay and, for the first time, with the world beyond.

Marais was the editor of *Land en Volk*, an Afrikaans-language weekly that launched scathing attacks at corrupt politicians. He considered himself the Mark Twain of the Transvaal. For this one occasion, though, he'd need to anesthetize his tongue.

What he'd drafted so far was not the beginning of a speech at all, he realized, but a political cartoon: an illustration of a steam train piloted by a clown in presidential garb. From the train's smokestack issued the words: "Was this a good use of a million South African Ponds?"

"Oh, for God's sake," he said to no one.

The winter wind gusted through the thatched roof. It poured through the linen ceilings, which billowed ghostlike above him. The lantern on the desk flickered. Its flame thinned. For a moment, his entire desk disappeared into blackness.

That's when he heard Lettie cry. He threw on his coat and sprinted down the hallway—mother's orders be damned. In his stockinged feet, he slid along the floor, a hard-baked manure that had been smoothed over and polished. He reached for the knob.

Before he could push it open, his mother slipped out of the bedroom and positioned herself in front of him.

A string of pearls ringed her neck, the one vestige of her former aristocratic life on the Cape. Her face was fully made, even at this late hour. A birth was about to take place, there would be a doctor in the house, and despite the inevitable blood and mucous, his mother was going to look her best. She stepped into the hall and shut the door behind her.

"Is she all right?" Marais asked.

In the moonlight that filtered into the hallway, his mother's mouth was tightly drawn. "Your wife, dear child, is perfectly fine. She's simply having a baby—like countless women before her."

There was no sound from the other side of the door.

"I'll just check on her."

"No need for that. Doctor Kriel will be here soon. And I should remind you, Eugene, that I know a thing or two about how babies come into this world."

"Mother, she's my wife. There's no reason I shouldn't see her."

He tried to make his way past, but his mother thrust her back against the door. She was a small, thin woman with a severe nose, and at seventy-one years old, still as stubborn as she'd been throughout his childhood.

"This is women's business, *laatlam*." That's what she'd always called him. He was the lamb born late and last, the youngest of thirteen children, ten of whom had survived past childhood. Their family came from the Jonkershoek Valley near Stellenbosch in the British Cape Colony, and generations earlier, from France and Holland. Eugene was the only born Transvaaler among them, the only native *landszoon*, son of the Boer country. Maybe it was this position in his family, the last in a long line of siblings and the only true Transvaaler, that had made him special. His mother had always treated him as if he were divinely blessed, and he'd grown to believe with a fierce degree of certainty that if he could just keep focused on the goal line, there was nothing that he couldn't accomplish. After all, this was what it meant to be modern and enlightened: to be unconstrained by your past.

"Men are not to see their wives this way," his mother said. "It's liable to make them fall out of love. You have other responsibilities preparing for tomorrow, and I know you couldn't possibly have finished yet. Now let us be and go write your speech."

There was a faint whimpering behind the door. It made him sick to hear Lettie in pain. Without thinking, he grabbed his mother's forearm and pulled her away. He meant only to peel her gently from the entrance, but the sleeve of her dress caught in his fingers and ripped all the way up to her elbow.

"Eugene!"

"I'm sorry," he said. "I'll go. Just please call if she needs me."

Reluctantly, he retreated to his study, to his books and writings, his maps and microscopes and preserved animal specimens. His pen holder was fashioned from a human skull that he'd acquired from a trader at the weekend market—the smooth skull of a pygmy.

Where in God's name was Dr. Kriel? He didn't know how much longer Lettie could wait. He didn't know how much longer *he* could wait.

He'd met Lettie at a dinner party just fifteen months earlier. Something about the delicate curve of her mouth and the flash of her eyes made it seem as if she were smiling throughout the entire party even when there was no real reason for it, as if she had some secret source of amusement. In the short time since they'd married, she'd helped settle him in ways he'd not thought possible. Gone were his brooding moods. He was even sleeping again. There were moments—more and more frequent—of something akin to joy.

Tonight, Lettie would bring their child into the world. He secretly hoped for a girl, a rambunctious little creature with Lettie's enormous brown eyes, her patience and pluck. The thought nearly suffocated him with delight. There was a solidity to his life, a permanence that comes from forging a family. He ran his skeleton key across the glass jars stacked on shelves behind his desk, vessels that housed specimens he'd collected from farms south and east of Pretoria. Talons, feathers, scorpions, tarantulas. The ossified eyeballs of venomous snakes. Each jar was pitched differently, and the tones rose up together and collided like notes from an organ.

"Wake up, my muses," he said. "We're all in this together tonight."

He wrapped a blanket around himself, on top of his house coat, and took pen back to paper.

His entire education—in the Cape, in the Free State, in Pretoria—had been in English. The speech he'd deliver tomorrow, though, would be in Afrikaans. Already he'd begun elevating the new language to a level of respectability within the Transvaal. His was the first newspaper to switch from English to Afrikaans, a language previously only spoken and long considered just a bastardized form of Dutch. Yes, there were papers in the Cape that had made the switch earlier, but Cape Afrikaans was a different language altogether, not the true Afrikaans of the Boers. Marais had formalized the spelling of many of the words himself. The initial switch was purely a business decision, a way to differentiate *Land en Volk* from the Transvaal's other weeklies. But it had become something more without his even intending it, the way that love too had caught him off-guard. The new language was now *his* cause, and every resident of Pretoria, from farmers to shopkeepers to the president himself, knew what Marais was up to, whether or not they approved.

Tomorrow, as much as it pained him, he'd need to pander to Kruger and his henchman. He recited the words aloud as he penned them:

"*Geagte Meneer die President.* Mr. President. Illustrious Ministers. Most Honorable Representatives of the Volksraad." Most Honorable! There was no honor to be found in Kruger's government. The very concepts of honesty and integrity had disappeared from the public buildings ages ago. The fundamentalist Doppers didn't want Marais participating at the inauguration of the railroad any more than Marais himself wanted to be there. But the Volksraad had launched a libel lawsuit against him for stories he'd recently printed. Marais couldn't afford a legal battle. He wasn't going to inflict upon Lettie and the child the same financial ruin that his father had brought upon the family years ago. Kruger's railroad needed positive coverage in the papers, and Kruger's advisors had hinted that if Marais, the president's most vocal critic, praised the government tomorrow, they might be willing to drop the suit.

"When our forefathers embarked on the Great Trek from the Cape Colony to the Transvaal in the eighteen thirties and forties, it was with faith in a singular destiny and in the promise of an independent Boer homeland in southern Africa, free from the crushing hand of the British crown. With President Kruger's vision, we have now arrived at that future."

Claptrap. This speech-writing exercise was thoroughly emasculating.

"Eugene. Please help!"

Marais dropped the paper and bolted down the hall. He threw open the door to their bedroom. The air was redolent of sweat and the wild roses he'd picked and cut and left by the bed earlier in the day. Lettie's head was propped against two pillows. A pile of gray woolen blankets hid all trace of her body. Her cropped brown hair was matted and wet and stuck to her forehead, her eyes squeezed shut. Shadows from the fireplace danced across her face. Marais bent down and kissed her cheek. He'd never loved anyone this deeply.

Lettie opened her eyes and smiled. "You're here," she said.

"Always and forever." He glanced around the room. "Where is Mother?"

"She's checking on Jan Nielen."

His stomach knotted. "She left you alone?"

"Your father needed her."

His *father*. Marais never used that term to reference Jan Nielen. That useless man. His mother had raised all ten of her children herself. She was the one who'd managed the family's finances.

"Say something kind to me, Eugene. Any sort of compliment. I don't feel whole right now. It's as if I were two people, and yet none at all."

"You look lovely, Aletta Marais," he said. It was true, even now, without color applied to her face and her hair plastered wet against her cheeks.

"That's a start."

"More beautiful than the day we married."

She smiled. "Now you're getting the hang of it."

"You smell like flowers, my love. Lilacs and roses."

"All right, that's enough," she said, laughing. "It's the roses you smell. It's definitely not me. My body wasn't fashioned for this. This is work for cattle and sheep, not for a woman."

"Baaaah," he crooned and kissed her again. "The loveliest sheep I've ever laid eyes on." He sat beside her on the bed. Through the blankets he caressed her leg, her thigh, her hip.

"Have you written the speech?" she asked.

"There's plenty of time still. Too much time. You know how I work. Panic is my great motivator. I'll probably just improvise anyway. A written speech is an oxymoron."

She gave him the growling face. "You haven't started."

"Of course I've started."

"Tell me you won't criticize Kruger. You know these men—they're not like other people. We can't risk a suit, Eugene. All you need to do is throw them a bone or two, and they promised that—"

Anger sparked and surged straight through him. "All they do is promise! When have their promises proven anything but worthless?"

A gust of wind rustled the pages of his father's old Dutch Bible. The air smelled of rain.

"They're politicians, Eugene. They're doing their jobs."

"Their jobs?" He glared at her. In broad daylight, Kruger was selling off concessions for all the major mining industries. And monopolies for alcohol, for dynamite. "He's not selling to Boers, Lettie. It's all going to foreigners. Why did we fight for our independence fifteen years ago? What did your own father fight for? So the government could just sell off our country?"

He was shouting all of a sudden. How could he be shouting at his wife while she lay here in labor with his child?

"Enough of this, Eugene. Listen to me. There's something I need to tell you." The clock on the wall chimed twice. She lowered her voice. "I've purchased a plot of land."

A what?

"With my own savings," she said. "Just a small plot. Ten miles east in Sunnyside. It's lovely country."

"Why would you do such a thing?"

"We can build a home there. We'll get you away from all the stress of Pretoria. You'll finally be able to pursue your first love—your naturalist studies."

"*You* are my first love. And we already have a home."

"This is your parents' house."

"There's plenty of room for us, even with the baby. You know that."

"It's not about room." Her eyes filled up, taking him by surprise. "It's too much for us here. Too much for you. I can't stand around any longer and watch you . . ." She glanced at his arm, then looked quickly away. ". . . hurt yourself. I need you to be healthy again. If I ever lose you, I wouldn't be able to bear it."

Her hands balled suddenly into fists, then snapped, elasticized against her face. Her entire body seized up. "Oh, God!" she cried through her teeth.

Marais squeezed her fists in his hands. He counted to himself, waiting for the contraction to pass. *Seventeen, eighteen, nineteen.* How could one minute last so long?

"I've sent three messages to Kriel," he said when she finally relaxed. "Where in hell could he possibly be?"

"It's the middle of the night. Who knows how many other patients he has? You can't control everything."

But he had to. There was no other choice. Without control, there was nothing but the violent pulse of nature. "He better be here soon."

"Of course he will."

But a terrible thought occurred to him now. What if something goes wrong tonight? What would he do if anything happened to Lettie?

He found the bottle of whiskey in the armoire and filled her water glass halfway. "Drink this. To help dull the pain."

She took the glass without protest. She squeezed her eyes shut and gulped down the liquor.

There was a pounding then at the back of the house. Three sharp knocks.

"Finally!" Marais said.

He shot through the kitchen. He threw open the door.

Kriel stood on the porch, grinning in the moonlight. His cheeks were a distinct shade of red.

"It's been hours!" Marais said.

"Look, I hadn't expected the kid to make an appearance tonight. She's weeks early, man. Weeks."

"Three times I sent for you!"

"I do my best, Marais." He sneezed into a handkerchief. "I'm a doctor. Not a saint."

"Just come inside. Quickly now."

As Kriel hurried forward, the toe of his boot hit the threshold. He toppled head-first into the house. Marais caught him by the shoulders just before he hit the floor. He was heavy like a mattress.

Kriel managed to pick himself up. He straightened his coat. "Damn good thing you're here," he said.

Marais smelled the liquor now. Kriel reeked of whiskey. Marais had never been a fighting man, but he could already hear the furious crunch of his knuckles against Kriel's cheekbone, the hump as Kriel's body hit the floor. He barely stopped himself from slugging him. There'd be no way to locate another doctor tonight. Kriel would have to suffice. Marais grabbed the doctor's bag. He led him into the bedroom.

Lettie had thrown off the blankets. She lay curled on her side in only her petticoat. In the dim glow of the fire, her skin was the color of water.

"I'll take it from here," Kriel said.

Marais saw the dark half-moons under Lettie's eyes. "I'll stay with you."

"No, it's all right," she said. "I'll be fine. You need to write. I'll see you in a little while. I'll have a small friend for you to meet."

Marais glared at Kriel and collected the whiskey bottle that he'd left on the nightstand. "I'll make you some coffee, Doctor."

"No need," Kriel called. "I can't drink the stuff. Too hard on the stomach."

Marais pursed his lips. "Tea then."

"Please, sweet," said Lettie. "Everything's fine here."

Something in the lightness of her voice reassured him.

September 1935, Cambridge, Massachusetts

When Charles throws open the church doors, the sun is bursting over the Yard. He blinks repeatedly as his eyes adjust to the light.

The scrum of students outside has grown to ten: nine young men and a girl capped in a gray fedora. He has barely reached the bottom step when the girl steps forward and points a finger in his direction. She says something he can't quite hear and twenty eyes seesaw upwards to meet his. A hush like a whisper slowly crescendos. The students, he realizes, are hissing at him.

Blindsided, he glowers at the group, his heart still pounding. "Mind your own business!"

The boys lower their eyes to their feet. But the girl with the hat does not. She steps forward and utters a single word. "Shame!"

A chill spreads through him, forcing itself through his bones, crawling across his skin.

"What did those men ask you to do for them?" she demands.

"Look, I don't even know who you are. I'm a teacher. I teach and research, that's all."

Her eyes bore into him. "What *sort* of 'research' are we talking about exactly?"

"I translate. Dead Indian languages that you've probably never heard of. Ancient texts on the verge of disappearing. Any of my students can tell you: Professor Marais has no secrets. Now if you'll excuse me, I need to get to my class." He hastens away, aware of her eyes as they follow him.

* * *

How does an orphaned Afrikaner wind up a scholar of ancient Indian languages at Harvard?

With the help of one good teacher who entered Charles's boyhood imagination and ignited a spark. Mr. Goldman was a bald and jowly Marxist with a prodigious beard who taught Charles literature and Classics during his fifth- and sixth-form years after he'd been sent away to school in London. Goldman took a liking to Charles. He shepherded him through Old, Middle, and Early Modern English literature, through *Beowulf* and Gawain, Chaucer and the Bard. They finished so quickly that Goldman decided to teach him Latin, navigating him through Virgil's *Aeneid* and Cicero's *First Catilinarian*. Goldman heaped praise upon him. He taught him to find and correct his own mistakes. As a boy, Charles didn't have a father to care for him, but for those two years, he thought he knew what life might have been like if he had.

Goldman told Charles what was already obvious to others: He had a gift for language. Later, when Charles arrived at university and enrolled in a linguistics class, he realized that he was particularly good with dead Indic languages, enormously complex grammatical systems that had been perfected and frozen in time. His interest had nothing to do with religion. He had no faith, not

Christianity, certainly not Buddhism. For Charles, the world was governed only by chance. But there was nothing he enjoyed more than poring over ancient stories that had been copied by hand again and again for hundreds or thousands of years. Centuries-old manuscripts became his personal skeleton keys to history's secrets. The scribes became his family.

And one sunny day, twelve years of graduate school later, he landed by chance right here in Harvard Yard. It was a turning point at last.

* * *

Three young men with blue blazers and crimson ties sit at small desks in Charles's classroom. New-dictionary smells of bleach and glue waft around them.

Dennis, William, and Harry. He received photos of each of them ahead of time. Upperclassmen from the physics and engineering departments who waited—or forgot—to fulfill their language requirements until now. With the modern language classes already full, Charles has been asked to teach Introductory Pāli to three twenty-one-year-old undergrads with no interest in the language apart from a desperate desire to graduate.

Harry, the plump blond one with slicked-back hair, is perched on his desk with his back to Charles, finishing off a joke with the others. The boy's oversized shoes dangle in the air.

The two boys in the rear snap to their feet when they spot Charles at the door.

Harry drops to the floor and spins around red-faced. "Pardon me, Professor."

Dennis, the youngest of the three, is reedy and starry-eyed, his jawline covered by a blanket of soft white hairs. To his right is William, brawny and handsome, front coat pocket impressed with the outline of a cigarette pack.

"Morning, gentlemen," Charles says. He gestures for them to sit.

"We weren't sure if you were coming," says William.

"But you decided to wait."

"Yes, of course."

"Then you've passed your first test."

All three smile back.

Charles slides a notebook from his briefcase. A faint splotch of blood has congealed on his palm. *The thorn on the rose stem.* Conant's face flares in his mind.

"Let's start the semester with a story," he says, shrugging off the image. "Once upon a time, there was a prince. His mother, the queen, died days after giving birth to him, and his aunt raised him as her own. This prince was wealthy beyond imagination. The prince's father, the king, loved him dearly. Determined that his son should become a great king himself, he kept the prince, Siddhārtha, confined to the royal palace, surrounded by earthly pleasures. But you know how boys are. One day after reaching maturity, the prince slips out of the palace for the first time. He sneaks into town in disguise and stumbles upon three sights that change his life forever. 'What are these things?' he asks his attendant. The attendant hesitates, knowing that he's in for it when he returns to the palace, but he gestures toward the men at whom Siddhārtha is gaping and tells the prince the truth: 'They are sickness, old age, and death. Eventually, they overtake every human being—one day, they'll even overtake you, your highness.'

"Devastated by this news, the prince vows to find a solution. Soon he stumbles upon a fourth sight, a wandering ascetic who has devoted himself to finding the root cause of suffering. This man's path, thinks Siddhārtha, is the one I must follow. In the dead of night, he escapes from the palace on horseback and journeys to the forest, leaving behind his infant son Rāhula, his little boy whose name means *fetter*.

"Years later, on the bank of a river, Siddhārtha realizes the truths of impermanence and selflessness. He attains *buddha* mind. He becomes awakened.

"This story is the prelude to our work. Over the next nine months, we'll be studying the language spoken by this Buddha two-and-a-half millennia ago. The grammar will prepare you to read the core Theravāda Buddhist literature: the stories of the Buddha's previous lives—the Jātaka Tales—and his teachings as the Buddha, the Sutras, or *suttas* in Pāli."

Charles has told this story at least a hundred times. He grabs a stick of chalk. He scratches the first five consonants of the Pāli alphabet across the top of the board in Roman characters.

"Ka. Kha. Ga. Gha. Nga," he says. "Now you." The boys repeat the sounds in unison, bungling the aspirates so badly that Charles can't help but smile. He scrawls the rest of the forty-one Pāli characters on the board in nine tight rows and tells the boys to repeat after him. They contort their mouths, struggling to replicate the gutturals. *At the end of the year*, he thinks, *when they look back on today, they won't be able to remember what it felt like not to know these letters. They won't remember not knowing how to read.*

A quiet rapping on the door. Charles checks his watch. "What is it?" he calls.

The door inches open and a young woman steps into the room, a rucksack slung over her shoulder. The girl with the fedora, the one who confronted him outside the church. Her hair bobbed and wavy. She has on a white skirt, stockings, and saddle shoes. Dennis, Harry, and William leap to their feet.

"I had trouble finding the classroom," she says, squeezing between the others and taking an empty seat. "First time I've been to this part of the Yard."

Charles can't seem to locate words. There's fire in his face.

"Sorry. I'm Hannah Tauber. Graduate student at Radcliffe. I'd like to enroll in your class."

"That's not possible," Dennis blurts. "Girls aren't allowed to enroll in classes at Harvard."

"Thank you, Dennis," says Charles. "We're all aware of the university's policy in that regard."

She casts the boy a withering look and turns back to Charles. Her earrings are mismatched—pearl on one side, small diamond on the other. "It's a funny thing. I've been wanting to learn something new. And then, just this morning, as I was walking through the Yard, I . . . remembered hearing about you." Charles thinks he detects a tinge of pleasure in her face. "They say you're one of the best Pāli teachers in the state."

"Actually, I'm the *only* Pāli teacher in the state. Look, Miss Tauber, I'm not wild about everything the university does, but we have to abide by the rules even if we don't agree with them." Conant's cobalt eyes shimmer again in his mind.

"Unless these fine young men are worried about a little competition," she says, "I'm hoping they'd be willing to keep this a secret."

"It's not a matter of secrets," said Charles. "It wouldn't be fair to them. They've all enrolled legally."

"It's fine with me, sir," William offers, a bit too eagerly.

"Us too," Harry and Dennis chorus.

He needs to end this here. He can't admit her to his class, not even secretly, not after she saw him at the chapel. But if he refuses, what would keep her from telling the others what she saw? How would he begin to explain that?

Outside, the bright sun still shines, the verdant paths loop through the Yard. There are still the manicured lawns, the thin-trunked trees—elm, maple, dogwood, ash. But he finds it impossible now to will back the good mood that suffused the day just ninety minutes ago. The talk of rules and instructions and secrets has transported him back to Memorial Church, to Conant, the consul, and the handshake, which he increasingly worries may have signified more than he intended.

Maybe the girl is just hoping to keep tabs on him, do a bit of private investigating. If she meant to expose him, she'd have done so already. The best approach might be to keep her close. She won't stay for more than a class or two anyway, he tells himself, not after she sees he really is just teaching Pāli. *Two weeks at most,* he thinks, *and I'll never see her again.*

"Miss Tauber, you're welcome to stay. As a silent auditor," he says. "You'll need one of these if you're joining us." He places a hardbound Pāli-English dictionary on her desk.

Her eyes are bright and green and flecked with gold. He seems to have surprised her. She slides her fingers along the spine of the dictionary. "Thank you, Professor. I appreciate it."

* * *

After class, Charles heads toward the small gate on the north side of the Yard. He's keen to put the morning behind him, to put distance between himself and campus. As he exits, he runs a hand along the Yard's massive fence, the sandstone piers, the elaborate brickwork, the imposing molded iron. For the first time he finds himself wondering: was this fence intended to keep the rest of the world from entering—or to keep men like him from leaving?

Outside the Yard, Memorial Hall looms with its gothic, buttressed windows and stained-glass panels, a tribute to alumni who fought for the Union in the Civil War. And so many others: Weld Hall, Straus Hall, Holworthy Hall, Widener Library, built in honor of an alumnus who drowned on the *Titanic*. Sometimes the entire university feels like one grand memorial to the deceased.

At the fire station, Charles cuts right and hastens along Cambridge Street, past the nursery, the vocational school, the paths that thread to the public library. His thoughts return to Hannah Tauber, though she no longer seems a threat. She'll realize soon enough that he's only a teacher, nothing more sinister than that.

By the time he reaches Inman Square, it's almost noon. Clutches of men in paint-stained trousers line both sides of the street, waiting for an odd job or a surprise act of charity. Charles has seen firsthand the toll of more than half a decade of sky-high unemployment. Shuttered storefronts. Endless soup kitchen lines. Daily street fights. Somehow these men still get out of bed each morning. They drag themselves to the same patch of concrete, despite near certainty that they'll end the day just as they began it, without a coin in their pockets.

A man with a young boy in tow tips his cap. Charles has seen this pair before.

"Good day, Professor," the man says with a hint of an Irish brogue.

"Any luck today?" Charles asks.

"Look at this little fellow. I'm the luckiest man in the world." He pulls his son close, tousles his hair. The young boy squeezes his features into a nose-wrinkled grin.

Charles glances at his own briefcase and pulls out a folded paper bag. "Why don't you take this? I'm not hungry today anyway."

"You happen to have a job in there?"

"Afraid not. Just a sandwich, some carrots, and an apple."

The man pauses as if weighing his options. "I suppose we could help you out with that."

Charles hands over the bag and starts to leave, then turns back. He has five dollars weighing down his pocket, money he won't miss for a second. "Take this too," he calls to the man. "For dessert."

At the end of the square, Charles veers into the maze of Somerville's streets where Cambridge's Victorians give way to boxy apartment buildings. Clotheslines are strung from house to house, an elaborate network tying the dilapidated town together.

Refuse litters the sidewalks. Laces from discarded work boots. Swatches of felt. Half-used spools of thread. Rubber bands. Shreds of newspaper. Leaves in a symphony of colors: garnet, saffron, coral, russet. He knows someone who can use the debris. He grabs the best of it, stuffs his pockets, and forges ahead to the next block.

Against the sky, his blue-brown building looks like a fresh bruise. The two lower windows are boarded up. Chipped paint peels away from the siding in *s*-shaped strips. He grabs the stack of letters from the mailbox, tucks them under his arm, and makes his way up the stairs.

His apartment was originally an attic before the owner squeezed a pair of dormers inside, laid down unfinished wood flooring, and slapped up some walls. A single man with his salary could afford to rent in Cambridge. He could live within minutes of the Yard by foot if he wanted to. His colleagues thumb their noses at Somerville, for its gross lapses in public sanitation, for the highest auto accident rate in the Commonwealth, and recently, for the packs of rabid dogs that roam the streets at night. For five years, Charles has remained here, tucked away at the far edges of the university. The long walk home each day brings him face-to-face with the real New England, the pulsing world outside the Yard. It reminds him how lucky he is.

He sets the mail on the desk. His walls are mostly bare, apart from an oil painting of a cactus that he picked up at a yard sale and the crisp cover of an eighteenth-century palm-leaf manuscript from Sri Lanka that he framed years ago.

A stray. That's what Williams called him. Perhaps, but what was the point of getting entangled in a place when you might soon be moving on again? That had been his thinking, though it never quite eclipsed the stubborn desire to belong. And, truly, where better to belong than Harvard? Where better to establish himself, to lay down roots, to forge a life? Winning tenure will be the final hurdle . . .

There's a rustling by the ficus. His South African weaver is hard at work on his latest nest. Earlier in the year, Charles had the small yellow bird delivered from Cape Town by steamer, his only extravagance in recent memory. He thought it would be good for him to have something to care for. The company that delivered the bird warned that it would be impossible to raise a weaver in New England. Charles took it as a challenge to prove them wrong. He's given the bird free rein of the apartment. He's kept the windows closed and the radiators on high, even in summer. The little bird has thrived.

Charles traipses over to the tree and empties his pockets onto the wood floor. "More supplies for you, Tonto."

The bird chirps back. He flaps his wings like a maniac.

Two weeks ago, Charles found him pulling threads from a kitchen towel and assembling them into a delicate, woven nest that hung bulb-like from the tip of the longest ficus branch. For twenty-four hours, the bird worked upside down, furiously constructing the interior of the nest and a tubular entryway at the bottom. Tonto was hatched in captivity and sent as a chick to the other side of the world without ever witnessing the construction of a typical weaver's nest. But he is as nimble and certain in this skill as any weaver raised in a wild South African flock. Charles can't bring himself to tell the little guy how few South African weavers inhabit North America, let alone the greater Boston area. No chance he'll ever find a mate here. Still, the bird has constructed increasingly elaborate homes, each built with the hope that his luck could change any moment. A dozen nests now dangle from the branches like Chinese lanterns.

"Maybe this next one will do the trick," Charles says encouragingly.

In the kitchen, he pours himself a Scotch and jiggles the dial on the Philco. The *William Tell* Overture booms through the little box, trumpets and French horns firing away. "Hi-yo, Silver! This is the legend of a man and a horse and how they met. The story of the Lone Ranger and his great horse Silver."

He listens to the story as he hunts through the day's mail. There's a notice from the WPA about upcoming street repairs, a rejection from a journal to which he submitted a proposal for a paper about the etymology of the Pāli verb "to sit." No more invitations at least.

At the bottom of the stack he finds an envelope postmarked three months earlier from his godmother Sophie's address in South Africa. Since he moved from London five years ago, he's heard from her just a handful of times.

But the writing on the envelope is small, tightly constructed, nearly illegible. It couldn't be more different from Sophie's elongated, flowery cursive. He peels open the letter.

Dear Dr. Marais,

We two worship at the feet of history. Only our vantage points differ: yours linguistic, mine psycho-evolutionary.

Charles flips over the sheet. The signature reads *Eugene Marais*. His own name but signed in another's hand.

He slows down, reads again. The name is not quite the same as his after all. It has the addition of a single character. Eugene *N.* Marais.

Deep within his chest, a subtle constriction. Eugene Nielen Marais is the man who fathered him. Since leaving Pretoria thirty years ago to attend school in London, Charles hasn't heard from Marais once. As a child, he barely knew the man. For as long as he can remember, he has considered himself an orphan.

He flips the paper back over.

As you must know, I've spent the past three decades researching the behavior of chacma baboons and South African termites in an effort to understand the origins of the human mind. Like the great thinkers of the Enlightenment, I'd always assumed that man's natural state is one of pure autonomy—that we are innately free agents with the ability to shape our future selves as we desire. The more I study the higher primates and the social insects, however, the more certain I've become that humans are ultimately constrained by the same forces of nature as the animal world. The notion of free will is the greatest lie ever perpetrated against humanity. This is not meant to exonerate me from the difficult decisions I've had to make since you were born or the fact that we haven't been in communication for an exceedingly long stretch. I have all the while taken delight in hearing from Sophie of your success in London and America. Delight and great pride. You are your father's son.

But this is just preamble. I am in need of your expertise. It is an awkward endeavor—seeking aid from one's child. And no, it's not money that I need. (I hope that thought didn't cross your mind.) The fact is your university is in the process of stealing my life's work, misusing my research to bolster a cause for which it was never intended. Please consider providing me with some assistance at this hour of need. Time is short . . .

Charles drops the paper on his desk.

Twice today this man's name has reared in front of him. Eugene Nielen Marais, who tossed him away at birth. The man must be mad. Marais has always had everything. What could Charles possibly do for him that Marais can't do for himself?

Tonto soars just above his head and dives for the ficus.

Charles has a strange feeling that if he closes his eyes he could find himself somewhere completely different when he opens them again. That the whole world could change with a single blink. The question is: how long can he keep from blinking?

He fishes out his pocketknife and snaps open a small pair of scissors. He folds the letter into a tight square and cuts into it until nothing remains but a clump of worm-like shreds.

"More building materials, Tonto," he says bitterly.

As he dumps the strips onto the pile of trash accumulating at the foot of the ficus, the little bird shrieks and pounces with delight.

Thus have I heard.

July 1895, Pretoria, South African Republic

Marais left Lettie with the doctor and trundled back down the hall past the kitchen. The larder was full to bursting—with flours, syrups, pouches of tea, packets of salt, boxes of nuts, tins of sugar. His mother maintained her kitchen meticulously. Every item was wiped clean and arranged in its proper place. The sheer quantity of food that she kept never failed to arrest him. There were dozens of jars of fruit, whole legs of cured meat, endless supplies of jams and pickled vegetables. Human-sized sacks of rice, coarse wheat, and beans. There were wheels of sheep cheese that a set of adult arms couldn't reach halfway around. Enough food to last through a war. They'd defeated the British fifteen years ago, but the memory of that war was still stuck deep in the blood of every Boer.

And for good reason. England had set its designs once again on forcefully unifying the Boer republics under the British flag. British interests in the Transvaal couldn't be more transparent—the English wanted total control of the Witwatersrand, the largest set of gold-bearing reefs in the world. Kruger had originally granted British investors and miners unrestricted access, but he'd since learned his lesson. London worried now that Kruger might cut Britain off completely and unionize the Transvaal with the other states of southern Africa. Or worse, cozy up to the Germans, who'd been making inroads along the western coast. Rumor had it that the British were preparing to raid the Transvaal under the direction of Cecil Rhodes—the diamond magnate and prime minister of the Cape Colony—and a doctor named Starr Jameson. According to the rumor, they would invade from the north via the Bechuanaland Protectorate, and simultaneously from the south by inciting a revolt among English gold miners in Johannesburg. The entire Transvaal was buzzing with the news.

Marais dropped into his chair. He poured himself a shot of whiskey and knocked it back. The British would come prepared this time. Kruger would never be able to fend off this attack.

From high on the wall, the head of a wildebeest that Marais had hunted stared down at him. His mind raced from Kriel to Kruger to his father and back again. Why was it always men who failed you?

He needed to finish the speech. He needed to calm his nerves. He couldn't bear to think of Lettie in pain. The urge crept up suddenly, as it always did. It started in his feet and rose through his bowels and stomach, then exploded into his chest. He forced up his sleeve, splashed whiskey across his left arm, and wiped it dry with a handkerchief. In his drawer was a silver case that held his syringe. He'd assured Lettie that he'd stopped. She'd seen right through him.

From a pouch in his pocket, he took two white tablets. He set them on a teaspoon with a few drops of water and held the spoon above the lantern's flame. The water began to bubble. The tablets melted and fizzed, the outer edges dissolving into the center. Soon all that remained was a pool of thickening liquid and the raw smell of vanilla. With a careful pull at the plunger, he drew the solution into the syringe. Then, on the count of three, he stabbed the needle into his vein.

With the cool, sudden rush, every muscle tightened, convulsed, then released. The clarity he'd been craving seeped into his head. It felt like donning a new set of eyeglasses, the prescription finally corrected. Morphine no longer sedated him. It made him euphoric. It made him create.

Pages began pouring from his hand now. He didn't need to think at all. His mind was *in* his fingers. He could hear his thoughts erupting in short, syncopated spurts. *Tick tick. Tick tick tick.*

The rest of the house had quieted. Lettie's anesthesia must have set in by now.

Tick tick.

The baby would come when it was ready. The world was safe and bright again. He couldn't imagine a more perfect life.

Tick tick tick.

That sound. He'd heard it before. He'd heard it while hiking past the conical mounds that dotted the countryside north of Pretoria. It wasn't his mind that he was hearing. It was insects. White ants. Termites.

Here in the house.

He placed the soles of his feet on the floor as quietly as he could, one after the other. He walked in whispers. He was hunting—listen and glide, listen and glide.

Tick tick tick.

They were here—in *this* room. At the far side of the study. They were here with him.

Ever since he was a boy, he'd been obsessed with the white ant. He had his own theories of how the termite queen controlled her colony from her isolated, stationary position. He was convinced that she exerted some invisible, magnetic pull, though he'd never viewed a queen for himself.

He touched his palms lightly against the mantle and held his breath.

Tick tick tick.

They'd burrowed into the walls. They'd surrounded the fireplace. The chimney was in disrepair. That's where they'd set up shop, directly behind the mantle. The opiates were coursing through him now. The noise intensified. It gushed over him like a wave.

How many would it take to create such a sound? Hundreds of thousands? Millions? How large must the queen be to sustain a colony of this size?

Marais took off through the living room. He scuttled through the front door, careful not to let the latch fall.

The first light of morning had painted the eastern sky a pale orange. He shot across the grass to the outbuilding where his father kept the tools. The axe he grabbed had a tapered wooden handle and a sharp iron head six inches high.

He whisked it back to the study and swept silently over to the mantle.

Tick tick tick.

The beat of his heart synchronized with the rhythm of the insects. How to approach them?

Tick tick. Pause. Tick tick tick.

He listened as they worked away behind the mantle. He lifted the axe quietly above his shoulder. All at once, he swung at the wall. The blade smashed into the dried mud with a *phlpt* and stuck there. He ripped out the head and swung again, landing a foot to the right this time. He cut once more, horizontally at the top of the first two incisions, then again at the bottom. The cuts formed a near-perfect square.

He stopped again to listen. The ticking had ceased. Were they listening for him too? He gripped the axe with both hands, barely breathing. He waited until he heard just one faint sound.

Tick.

With the edge of the axe, he pried at the right side of the square. He worked the blade back and forth into the cut, then pushed against the levered handle and wrested out an entire block of wall.

With the brick of dried mud clasped in his hands, he squinted inside. Too dark to see. He grabbed the lantern from the desk, held it to the hole. There, his heart stopped. The intricate workings of a maze fanned out in front of him. Hundreds of tiny canals spreading in all directions. Through each canal flowed a dark stream of water, all the channels moving steadily in the same direction.

Marais brought the lantern closer.

It wasn't water after all. It was the steady flow of white ants, thousands of insects at work in this one small square alone.

His breath quickened. All he had to do was follow these insects, and they would lead him to the queen.

He raised the axe again. On the count of three, he swung as hard as he could. The blade bit into the mud. His eyes toured madly over the surface. He would bring the entire wall down. Whatever it took to find her. He crashed the axe into the mud again and again.

He'd taken down two-thirds of the wall by the time he heard the knocking at the door of the study. A hard fist-driven knocking.

Kriel's white shirt was streaked with blood. The doctor's cheeks were drained of color. He looked first at Marais, then at the wall, then down at Marais's hand which still clung to the axe handle.

"Jesus," he said. "You've got one hell of a termite problem."

"Never mind that. How is she?"

Kriel wiped the perspiration from his lip. His Adam's apple disappeared for a moment, then bobbed back up. "Breach." He didn't look Marais in the eye. "I had to operate."

Marais couldn't draw a breath.

"They've both pulled through," said Kriel. "It's a boy. He's perfectly healthy. Mother and child are sleeping."

Marais set down the axe. He rolled his shirtsleeve back over his arm and attached his cufflinks. He shook the doctor's hand.

He had a son. Not what he'd expected, but he was thrilled nonetheless. He was a father. It occurred to him that he'd never actually seen a newborn child close up. A baby boy. How small it must be.

He started from the room. He wanted to make sure his wife had everything she needed. He wanted to meet his child.

Lettie was breathing peacefully, her eyes loosely shut. On her chest, beneath the blankets, lay a large, egg-shaped bundle. The baby was suckling, nestled with its mama. Marais's own mother sat beside them, cooing at the baby with quiet delight. Marais's heart nearly burst.

He glanced at the clock above the bed. Half-past eight and he hadn't bathed or dressed. He wouldn't disturb her now. She needed to sleep. He'd wait until the afternoon and meet the child then. He'd be lucky to make it into town in time to deliver the speech.

He would never meet the queen.

* * *

Pretoria Station was bustling. The day was windy and cold, the sky gently marbled. A sparkling steam engine bearing the Transvaal crest and the Vierkleur, the Republic's flag, was parked at the end of the line, coupled to two black coaches. A set of gleaming tracks extended southward, two thin lines disappearing amid the farmland.

From where Marais sat, he could just make out the right side of Kruger's face, the gray wisps of beard, the forehead protruding below his top hat, hair matted down with coconut oil. Thick brows sprouted above his eyes. Kruger's sole education was the Bible. The man still believed that the world was flat!

Kruger's hand, with its thumbless stump, rested on his knee. When Kruger was twenty, the story went, his elephant gun had blown up in his hand during a rhino-hunting expedition. With his jackknife, he'd cut away his own thumb at the second joint to save the arm. Gangrene had set in, but Kruger, unfazed, resorted to an old Boer remedy: he plunged his hand into a goat's hot stomach. This same man, thick-nosed and thumbless, now sat on the platform beside a brand new railway line, beaming.

Four thousand Pretorians spread out below, contained by mounted police and the Johannesburg lancers and cavalry. Marais knew most of them—advocates and mayors from across the Transvaal, teachers and shopkeepers. Every newspaperman in the country was here.

When it was Marais's turn to speak, he strode to the front of the platform. He gazed over the crowd, then turned briefly to Kruger, the corrupt beast. This was his chance to expose Kruger for what he was. Marais would never have a larger soapbox.

The president bore into him with his dark lion's eyes. He nodded almost imperceptibly.

Marais turned to the crowd. Cameras fired. The entire Volksraad was seated on the platform behind him.

But as he cast his gaze among the crowd, he remembered Lettie in bed, cradling their newborn son, and he remembered his promise. He inhaled a deep breath of Pretorian air.

"Two decades ago," he shouted, glancing at the notes he'd jotted down minutes earlier, "Pretoria was a speck of a village. Johannesburg did not yet exist." His voice rippled through the crowd and echoed back at him.

"The Zuid-Afrikaansche Republiek is an infant relative to the powers of Europe: Holland, Belgium, Germany, England. For forty years after our ancestors founded this nation—a Boer republic in the heart of southern Africa—we remained independent. Then diamonds were discovered and along came the British. The most powerful empire in the history of the world rode into Pretoria and annexed the Transvaal as you'd scoop up an errant child. But fifteen years ago, we defeated the British in our War of Independence. We fought with our hearts and drove the bastards out. Our determination has been steadfast, our national identity forged with a sense of purpose unmatched since the founding of America across the Atlantic.

"But make no mistake, my brothers. The threats to our sovereignty are greater than ever. The Brits have come again, this time for our gold. We've allowed them to pillage Johannesburg and extract our treasure. But even this is not enough for them. What they thirst for now is absolute control. With the railway that we inaugurate today between our great Republic and the sea at Delagoa Bay in Mozambique, the Transvaal is no longer dependent on British colonial ports. For the first time in history, we're connected directly to Asia and Europe. Britain fears what this will mean for them. And fear and greed, when coupled, lead in only one direction. To war. Know this, Pretoria: a second war with Britain is coming, a Second War of Freedom, and it will be the great test we've ever faced. We must remain vigilant. We must prepare for the fight. With Oom Paul's leadership, we shall be victorious. From here to forever, we Boers shall be the makers of our own history. *Lank lewe Oom Paul*!"

Before he even finished the speech, the crowd erupted in cheer. "Kru-ger. Kru-ger."

Marais glanced over his shoulder. Kruger raised a massive finger, pointed at him, and winked a fleshy eyelid. His lips parted just slightly, revealing a set of sharp gray teeth. The president, Marais realized, was smiling at him. The legal suit would be dropped. Marais's knees nearly gave way beneath him.

After the ceremony, four black steeds, hooves clipping against the dirt, whisked Kruger in his landau toward his house a few blocks away. Marais stepped off the platform, twirled his cane, and practically danced the six blocks home. The wind had died down, and the sun shone brightly along the north side of Jacob Mare Street. All the storefronts were still shuttered in honor of the day. Truter the assessor. De Wet's barbershop. Koch's pharmacy. Every building was dark.

At the corner of Prinsloo, the cottage's thatched roof peeked out above the hedges. Marais felt a smile pull across his mouth. He *could* make anything happen. He looked at the sky and laughed out loud, then broke into a run. He was shouting the news before he even opened the front door.

"Lettie, we've done it. We've done it!"

Kriel was sitting in the old rocking chair. When he looked up, Marais noticed something strange in his face.

The doctor cleared his throat. "I'm afraid she has the fever."

A fly landed on Marais's hand.

"I forgot my cleansing solution last night," said Kriel.

"I don't understand."

"It was so late. I wasn't thinking clearly."

"Lettie is the strongest woman I've ever known. She'll be better soon enough."

The doctor looked at his shoes. "It's childbed fever. I've been doing everything possible to bring down the temperature."

Marais's hands began to tremble. "You've initiated treatment already."

Marais could hear the man's breathing, a curdle of phlegm in his throat. "Marais," he said, "once contracted, puerperal fever is fatal. There is no treatment."

What was he saying? Marais's cane dropped to the floor behind him as he shot from the room.

"She's sleeping!" Kriel called after him. "She needs to rest."

His mother was standing just outside the bedroom, rocking the baby. She'd changed her dress since last night, but the pearls still hung from her neck. Marais could see that she'd been crying.

"Come meet your son," she said.

Marais parted the blankets with his fingers. He peered inside.

The baby's tiny head was covered with thin strings of dark hair. It blinked its filmy, blue-black eyes at him. Marais touched its nose with the tip of his finger. He touched its pink lips, its chin and ears. The baby's skin was as soft as dough.

She laid the boy in a small basket and embraced Marais. Her head barely reached his shoulders. He felt like a child again. It embarrassed him to be caressed like this, to be held by his mother near his own bedroom. But he didn't want her to let go.

"It seems there's nothing to be done now," she whispered. "But we soldier on, don't we, Eugene? You and I, we always soldier on." She loosened her grip and kissed him, then carried the baby into the kitchen.

He nudged open the door. A thick cloth was draped across Lettie's forehead. Marais couldn't tell whether the moisture on her cheeks was water or perspiration.

"I'm not as bad off as I look," she said.

She was so hot when he kissed her face that instinctively he pulled away. He took the cloth and dunked it into the bucket of water on the side table, then wrung it out and spread it back across her forehead.

"Mmm, that's better," she said. "He's beautiful, don't you think? Our sweet little boy. We should name him after your father."

Marais shook his head. "Never. We can name him after Charles." Marais's brother. The closest thing he'd ever had to a real father. "Eugene Charles Gerard Marais."

Lettie brushed a strand of hair from her face. "Yes." She forced a smile. "It's always been perfect with you. Every minute together."

She took his left hand between both of hers. It felt as if he was being cooked inside her.

"What is it that you want from this life?" she asked.

Marais couldn't think clearly. "I don't know, sweet." His head was swimming. "To make a mark on the world, I suppose. To leave myself somehow embedded in this planet. There was always so much time."

"What I wanted, Eugene, was to marry a good man, a kind man. I've done that." She brought his hand to her face and held his palm against her cheek. "There are only two things that I still want. Imagine that. Two is so few, don't you think? I want you to go and make your mark on the world. I truly do. But above all else, I want you to love our little boy."

Marais could feel the pulse in her neck. Her eyes shot wide open. Her whole body shivered. "Look how these things happen, Eugene. So quickly it all changes."

"Don't talk like that, Lettie." His voice didn't sound like his. "There's nothing to worry about. It's only good news. That's what I came to tell you—they're dropping the suit."

Her body seemed to relax at this. "I knew you would do it. As long as we've known each other, I've never doubted you. Now you can do me one last favor."

"Anything."

"Go to your study. Open your drawer. And throw away the medicine. There's no need for that wretched stuff anymore. Get rid of it now, before it kills you."

Gently, he touched her lips—she didn't mean this—but she thrust his hand away. "I want it out of my house," she cried. "All of it!"

"Lettie!" She was struggling so hard against him that he pinned her shoulders to keep her from hurting herself. "Please, sweet. Please calm down."

Her frame went limp. "I'm sorry," she said. "I think I need to sleep."

He felt himself falling then. The floor was still solid, his feet firmly planted, and yet, he had the sudden feeling of dropping. "No, no, Lettie. Not now," he said, gasping. "We can't have this now."

"Shush. Don't be silly. Only for a little while. I just need to rest. Then we'll talk about that medicine."

She closed her eyes. Soon her breathing deepened. Marais sat next to her on the bed. He pulled up the blankets and tucked them around her shoulders. He ran his thumbs over her forehead. With her eyes shut like this, with everything covered but the white of her neck, her head, and chin, there was something saintly about her. He smoothed out the wrinkled blankets. He pushed them gently along her belly, her hips, knees, and legs. She was so small all of a sudden, so fragile he could hardly breathe.

He must have fallen asleep himself. He was certain that he'd reached the queen. He'd finally found the bloated insect, cloistered in the heart of her termitary, bulbous and mucousy. Her face was that of Queen Victoria. And all around her, British soldiers were swarming. She commanded them to attack. With his knife, Marais reached for her neck . . .

When he awoke, a thin stream of saliva was running down his cheek and stark gray light flooded the room. Marais wiped at his mouth. His lips were dry, his temples throbbed, and Lettie, his sweet wife, was dead.

September 1935, Cambridge, Massachusetts

Charles's eyes snap open. Two in the morning and there's an intruder in his apartment. A rustling sound followed by searing screams. He takes a breath, creeps from his bed to the kitchen in only his underwear, palming his Swiss Army knife.

What he finds is Tonto, perched at the top of the ficus like an angel atop a Christmas tree. A dozen nests bob around him like homemade ornaments.

The bird blinks twice. The yellow crest droops to the side of his head. He opens his beak slowly, the start of what looks like a bird-sized yawn. He ogles Charles, waggles his head. Then he starts to bawl. It's the loneliest crying Charles has ever heard.

Charles cages the little bird to try to comfort him. He tosses a blanket over the bars. The bird immediately quiets.

Hours tick by. Charles vowed to keep the bird out of its cage, wild within the confines of his flat. The silence grows unbearable. He removes the cover, unlatches the door. The little bird flies back to the ficus. Within minutes, his construction work hits a manic pitch. He shrieks so loudly that Charles begins wondering where he'll move after the inevitable eviction notice arrives. How many houses can one weaver build?

* * *

Charles never had a home. Not one that felt like his own, with childhood rooms that would appear years later in his dreams. There were no family relations to anchor him, to keep him from drifting across oceans—to one life and then another. The letter from Marais only served to remind him of what he missed. Five years in the States, the preceding twenty-five in Britain, his first ten in South Africa. What does this make him? Afrimeritish? Amenglikaner?

He still holds faint memories of Pretoria. Sophie, his aunt and godmother, owned a boarding house, a two-story wooden structure with five spare rooms that she let to anyone passing through—failed gold prospectors who'd given up on the Witwatersrand and fled north while they figured out where to go next, Jewish peddlers who drove wagons full of fabrics and cooking pots and hand tools from farm to farm until they depleted their stock and returned to Durban or Port Elizabeth or Delagoa Bay to refill. On any given night, Charles had to share his attic room with one of Sophie's itinerants, an old braided rug the only thing separating their beds. He was too shy to converse with most of them. There were a few drawers for his clothes and a shelf for books. He had a penchant for the adventurers, Kipling and Jack London.

After dinner, Sophie and her son and two daughters, Charles's cousins, would say their goodnights to Charles. He tried not to look them in the eye at these times—the last thing he wanted was for any of them to feel sorry for him. Why should they? He could take care of himself. He would stand at the doorway to the circular dining room with his arms stiff by his sides and endure their hugs and the pecks on his cheek. Then the others would retire to the east side of the house to prepare for bed, and he'd climb the wooden staircase to the attic, where he combed his hair and changed out of his clothes, and reminded himself that at six years old he was nearly a man and that there was nothing about nighttime that need sadden or scare him. But even with the covers pulled over his head and the space of the house between him and the others, as he drifted off to sleep, he sometimes heard his cousins joke and laugh—in the ordinary manner that siblings do when the lights wink off at the end of a day—and this made him saddest of all.

War loomed over the Transvaal during his childhood. Fortunately, the raid by the British doctor Starr Jameson had amounted to nothing—Jameson and Cecil Rhodes bungled the operation, failing to incite a revolt among the English miners in Johannesburg. Disgraced, Rhodes resigned as prime minister. Jameson got jail time. But twenty-four months later, thousands of British troops were assembling in Natal along the Transvaal's southeastern border. Charles had the sense that something terrible might befall his city any day. What he didn't know was that President Kruger would declare war first.

Charles listened intently to Sophie's conversations with her guests each night. Journalists and prostitutes from London, they said, were sailing for Cape Town in droves. Gambling rings sprang up across the imperial city so men could wager on the number of days until the Transvaal and the Free State, the other Boer Republic, finally fell. English papers dismissed the entire event, predicting an excessively short "teatime war."

To everyone's surprise, the war started out well for the Boers. Kruger's men laid siege to Ladysmith in Natal, Mafeking in the northern Cape Colony, and Kimberley on the border of the Free State. Hundreds of British died. Dozens more were taken captive. It would be weeks before reinforcements could arrive. Charles overheard Sophie's guests debating whether they'd overestimated

English military prowess after all. The Brits were being routed by small ill-equipped troops of untrained Boer farmers.

By January, though, great hordes of British reinforcements began to arrive. More than a hundred thousand descended on Natal and the Cape Colony, and there were rumors of another hundred and fifty thousand to come. Battalions of lancers, rifle brigades, cavalry, and the Royal Navy all sailed to the southern tip of Africa to quash the tiny wayward republics. They brought with them howitzers and maxims and boatloads of heavy cannon.

In June, Pretoria surrendered. The British paraded into the capital on horseback and hoisted the Union Jack in the middle of Church Square. Charles had never seen the British flag close up. It had been twenty years since it last flew in the Transvaal. Kruger fled for Europe through Mozambique. In November, Britain declared the war over.

But the Volksraad's concession of defeat meant little to the Boers. Charles watched from his window as all the men of fighting age left Pretoria. There was nothing they wouldn't do, Sophie told him, to protect their farms and their families. The Boers' guerrilla resistance proved much more potent than the Transvaal's original, "organized" forces.

To combat the commandos, Lord Kitchener cooked up a more sinister strategy. British troops set off across the countryside setting fire to every farm they passed. They ravaged crops, burned down homes, and rendered the fields uncultivable. They slaughtered three quarters of the Transvaal's cattle and sheep in a single year.

One spring night, Charles was awakened by the shatter of glass and the sound of military boots clomping up the stairs. Timbers rattled through the wood-framed house. Men bellowed in thick English and Irish accents. "Mandatory evacuation, mum.

For your own safety. There's no choice but compliance." He lay frozen in bed, listening as Sophie unleashed a hailstorm of obscenities.

Then Charles's own door burst open. Three British troops plowed into the room. "Get the boy!" they shouted. Before Charles could throw off the covers, one of the men scooped him up, locked his head under his arm, and wrangled him down the stairs, his feet flailing in the air behind him. The tang of their sweat stung his eyes.

Outside, in the damp night, the first person Charles saw after his aunt and cousins was his favorite neighbor, Van der Vetter, the sixty-year-old carpenter who always gave the local children sweets when their parents weren't looking. Van der Vetter was lying in the road, his face shimmering in the torchlight. He was dead and bleeding from the eyes. All of Charles's schoolmates, along with their mothers, were corralled into a line that stretched as far as he could see in both directions. The parade of mothers and children began to march eastward.

That night, Charles slept in the dirt under a bell tent with a dozen neighbors packed in so thickly that he couldn't roll onto his back. His neck bristled with pain. When day finally broke, he sat in the sun, trying to spit the mud from his mouth, while a soldier with a khaki helmet and shoulder stripes explained that they were now all happily safe. They were being concentrated in camps where they'd be shielded from Boer fire and out of harm's way. The Queen, the soldier said, encouraged them to go about their lives in the camp as best they could. They should consider themselves her guests.

A five-strand, steel-wire fence with barbed tips enclosed the compound. They were being imprisoned in a highly patrolled chicken coop. The northwestern corner of the camp was designated for toileting. Eating facilities were erected in the northeast. The British would soon provide them with beds in the tents, they were told, and two hot meals a day. These turned out to be maize mixed occasionally with shreds of unidentifiable meat. Charles and the other children passed the afternoons scavenging through trash heaps outside the soldiers' mess hall, hunting for burnt onions or air-dried potato peelings, or just an eggshell to lick clean.

Each of the Queen's guests received one cup of drinking water per day. The soldiers said they expected to increase that ration over time. They never did.

One by one, the Queen's guests died. Of dehydration and dysentery. Of heat stroke and malnutrition, measles and typhoid. Twenty-six thousand in all, most under the age of sixteen. Charles watched them die. One day a child was there—the next she would be gone. The British had nowhere to dispose of the bodies, so they heaped them in the far corner of the camp where the flies were as thick as termite storms, and rats plucked out eyeballs and noodle-like intestines. There were piles of boys. Mountains of girls. From time to time, Charles spotted a corpse that looked familiar. Sophie told him not to look, but he couldn't help but stray to the camp's edge. The shape of so many bodies stacked together was mesmerizing. The British were transforming his neighbors into a towering sculpture of flesh.

* * *

From outside the classroom, Charles hears the hum of student voices. He listens to the rise and fall of their speech, as opaque as the burbling of a foreign language. Three voices, all male. As he suspected, Hannah Tauber decided not to return. He's relieved that the girl, who witnessed his attendance at Conant's memorial service, has disappeared quietly from his life, and at the same time, surprised by his own disappointment.

Thankfully, he's heard nothing from Conant since that service. The president must have come to his senses and abandoned his plans.

When Charles opens the door, Dennis, Harry, and William sit at attention in the front row of chairs. The room smells vaguely of decay. The building's age has seeped into the floorboards and settled in the plaster.

"You're late again, sir," says William cheerfully. He has on a black linen jacket and pinstriped trousers, a pencil tucked into the fold of his ear. Charles likes these students. He likes their youth and their unexpected enthusiasm for this ancient language. Every semester he teaches a handful of classes, but Pāli has always been his favorite.

As he turns to his desk, he realizes he was mistaken. Hannah Tauber sits by the window, paging through a dictionary, hair tied up with a blue ribbon. A cotton blazer flares gracefully over her hips.

"I didn't expect to see you again, Miss Tauber."

"To tell you the truth, I didn't expect it either. The last class intrigued me—I've been reading up on Buddhism all week. Plus, I figured these fellows could use some reinforcements."

"That is so thoughtful," says Harry, flashing his teeth at her.

"I'm sure they'll appreciate any help they can get," Charles says. "We have an entire language to learn."

On the blackboard he chalks the words, "Case endings for A-stem nouns," then sketches a table with two columns marked "Singular" and "Plural," and begins filling in the cells. Nominative.

Accusative. Instrumental. Eight cases in all. Behind him, pens whisper across paper.

He turns to face them. "You may recall the context for this language, for this entire course really: how Prince Siddhārtha left his home, his entire family, to pursue enlightenment unfettered—"

Hannah's hand flies up, delicate fingers fluttering at the ceiling.

"Miss Tauber?"

"I hate to ask this, as it was generous of you just to admit me—"

"As a silent auditor," says Charles.

"Fair point." She tucks her hair behind her ear. "It's just that last year, I lost both of my parents. I need a new way of looking at the world, one that can provide a reasonable explanation for what I've been going through. I know we're focusing on grammar, but will we also get to read what the Buddha taught, in his own language, about the nature of truth—at least eventually?"

She's an orphan, he thinks. *Like me.* So that's the reason she's come to his class. "From what you've read so far, what *did* the Buddha teach about the nature of truth, Miss Tauber, in *your* language?"

She considers the question. "He taught that life is suffering. That there is a cause to this suffering. That there is an end to this suffering—"

"What is the cause of suffering, Miss Tauber?"

Her cheeks flush, but only for a moment. Then her eyes meet his, and for the first time since he's known her, she smiles. "I guess that's what I'm here to find out."

"Desire," he says. "The cause of suffering is desire."

* * *

Charles walks everywhere. Unlike his colleagues, who exit their Cambridge homes, unlock their polished cars, and drive, even if their destination is a hundred yards away. They drive past the beggars, the missionary kitchens, commercial districts that look bombed apart. They drive right past the throngs of men who squat on the sidewalks of Inman and Kendall Squares playing cards on oil drums and drinking from paper bags until sunset falls and they jump turnstiles to get back onto the subway and find their way home. Charles is captivated by the streets. If you never leave your car or the Yard, if you never leave your palace—he thinks of the story of that wayward Indian prince—how can you know the world?

The last day of September, he hikes to Central Square to grade papers and plan lessons. Six months ago, his favorite coffee counter was shuttered. With the economy as it is, he expected it to remain boarded up for years, but today an OPEN sign hangs like a set of teeth in the pharmacy window. The original owner apparently used a strong adhesive when he plastered the walls with posters of Ireland's greatest writers, so strong that the new owner, instead of removing them, has tacked his Red Sox paraphernalia right over their faces. The place reminds Charles of how much he likes living here—it doesn't get more Boston than this. He takes an empty stool at the back of the counter, and as he knocks back mugs of iced tea, he becomes increasingly certain that what's staring back at him from beneath Lefty Grove's pitching arm is, in fact, James Joyce's good eye.

The afternoon swelter slowly abates. The sun sinks into a blood spot. Charles buys a scoop of ice cream and rambles back along the side streets that lead to his apartment in Somerville.

He grabs the mail from the box on the porch that says "Marais" in stenciled white letters. He climbs the three stories. He unlocks his door. It's good to be home.

Bright orange light spills through the blinds and paints stripes across the wood floor and the old dresser and the closet door that hides his Murphy bed during the day.

"Where's my favorite bird?" he calls.

He kicks off his loafers and hangs his hat on the peg. He strolls into the kitchen. Tonto has started on a new nest constructed of colored rubber bands, which threaten to send him hurtling into the wall each time he snaps one back and lets go. When the bird sees him, he stops. He squints at Charles with an expression that looks like a reprimand, then plucks a twig from the pile on the floor and begins weaving it through the nest.

Charles fans the mail across the kitchen table. He finds a letter from the Union of South Africa with an ox-wagon emblazoned on the stamp. He peels open the envelope, unfolds the linen paper.

Dear Dr. Marais,

I realize that it may be months before your response to my initial correspondence finds its way back to me. I'm also well aware that our shared blood offers me no entitlement. But on the off-chance that you have not yet replied, or worse, thought against replying at all, I petition again for your assistance. My words are being stolen from me. And I am, alas, not currently in a state to recover them myself. Our family name is at stake. A name that you share.

Beneath more of the same entreaty and the signature is a faint patch of lines with arcs that spiral toward the center. Lines that look like an oily thumbprint. Charles folds up the paper, and as he does, his own thumb slides over the mark. Here he pauses. He presses down. There's a sort of tack to the print, and heat—like the heat of another's skin against his own. For a split second, he feels as if he's actually touching Marais's hand.

A thought occurs to him. Is Marais—his one living parent, the man who abandoned him—so calculating that he left this print intentionally?

One of the drawbacks of a letter is that you can destroy it only once. Charles crumples the paper in his fist and pitches it down the metal trash chute. He clicks on the Philco and dials through the stations, but he isn't in the mood for music or news. He tries grading papers but can't concentrate for more than a few seconds at a time. In his mind, he can still see the thumbprint marring the crumpled letter. It will be three days before the trash gets picked up.

At the bottom of the rickety staircase to the basement, he finds the paper perched on top of carrot peelings and used tea bags and melon rinds. He grabs the letter. He takes it outside. With a single match-strike, he sets the ball on fire.

* * *

As the semester burns on, Charles leads the class at a ferocious pace through the foundations of Pāli grammar, through declensions and persons and tenses and moods. So much white chalk accumulates on his right palm and fingers that it's hard to wash off at the end of the day. His own prints seem to linger on everything he touches.

"Most suttas," he tells his students, "begin the same exact way, with the same three-word formula: Evaṃ me sutaṃ. 'Thus have I heard.' A question for you: who is this invisible I who's heard all the Buddha's teachings?"

William's hand shoots up. "It's one of his disciples. Ananda, I think."

"That's right. It's said that after the Buddha died, Ananda memorized every *sutta*—the equivalent of thousands of pages. He seared them into his memory for the community's benefit. Without paper, there was no other way to keep the teachings alive."

"I've been toying with a different theory," Hannah says.

"Miss Tauber, you may be the most vocal silent auditor ever to set foot on this campus."

"It's very kind of you to say so. But if I may, the Buddha was like a father to Ananda, right?"

"In a sense . . ."

"When the Buddha got sick and died, Ananda must have been devastated. He must have been terrified of forgetting him. What better way to remember his father—to keep him vivid in his mind—than to tell the stories again and again? So I keep thinking: maybe Ananda didn't recite the *suttas* for the community's benefit after all, at least not primarily."

"Why else would he have done all that work?"

"What I'm saying is that maybe it was *personal*. Maybe it was just for him."

The boys consider this for a moment. One by one, they begin scratching away in their notebooks.

Terrified of forgetting his father? All his life, Charles has been *trying* to forget Marais. But as he mulls over her words, he realizes he has never questioned the standard interpretation.

He sits on the corner of his desk, folds his arms over his chest, and observes her. She reminds him of himself as a graduate student. She won't accept anything as given. She won't let go of an idea until she's considered it from every angle. "Your theory, Miss Tauber, is unconventional. At the same time, it seems plausible."

Dust motes shimmer in the golden afternoon. Her smile flashes quick and radiant as the three young men look on with unconcealed adoration.

* * *

The next week, they move on to nominal compounds, the building blocks of Pāli and Sanskrit—*karmadhārayas, tatpuruṣas, dvandvas.* He's pleasantly surprised at his students' interest.

"The one that holds the special place in my heart," Charles tells them, "is the *bahuvrīhi.* A compound noun that refers to something completely separate from any of the elements in the compound. In English, a 'bigshot' isn't necessarily big and is definitely not a shot. But when the two words combine, they take on a new meaning. In this case, the compound connotes a certain type of person."

Harry hoists his hand. "A person not unlike yourself, sir."

Charles raises his brow at the flagrant brown-nosing. He turns to the others. "Okay, who has another?"

"You're pretty nice too," says Hannah. "For a professor, I mean."

"I meant another example," he says, unable to suppress a smile. "But I'll take the compliment."

Dennis nods toward William, whose chair sits directly between his and Hannah's. "Girl-crazy," he says. William punches Dennis in the thigh.

"Not quite," Charles corrects. "That's an adjectival compound. To be a *bahuvrīhi*, it has to be a noun."

Out of nowhere, a chorus of trumpets erupts. The windows are all flung open because of the heat, and the blaring horns and snare drums reverberate against the classroom walls.

The three boys jump from their seats to have a look.

"What's the Salvation Army doing in Harvard Yard?" says Harry.

Charles gazes through the open window. In the middle of Tercentenary Theatre, just west of Sever, a couple dozen students in blue military uniforms are parading in formation. A small band pounds out a military march. The line rotates in a slowly swelling spiral. At the very front, a teenage boy brandishes a red flag. Each time he tugs at the pole, the fabric snaps like a gunshot. *That isn't the Salvation Army*, thinks Charles.

In the center of the flag, a stark white circle enshrouds a black swastika.

He's seen the new Nazi flag in the papers. But the sight of it this close up jolts him. Memories of the church service flare in his mind.

"Jesus," says Dennis. "That one in the front is an editor for the Harvard *Crimson*. I *know* him."

The kid with the flag has on tall black boots with thick, double-knotted laces.

Small crowds have gathered to stare from the walkways that cut through the lawn. Charles can't pull his eyes away. The boys on the grass look like marionettes with their sharp, jolting movements. Their knees pull unnaturally high.

The music explodes. The parade accelerates. Can this be happening in broad daylight, in the middle of Harvard Yard?

The sun pours through the window. Charles wipes at the sweat on his forehead. He turns to find Hannah sitting at her desk, staring straight ahead. At first he thinks she's studying the examples on the board. But the rims of her eyes have reddened.

"Is everything all right, Miss Tauber?"

The boys drift back to their seats. The girl claps a palm to her lips and barely suppresses a cry.

"Ms. Tauber?" says Charles.

Trumpets erupt again. A fanfare from Wagner. Her chin is trembling.

William reaches into his pocket and offers her a handkerchief. "Hannah," he says quietly. "It's going to be okay."

She takes the cloth. She wipes her nose. "'Lowlifes,'" she says under her breath.

"Excuse me?" says Charles.

"It's a *bahuvrīhi*, isn't it? 'Lowlifes'?"

It takes a moment before he understands. "Yes, that's a good example."

"Blockheads," she says, her voice rising.

"Also correct," says Charles. He leans on the edge of the desk, crosses his arms around himself. There's a tightening in his chest.

Hannah's hair seems suddenly disheveled. She pushes it from her eyes. "Halfwits. Hateful, ignorant halfwits."

"Thank you. We get the idea. I think we can safely say we're okay with compounds at this point."

"No, Professor! None of this is okay. We're no different from Europe. We tell ourselves we're safe here only because it makes us feel better."

"She's just upset," William says. "It's a bit of a shock for all of us to see them right here on campus."

"Keep out of this," says Charles sharply. His voice doesn't sound like his.

William's face darkens, and Charles knows he's crossed a line. He wants William and the others to disappear. He wants to focus on Hannah. He wants to defend the university, New England, an entire country that is not even his, but to whose unsullied image he's been clinging for years.

"I disagree, Miss Tauber," he says. "We *are* different from Europe. In this country, those students are permitted to voice their opinions peacefully just as we're free to disagree with their politics. It doesn't make us any less safe."

Hannah stares at him in disbelief. "If you actually believe that, you're deluding yourself." She slaps her dictionary closed and storms out of the room, and he realizes that nothing he's said to her, nothing he's told himself, has made him feel safer or better at all.

* * *

There have been women in Charles's life, though few of his past relationships could be counted real successes. British girls always seemed to try too hard in conversation, and when it came to romance, to try barely at all. As a university student in London, he sometimes felt as if he was expected to run the entire operation himself, even as he was still learning how a number of the most important female parts worked.

At the end of his sixth-form year, he found himself with a tall, athletic girl named Laura. She visited him in his dorm room one night, and after only a couple minutes of necking, unfastened her dress and peeled off her shirts. He told her that she was beautiful, which struck him as a ridiculous understatement.

Afterwards, he lay next to her, marveling at the miracle of her body. Laura raked her fingers through her tangled hair. His sweat glistened on her pale chest. It was the closest he'd ever felt to another person. In a burst of optimism, he rolled onto his side, took her hand, and asked how their petting had been for her.

A faint shadow passed behind her distracted eyes as she returned to the present. "Oh. Well . . . you know. It was brilliant, love," she said with considerably too much enthusiasm, dashing any hope that he might see her again.

When he first moved to America, he dated a handful of women, a librarian from Boston, a teacher at the elementary school on Cambridge Street, a secretary in Harvard's English department. They were fine women with interests in literature and history. But the relationships petered out without any real discussion of what was ending or why. On some level, they could never measure up to that other woman, the one he'd lost before all of them.

Stashed at the bottom of his closet is a picture he's kept since childhood, a framed, sepia-toned photograph whose details he's burned to memory. In the photo, his mother, Aletta Marais, is reclining on a four-poster bed amid a mess of pillows, suckling her newborn child. There's a radiance about her. And anyone could see that, although she'd known her baby for only a few hours, she already loved him more than the world.

* * *

Before the next class, Charles swings by the department and grabs his campus mail. The note in his box is handwritten on ivory stationery.

Dear Dr. Marais,

We're nearly ready to progress with the new committee I mentioned. Such exciting times. Let's schedule a date to meet and identify a suitable role for you. Contact my office at your earliest convenience. I look forward to a productive collaboration.

—Your most humble servant, JBC

Charles folds up the paper. He stashes it gingerly in his briefcase. He feels positively ill. Is it possible he misunderstood the conversation with Conant at Memorial Church? Maybe he misinterpreted the purpose of the committee, though he can't imagine how. One way or another, there has been a mistake. If nothing else, Conant has mistaken him for a different sort of person. He needs time to sort this out, to disentangle himself. There has to be a way to correct the misunderstanding without threatening his career.

He decides to skip his next Pāli class. He has the department secretary tell his students that he's guest lecturing in Boston on short notice. No one asks questions. These things happen: last minute invitations from neighboring institutions when some bigger-name speaker happens to cancel. You scramble to patch together a lecture, catch a series of trains to reach the school, search for the address among labyrinthine halls with inadequate signage, and find yourself at last in a small, remote room, sometimes barely more than an office, with half a dozen students and faculty, a few of whom might have some real interest in your topic, while the rest have been pressured into attending. You deliver your talk amid yawns and distracted glances, receive a pittance of an honorarium. This is success in the sport of academic ladder-climbing.

When the class reconvenes, Hannah is curt and aloof. William won't quite meet his gaze. Charles suspects that if he offers a formal apology for his outburst in the last class it will only make matters worse, so he plows ahead, focusing squarely on teaching.

Hannah was right: no one stands up to the Nazis. No one asks them to stop. Not the deans, not the police, not Conant. The outdoor music concerts soon migrate to Harvard Square, a backdrop against which Charles tries his best to carry on with his routine. The weather cools, and with the windows shut and locked, it's almost possible to pretend that nothing out of the ordinary is occurring, that it's just another typical fall semester at Harvard—like 1934 and 1933 and the several hundred years before that. Except when the smack of a bass drum bursts its way inside. When the floor rattles and the walls start to sway.

* * *

Two more letters from Marais arrive at his home in October, another three before Thanksgiving. Marais has no right to inject himself into Charles's life after so long. What right does he have to ask for help? Charles doesn't owe him anything.

By December, letters from South Africa are arriving almost daily. Charles tosses them unopened onto a shelf in the corner where they form the foundation of a minor mountain. He can't focus on work. During class, he loses his train of thought mid-sentence. His students look on uneasily, as if he's just lost a limb. Or contracted the plague.

With a week left before winter break, a wooden sign appears tacked to a tree in the Yard. Harvard's history department, it announces, is planning a mock public trial of Hitler. The university's faculty is finally preparing to put this to rest. His colleagues are going to take a stand and reaffirm the institution's essential decency.

Re-energized, Charles vows to take the class through at least one full text this semester. On a whim, he decides on the *Vessantara Jātaka*. "Do any of you know this story?" he asks.

The first snow of the year is falling on the other side of the window, descending so slowly that you can follow a single flake from the point in the sky where it first breaks through to the spot on the ground where it settles.

As Hannah raises her hand, the other three drop theirs and turn to her. Her nails are polished, colored a deep coral. Increasingly, Charles senses, the boys are in awe of her.

"It's the most famous of the Buddha's birth stories," she says. "His penultimate incarnation."

"In which . . . ?"

"He perfects the practice of generosity. As a result, he's reborn in his next life as Siddhārtha Gautama."

"I'm impressed. Go on."

"I'd love to, but that's as much as I know so far on this particular topic."

Charles leads them through the story of how Prince Vessantara gives up his kingdom and moves to the forest to live as a hermit with his wife and his two young children. A greedy Brahmin named Jūjaka lives nearby. Jūjaka is looking for slaves to care for his house, and hearing about the generosity of the new hermit in town, he hunts down Vessantara in the forest and asks for his son and daughter. With his wife away at the river, Vessantara gladly hands over his children. Jūjaka binds Vessantara's son and daughter with leather straps and hauls them away as they cry out, begging their father to save them from slavery. But Vessantara turns his back and returns to his hut, having completed this greatest act of generosity.

Condensation drips down the windows with steady, staccato plinks and pools on the sills. The radiator in the far corner of the room clangs and whistles. Dennis shuffles in his seat.

"I don't understand," says Harry. "You're saying the Buddha does this?"

"Technically, he's Prince Vessantara," Charles says. "Because of this act, he'll be reborn as Siddhārtha Gautama, who will then become the Buddha."

"Because he gives away his children?" Dennis asks.

"That's right."

"To a man he knows will abuse them?"

"Correct."

Dennis drops his chin in his palms. They all look confused. "This represents Buddhist generosity?" William asks.

"More than any other story."

"To give away your child without concern for what will happen to him?"

"It's a complicated story, I'll grant you that."

"It's criminal," Hannah protests. "His kids are going to be enslaved. They'll be beaten. Vessantara *knows* this."

"Think of it this way," says Charles. "What if Vessantara has to perform this one act in order to become a Buddha? And what if becoming a Buddha is the only way to save the world's countless beings? What if he has no choice?"

She rolls her eyes at this explanation. "Of course he has a choice. Every father has a choice. No one *has* to give away his child."

He could have chosen a hundred other stories. Why did he have to select this one? With five words, she has yanked the ground from under him. *Every father has a choice.* "What are you saying?" he asks. "What does that make him?" His composure has vanished.

"Honestly, I don't know, Professor."

But Charles knows. He answers his own question. *A selfish son of a bitch.*

He has read the story dozens of times. But these are the words that ring through his mind now—nothing that he'd ever utter within the bounds of Harvard Yard, in a classroom on the top floor of Sever Hall with the snow falling outside and winter break approaching and tenure at last on the horizon. The problem with living alone for so long is that the line between thought and speech sometimes blurs to the point of dissolving entirely, and he finds himself face-to-face now with four students gaping at him.

"Did you just say what I think you said?" Dennis asks. "About the *Buddha*?"

Charles takes off his glasses.

"Are you even allowed to say that at Harvard?"

Charles blows on the lenses. He wipes them with a handkerchief. He feels four pairs of eyes lock onto him. That's half the problem, he thinks. No one seems to care anymore who says what on this campus. He rubs his hand along his face. Two days' worth of stubble scratch against his palm. He forgot to shave again this morning.

* * *

Across the Yard, Charles downs a third cup of coffee as he works his way through a medieval palm-leaf manuscript from Burma and tries not to think about fathers who abandon their children.

Only a fraction of his office could be considered usable by an average-sized human. The ceiling slants viciously toward the nook where the floor meets the ceiling, so he has turned his bookcases on their sides. The hundreds of volumes that don't fit on the shelves he has stacked in piles along the room's perimeter.

As he forges a path through the text, it strikes him for the thousandth time that translation is ultimately just a game of guesswork. With every translation, there are multiple considerations: historical context, presumed authorial intent, the interplay of one text with another. He recalls a joke familiar to all Sanskritists: every Sanskrit word means itself, its opposite, and "elephant." And then there are the scribes. He feels as if he's come to know the men who produced these copies of the ancient manuscripts. He knows their individual handwriting, subtle lexical preferences, their typical spelling mistakes. Over time, he's given names to his favorites: Gus, Townshend, Leroy, Monsieur Stylo. On certain leaves, he thinks he can make out traces of curries or oil or fruit stains. He knows what they liked to eat. He can smell them on the leaves.

He flips through the pages, unable to focus for more than a few seconds at a time. The fact that he hasn't responded to Marais has only made the problem worse. The letters keep coming. Maybe he should leave Somerville entirely. If he moves, it could take Marais years to find him again.

A flash of color catches his eye. Hannah whirls through the doorway. She's bundled in a peacoat and a blue wool hat with a moose embroidered on the front. Her lips and cheeks are nearly as white as the snow that clings to her stockings.

"May I come in?" she asks.

Charles rises, narrowly avoids knocking his head against the ceiling. He pulls out the other ladder-back chair. "You don't look well," he says.

"You haven't heard then . . ."

News of the mock public trial gushes from her. Faculty in the history department have pronounced Hitler innocent of all charges. Of persecuting Jews, invading homes without a warrant, ordering the murder of dozens, if not hundreds, of Germans.

"Innocent!" she cries. "On what basis could a reasonable person come to that conclusion?"

Charles is stunned. For the first time, he starts to wonder if this is how fascism takes root. Not in the shadows, but where you'd least expect it—in the most visible of places. He can't bring himself to tell her how high up the Olympus of Harvard the matter extends.

"They're smart people," he says. "Good people. If they made a statement like that, we must not have the whole story. There has to be an explanation."

"I *know* the explanation." The frustration in her eyes is followed by a flicker of suspicion. "The first time I saw you was at Memorial Church." She lowers her voice to nearly a whisper. "I knew who was inside with you, Professor. I decided not to ask what you were doing there. I wanted to give you the benefit of the doubt."

His face begins to burn. "The president of the university invited me—"

"To do what for them?"

He has no good answer. He can't tell her about his conversation with Conant, regardless of how much he wishes he could. She's his student. He is inches away from tenure.

"Did you promise them something?"

"Is that what you think? That I'd sell myself out?"

"What should I think? I'm Jewish. I believe they want to eliminate us."

Judenfrei. Conant's word ricochets through his mind. "It was a mistake. I would never have attended if I'd known what they were up to."

"Well, now you know. And because you know, you have to do something. You have to stand up to them. Report them to the Board of Overseers. If that doesn't work, escalate the matter to the Bureau of Investigation. The whole country needs to know what's happening on this campus. You have a responsibility."

"They haven't broken any laws, Hannah. And I can't just . . . I have a career to think of. I'm nearly tenured. Do you know what that means for someone like me?"

She stops as if to reassess him. "You would compromise everything you believe in just to stay at Harvard?"

"No, of course not." He can feel the shame smeared across his face. "I just mean that I need to act sensibly."

"Professor, there's no time left for acting sensibly. I am terrified by what's happening here. I came to tell you that I'm thinking about leaving."

She would leave? "There's no need for that." The urgency in his voice surprises him. "I know what you're saying, but I'm not ready to give up here. I've made it through worse before. Hell, do you know what happened in South Africa when I was a child? The whole place was nearly razed to the ground. And now? It couldn't be safer."

"For Jews, you mean?" Her green eyes dissect him.

"That's not what I meant, but sure. When I was a boy, there were Jews living throughout the Transvaal. I've heard a hundred thousand have already immigrated there."

"To South Africa?"

He nods.

"A hundred thousand?"

"Probably more."

Her chair creaks as she leans back. "I had no idea," she says. Her shoulders seem to soften. She looks at him with a sense of trust that he's not sure he deserves. "It's good to know there are options out there at least. That makes me feel a little better."

"I have that effect on people."

When she laughs, it seems as if the room itself has brightened. "Then you won't be surprised if I decide to return in a few minutes."

In the orange light, he notices the faintest birthmark imprinted above her left ear, a tiny half-moon. She sits feet away, but he feels somehow affixed, nearly buoyed in her presence.

"Come back whenever you like, Hannah Tauber. You're always welcome."

"I shall happily take you up on that offer." She rises, squeaks her chair into place. As she turns to leave, the back of her hand stirs against him. It feathers across his arm, his hand, his fingers.

What he meant to say was, "Why don't you stay a bit longer?" But he blinked and she's already gone.

The moment, like all moments, is fleeting. He didn't tell Hannah about the conversation with Conant. He didn't tell her about the president's latest letter, which he deposited like an explosive in his briefcase. He hasn't scheduled a meeting with Conant. He tries to convince himself that the university's flirtation with Germany might be a passing fad. If he keeps quiet, he tells himself, surely he can ride it out. Harvard is his home. He belongs here as much as any of them do.

Afternoon tumbles into evening, and he craves a decent dinner. He invites his friend, Frank Williams, but Williams says he has a date—he'll be untangling an arcane linguistic mystery in a Sanskrit text he's been grappling with.

Charles returns to Somerville alone. He boils yams on one burner and steams greens on the other. In the oven, he roasts a small chicken. He salts and peppers the hen and stuffs garlic and herbs between the skin and muscle and lets it cook in its juices until the room is awash with the smell of the roast. When the food is ready, he lights a pair of candles, uncorks a bottle of red wine, and sets about his meal in silence.

Tonto stares at him, gaping from his branch. So judgmental, this bird.

As he polishes off his fourth glass, a nagging thought occurs to him: if he were to disappear, would anyone even notice? Would Hannah? He forks the greens around his plate. He thought he'd finally banished this loneliness. But here it is again with its unstomachable gristle. He knocks around the cupboard until he finds the gin. He doesn't even bother to pour, just swigs from the bottle, which is redolent of medicine and herbs.

Hours later, he manages to pull himself from the floor, head pounding. He washes and dries the dishes, restocks them in the cupboard. He exits the kitchen to undress and read in bed. On the way, he skids over an envelope that looks exactly like the others from Marais. Someone must have slipped it under the entrance. He throws open the door. No one is there.

Three letters are inscribed on the corner of the envelope. *SOS*. Charles tosses the letter on the desk. He brushes his teeth, washes his face. It's only after he shuts off the reading light and tucks the sheet around his neck and rolls to his side—always his left, where he can feel the beat of his heart through his skin—that he remembers the letter again.

He pulls the switch and the light winks on. At his desk, he slits open the envelope, unfolds the paper:

Dear Dr. Marais:

Each day I await your response, and still there's no word. I should disclose to you that I've received communications from your university extolling my research on the white ants, and corrupting it in the name of racialism. Imagine losing control of your own ideas. As if I have ever suggested that the queen's role in the hive supports the theory of a master race among humans. They are perverting our name—yours and mine. My unpublished field notes would disprove their thesis, but given my current state, there is nothing I can do about this, at least not alone. This is an attack not just on our family, but on all of South Africa. I feel as if we are at war once again.

Oh Charles—please don't take offense at this informality—I've never been a desperate man. And I don't reach out for help lightly. But I'm afraid I can't go on from here. Son, I need you . . .

Charles does not make it past this last line. "Son" is a name by which he's never been addressed, not once in forty years, and the word chokes in his throat as he recites it again and again and again. He has never been son to anyone.

Thus have I heard.

April 1902, Brussels, Belgium

It was clear and cold the day Marais reached Brussels, the sky awash with blue-gray glaze. The paper he clutched in his hand contained the address of the Transvaal embassy.

From what Marais had pieced together, the Boer commando units in the Transvaal were, after two years, finally on the brink of collapse. They'd been scattered throughout the veld, the men shoeless and pox-ridden, their caches of ammunition nearly exhausted. Without reinforcements, there was no way they'd be able to continue the fight. Tens of thousands of Boer women and children had been rounded up to die in Britain's "concentration camps"—of malnutrition and dysentery and dehydration. Conditions that were completely avoidable. He couldn't help but think that this was the Crown's unspoken intention: to exterminate the Boers once and for all. No other direct military support was forthcoming—not from the Dutch, or the French, or the Germans. Marais had abandoned the Transvaal for London more than five years earlier. He hadn't intended ever to return. But if the commandos fell now, the Transvaal would be lost forever.

Britain would control virtually all of southern Africa. This expedition—*his* expedition—would be the Boers' last chance.

Marais hailed a cab and offered to double the driver's normal fee if he could get him to the embassy in less than half an hour. The cart's wheels plunged through a layer of slush and grime. Mud-brown dogs raced through the street in the opposite direction.

The embassy was housed on a side road in a dilapidated stone building that felt strangely segregated from the city's heart and bustle. The afternoon was windless. The Vierkleur, the Transvaal's flag, drooped from the corner of the roof like a dead fish.

The ambassador, a starched white Boer with a copper head of hair, poured two glasses of brandy and handed one to Marais. "It's a pleasure to welcome one of our shining lights to Brussels," he said, knocking back his liquor and wiping his mouth with his sleeve, "a city that is, I regret to say, otherwise devoid of light or shine."

It was not the ambassador's first drink of the day.

"I tell you, Marais, this godforsaken post in Brussels is equivalent to riding third class on the world's diplomatic railway. Now London, on the other hand—London is the ultimate post city. You've been residing there for years already, I hear, right in the pulsing thick of it. You realize that if all this nasty business with the British had never occurred, I'd be stationed in London right now as Kruger's ambassador to Britain and living in considerably more accommodating surroundings." With a disgusted look, he rubbed vigorously at a spot on the corner of the desk. "Tell me about London. Tell me what I've missed."

The day Marais had arrived at the port of London five years earlier, dozens of ships were plowing through the harbor, horns blaring. Cranes groaned under the weight of steel beams and crates packed with coal. Workers cursed each other, sprinting across the quays to secure their freight. When the ship moored and the gangway was lowered, porters swarmed the pier. Marais took his overcoat and his bags and pushed his way through the crowd—past sandwichmen and hawkers and barrel organists—until he reached land. For the first time he felt London under his feet, the most solid ground he'd ever set foot upon. He had reached the center of the world.

He soon enrolled in law classes at the Inns of Court and medical school at Guy's Hospital. To do so, he had to forge his own undergraduate diploma. He'd never been to college. He was completely self-educated—in the sciences, in literature, in history. He just never stopped reading.

But it wasn't long before the war that he had predicted finally enveloped the Transvaal. British atrocities weren't reported in London's papers. Marais had the stories sent to him from the Cape. With each new report from the concentration camps, he felt a part of himself die. The British, for all their gloss and sophistication, their teatime and glittering palaces, were, as he'd always suspected, the most savage creatures on the planet.

He increased his morphine dosage to four tablets—two grains, nearly five times what it had previously been. He could smell the morphine on his body even after his morning baths. So he began dressing the odor with a perfume that he concocted from cloves and cinnamon and sage. But the increased dosage did little to quell his torment. With each waking minute, the Transvaal, his homeland, was being torn further apart.

It was a university classmate who caught wind of the clandestine expedition leaving from Brussels to deliver crates of ammunition to the guerrillas in the Transvaal. The whole enterprise was top secret, led by a medical doctor named Schultz who'd been trained by the German secret service. The last remaining hope for the Boers.

Marais hadn't considered actually returning to Africa. Or rather, he'd thought of it, but only in a fleeting sort of way. While he'd always be a Boer, London had become his home. He and his family were better off with great distances spilling out between them. He'd planned to remain implanted in the heart of the British metropolis for the rest of his life. But mental images of emaciated Boers, of bones protruding through joints, stoked the coals of his combustible imagination. Lettie, his greatest love, was dead. But his country, his fatherland—for now, that was still intact. It was up to him to go and save the Transvaal while there was still time.

Marais glanced up at the ambassador. "I've come about the expedition."

The ambassador helped himself to a refill. "I'm afraid I don't know what you're referring to."

"The expedition to the northern Transvaal to reinforce the commandos. I've come to join up."

The ambassador opened his eyes wide in mock amazement. "A secret expedition to the Transvaal? My goodness." He began to laugh. "What a marvelously fanciful idea! But seriously, even if we had the will for such an endeavor, how do you think we'd ever fund such a thing? Have you looked at this shack of a building? My staff has been slashed to a mere skeleton. For God's sake," he said, "these days we have to buy our own liquor!"

"I have it on good authority that the Germans are funding an expedition and that it's being mounted from this office." In fact, Marais knew nothing apart from the scant information that he'd gleaned in London, but the more the ambassador denied it, the more certain Marais became of the expedition's existence. "Time is short. I have medical training. I know the geography of the northern Transvaal inside and out. I'll be of great use to our leaders—Botha, Smuts, de la Rey, de Wet."

"I hate to tell you, Mr. Marais, but if this is the reason you've come, I'm afraid you've left London for naught."

The ambassador shook his head with staged pity, reminding Marais of his long-held distaste for civil servants. He was not going to be sent away, not by a goose-headed bureaucrat. "Seeing as I have nowhere else to go, I trust you won't mind if I settle in here for a while."

Marais dropped his bag in the middle of the floor. He helped himself to a generous pour of the brandy, and as the ambassador watched with increasing concern, reclined in the leather armchair and took out his cigarette papers.

"I'm sorry, but I have a great deal of work ahead of me," the ambassador said, aghast at the sight of Marais's shoes on his furniture.

"Don't let me keep you from it."

Marais lit the cigarette and tried to suppress his frustration. He exhaled a series of smoke rings that wafted across the ambassador's desk. With each passing minute, Schultz, the expedition's leader, was moving farther away.

"I do so enjoy reading aloud," said Marais. "I hope this won't bother you." He pulled Darwin from his bag, opened to the beginning, and began reading at a volume fit for the stage. "'After having been twice driven back by heavy southwestern gales, Her Majesty's ship *Beagle*, a ten-gun brig, under the command of Captain Fitz Roy, R. N., sailed from Devonport on the twenty-seventh of December, 1831 . . .'"

The ambassador let out a sigh. "How do you expect me to work while you're 'performing' like this?"

"Not to worry if you miss a passage or two. I plan to read Darwin's entire oeuvre. You'll have no problem catching up. From there, we can move on to Freud."

Marais knew the man would never contact the police and risk calling attention to the embassy's secret mission. If the British discovered that Boer renegades were receiving assistance from within Brussels, the Belgian authorities would shutter the embassy's doors and expel the ambassador. If he wasn't fond of his current post, he really wasn't going to like being shipped back to Pretoria.

The ambassador went about signing the papers on his desk. He twirled nervously with the edge of his mustache and periodically barked inane orders at his staff.

When the embassy closed for the day, Marais adjourned to a small pension around the corner. He took a dinner of sausage and pastries in his room, and pored over the local papers. Britain had now deployed four hundred and fifty thousand imperial troops in southern Africa—more than the entire Boer population of the Transvaal. The commandos' position was growing more tenuous each day. Worse was the damage to the Boer people. Thirteen thousand Boer women and children were homeless, wandering across the barren veld without water or provisions. Open wounds were being sutured with fishing line, lesions bandaged with leaves.

What had become of the boy? Marais grew increasingly desperate at the thought.

He arrived at the embassy the next morning before the doors opened. He wore a pressed suit and carried his steel-tipped cane in one hand and his luggage in the other. When the ambassador arrived, Marais again set up shop in the man's office and refused to budge. He'd brought with him tins of sardines, which he consumed slowly throughout the day.

The ambassador couldn't conceal his exasperation. "I suppose it's safe to tell you," he said at last. "It's clear that you're not an English spy—you're much too recalcitrant for their taste. And in any event, you're too late. The expedition has already left. Doctor Shultz reached Paris last week with explosives and medical supplies arranged for him by our European supporters. He'll be sailing for Dar-es-Salaam any moment, and then for Delagoa Bay, Mozambique. From there, he'll find a way to rendezvous with the Boer commandos. Schultz is long gone. From here on out, he's completely invisible. You might as well return to London—"

But Marais was already sprinting from the ambassador's office. He raced down the steps and leaped into the street to hail a taxi. If he hurried, he could still catch Schultz in Mozambique before the man disappeared forever into the African interior.

At the port, Marais secured himself a berth on the next ship headed to East Africa, a dilapidated old steamer called the *Admiral*. He embarked with one small bag and a stockpile of chocolates and wine. He was soon the most popular passenger on board.

It was blisteringly hot by the time they sailed through Suez, a raging biblical heat that made the bronze sea appear to be steaming. At Dar-es-Salaam the ship docked. The passengers, dripping under their sun hats, disembarked in a great wave. Marais caught the arm of a steward wheeling a stack of wooden crates toward the gangway.

"Where is everyone going?"

"In search of shade and fans."

"But they'll be left behind."

"Didn't you know, sir? We have a full day in port."

"A full day! That can't be."

"Plenty of time to enjoy the market. Try to stay cool." The steward wiped at his brow, and with a grunt, shoved the crates forward.

A patch of flies buzzed past Marais's ear. It killed him to think of the precious time that he was going to lose. Schultz would only increase his distance. But there was nothing to be done—he had no way of reaching Delagoa Bay any sooner.

A suffocating odor of cumin and roasting lamb blanketed the town. The air was thick and clung to his skin as Marais forced his way through throngs of white-clad hawkers. Sweat leaked through his shirt and darkened his suit. Clutches of men in cotton kaftans played cards on wooden crates, shouting at one another. It didn't take Marais long to learn that a German doctor had been seen provisioning himself in the central market the week before. A shopkeeper told him he'd overheard the doctor say that he was headed south, not all the way to Delagoa Bay, as the ambassador had told Marais, but to Beira. If the shopkeeper was right, then either the ambassador had lied to throw Marais off the trail, or Shultz had changed plans mid-route. Either way, Marais was going to find him.

A few days later, the *Admiral* docked on the edge of a great sand spit at the port of Beira, where the Pungwe River emptied its dark brown contents into the sea. The city was stuck deep in sand. Small trucks veered along narrow rails that spread inland from the port, hauling vegetables and dried fish, stones and lumber.

Marais debarked with his bag. He crossed the railway tracks and found his way to the market.

A man in a cream-colored robe stood by a stall stacked high with kudu heads, pink tongues lolling from their lips. He was calling out prices.

"I look for doctor," Marais managed to say in Portuguese.

The shopkeeper's eyes brushed over him. The man reached into the box he'd been sitting on. He dug around, then stuck a desiccated hand out to Marais with what looked like two small, dried animal turds. "You eat these," he said. "Feel better."

"No medicine. I look for doctor. A white man. German."

The shopkeeper seemed to understand. "Paiva Coucerio Rua. Try there."

Marais located the street, which he followed to a small hotel at the eastern edge of the city. The proprietor showed him to a room on the second story, and Marais dropped a coin into his gnarled palm.

As soon as the proprietor disappeared, Marais rapped on the wooden door. "Doctor Shultz!"

The door cracked open. A man with a thick yellow beard and fiery blue eyes peered out at him. "What do you want?" he snapped in English.

"I've come to join you."

"I'm sleeping, and I don't require any joining right now."

As he shut the door, Marais wedged his foot in the jamb. "I've traveled all the way from Brussels. I know what you're up to. I can help."

The doctor stared at Marais from beneath hooded eyes. "Let's say, hypothetically, that any of what you *know* is true, which by the way it is not. Why would I let you accompany me?"

"I'm a legal man."

"Oh, please."

"With medical training."

"Which is what help to me? I'm a physician myself."

"I'm conversant in twelve languages," Marais said, though "conversant" was a generous term for describing his knowledge of more than half of them, and French, Latin, and Greek weren't going to help them get through the tribal areas of southeastern Africa any more than an English law degree would. "And I know the countryside of the northern Transvaal better than any man you'll ever meet."

The doctor unlatched the chain. He opened the door and glanced in both directions. "Come in. Quickly."

Schultz was a stocky, ursine man of forty whose eyes never seemed to stop moving. "You're a Boer," he said.

"Yes."

"The accent is unmistakable. From the Transvaal?"

"Born and raised."

"You have family there?"

"I had nine siblings before the war. How many have survived I don't know."

"Wife?"

Marais shifted his weight to the other foot. "Dead."

"What about children?"

Out on the street, stray dogs howled and squabbled. Five years earlier, Marais had decided to abandon Pretoria for London. It had already been eighteen months since he'd lost Lettie, but the wound felt as fresh as if no time at all had passed. His father had died—physically and mentally broken—shortly after Lettie. And his dear mother had followed soon after, her heart having ceased to beat one evening. Marais had been typesetting all day at the newspaper office. When he'd finished his printing run, he packed up his cast-metal sorts and hiked back along Koch Street, past the train station and the old schoolhouse and the string of steepled churches, until he reached Lynnwood House. In the nursery, a voice was whispering. He tiptoed to the doorway and peered inside. Sophie, his sister, was feeding the baby.

"Watch him for me, will you?" she asked when she saw Marais.

The baby was nursing a small glass bottle that Sophie held to its mouth. It squeezed its eyes shut in concentration and grasped the bottle between its fat fists to ensure that the milk would not be taken from him. The throated gulping reminded Marais of a farm animal.

"Of course. I'd like to. But it will have to wait for another time when my next deadline is not snapping at my heels."

"Only for an hour, Eugene. Just so I can get my hair washed and cut."

She practically tossed the child at him then. When he looked up, Sophie was gone.

In his arms, the boy felt dense like a bread loaf. He peered suspiciously at Marais with brown, moon-like eyes. Marais held him at a distance. He examined the way the boy's hair streamed over the scallops of his ears. The child started to shake in his arms.

"There, there," Marais said tentatively as he bounced the little monster. The boy began to cry. It started as a quiet sort of whimper, but the crying quickly grew louder. Marais looked around for help. Of course, no one was there. Soon the child was sobbing in terrible, bleating gasps.

"Shh!" Marais scolded, and he shook the child firmly. Strings of tears ran down the boy's round face as he stared at Marais. There was mucous around the child's nostrils and fat at his neck and elbows, and something about the boy's sweet smell sickened him. The crying worsened. Marais raised his voice. He shook him even harder. Now the boy was positively wailing.

Marais realized then that he hated the child. And he hated that he couldn't comfort him. It struck him with a blunt sort of force that Lettie would still be alive if it weren't for this fat milky creature. He ran from the room with the boy like a rugby ball in the crook of his arm and burst out the door. Clouds eclipsed the sun and wind tore at his hair. He raced down Prinsloo street, shouting at his sister's back.

"Take it, Sophie! Take it from me before I do something I'll regret."

Sophie turned and stared at him, her mouth agape. "Thank God Mother is not alive to see you now, Eugene."

She took the child. The crying stopped immediately. Marais couldn't remember ever feeling such relief.

He couldn't stay in South Africa any longer. The child would be a constant reminder of everything he'd lost. There was still the whole warm, pulsing world. There was still the future. Only his heart had broken—not his brain, not his body—and surely that could be repaired. He had been thinking of London. He'd been thinking about medicine and law. Now was the time.

That same week, he left the paper in the hands of another editor, Gustav Preller, packed two canvas bags, and set off by train for the port at Cape Town where steamers collected, stocked with weeks' worth of food and bound for Europe.

* * *

"There's a boy," Marais said to the doctor. "I haven't seen him for five years. He was a baby when I left."

The doctor slapped a mosquito on his forearm, picked it off, and flicked it onto the floor. "There's a good chance we won't ever reach Pretoria. The British are infinitely better armed. The natives in the countryside are emboldened by the English presence. The route we're envisioning is exceedingly dangerous. The land is overrun with malaria. Go buy yourself a ticket on the Delagoa Bay rail line while it's still running. Go back to Pretoria and take up with your son. Think how he must miss you."

Marais had abandoned London for this cause. He'd sailed halfway around the African continent to track down this doctor in a remote corner of a Mozambican town. And he didn't know if Charles would even want to see him again. "Doctor, the boy is one person. I barely know him. We're speaking of the fate of my country."

Schultz chewed on these words. "If that's what you really want, you're welcome to accompany me." He held out his hand to Marais.

"You mean accompany the expedition."

"I *am* the expedition. There were a couple of others, but they're worse than worthless. I'm abandoning them here in Beira. It's just the two of us now. Let me show you the supplies."

Stacked along the baked-mud walls of Schultz's hotel room were several dozen trunks and mountains of wooden crates—the provisions that he'd secreted from Paris to Beira. Five of the crates contained champagne for bribing Portuguese officials, he said. The others were filled with bandages, syringes, disinfectants, and medical equipment.

"This is everything you have? It's only a humanitarian mission then?"

Schultz smiled darkly. "Well, there are a *few* other items." With an awl, he pried open the tops of several crates and dug into the contents. Concealed beneath a shallow layer of bandages were the components of Mausers and Krag-Jorgensons, Martini-Henrys, and Maxim machine guns. There was a vast range of shells and bullets, insulated fuses and gunpowder. There had to be a dozen tons of weaponry in this one hotel room. On each trunk was a handwritten label that said, "Horse medicine and grease."

Marais felt a bursting within his chest. He and Schultz could singlehandedly change the course of the war. The reinforcements would buy the insurgents the time they needed until the Transvaal convinced the Germans to protect their interests in southern Africa and take up arms against the Brits, their common enemy.

Schultz poured two tall glasses of bean-red port and sat down with Marais to map their route for gaining entrance to the Transvaal.

"A dhow," said Schultz, "will sail us a hundred and fifty miles south of Beira to the mouth of the Save river. From there, we'll boat inland as far as the river is navigable, then assemble a team of local porters and pack animals to continue overland with us. When we reach the Limpopo, we'll cross by canoe and head south on foot through the wilds of the northern Transvaal to rendezvous with the commandos near Pietersburg. God help us, we'll reach the Boer forces outside Pretoria by July. We don't have a moment to lose."

The plan was far-fetched at best, but it was not quite impossible.

* * *

While Schultz set about hiring a sailing vessel, Marais prowled the markets, provisioning the supplies they'd need to break into the northern Transvaal: tents and ropes, buckets of fuel, compasses, dried beef and fish, maize, millet, cassava, potatoes, sugar, fruit, liquor, port, tea, hunting knives, half a dozen rifles, piles of tobacco. And three pouches of morphine tablets.

Every night for a week, Marais and Schultz mounted several crates on a pair of mules. They led the animals along the darkened side streets to the edge of the port, where the captain of the dhow they'd hired stashed the supplies below deck under canvas sheets and fishing nets.

The wait was unbearable. The night before their departure, Marais injected himself twice just to get a few hours of sleep. He managed to finish packing before dawn, but he kept to his room until the sun was broiling in the morning sky. He and Schultz were scheduled to set sail in the late afternoon. To avoid arousing suspicion, they'd agreed to wait until then to meet.

Marais ate a solid breakfast of eggs and bread, fish and coffee. He settled his bill, then left the hotel with only his bag, his hat, and cane. He strode as casually as he could through town, past rows of coconut palms and eucalyptus. Wild ducks veed over the maze of streets. Small wooden fishing boats fanned out like seaweed across the harbor. How far this all seemed from London with its traffic and filth and swarming crowds.

He thought once again about Charles. He'd be almost seven years old by now. Would the boy even remember him? Certainly not. It was a ludicrous question. Freud claimed that humans retained no actual memories from early childhood. The memory faculty didn't fully develop until later on. But Freud had recently documented a fascinating phenomenon: in the case of a particularly painful experience, a "screen memory" could arise, a recollection not of the experience itself but of other elements closely associated with it. Everything essential from childhood could be recorded in that single screen memory. Charles had lived through a war. What did the boy remember of his early years? Had he twisted up the facts of his own history? Would he be pleased to finally have his father home? No, of course not. The boy would have grown into his own life by now—there was nothing about Marais that he missed or needed. That much Marais was sure of.

At the far end of the port, the dhow rose up from the bay, its two masts jutting into the sky like temple pillars. The crew was racing about, securing the rigging. Marais strode feverishly along the gangway, trying not to break into a run. Schultz was already on the boat, seated cross-legged near the prow, swinging a near-empty wine bottle. As he swayed from side to side, he sang at the top of his loud German lungs.

"A sailor I'm— I sail the seas, she pleases me from both her knees!"

"Quiet!" Marais snapped. "Have you lost your mind?"

Schultz glanced up and laughed. He laughed until his eyes leaked water. When he finally composed himself, he tossed the newspaper in Marais's direction. Marais caught the paper just before it plummeted into the water.

It was a special edition of the one English daily printed in Beira. Plastered across the top half of the front page in huge block letters were the words *PEACE SIGNED.*

"What is this supposed to mean?" Marais asked.

"It means we're finished." The doctor sucked at what remained in his bottle, then pitched it into the sea.

"That's ridiculous. It's been 'over' for nearly two years. We're still fighting though—from the veld, from the forests, from the koppies. The Boers won't give up until the British are gone. Now let's get going."

"On the contrary, my friend, they *have* given up. This time it really is over. Our entire expedition is for naught."

"I don't believe that for a moment."

But as Marais scoured the paper, he saw that the doctor was right. The military leaders of the Transvaal and the Free State had conceded. The *bittereinder* commandos had finally laid down their weapons. The British had moved in and taken permanent control of both the Transvaal and the Free State. From now on, they would be run by a British military administration. The Boers had agreed to acknowledge King Edward VII as their lawful sovereign. He could not even imagine it.

Schultz tipped over on his side and began snoring like an engine.

Marais felt a cracking inside him. A pain worse than anything he'd experienced since the day Lettie died. Like a spouse—or a child—the Transvaal was an integral part of him, an essential organ. He hadn't been able to save Lettie. He had left Charles behind forever. He'd given up on fatherhood, but there had still been the possibility of salvaging his fatherland. He had packed hope within hope. He had focused everything on this one opening, this last chance to save himself.

There was nothing left to be done. They'd already paid for the trip. Marais didn't even bother to tell the captain that there was no longer a point to their journey.

The crew hoisted anchor and raised the sails, a pair of brown lateen triangles. As they started southward, a warm fog rolled in, blanketing the Mozambican coast and propelling them forward through the chop. When they reached the Save, they turned inward and began the journey straight into the heart of Africa.

West of Beira was wild country. Huge packs of black hippos hid in the mangrove swamps by day, and by moonlight cruised upriver to graze above the district of Machanga. Leopards, hyenas, and lionesses slinked behind papaya trees along the marshy banks.

When the morphine wore off, panic overtook Marais. The futility of the expedition, the loss of his country, the grim finality of the war's end. He thought he might wait until nighttime, when the crew was asleep, and hurl himself into the depths of the river with one quick splash.

Below deck, next to the main hold, was a dark nook where he performed his injections, gasping at the sensation of ice thickening in his veins. He found that if he got his plug every few hours, the days streamed by rather painlessly. There were pockets of feeling—each night's flash and shock as the sun dropped into the Save, the bracing sense of smallness amid the endless blue-black water—but it was as if the edges of feeling were shorn off. He could just as well have been on his way to a dinner party in London as to the remote border of his tiny conquered country.

At some point, the wrong mosquito alighted on his body. It hid itself unnoticed at the nape of his neck or in the bend of his knee, and stuck him with its needle without his feeling the prick. For days, Marais was feverish. He had a sense that his bones had become brittle and wouldn't stop rattling from the wretched chill and heat until they'd splintered into a million bits. Schultz administered quinine and laudanum and compresses, all the while swatting at the mosquitoes that swarmed overhead.

"Tell me, Schultz, what's wrong with the human mind?" Marais asked in a moment of lucidity. "How can we be so unskilled at containing our suffering when the lower orders of animals manage it so easily? Slaughter a pig or a goat, and its siblings seem barely to notice. But rip a man's freedom from him, take away his nation, remove the love of his life, and the pain is worse than daggers." The thought that he would die here—worlds away from the country that he'd failed to rescue—was his one small comfort.

* * *

Weeks later, he found himself washed, clean-shaven, and suited up, gazing from the window of a steam train as the brown-green veld rolled past. He was on his way from Delagoa Bay to Pretoria, on the same rail line that he'd helped Kruger inaugurate the day Charles was born. Outside, bare-chested African men hacked with sickles at the fibrous brush that encroached along the track. The train chugged into the mountains and edged along a series of craggy precipices. The car rocked so fiercely that at one point Marais was sure they were plummeting over the side. But the track gradually uncoiled and headed lower. The train dipped into a lush valley and paralleled the serpentine course of the Crocodile River, then climbed again, spiraling up between cliff and boulder. Sun streamed in and warmed his face. The end of winter was near.

He could remember only images from the preceding days, a series of dull-edged pictures. The look of relief on Schultz's face the day Marais's fever broke. The boat's emergence from the mouth of the Save back into the frothy whirlpool of ocean. Mud and grass huts dotting the shore of Delagoa Bay far in the distance. He could remember stepping off the boat and onto the spongy ground, Schultz saluting him one final time from the deck of a Castle steamer bound for Europe. He could remember standing in line at the train station to purchase a ticket, one way to Pretoria.

The train passed through blackened fields, formerly fertile land that the British had incinerated. The hillsides were crater-scarred, gorged from cannon fire. There were few farmhouses still standing. The countryside was deserted, completely unpeopled. A bitter odor lingered across the veld. The koppies were charred and redolent with smoke. It could have been Pompeii.

But in the morning, the sun broke through a gray mist. Church steeples rose in the distance, followed by a skyline of government buildings. Two young African boys waved wildly at the train and jumped up and down. Marais waved back at them.

A whistle sounded when the train entered Pretoria. The wheels shrieked to a stop. The doors opened. Marais took his bag and stepped down from the carriage. The city was exploding with purple jacarandas. It felt like spring.

Sophie was waiting on the platform, barely five feet tall, in a plain wool frock and a blue felt hat. Marais and Schultz had wired ahead to her. She looked gaunt, almost stick-like.

"Welcome home, Eugene." Her gaze was stern, her lips pursed.

Above the station roof, the Union Jack snapped in the wind. How strange to be welcomed back to a country that was no longer his. Marais leaned down and kissed Sophie's cheek. "It's a relief to see you in one piece."

"No need for concern. We've all pulled through. Not one Marais lost. We're likely the only family in all of Pretoria to fare so well. Luck has always stuck close to us."

A child, he noticed, was crouching to her left. A skinny child with chestnut eyes and a narrow, delicate face, who seemed to be trying to hide himself behind Sophie's small frame.

"Is this the boy?" Marais asked, astonished.

Sophie nodded. "Eugene, this is Charles."

The boy was alive then. Alive and walking, a whole small person. Did he speak? With what sort of voice?

Marais stepped around to observe him. The child was a runt. He had light brown hair that hung limply beneath his hat and old beaten-up boots. Frayed suspenders held up his khakis. He had no waist or bottom to speak of.

"How old are you, Charles?"

"Seven, sir," the boy said quietly.

"You may call me 'Oom Eugene.'"

The boy blinked. "Yes, sir."

"You're small for your age, aren't you?"

"I'm about average, sir," he said, looking at the ground.

"Is that right? Well, let's see a muscle then."

The boy glanced at Sophie, who nodded back at him. Charles turned bashfully to Marais, pulled his small fist toward his head, and made a face from the exertion.

"Look at that," Marais said. He pretended to examine the skin where the child's biceps should be. He didn't touch the boy, though. He didn't feel his arm, or tousle his hair, or stroke his cheek. "Not bad. Perhaps you *are* about average. You are only seven after all."

Marais stood there studying the child, searching for some trace of himself in the boy. Was this one small creature what had pushed him away to London more than five years ago? Was it really on account of this small child that Lettie had died?

"You'll stay with Jess for now," Sophie said to Marais.

"No, no, I can find my own place."

"Just until you get on your feet. A room has opened up in her boarding house. She's already made up a bed."

Marais hadn't considered the possibility that he might be thrust back into the suffocating world of his siblings with their routines and expectations. But wisps of the fever were still with him, his money was nearly spent, and he had no other choice.

"Very well," he said. And to Charles, "Young man, it looks like we shall be neighbors."

The boy shrank back. There was fear in his eyes, which were dark and moonlike, as impossibly large as Lettie's had been.

December 1935, Cambridge, Massachusetts

Charles dashes along Cambridge Street in the dark, predawn hours with Marais's last letter crumpled in his briefcase. This morning he's on a mission. The wind whips at his eyes. The air freezes in his lungs like glass. According to the papers, gangs of dogs have been roving the streets of Somerville, and he's armed himself with pockets full of dog biscuits, just in case.

In his coat is a key to a side door of Widener library—a key that he obtained not entirely legally—and well before opening hours, he's climbing through the stacks to the northeast corner of the library's sixth floor where South African periodicals are stored. Boxes upon boxes of them.

He gathers piles of Afrikaans language weeklies from the previous decade—1923, 1924, 1925—and settles into the nearest carrel. He wipes off layers of dust, scrapes away pockets of insect larvae. He hunts through *Die Huisgenoot* and the *Johannesburg Star*, searching for his surname. Newsprint tattoos his palms. 1926. 1927. Marais claims that Harvard is perverting his work in the name of "racialism," that his actual findings would never support such a theory. But Charles has no reason to trust the man's word. He scours article after article. He needs to see for himself.

To his surprise, Marais is everywhere in the South African papers. Marais the journalist. Marais the poet. Marais the scientist. How many lives has he led? The man is an illusionist, a shapeshifter. Charles flips through pages, struggling to ward off a whirlwind of images from his childhood in the Transvaal, a childhood bereft of a father.

Shadows of the concentration camp where he was imprisoned rear up before him. An English soldier, barely eighteen years old, guarded Charles's section of the camp each night. Charles suspected that the man's job was to ensure that Boer prisoners didn't become too comfortable. But six months into their confinement, this all changed. The soldier began doling out to Charles and his cousins an extra cup of water each day, and occasionally, a slice of fresh fruit—remnants of a pear or a tangerine from the soldiers' mess hall. Charles couldn't understand why the guard would direct such kindness to his family alone. It wasn't fair to the other children whose ribs were growing more visible each day. But he also couldn't imagine giving up these small luxuries.

One night he hid behind a tent and watched as a small, hooded figure slipped six bright coins into the soldier's pocket, then scurried away. Charles couldn't see the stranger's face, but for the first time—the only time—he felt as if someone was watching out for him. If not for that mysterious figure, he would have been long dead.

On a sunny morning in late May, the southern gate to the camp was left open. British soldiers stood nearby, smoking. They'd left their helmets on the ground. A pair of ragged Boer boys padded barefoot toward the gate. One limped along on a swollen, swamp-colored leg. The left arm of the other boy was bent as if it had two elbow joints. The boys stopped a hundred feet away and glanced at the Brits. The soldiers didn't seem to notice. The boys stared at each other, trembling, with gaping eyes. Then, on the count of three, they lunged forward, scrambling as best they could through the gate and out of the camp. The soldiers kept smoking. The war was over.

Charles, his cousins, and Sophie walked back across town to her house. They swept out cobwebs, bandaged splintered windows, plugged up bullet holes. More than twenty-six thousand had died. One out of every ten Boers, though the percentage was much higher among children. Charles was one of the lucky ones.

"Charles Marais?"

A deep voice cuts through the edges of his thoughts.

"It *is* you!" the voice says.

The sunlight streaming through the library window splashes a bright triangle across the face of the man next to him. He's older, maybe sixty. English-style mustache. Full, rounded belly. White tennis shoes.

"Too cold to exercise outside today," he says. "Thought I'd give the steps a try. I started three stories below ground level and just kept walking up. Honestly," he gasps for air, "I had no idea that this floor even existed." The man's cheeks glow with perspiration.

"Sorry, do I—?"

"I'm disturbing you," the man says. "My apologies. What a pleasant surprise though . . ." He gasps again. "To stumble upon Doctor Charles Marais all the way up here."

Far across the room, a second hand ticks unrelentingly.

How does he know me?

"You don't remember. We met earlier in the year, albeit briefly and under unusual circumstances." The man smiles broadly. "At a church service."

Memorial Church shoulders its way into his head. Charles glances around the stacks to make sure no one else has overheard. Casually, he covers the periodicals with his briefcase. When he looks up again, the man's face reconfigures itself: Arnold Sizemore, chair of the biology department. "So sorry, Professor," says Charles. "Of course."

"Please, it's Arnold." Sizemore takes a blue handkerchief from his pocket and dabs at his forehead. "President Conant speaks highly of you. He's not easily impressed, you know."

Charles swallows as quietly as he can, which is not quietly at all.

"Actually, a number of us have taken an interest," says Sizemore. "Perhaps you've heard: I'll be a reviewer for your tenure case this spring."

"I hadn't known," Charles manages to say. He's heard nothing about this. Harvard is notorious for keeping the evaluation process opaque, replete with mystery reviews and secret correspondence.

Sizemore pulls at his red fingers. "I was just today thinking about the parallels between our research. I have an endless fascination for interdisciplinary affinities, you see. I guess I never outgrew the childhood obsession with connecting dots."

Charles tries to conceal his ballooning confusion. He has spent the last year translating a series of Burmese Pāli texts, an anthology of legal treatises from hundreds of years ago that sets out with painstaking precision the appropriate social and political behavior for the ruling classes. How to greet members of various castes. Which meats to avoid. The best times of the year for mass executions. Emily Post for a medieval Burmese aristocracy. His work has nothing at all to do with science. "Not to be rude, Professor Sizemore—"

"Arnold."

"Right. Sorry. But I can't imagine a connection between the biological sciences and ancient Pāli texts."

Sizemore looks tickled. "I didn't mean *your* research. I meant your family's—your father's. I ought to explain. Or better yet"—he's struck by some new thought—"give me an hour of your time. Come to my lab and I'll show you firsthand."

Charles can think of a thousand things he'd rather do. Feed his arm through a meat grinder, for example. "Maybe we can find a time once the semester ends."

Sizemore's features are practically paleolithic. "I'm free right now," he says with a significant look. "It's probably best if we start getting to know each other before your review begins, don't you think?"

Charles feels as if he's observing the unfolding of a future memory, as if one day he'll look back on this particular moment, colored by the days that follow, and recognize it as a turning. He slips the newspaper from the top of the pile into his coat. He hears his own voice echo back through an endless tunnel: *The morning I walked to the laboratory of Arnold Sizemore, the man who would determine my professional fate, the ground outside was frozen solid.*

They stride briskly through the Yard together, wading through ankle-deep drifts, flannel scarves wrapped around their faces to cut the bite of the wind. The sky is gray and hostile. The snow comes down in fat flakes.

Sizemore's laboratories occupy a chunk of building on the north side of campus at the top of an ornately balustraded staircase. In the five years that Charles has worked at Harvard, he has never set foot inside the natural sciences buildings. He's struck by the freshly stained wood, the crystal chandelier, the Persian carpets.

At the end of the hall, a steel padlock joins a set of double doors with a heavy chain. Sizemore maneuvers a key in the lock, hefts open the doors. He leads Charles down a narrow hallway with neither windows nor carpets. The only sound is the clap of their shoes against the floorboards.

The next door reads, "LABORATORY RESEARCH IN PROGRESS." Sizemore removes this lock too.

"Home sweet home," he says cheerfully. He reaches an arm inside the dark room, and rows of lights burst on, one after another, in tiny explosions.

As he enters the lab, Charles is smacked by a burst of hot air. The radiators along the opposite wall clatter and bang, sending steam hissing up. A familiar odor wafts through the room.

Sizemore drops his scarf and coat on an iron rack. In his shirtsleeves and exercise trousers, he looks frailer, older. He looks like someone's grandfather.

Half a dozen lab tables crowd the center of the room. Charts propped on wooden easels announce a series of measurements: "diastolic," "systolic," "heart rate," "oxygen saturation," "temperature," "pupil size." There are figures recorded for each of the last thirty days.

A vase with three dried sunflowers stands on the edge of Sizemore's desk next to a framed photograph of a couple sitting in a cherry-red Model A Duesenberg with a classic, bow-tied front bumper. The man's arm is draped around the shoulders of a woman with abundant braided hair. His fingers float over the butterfly brooch pinned to her dress. They both smile broadly. Charles thinks he detects in the man a younger, pre-balding Sizemore. He hangs his coat next to Sizemore's and exhales. It's good that he's come after all. He can forge a connection with this man. He can lay the necessary groundwork for his review.

"Is this your wife?" Charles asks, pointing to the photo.

Sizemore lumbers up beside him. "Wasn't she beautiful?"

Charles can picture the elegant couple, motoring the Duesenberg across the Bourne and the Sagamore—the gleaming new bridges that connect the mainland to Cape Cod. He can imagine them ferrying that perfect car to Martha's Vineyard for summer vacation.

"She passed several years ago. We had an accident in that car. Her skull was completely crushed. Just before our first grandchild was born."

"Jesus, I am so sorry," says Charles.

"It was unspeakably difficult in the beginning. The way I pulled through those first few months was to tell myself that the next few would be easier, and the few after that even more so. The funny thing is I was wrong. It's no easier now than it was the morning after I lost her. Some days I still can't get out of bed."

Charles's sympathy for the old man clenches like a fist inside him.

"But enough gloom and doom for one day," Sizemore says. "Let's have a look at my puppies."

"You keep puppies here?"

"That's what I wanted to show you!"

Charles glances among the stone lab tables, wondering if he's about to witness disfigured dogs with severed limbs, or multiple, hairless heads. But of course, Sizemore doesn't conduct those sorts of experiments. The man keeps sunflowers on his desk.

Six metal cages lined with mats of straw house five mice each, barely the size of plums. Charles peers into a cage. The odor that he noticed when he first arrived is more pungent here. He tries breathing through his mouth, but it's as if the aroma—a sweet and sour smell of vanilla and pickled meat—has implanted itself in his nostrils.

Inside the cage, tiny levers are fastened to the spouts of five stainless steel pipettes. Rubber tubes snake around, connecting the pipettes to a glass bottle that's hooked to the bars. The mice lie still, curled like commas. Their pink noses barely poke out from the straw. Their eyes, however, are open and capacious, their pupils glazed.

Charles taps against the side of the cage. The mice—the same skittish creatures that overrun every apartment in the greater Boston area—don't budge. He taps again, harder. Not a twitch. You could barely tell the difference between these mice and the taxidermied versions in the Comparative Zoology Museum. Mice shouldn't be this still. They should be cowering in the corners. He knocks his hand hard against the bars.

From the corner of his eye, he catches Sizemore, delight filling his face.

"Are they always this quiet?" Charles asks.

"They are models of docility." Sizemore nearly skips to Charles's side of the table. "Have a look at this." He unhooks the latch on the cage. He pulls up the door.

The five mice lift their heads and glance dully through the open cage—they don't even consider breaking free.

"Come on out, my little ones," Sizemore says. "There's a whole world to explore out here."

The smallest mouse stretches its pink nose toward the door. It rocks from side to side, staring glumly at the obvious escape hatch. Its rear legs twitch as if palsied. After a moment, the little creature lowers its head. It tucks its chin back into the straw.

A strange lightheadedness overtakes Charles. The odor strikes him now with the blunt force of a baseball bat. The last time he smelled that odor was the week before he was to leave South Africa forever. He was ten years old, and Sophie had arranged for him to attend boarding school in London. It had been several years since the end of the war, and half the population of Pretoria was now English. Pretoria's Boers had not forgotten the atrocities of the concentration camps, and they seethed at the British occupation and at the insult of having to submit to foreign rule. But Sophie was intent on sending Charles to England. The Marais family had always thought of themselves as heirs to greatness. Since London was still the center of the world, that's where Charles would study.

Most Boer children would have resented being sent away, and to England of all places, but Charles was exhilarated at the prospect of travel, his belly aflutter as he ticked off the days on his calendar. He could bring only a single trunk on the ship, and Sophie said that he was free to pack anything he could fit inside, apart from his rifle, as firearms were not permitted in London's schools. He'd nearly filled the trunk already with three white shirts, two coats, a cotton suit, two pairs of khaki trousers, five pairs each of underpants and socks, one change of boots, a tin of chocolates that he'd saved up to purchase for the trip, a miniature tool set, his hunting knife, several books by Rudyard Kipling, Sam the Lion (the only doll that had survived his early childhood—though its mane had long since fallen off and the hay with which it was stuffed continuously seeped out), and a framed photograph that his grandmother had taken and that he kept wrapped in muslin, as if mummified: the photo of his mother, Aletta Marais, lying in bed amid a pile of pillows, cradling the newborn child that was Charles.

That Saturday morning Sophie asked him to pick up a sack of flour at the weekend market. Like the rest of his aunts on the Marais side, nearly all of them now single, Sophie was a savvy, hardened woman who earned her own money and managed her own finances. She dropped a few coins into Charles's hand. He took his hat and coat and sloughed off toward town.

He'd always liked the weekend market. He'd troll silently along the dusty rows, watching the traders from the northern towns of Waterberg hawk their exotic wares—gilded rhinoceros horns, whips fashioned from giraffe tails, tanned hippopotamus hides, massive chunks of ivory. Waterberg was the Transvaal's Wild West, a land of fantasy and riches.

The day was cold, the breeze mild, and the sun shone through the jacaranda leaves, casting flickering shadows along the road, which made Charles feel as if he were walking underwater. He passed white steepled churches, de Wet's Inn, the old tailor's shop with its green corrugated roof, and the former makeshift armory, and he thought about cannons and ships and the limitlessness of the sea. As he approached the plot where Lynnwood House once stood—the house where he was born—he broke into a jog. He kept his eyes glued to the gravel road ahead, trying not to glance at the plot.

Around the corner, two blocks up, was his aunt Jess Rex's boarding house where Oom Eugene resided. In Charles's presence, people referred to him as Oom Eugene, though everyone knew that he was both more and less than Charles's uncle. In the three years since Oom Eugene had returned from London, he'd never acted in any way avuncular toward Charles, let alone fatherly. Marais made it clear that he was thoroughly occupied by his work. He had no time to engage with a child. During their few staccato exchanges—at Christmas dinner or the funeral of a distant cousin—*father* was not a word that either of them ever uttered.

The market would be open for some time, and as Charles passed the boarding house, he had an idea.

Marais would have left for his office already. Charles took a chance, sprang across the slabs of blue slate that wound through the garden of orchids and agapanthus, and slipped inside the front door of the house.

There was no one in the parlor.

He scurried past the china cabinet, ran his fingers along the side of the upright piano. Next to the third door on the left, he found a small pine plaque that read *Eugene Marais, Advocate.* Charles knocked softly on the door. He knocked a second time. No answer. He turned the handle until it clicked and let himself in. He was hoping to find an article of interest to take to London for a keepsake, ideally something of value that Marais would miss. His sense of abandonment had crystallized inside him into something knife-like. He wanted Marais to feel the hurt that he did.

The room was no more than twelve by fifteen feet, with hundreds of books heaped into tall piles. There was a plain pine bed, a single set of drawers, a small oak desk. Rows of jarred animal fetuses and plant specimens crowded the shelves that ran along three of the walls. All the jars were meticulously labeled but not categorized according to any system that Charles could decipher. He pawed through stacks of anatomical sketches and notebooks of handwritten Afrikaans poetry and all sorts of medical instruments, searching for the right item to steal, but the sheer wildness of the collection stalled him.

In the desk, he came across a peculiar leather case, which he removed and unlaced. Inside was a silver syringe. A bead of liquid still clung to the tip of the needle, and it carried an odor, an odd pungency that he'd never smelled before.

Charles grasped the syringe while the air thickened. As his eyes toured the room, he grew increasingly certain that Marais was about to return and discover him there, having broken into his chambers. His heart thundered. What would he say if Marais appeared in the doorway—that he intended to rob his father? The longer his legs kept him there, the more oppressive and asphyxiating the odor became, until Charles thought he would faint. He dropped the syringe where he stood. He fled the room without taking a thing.

Charles notices the soft white fuzz that extends like lichen along Sizemore's cheeks and jaw line. The odor in the laboratory, he realizes, is the same as what he smelled thirty years ago in Marais's room.

"What is it?" he asks, nearly choking.

"My puppies? Aren't they wonderful?"

"No, the smell. That odor."

Sizemore's pink mouth balloons into the grin of a mischievous schoolboy. "Professor, that's the smell of morphine, distilled from pure, high-grade opium."

Blood thrums in Charles's ears. The sound might have been there all along, but he notices it only now, ringing with the force of the noon-time bells. "I think I'd better sit down."

He squats on the wood floor. He brings his knees to his chest. Marais the journalist, the lawyer, the poet. Marais, who never had any use for a child. The last time Charles saw him before leaving for London was at Pretoria Station. Marais had come with Sophie to send him off. Charles hadn't expected to see him, but Marais had found time to send Charles away yet again. Charles waved to Sophie through the window of the train and glanced shyly at Marais. As he looked down, his eyes happened to fall on Marais's leg, which was shaking: a mild but distinct tremor. Charles must have been staring, because Marais looked at him uncomfortably, shifted his cane, and stepped to the left such that his leg was obscured behind Sophie. He waved at Charles then, in an excessively casual manner, and Charles realized that Marais was trying to conceal the trembling.

Charles has no proof, but he has all the suspicion in the world now: Marais was a morphine addict. He probably still is.

"We've trained the mice to self-administer." Sizemore's baritone rings out. "The beauty is we're no longer needed. The little fellows sedate themselves. And it's all completely natural. Just imagine the potential applications."

What Charles imagines are Marais's hands as they must be now, the hands of a sixty-four-year-old addict, wrinkled and palsied. He imagines the sheer effort it must have taken to steady his fingers enough to pen those dozens of letters and sign his name to every one. How many drafts did he mangle before he finally crafted a letter that was legible, sealed the lip of the envelope with wax, and sent it to the other side of the world? For the sole purpose of reaching Charles. Despite decades of anger, the thought of his father in so much pain crushes him.

Charles gets to his feet, unsure how to explain his behavior to this man who will soon decide his professional future. He can't tell Sizemore what he's just discovered, that his own father may be an addict.

"Haven't you dreamed of changing the world, Charles? I don't need to ask. You and I share the same dream. I'm certain of this. You are your father's son after all." He rocks onto his toes. His round face shines like the headlight of a train. "This is where my work converges with his."

"I don't understand."

"Let's be frank with one another. There are two schools of thought concerning a resolution to the Jewish question. The one coming out of Germany is veering inexorably toward violence. Personally, I find the rumors horrifying. Imagine trying to wipe out an entire race. It would be no different from the English treatment of your own Boer people thirty-five years ago. I can only hope that your family wasn't affected by those concentration camps. It was completely unconscionable. That's not who we are. We're a civilized race, Charles, the most civilized race in history."

Charles glances through the window. The snow has stopped. A woman cracks off an icicle. She hands it to a small, snow-suited boy.

Then this *is* the line of thought brewing among the German leadership. Nuremberg was not their end goal—discriminatory policy was just the first step. The next is extermination. To rub out an entire people as you would a mouse infestation.

The little boy accepts the spear of ice from his mother with a look of wonder. He brings his tongue to the glistening tip.

What about Hannah? She's one of the best students he's ever had. A compassionate thinker. A beautiful human. How could anyone want to hurt a person like that? He is nearly slain by the thought.

"There's a second approach, Charles, a 'humanist' approach, that I'm pioneering right here," says Sizemore. "I'm of the opinion that a rebalancing of power can be achieved without resorting to violence at all. At the proper levels of concentration and frequency, morphine is endowed with the ideal qualities necessary to facilitate addiction. The human body is a miraculous machine. The drug incapacitates but in a most pleasant way. If the Germans were to manage the program at the national level, it could mean just a few compulsory injections for certain segments of the population—mere pokes in the arm, mind you—and then ensuring that an adequate supply is made available. It would be largely a project of marketing. And infinitely more humane than the alternative. Don't you see? They'll sedate themselves."

"The Jews?" Charles barely whispers.

The boy licks at the ice spear, nurses it, cracks off a chunk with his teeth.

"We could save millions of lives in Europe alone. Imagine how tractable society's least desirable elements would suddenly become. And without having to spill a drop of blood. If we can secure the necessary support, I hope to begin the first human trials within a year. I'm tickled that I can confide in you, Charles. We all have our roles to play in the construction of the new Aryan nation. It was your father's research on the termites' communal mind, the *hive* as it were, that inspired me to evolve my own thinking in this regard. Indeed, it's been thrilling to track the evolution of *his* mind—from his exploration of individual memory to his more recent obsession with the social insects and the power of the collective mentality. We'll soon have the ability to harness that power, to foster the same sort of communal mind that functions so perfectly in the natural world. And with this, to establish the lower races in peaceful subservience to those, like us, who were meant to lead."

"You have it all wrong," Charles says. "I'm certain he never suggested anesthetizing whole segments of the population."

Sizemore frowns at him. "Not directly. I said his thinking *inspired* me. Actually, I'd been saving this as a surprise, but I might as well tell you now. We'd like your father to present his research at Harvard next quarter. It's not just his work that we want. It's *him*. His reputation. His life story. How he helped found a white nation against all odds. Eugene Nielen Marais is the symbol we need for this institution—you know how effective a good symbol can be. He is the perfect Übermensch. Master of his domain in the cities of Europe and Africa alike. Even in the jungle—in the very heart of darkness."

The ceiling above Charles is spinning now. "You'll have to excuse me." He scrambles for his coat. He nearly knocks over the photograph of Sizemore's wife and the vase of sunflowers.

"He brought his research to our attention some time ago but hasn't responded to our invitations since. We've tried for months to track him down to no avail."

Charles quickens his pace. It takes half a dozen steps to clear the threshold. *They're animals*, he thinks. *Harvard has become infested.*

Sizemore calls after him. "We'd like you to escort him to Cambridge this spring. Your family name will be of tremendous value to this initiative. And you know what it could mean for you and your tenure review."

"These are human beings we're talking about," Charles calls back, "not mice, not termites."

"Your father would say they're not so different in certain respects."

"I won't be a party to this. Not for tenure. Not for anything."

"Don't be pig-headed," Sizemore bellows. "Do you realize what you'd be giving up?"

As Charles breaks outside, the winter air stings his face, and though the day is gray and heavy with moisture, the brightness of the sky nearly blinds him.

* * *

All night long Charles's eyes burn holes in the ceiling as Tonto shrieks and dives into the moonbeam that cuts through the room above his head. Each time the bird passes through the cone of light, he materializes and then vanishes, zagging over and over like an aging, busted zoetrope.

The university is seeded with Conant's ideologues. Charles has stood by as the storm clouds have gathered and rained down around him. This isn't why he took the job at Harvard. It's not why he came to America, the land of stability and freedom and reason.

When he bursts into Sever Hall the next morning, his hands are shaking. It's the final class of the semester. The three boys shift in their seats when they see him. Hannah tilts her head and regards him strangely. "Looks like someone had a late night," she says.

"It wasn't a late night," Charles replies. "At least not that kind." His patience is edged. His nerves are jangled.

"That was a joke," says Hannah. "Are you all right?"

"I'm . . . fine. Time is in short supply, though. If there are no other questions, let's begin our final *sutta*."

He scans his students' faces. His eyes lock on Dennis, the one who is always the least prepared. The young man looks quickly away, hoping to be rescued by one of the others. "Why don't you start, Dennis?" Charles says.

The boy opens his primer and, with some effort, locates the page. He loosens his tie at the collar, unbuttons the small white button at the top. Slowly, he begins to read. "'*Evaṃ me sutaṃ*' . . ."

The radiator drips with the precision of a metronome. The room is swelteringly hot. Charles glances at his watch. He needs this day to end. He needs time to gather his thoughts, to plan his next move.

Dennis squints at the book. His eyes wander over the length of the page as if he's lost his place. He looks up at Charles with embarrassment. "Excuse me, Professor," he falters. "I can't seem to remember how to translate this phrase."

Clouds of steam float toward the ceiling.

"*Evaṃ me sutaṃ*," says Charles. "You know this."

The boy wipes a wrist across his forehead. He stares at his book with a desperate sort of hope. "I'm sorry, sir," he says quietly.

"For Christsake, Dennis, nearly every Pāli *sutta* begins the exact same way."

Dennis's lip starts to quiver. "I know. I just can't remember what it means exactly. It's hard to focus when it's so hot."

Charles is incredulous. What have they been doing for the past three months? Hasn't he taught them anything? "'Thus have I heard,' Dennis. It means, 'Thus have I *heard*!'"

The boy's face burns crimson. "You don't have to yell at us," Hannah scolds. She turns to Dennis. Her voice lightens. "It's just Ananda's standard preface before he recounts something that the Buddha said."

At this, Charles can't stop himself. "Is that what you believe? Then allow me to enlighten you. We don't know what the hell the Buddha said. We don't have a clue. All we know is what Ananda, his disciple, says he *remembers* hearing the Buddha say, long after the fact. Or worse, remembers hearing others tell him what they *thought* they heard the Buddha say. It's all just hearsay. Ananda hears it said and then says what he remembers hearing. And the stories themselves have been copied over and over. The texts we have are copies of copies of copies of copies. When mistakes were made, the mistakes were copied too. Don't you see? Everything we think the Buddha said is the product of a twenty-five-hundred-year-old game of telephone. After all this time, nothing we thought to be true is necessarily so."

Through the closed windows, Charles can hear the band, slow flourishes that sound like the second movement of Beethoven's *Eroica* symphony, the funeral march. The music grates against his bones. Nothing good will come if he remains in the classroom. He needs to get out now before he makes a fatal mistake.

"I'm afraid that's all for today. Class dismissed. Final papers are due on my desk in three weeks." To Hannah, who stares at him in disbelief, he mouths the words, "I'm sorry."

He exits the classroom, hurries down the stairs, retreats across the Yard toward his office.

Outside, the band is marching directly toward him.

"It's colder than Mrs. Roosevelt's tits out here," says a blue-lipped kid with a tuba. He has the smooth, creaseless face of a high school student and dozens of little white teeth. The band strikes up Wagner's *Kaisermarsch*. The tuba player brings his instrument to his mouth. The boy at the front of the formation brandishes the new German flag.

How much longer can Charles pretend otherwise? How much longer can he walk right past them? There are *Nazis* in Harvard Yard.

He steps forward and positions his body directly in their path. The music comes to a sudden halt.

"This is an institution for higher learning," he says as calmly as he can. "You have no place on this campus."

Half a dozen musicians collect around him. They're still holding their instruments, but they wield them now like clubs and spears.

"Who are you to talk, Professor Marais?" the tuba player demands. "You think we don't know where you came from? You think people haven't been watching you? You have no place in this *country.* Why don't you turn around and go back to Africa." A horrible smile passes over his lips. "White nigger."

The tuba player turns to the other musicians, expecting guffaws of support. But they won't meet his eyes. Even his friends know he's gone too far.

Charles should pummel this kid, teach him a lesson about respect and propriety. He should wrap the thug's instrument around his neck.

He glances from one to the next, from peach face to peach face. They're boys, he realizes. Children. As he reaches inside his coat pocket, he sees fear creeping into the tuba player's eyes. *He thinks I've got a gun.* The feeling of power brings a certain fleeting pleasure.

Charles pulls out a handful of dog biscuits. He squeezes them into crumbs and stuffs them into the boy's tuba. "Go home to your mothers," he says. "Before the local dogcatchers round you up like the curs that you are." He leaves the musicians in the snow, disarmed and gaping at him.

Rolled up on the floor outside his office is today's *Boston Post.* Charles grabs the paper, slams the door behind him, shuts himself inside. The violent knocking beneath his ribs has not abated. Harvard was not supposed to be like this. His life was not supposed to be like this.

Footsteps approach from behind. The door creaks as it opens. He barely has time to straighten his coat.

"That was amazing," Hannah says. "The way you stood up to them back there. I saw the whole thing."

"You said it first. We can't pretend this isn't happening. Not any longer."

She unbuttons and removes her coat, folds it neatly over the back of a chair. Her dress fits tightly to the curves of her body, and for a moment, Charles is overcome. He tries to find a place to rest his eyes.

"I need to know what's going on," she says. "And don't tell me that everything is fine. I'm not a stupid woman."

He needs to tell someone—he longs to tell *her*—about the library of correspondence from Marais. About his morphine addiction. About Sizemore's experiments. About the danger that may lie ahead for her. Maybe he can.

He shuts the door and pulls out a chair. "Take a seat."

Hannah doesn't budge. "Have I done something to anger you? Because that was never my intention."

Through the window, the sizzle of snowfall, the dimming of daylight.

She thinks he's angry with *her*? His anger from this morning melts into regret, then flows into a river of guilt.

"You haven't done anything, Hannah. It's not you at all. I'm just having trouble remembering why I entered the academy in the first place."

Her eyes soften slightly. "For the same reason I did, I'm sure. To understand the complexity—the insanity—of human history."

Charles considers this, how easy it sounds, and it strikes him for the first time that this is the opposite of the truth. He told himself he'd entered in search of a home, but that's not the case at all. What he has been seeking is *refuge* from history, refuge from his past. The way that Buddhist monks go forth from home to homelessness. *Agārasmā anagāriyaṃ pabbajja.* This is his life, which despite his meticulous planning and coordination, has somehow turned out all wrong.

"I owe you an apology," he says.

She eyes him. "Well, *that's* the truth." He can see she didn't expect him to apologize, but she hasn't forgiven him either.

"It is, but only part of it," he says. "Here's the other part: having you in my class is what has sustained me this year."

Her mouth parts just slightly. When she returns his gaze, her green eyes are shining. "I could say the same to you."

Silence squeezes the air from the room. All he can hear is the clock's ticking.

"It's getting dark," he finally says. "You should head home. I still have a few things to finish up." He straightens his back, extends his hand. "Merry Chanukah."

She smiles and takes his hand in hers. Her nails have changed—today they're the color of pomegranates. "Happy Christmas to you."

Without thinking, he leans in. He brushes his lips against her cheek. It's not unlike those European kisses of hello and goodbye, except that this kiss lasts longer, a good several seconds, perhaps because she's as surprised by their sudden proximity as he is. Her head turns, eyes close. Her lips graze his face. Her breath is warm against his neck. Her hand touches his shoulder.

He barely pulls himself away. "I should be getting back to my . . ."

She tucks her hair behind her ear. "Right," she says. "Me too . . ." She gathers her coat, buttons herself up, turns back to him. "Just so you know, I'm an excellent listener. And conveniently located in the directory."

She leaves him there, a statue stuck in the doorway.

Sweat trickles down his spine. He cracks open the window, loosens his tie.

His books rise in towers along the periphery of the room like military fencing. Flashes of the concentration camp in Pretoria, and of Harvard Yard, its fortress-like fence, the wrought-iron gates.

Blood ticks in his ears. His mind returns to Sizemore's little mice, drugged and pliant. How helpless they looked. As he rises, the periodical that he swiped from the library—the 1927 Christmas Eve edition of the *Johannesburg Star*—knocks against his chest. He unrolls the book, flips the pages. Halfway through, a headline in the top left corner catches his attention. Words pop from the page: Termites. Corpuscles. Blood. Soldiers. Haemorrhage. Animal mind. The story reads like a plea. It's almost as if Marais knew that Charles would find it exactly eight years later. *As if he wrote this to me.*

The act of crossing an unthinkable line is rarely as abrupt as it seems. The men who leapt from the top floors of financial buildings after the Crash didn't just wake up one morning, make for a window, and jump into space. They approached gradually, incremental step by incremental step, until one movement in the protracted sequence tipped them over the edge. From a distance, that final moment only *looked* like a sudden wild leap. It only *looked* random and inexplicable.

It's become increasingly clear just how much damage this one small group of intellectuals could cause. Charles refuses to enlist in service to Conant and Sizemore. But if he stays here, he'll have no choice. He has to leave this madness. He has to help disarm them if he can. Marais is *his* father.

His finger runs slowly along the graying pages of the journal. He underlines Marais's name. Maybe Marais's field notes really can defuse their plans.

It's a matter of physics. The forces pulling him away are more powerful than the ones keeping him in place. He'll go to South Africa. He'll go and find Marais. He'll leave and find the truth.

The *Post* lists every form of transportation on offer for local and far-flung travel—train, taxi, bus, steamship. There's a steamer leaving at midnight tonight. High-quality, affordable berths still available. The last ship of the year from Boston to England. He circles the advertisement in black ink.

Then he takes a pen and a sheet of letterhead. In less than a minute, he drafts a note to his department chairman—ten simple lines requesting a leave of absence on account of "family emergency."

Back at the apartment, Charles rummages through the contents of his closet, his desk, the cupboards. Journals he's never read, phonograph records he's not yet listened to, ties, socks, ancient cans of food—all of it he dispatches down the metal trash chute. Half of his possessions are still stored in his green duffle and in two brown cartons. Maybe a part of him has always known this day would come. He scrawls his name across the tops of the cartons and stashes them behind the boiler in the far corner of the building's basement next to long-abandoned bicycles, an assortment of cast-iron cookware, and some student's papier-mâché sculpture of a nun feeding what looks like a baby otter. A handful of items he stuffs into his bag—some toiletries, his passport, Sophie's address, the photo of his mother, and the magnifying glass that Marais gave him when he was a child.

When he's cleared his belongings from the apartment, he sits on the edge of the bed and surveys the empty room. This place that was to be his permanent home. It has been five years since he last saw it so denuded.

There's a rustling in the ficus.

Tonto perches on an upper branch, twig in beak, peering out at Charles.

He forgot about the bird.

The feathers on Tonto's crest have fanned out from the humidity.

Charles stares at his bag. *I haven't thought this through.* He reconsiders his plans. None of his colleagues is an animal person, not even Frank Williams. They'd never be able to care for a South African weaver. He has no one he can give the bird to.

Marais kept yellow weavers, Charles remembers hearing. He experimented on them, as he did with virtually every species he encountered. Charles can't help but wonder now whether this was the real reason he purchased Tonto: as a reminder of his father.

In the kitchen, the refrigerator drones like a sitar.

The longer he stares at Tonto, the clearer it becomes that there is only one option.

He ambles over to the window as casually as he can. He forces up the lower sash. Night wind gusts in and whips at his face. It's seventy degrees colder outside.

"I'm truly sorry," he says.

Tonto stares unblinking at him. He pokes his beak under his wing and scratches himself.

"Don't look at me like that. What choice do I have? I can't take you on the ship. And I can't leave you alone in the apartment. You'll be safer out there. At least you'll have a chance to fend for yourself." They both know the magnitude of this lie. Charles takes Tonto in his hand and strokes the edges of his tail feathers. "You've been a good pet." He sets the bird on the sill of the window. "Go on now. Think of all the new nests you're going to build. Think of all the ladies you're finally going to meet."

Tonto glances out incredulously, then turns and shuffles back inside.

With his knuckle, Charles nudges him out onto the ledge again.

Tonto looks down. His wings flap manically.

Charles starts to shut the window behind him, but Tonto slips back inside. He noses his way under the sash, and Charles nearly catches his wing in the frame.

When he pushes the bird out again, Tonto pecks angrily at his thumb.

Charles draws back his hand. A red dot widens into a small pool. He sucks at the blood.

When the bird isn't expecting it, he shoves him hard onto the ledge. This time he manages to shut the window. He flips the lock and secures it.

Tonto stares at him through the glass. He looks incredibly small. He looks betrayed.

Charles draws the curtains. The bird will be okay, he tells himself. Maybe he'll meet up with a flock of Canada Geese and be taken in as one of their own—like that girl who was raised by wolves. He might even find a mate, put his nest-building skills to good use.

A hammering starts up against the glass. *Tap tap tap.* Tonto begins shrieking. He raps again, then again. He raps so hard that it seems the window might crack.

"Stop it!" Charles shouts. "Please stop already."

He can't abandon Tonto here. When he cracks open the window, the bird wings itself inside, sails over to Charles, and finds a home on his shoulder. He doesn't resist even as Charles places him, gently, back in the cage.

Charles hunts through the Radcliffe directory until he finds Hannah's address. He leaves the rent and his key on the kitchen table, hauls the duffle over his shoulder, and hurries down the three flights of steps, the cage clenched under his arm. The door to the building slams behind him.

The sky is sharp and clear, and it doesn't take long to hail a cab. First stop is Hannah's apartment. Charles stands on her porch with the bird and a note and wonders if it's Hannah who's singing inside. He could at least say goodbye. He could tell her not to worry. He could touch her hand one more time. Instead, he leaves the caged bird on the porch with the note. He taps on the door, just once, and climbs back into the cab before anyone can answer.

The car rattles over potholes the size of cannonballs, as Charles lets himself sink deep into the leather seat. Along the sidewalk, groups of men stream by, huddling in patches around oil-drum fires. They hold up their frostbitten hands to warm them, and the flames lap in their eyes.

As his taxi crosses the Charles River—*his* river—spiraling silver below the bridge, on his way to the harbor and to England and Cape Town beyond, the thought of the future in all its unknowableness is oddly comforting. It's the present that scares him shitless.

Thus have I heard.

August 1902, Pretoria, Transvaal Colony, British Empire

Eugene Marais wandered through postwar Pretoria like a tourist who'd lost his map. A village of bell tents sprawled across the eastern edges of town. Women plodded barefoot through the streets with filthy, malnourished infants. A pair of ragged men picked at the filaments of a zebra carcass, attempting to scrape together the makings of supper. British regiments marched past them in formation, ignoring pleas for a few pence or a bowl of food. At the top of every public building—schoolhouses, banks, the Old Council Chamber—the Union Jack beat hideously in the wind. London, a city thousands of miles away, had muscled its way into Pretoria and crushed it once and for all. Marais had crossed oceans and continents to reach home. But now that he'd arrived, home was no longer here.

Still, the whole town wanted to see him, Pretoria's prodigal son finally returned from London with his deerstalker cap and European suits. He let an office in the Netherlands Bank building and set off to find legal work. He tapped everyone he knew in an attempt to land a single significant case. But the city was paralyzed from the war. His neighbors could focus only on trying to put food on their tables each night. Legal suits were an unaffordable luxury. People were so uncertain of their rights under the British that even those who had the means didn't bother to rebuild. They couldn't bear to have it all ripped from them again.

At night he'd return to his sister Jess's boarding house, a rambling two-story structure that backed up on a set of stables where she kept a small dairy. Jess was forty-eight now and as hardened as Sophie. Years earlier, her husband had divorced her, just as Sophie's husband had left her, and Polly's as well. Lizzie, Marais's oldest sister, had lost her husband to suicide. A single gunshot to the head. Four of Marais's six sisters had been deserted by their husbands. And he had lost his wife to the ministrations of a drunken doctor. Was this the family "luck" to which Sophie had alluded?

Early one Saturday morning, Marais led Gustav Preller down Koch Street to his old office with the small blue door. A hairless dog with half a tail and an oozing skin infection was curled on the stoop. Marais nudged the animal with his foot. The dog let out a half-hearted growl and slinked away.

Marais unlocked the door and ushered Preller up the narrow staircase. The walls were peppered with perfectly rounded bullet holes. Hunks of shrapnel marbled the floor. Everything that had previously hung from the walls—paintings, editorial schedules, budget projections—had fallen. His mahogany desk still stood by the window with a pile of stories from five years earlier that he'd never finished writing. All of this he dumped into the trash.

The British authorities had decided to allow *Land en Volk* to reopen. They'd even offered to subsidize its operations. Of course, Marais was under no illusions—in exchange, the English would expect favorable treatment. But he needed the money. While he was in no condition to manage the paper alone, Preller, his old friend and editor, had good business sense and a hatred of the British that rivaled his own.

In the corner of the room, a sheet of canvas was draped over his printing machine, covered with a layer of broken glass that sparkled in the morning light. Marais yanked off the canvas. A thousand shards jangled to the floor. He slid his hands along the steel casing. The machine was as good as new. "Pretoria is dying to have news in Afrikaans again," he said. "You're going to be famous, Gustav."

Preller grinned mischievously. "I'd rather be *in*famous."

"I think we'll find that in the eyes of the empire, there's little difference between the two."

Together, they published leaders condemning the British for coercing Boers into mortgage default and then buying out their farms, for making English the sole language of instruction in Boer schools. They condemned the empire for resettling English citizens in the Transvaal in order to outnumber and anglicize the Boers. They decried the measly "war reparations" that the British provided to Boers whose farms they'd destroyed: diseased donkeys that died immediately upon receipt.

It didn't take long for Marais to outrage the authorities. Lord Alfred Milner, High Commissioner for South Africa, and Governor of the Transvaal and Orange River Colony, summoned Marais to his residence in Johannesburg. Milner had been the architect of the war. He more than anyone was responsible for the tragedy that had engulfed the Transvaal.

Marais's train arrived at noon. A polished Cape cart was waiting for him at the station. His malarial fever had returned during the trip, and his legs shook now as he climbed into the cart. The driver wheeled him through the Rand, past cantilevered mining shafts and corridors of chimneys belching smoke. He dropped Marais in front of Milner's brick home in Sunnyside.

Marais stood in front of the property, surrounded by a sea of red and yellow roses and thought that he'd been plunked down in a fairy tale. He stared at the peaked roofs and the turret, at the perfectly painted stoep, and tried to will his temperature back down.

Milner met him in the parlor. The High Commissioner was smartly dressed. He had a thick-bristled mustache and a head of thin hair that was oiled and turned to the side. It was lunchtime, and Milner's servant laid out trays of salads, meats, pasties, and tiny sandwiches with the crusts cut off. Verdi blared on a phonograph.

"Please," Milner said, gesturing toward the spread. "Food makes friends of foes." He balled up a slice of ham, popped it in his mouth, and finished it off in one swallow. "I'm glad you've come. As I'm sure you know, it's been a difficult few years for the English."

Marais might have found the irony amusing if his bones weren't rattling from fever. "I can only imagine," he said.

"Britain faces an array of challenges with reputation and public perception. We need your assistance, Marais. That's why I asked you here."

Marais's stomach was sour and churning. The smell of the food sickened him.

The servant, a native, was still standing in the corner of the room, watching them, with a napkin draped over his forearm.

"If the English and the Boers are ever going to reconcile, and we must," Milner said, "we have to find some common ground."

A mob of violins shrieked through the room. "Which ground would you like?" Marais asked. "The smoldering hillsides, the city streets mired in rubble, or the thousands of Boer farms that your men incinerated? Have your pick of the prime real estate."

Milner smiled coldly. "We've allowed you to re-open *Land en Volk*. We believe in the importance of a free press. We also believe in the unifying power of language—it's the framework that will bind our peoples together. From now on, we want you to devote a portion of each issue, a significant portion, to teaching English to your Boers. They'll grow naturally to appreciate the majesty of English—the language of Shakespeare and Chaucer—and in turn, to improve their understanding of the basic principles of the Empire. Down the road, once we're all speaking the same language, *Land en Volk* can become an English-only paper. Ultimately, and I trust that you won't take offense at this, there will be no need for your kitchen Dutch at all."

Marais was shocked. How could Milner even suggest such a thing? "Afrikaans is the language in which Boers learn to count as children," Marais explained. "It's the language in which we learn to say prayers. It's the language in which we're taught to say 'I love you' to our mothers. That language is all we have left of our identity."

The clock on the wall chimed twice. Milner checked his watch. "You're a student of evolution, Marais, aren't you? Darwin taught us that languages compete just as individuals within a species compete. The most evolved languages, like English, must eventually lead to the domination of the lesser languages, like your own. That's just the way of the world."

"You must also understand that when a language, like a species, goes extinct, it is gone forever."

"More's the pity," said Milner. He clapped once and the servant glided to his side. "What do you think, Leopold? Would your people ever speak kitchen Dutch?"

"No, sir. That language sounds like wild Boers tupping. Excuse me—wild *boars*, I mean." The man laughed venomously. "We're English now. We don't need another tongue."

"See there?" Milner said. "It's a nasty language, Marais. Even the natives think so. You're a well-heeled man. You lived in London. Your 'Afrikaans' has no standards. There is no literature to speak of. It would be generous to call it a poor bastardization of Dutch, which is itself vastly inferior to English. Frankly, Afrikaans marks your people as backward. We'll all be better off once the Boers are speaking English."

Marais's eyes were dripping with fever. He wiped his brow with his sleeve. "I'm sorry," he said. "I'm not well." He thought he was going to be sick.

"I'm not offering this as a choice. But I can assure you we won't be ungrateful financially."

The breath in Marais's mouth came up in short, hot spurts. "I'm sorry. I can't discuss this now. I need to get home."

"This is not up for discussion, Marais. This is imperial policy."

Marais felt himself bend forward. "You can't expect me to . . ."

But he didn't get a chance to finish his thought. The contents of his stomach rose through his throat, and in one roiling flume, spilled over the tray of salads and pasties and little white sandwiches, and across the gleaming black shoes of the British High Commissioner for South Africa.

* * *

At their office on Koch Street the next day, Preller gave Marais a glacial stare. "You're giving in to them?"

"Not giving in," Marais said. "We just need to be a bit less conspicuous."

Preller looked skeptical.

"We won't stop printing political leaders," Marais said. "But we can't risk being shut down either. Subtlety and grace—that's our new game."

They had urgent work ahead of them. If Afrikaans was to survive Milner's plans, it would have to be able to compete. They needed to elevate Afrikaans to a literary language. How long would it take to create a national body of literature from scratch? Marais intended to find out.

He penned a poem, "Winternag,"—the first real poetry in Afrikaans—and ran it in the paper to prove what could be done. Then he and Preller sought out every Boer writer that they knew—in Pretoria, Johannesburg, Cape Town, Bloemfontein. They urged anyone with nascent literary skills to submit work to them in Afrikaans. They ran weekly contests for original short stories and poetry. As prizes, they awarded whatever they could get their hands on—a sack of wheat, a barrow of melons, a battered hunting rifle. They stuffed each issue with all the Afrikaans writing they could generate.

For Marais, it was like witnessing the emergence of his people from the Dark Ages. Like the process that England itself had undergone at the hands of the French six hundred years earlier—England had emerged from the Norman invasion a stronger nation with the richest language in the world. If he managed the process correctly, the Boers—the *Afrikaners*—could emerge from Britain's shackles the same way.

But Marais was running out of money. He'd spent most of his savings in London and the rest on the ill-fated mission with Schultz. He hadn't paid Jess for a single month of room or board since he arrived. He was overdue on rent and paper and ink, on postage and distribution. Creditors were threatening to cut him off. This month's advertising revenue combined with the British subsidy would pay for less than half the paper's total expenses. Next month looked worse.

Who was he trying to fool? A few dozen stories in Afrikaans? A hundred sonnets? None of this would mean anything to England. It would never lead to independence.

Wherever he looked, he apprehended a terrible absence. The war had torn a permanent hole in this country, and he had let it tear a hole inside himself too. He couldn't sit by any longer and watch as British regiments trampled on his city. Pretoria was suffocating him. There was no solace to be found here apart from the repeated stabbing of needle into vein.

* * *

7 NOVEMBER 1905

TRACKED YOU DOWN VIA SOPHIE STOP
ITS GLORIOUS HERE IN WATERBERG STOP
TIN AND OTHER MINERALS ABOUND
PLUS TRACES OF FLUORSPAR AND
PLATINUM STOP THIS IS THE RAND OF
THE FUTURE STOP YOU MUST TRY YOUR
HAND AT PROSPECTING MARAIS ENOUGH
DITHERING IN THOSE WRETCHED BRITISH

CITIES STOP I COULD USE SOME MORE GOOD MEN STOP HOLDING A PLOT FOR YOU STOP NOW IS THE TIME

DOLF ERASMUS

Marais found the telegram from his old schoolmate slipped under his bedroom door. Dolf had been a big child with a huge gap between his front teeth, a very average brain, and a predilection for European pornography that he believed made him worldly. As a boy, Marais had never felt that he could trust Dolf completely. He'd heard that Dolf had resettled up north in Waterberg, but it had been years since he'd last seen him.

Marais struggled to steady the paper and confirm that he'd read the message correctly. He'd never seen Waterberg firsthand. Here was his chance to escape life under the yoke of the British. Waterberg was barely regulated. If the British could bore into this land and extract its natural riches, why shouldn't he, an Afrikaner, profit too? The southern Transvaal would always remind him of Lettie and of a country that had ceased to exist. There was no room in Pretoria even to think anymore. Here was his chance to lose himself to prospecting. Here was his chance to forget—to forge a lasting future, to unbind himself from the past.

He wired back to Dolf.

PREPARED TO JOIN YOU NEXT SATURDAY STOP WILL BE ON THE MIDNIGHT TRAIN AT NYLSTROOM STOP HAVE NOT FELT SUCH HOPE IN A LONG TIME

Marais decided to pay a final visit to his sister and the boy before leaving for Waterberg. Since returning to Pretoria, he'd barely seen Charles—only on Christmas and Good Friday and Dingaan's Day, when Marais made the obligatory rounds to his siblings' households. On those occasions, the boy had shied away from him. He'd tracked Marais's movements peripherally, like a young, wary cheetah.

Charles, he'd heard, would soon be departing for boarding school in London. For all he knew, he'd never see the child again. He thought he should give the boy a gift. While packing, he'd come across a small magnifying glass that his sister Sophie had given him as a child for his insect studies. Marais engraved his own initials, ENM, into the beveled wooden handle—perhaps it would help Charles remember him.

The boy was preparing for bed when Marais reached Sophie's house. He was seated in the kitchen in an old flannel robe, sipping a cup of steaming milk.

"It helps Charles sleep," Sophie said. "Maybe you'd like to put him to bed tonight, Eugene?"

Marais thought he detected a note of scorn in his sister's voice.

"Oh, that's all right," said Charles. He looked horrified at the suggestion.

"Of course I would," Marais said. "It would be a pleasure."

There was an earthenware jar of water in the corner, and Marais ladled a drink for himself. Then he turned to Charles. "I'll tell you about London, so you'll be ready when you arrive."

"I can put myself to sleep," said Charles.

"Also," Marais said. "I brought you something. Something special."

Light flickered in the boy's face. He took a breath and squared his shoulders. "Okay, you can come." Charles rinsed both their cups and led Marais up the little staircase to his bedroom.

The magnifying glass enraptured Charles. He practically cradled it in his palms. "Can I take it with me to London?"

The clock on the wall chimed eight.

"That's the idea," said Marais. "Now it's time for bed."

Charles smiled and wriggled his way under the covers.

Marais snuffed out the lamp with his fingers and began to leave.

"Wait!" cried Charles. He was frantic all of a sudden. "We leave the light on at night. I can't sleep without it."

"Don't be silly. You're ten years old already. You'll be leaving on a great adventure soon. Bravery is in order."

Charles bit his lip in the faint moonlight that seeped into the room. "But—"

"No buts." Marais pulled the quilt up to the boy's neck and tucked the edge under the mattress. "There you are. Sweet dreams or no dreams at all." He strode toward the door with a budding sense of accomplishment.

"Oom Eugene!" the boy called.

Marais turned back. "What is it?"

"Please turn the light back on."

"Charles, you're old enough to sleep in the dark."

"What if someone comes in . . . and takes me? I wouldn't be able to see."

"Where in the world would someone take you?"

The boy paused. "Back to the camps."

The words nearly slayed Marais. "The camps have all been shuttered. There's nothing to be scared of. Dream of London and the sea."

The boy wasn't convinced. "I wish there was no such thing as nighttime," he whispered.

Marais padded back over and knelt by the edge of the bed. He'd help Charles follow his line of thought to its logical conclusion. The boy would come to see the folly of his own thinking. "We're diurnal creatures. Imagine how exhausted we'd be if we didn't sleep at night."

In the dark, Charles's eyes looked like the barrel end of a shotgun. He lowered his voice still further. "Then I wish that there was no such thing as being scared."

Marais could hear the boy's quick breaths, and something about the sound rattled him. Should he relight the paraffin lamp as Charles had asked?

He grabbed Charles then. He gathered him in his arms, as he should have done a thousand times before, and smothered him against his chest and whispered to him that his father was here now. There was nothing wrong with being scared. But there was no reason for fear now that his father was with him. Charles seemed as startled as he was.

For a while he held onto the boy—bearing the child's soft, dense frame. Once he released him, he regarded the boy closely. If it weren't for this child, Lettie would still be alive. Marais would still have his life.

"You'll be perfectly safe, Charles," he said. "Goodnight now."

Marais rose from the bed. He hastened from the room and pushed his weight against the door until he heard the latch click into place.

* * *

The train from Pretoria to Nylstroom was nearly empty. Marais stretched out across two seats and watched through the window as the car's shadow painted the edges of the veld a dark gray. He was, at last, heading to Waterberg and to a new chapter. Everywhere he looked was wide open space. Wildflowers bloomed with spring. Small clusters of birds and sheep bled into land that stretched to the horizon. He'd packed some rusks and dried beef for the trip, and he ate these now as the wheels roared against the tracks and the sun fell away with the onset of evening.

By the time the train approached Nylstroom, the sky was chocolate-black and the air scented with the aftermath of rain. A faint patch of light shimmered along the side of the car. Marais squinted through the window. Dozens of men and women were circling a white stone monument with candles in their hands.

"*Wat is dit*?" he asked when the conductor loped down the aisle.

"Church grave," the conductor replied in Afrikaans. "Nine hundred women and children buried here. Barely a drop compared to all those killed in the camps. But every week the villagers come to remember their dead. Makes no sense to me. Far as I'm concerned, nothing about that war's worth remembering."

The conductor shambled on to the next car. The floor of the train hummed, the vibrations winding through Marais's legs. Tens of thousands of Boers had been erased from the earth. The British had devastated this country, even all the way up here.

At least the English *people* had responded, though. When the truth of British imperial crimes was finally revealed in the papers, there'd been a worldwide uproar, in England more than anywhere else. That was something. Londoners were appalled to learn how their own government, their own military, had treated other human beings, however inferior they believed the

Afrikaners to be. It had been the world's first full-scale experiment with concentration camps. God willing, it would also be the last. England had learned. The world had learned. Humanity would have to evolve now.

The train was empty by the time it pulled into Nylstroom station, which was barely a station at all. There was no platform, no ticket office, no staff. And no one was waiting to meet him.

It was hours past midnight already as Marais climbed down from the car into the cold sodden air. He stretched his coat tightly around his neck. The train whistled, jerked forward, and chugged off again. He watched as the light shrank to a point and disappeared into the night ahead. Darkness enveloped him. His bags seemed heavier than when he'd packed them. He'd assumed that Dolf would meet him at the station.

He began walking eastward along the road, the treads of his shoes crunching against the sandy grit, while dust stormed at his face. When his eyes adjusted, he could just make out the silhouette of a horse cart ahead of him. The man at the reins wore a floppy, wide-brimmed hat, which he removed to make a show of bowing.

"Welcome to paradise, Marais."

Marais knew the voice immediately. "Is that where I am then?"

"You'll see for yourself come sunrise."

Marais strode across the street. Dolf looked exactly as he remembered, except his hair had thinned to wisps of string, and between his suspenders, his belly jutted over the waist of his khakis. The hand that Dolf extended was as large as a meat slab. Marais grabbed hold and climbed into the cart next to his old friend.

"It's a damn fine thing to lay eyes on you again," said Dolf.

"You're a good man for thinking of me." He threw an arm around Dolf's shoulder.

"All right, all right. Let's get going before we embarrass ourselves." With a gruff chuckle, Dolf snapped the reins.

"How can you even tell where we're going?" Marais asked as they picked up speed. "I can't see a thing." He'd heard of Waterberg's stark cliff faces. How often did carts like this one plunge over the side, wheels, hooves, bags, and all? The only sound was the clap of horseshoes echoing in the darkness.

"Don't you know where we are? This is the road of the Great Trek, man—same road our forefathers took from the Cape seventy years ago to escape British rule. And here we are, doing the same thing—forging a new country in the promised land. This route is baked into my blood. It's in yours too."

Dolf snapped the reins again. He began humming to the rhythm of the horses' hooves. A billion stars kindled the dark sky overhead: Canopus, Betelgeux, Kappa, Rigel, Eridanus. Marais craned his neck and searched from constellation to constellation. The Cross hadn't risen yet, but he calculated exactly where it would appear. He searched for the two milky patches—the Magellanic clouds—then located a third point below which formed an equilateral triangle. That's where he kept his eyes as Dolf hummed and the horses clomped and moisture from the night air bathed his skin. Slowly, the arm of the Cross hoisted itself into the sky.

Marais dreamed that he was riding a chariot. When he opened his eyes, a crescent of sun had arched up, and the horses were huffing them over a steep pass. At the top of the mountain, Dolf pulled on the reins. The cart slowed to a quiet rumble and stopped.

Below them, hills of farmland, gold with morning, rolled all the way to the horizon. Countless fruit and nut trees spread out before them. The fields were springing with every sort of grain and rainbows of vegetables. On the side of the road, a clutch of ostriches huddled in the shade. A hundred yards to the left, the horns of a giraffe peeked out from a stand of conifers. Nature's only sounds were horse breath and the trill of songbirds. It was as if the world had opened up and ripened, welcoming him with a riot of color.

"This is it!" Marais said, unable to contain his excitement. "This is the Waterberg of my childhood dreams."

"What did I tell you?" said Dolf, grinning. "Just wait till you start prospecting. I swear you're going to love this place."

They continued left, veering off the main road. The cart bumped over a trench onto a narrow dirt path that unraveled gently ahead. They wound their way up the red mountain toward peaks that floated in the distance.

The path took them through a thick forest of timber trees, high tambotie grass, and wild figs, the trunks smooth and silver. Great canopies of glossy leaves crisscrossed high overhead. At the base of one tree, Marais could make out the rotted remains of another older tree. The same was true of the next tree. And the next. The forest was teeming with figs. They had glommed onto the trunks of trees that had burned out or died of disease or old age. The wild figs had sought out death. They'd taken over the old root systems and thrived on them. Where there had been decay and destruction, a forest now flourished.

"Welcome to Doornhoek," said Dolf.

The trail turned steeper. The horses whinnied and slowed but continued dragging them up the mountain. Every so often something large rustled behind a tree a hundred feet from the cart.

Marais caught a streak of silver fur. Halfway to the ridge, the path was washed out by a silted brown stream, and they had to get down and push from the rear of the cart to help the horses along. The water reached to Marais's knees, but it was warm where his feet disappeared.

In the distance, a dozen makeshift cabins and another ten canvas tents were set back from the ridge under a cluster of red milkwood trees. Wooden claim markers extended from a patch of silver oaks all the way down the west side of the mountain.

"I've kept one of the most productive claims for you," Dolf said. "Work hard and you're going to make yourself rich."

"I sure do like the sound of that."

"Prospectors are charged just twenty quid a month for rights, payable in advance."

"Twenty quid? Payable to whom?" Marais asked. It was the first time Dolf had mentioned a fee.

"To me, old friend."

Off to the right of the path was a rocky kloof that had been carved into the middle of the mountain by a falling stream. It was bordered by a steep krantz, which towered several hundred feet above them. At the mouth of the kloof, a young man with suspenders, boots, and several days' worth of beard was digging in the stream bed with a trowel, hammer, and chisel.

"We work in pairs," Dolf said. "You two will be working and living together." He lowered his voice. "The fellow recently fled Jo'burg. There's a court order for his arrest. Charged him with theft. No need to get into details—suffice it to say, the charges are completely unfounded. He's a good man, hates the Brits as much as you and I do. Came to Doornhoek to seek his fortune. You'll get along swimmingly."

When the man looked up and saw them, he dropped his tools on the bank and jogged over. “Alec Austin of the mighty Transvaal,” he said and shook Marais’s hand vigorously. “I been waiting for yer to arrive. ” He was a strapping, laconic man with the widest smile Marais had ever seen. “Dolf says you’re the smartest Boer he knows. Hoping that applies to house-building too, cause I’m about ready to set fire to that tent.”

Early the next morning, after a night on a rocky bed of blankets, Marais got to work with Austin. They decided to build two small huts near the mouth of the kloof, close enough to shelter from the wind but far enough to avoid rock falls. They scavenged for hunks of granite and chiseled them into square blocks, which they stacked into rectangular, foot-high foundations. Next, Marais had them haul down logs that they felled near the mountain top—from Silver Leaf Vaalbos trees impervious to the appetites of insects—and sawed them to size.

“Mind where yer leave the tools,” Austin cautioned. “The kloof is infested with baboons. Terrible fellows, the lot of them. They’ll make off with our saws and hammers if you take your eyes off them, and if they do, we’re tent-bound again.”

Those first nights, they camped along the stream. But within a few days, they’d finished the outer walls. The huts stood six-and-a-half feet high, the logs cleanly notched. Marais readied an infrastructure of branches at the top of his hut, peaked to support a heavy thatch.

Austin was strong and able-bodied, but he had a tendency to cut corners or commit outrageous oversights. He sawed one of the logs on the west side of his hut a full six inches short. When Marais pointed out the error, Austin said he had no interest in felling and recutting another.

Marais was incredulous. The stability of the entire structure was compromised. "You have to fix that," he said.

"Not so. That's why I came to Waterberg. No one to tell me what I 'ave and 'ave not to do."

"One strong wind and the whole house will come down on you. Is there something wrong with your brain, man?"

Austin looked up and made a face. "Aye, indeed there is. I'll tell yer a story. When I was a boy, I 'ad a terrible lisp. They said my speech was a 'bomination. I said *sh* when I was supposed to say *s*. Instead of 'Sue,' it was 'shoe.' Instead of 'sigh,' it was 'shy.' Maybe that don't seem like it could do a kid 'arm. But picture this: one day at Catholic school, they set me in front of all the students for a spring performance—parents were there too, my mother dressed 'ead to foot in 'er Sunday best, and all the effin' priests and nuns lined up in vestments. 'Sing "God Save the Queen" for the mums and dads, Alec,' the head priest says. 'No, Father,' I whisper. 'I best not. I'll mangle the words.' The priest looks like 'e's never heard such incense. 'Aye, you shall boy or you'll take it on the backside,' 'e says, readying to whack my arse with his cane. Well, I never enjoyed a licking, so I up and did as I was told. Sang with as much enthusiasm as I could muster: 'God shave the queen!' Yer can picture the scolding I got for that one. The next year it was nursery rhymes. 'umpty Dumpty shat on a wall.' I can tell you—the nuns' gasps alone were enough to do permanent damage to the marble." Austin made a gun with his thumb and forefinger, aimed at the side of his head, and fired. He crossed his eyes and let his tongue loll about.

Marais liked his claim mate already.

The first night in the hut was paradise. Marais hadn't fashioned a bed for himself yet, and his two windows were just square holes in the walls of the tiny one-room home. He lay on the dried mud floor under a stack of cast-off army blankets and watched the starlight flood in. The newly felled logs smelled of mint. The crickets sang ceaselessly.

Shortly before dawn, a terrible screeching shook him awake. He threw off the blankets and jumped to his feet. A shadow passed under the window. He grabbed his Mauser, cocked it, and kicked open the door. Heart thumping, he braced himself for an attack.

Twenty feet away, at the mouth of the kloof, a baboon was squatting on the rocks, gaping back at him. It was a large adult male with silver-gray fur. Marais knew the breed from its beak-like snout, small black eyes, flared nostrils. A chacma. He lowered his gun.

In the chacma's hand was a brown glass bottle. It took a minute before Marais recognized the whiskey that he and Austin had shared the night before. They'd finished less than half. Marais had stowed the bottle inside his hut near the window before retiring to bed.

The chacma brought the bottle to its lips and sucked at the whiskey, then pounded the bottom on the ground with an awful screech. His whole body writhed from the acrid taste. Seconds later, though, he grabbed the bottle again and swallowed another gulp. This time he screamed even louder.

It made little sense. Why would the creature continue drinking something that tasted so vile to him? Only humans used intoxicants. Only humans experienced pain profound enough to make the taste worth enduring.

Marais looked directly at the animal and stuck out his hand. "That belongs to me."

The chacma stared back. He gulped down another swig.

"Give it," said Marais.

The chacma puckered his lips and made a grotesque kissing noise. He guzzled again from the bottle.

"Either you return it to me, or I'll take it back myself," said Marais. He began walking slowly toward the chacma. Fallen leaves crackled underfoot. The animal didn't budge.

Ten feet away, Marais broke into a run. He headed straight for the baboon.

The chacma screeched, dropped the bottle, and galloped off through the figs. He clambered up into the kloof and bouldered over the rocks and onto a flat shelf halfway up the gorge. Marais shielded his eyes from the sun. Above him, two dozen other baboons were squatting on the shelf, observing him from the tops of their great distended noses. He'd just met his new neighbors.

A line he'd read from one of Darwin's notebooks came to him like a song. "Origin of man now proved . . . He who understands baboon would do more towards metaphysics than Locke." What was it about the baboon? Marais had wondered at the time. Here was the answer. Right in front of him, the chacma had learned about the somatic effects of whiskey. He'd learned that liquor dulled the pain of consciousness. The creature had weighed the benefits against the cost. He'd grasped the effect that stemmed from the cause. There was a system to his thinking. It was just a matter of decoding the rules. The chacma was closer to man than to beast. If one wanted to understand the human mind, thought Marais, the origins of the human psyche, the cause of human suffering, the chacma would be the perfect subject. *This* was what Darwin meant.

There was a pulsing in his forehead—it had been there for as long as Marais could remember, but he felt it quicken now.

"Austin!" he shouted. "Come here, right away."

There was a clattering of tools and cups in his neighbor's hut. The door flew open, and Austin bounded outside in only his underwear, his hair matted against his face. "What's all the noise? I thought yer'd been attacked." He tromped through the mud with his bare white feet, cursing at the rocks underfoot.

"I need your help. With a research project."

Austin rubbed at his eyes. "It's barely morning. There I was chewing on the loveliest dream. If only you'd seen this girl. Christ, was she shapely—"

"There's an entire troop of chacmas living on the shelf above us. Do you know what this means?"

Austin looked disgusted. "I do not and shall not eat monkey meat."

"I'm not talking about *eating* them, man. We're going to *study* them. In the wild. We're going to document everything about them—how they procure their food, how they rear their children. We're going to study the chacma psyche. We're going to learn how they learn."

Austin glanced at the empty bottle by Marais's feet and looked at him suspiciously. "The baboons you're sayin' . . ."

"It's about more than just baboons. Freud has got it all wrong. It's not sexual obsession or hatred of our fathers that drives us. We're moved by something deeper, something locked secretly away within us. The human mind can't grasp the human mind directly—but we *can* study the higher primates, the animals that are most like ourselves."

The irony didn't escape him. The chacmas were only here—in such numbers and such close proximity—because the British had un-peopled the Waterberg. In the absence of humans, the chacmas had proliferated. They'd forgotten their fear of humans. It was the war that had brought this opportunity.

Austin belched. "Who the fark is Freud?"

"Haven't you been listening?"

"You're sayin' you want me to *study* the effin' baboons?"

"I want you to assist me in studying them."

Austin shook his head. "Ain't no money in that, Marais. We came for metals, not monkeys. What's in it for Alec Austin?"

Marais was going to grab hold of the planet. He was going to shake it with all his might until the fruit that was rightfully his rained down all around him. "What's in it? What's in it? Everything! The entire world. Don't you see? The hunt for truth. And boundless adventure."

A trio of mottled bush chickens scampered past and vanished into the brush. Austin kicked his big toe into the mud. Then he looked up and eyed Marais. A grin peeled slowly across his face. "Did I 'ear yer say . . . adventure?"

December 1935, Boston, Massachusetts

At nine o'clock, Charles's taxi wheels up to Boston Harbor for the midnight sailing. Red and blue lanterns dance on the inky water. The night is clear and shot through with stars, the air full of seaweed smells and the croaking of gulls.

Charles buttons his coat collar and hauls the duffle over his shoulder. He glances back toward the taxi as it speeds away. Sometimes giant steps are in order, he tells himself. He takes a breath and muscles his way through the crowd of porters and beggars and hawkers, between carts steaming with chestnuts and pretzels, and through the glass doors to the terminal where trans-Atlantic passage is sold.

The line of travelers inches toward the ticket window, and as he waits, doubts careen through his mind. Is he really ready to abandon his career at Harvard? He's not this impetuous. He can still turn around, catch a taxi back to his apartment, get a solid night's sleep. No one but Hannah would ever know he'd nearly skipped town.

But giant steps, he thinks, mask smaller strides—and smaller strides are, surely, possible. If he can make it to Boston Harbor, he can make it to Southampton. If he makes it to Southampton, then he can make it to Cape Town. If he reaches Cape Town, one way or another, he will find Marais, wherever he is. Marais suggested that his field notes would undermine Sizemore's project. His family's name is at stake. Still, a question nags at him: *what if this is all just a ruse compelling me to journey halfway across the planet?*

There's no time left for second guessing. At the ticket booth, he doles out a month of his salary for a tourist-class cabin, full board included, which still leaves plenty of reserves for the second half of the trip.

The ship doesn't sail for hours. The chairs in the waiting room overflow with fidgeting passengers. Charles buys a Scotch and soda at the bar, finds a space on the floor in the far corner, and settles onto his duffle. Across the aisle, two American businessmen thumb through issues of *Esquire* and smoke capacious cigars. A young woman chews voraciously on her nails. Mothers turn their laps into berths for crying children. Charles scans their faces. Every one of them has a story. Like him, each has their own reason for setting sail tonight.

In his rush to pack, he has brought nothing to read. He left his palm leaf manuscripts wrapped and boxed in his basement. Thousands of pages that were hand-copied and re-copied by individual monks over the centuries. He left behind his family of scribes. Another ripple of regret. Another dose of doubt.

Ice cubes clink against the sides of his glass. He leans back against the wall and tries to calm his nerves. Soon he is rekindling South African memories.

For his tenth birthday, his aunt Sophie gave him an old sporting rifle that had belonged to her husband, along with a single, sobering dose of caution. Later that day, Charles started shooting rabbits. He can still recall how the sun lit up the river where it eddied half a mile from the house, as he crossed the wooden bridge to the east side with the rifle slung across his shoulder, pretending he was a Boer commando fighting the British. All that afternoon he hid low in the green brush with his floppy, wide-brimmed hat pulled down over his eyes and waited until he noticed a movement in the grass near the water—the quick white flash of a foot or an ear. Each time he shut his eyes and squeezed the trigger, his heart clutched like a fist in his throat. He didn't want to kill the rabbits. He hated thinking of the pain he must be causing. But he needed to grow up, he needed to know his own mettle, and each successive shot came a bit more easily than the last. Maybe this meant he was on his way to becoming a man. At dusk, he returned to the house with a bouquet of little rabbits strung together—his shoelaces threaded through their pelts. Sophie skinned and roasted them and said that the meat was sweeter than she'd ever tasted. She was trying, he knew, to provide a home for him. But the fact that she had to try, the idea that she'd been forced to care for him, was a constant reminder of the real parents he lacked.

When Sophie offered him the chance to go to school in London, he seized it. He could finally leave South Africa and all his festering anger behind him. He could finally start again. He still remembers his first pint of bitter, warm and flat in classic English style. He remembers his first kiss—with the sister of a roommate he visited during fifth-form holidays. He can no longer recall the girl's name, but tonight he remembers her clearly, her soft curls in his hands, her breath on his face.

A whistle blasts through the terminal's commotion. He checks his watch. Eleven o'clock. In a single, sprawling motion, the entire crowd—passengers, visitors, shore staff—rises and heads for the door. Tugs, buoys, and skiffs bob around the steamer's hull. Silver lights stretch from bow to stern. As Charles boards the ship, the gangway flexes and rocks underfoot. He's on the verge of leaving the continent, perhaps forever.

Armies of parents fan out across the embarkation hall, eager to put their children to bed and return to the ballroom for the midnight sendoff. Porters and longshoremen fumble with trunks, golf clubs, and handcarts. Stewards thread through the crowd with telegrams and trays of champagne.

This old ship will transport him one step closer to South Africa. It will take him one step closer to Marais. After all this time, he is going to face the man who gave him away.

First things will be first. Marais will turn over his field notes. Charles will scour through every document the man has produced. Once he finds what he needs there, he'll give Marais the assistance he's requested. Quid pro quo.

And if the field notes don't vindicate him? Well, he'll have to cross that bridge . . .

Worn crimson runners line the corridor two flights below deck. Brown water stains pock the baseboards. Charles navigates to a row of tourist-class cabins and follows the signs to 267. To the right of the door, a handwritten placard reads *Marais*.

The cabin is nearly bare apart from a simple bed, a set of drawers, an armoire, and a small porcelain sink. Everything is shrunk and self-contained in a way that reminds him of the attic room he occupied as a child in Sophie's boarding house in Pretoria. A thermos hangs from brackets mounted to the wall. A strange amalgamation of smells—rose petals, floor wax, tea, and detergent—wafts through the cabin. Every few seconds, the light bulb above his head sizzles and flickers.

He gazes through the porthole at the docks silhouetted against the shoreline. Everything sways with the tide. Within him, tiny sparks of hope begin to fire.

He stows his clothing, kicks off his shoes. He unbuttons his shirt, pulls out the tails, turns on the tap, and splashes his face and neck with water. The mirror reveals the fatigue that has been compounding over time. The last few months have worn him down. But he's increasingly certain that he's made the right decision. He is no longer complicit in Harvard's love affair with Germany. He is going to find the truth about Marais.

Behind him, the door to his cabin creaks open. Engines rumble beneath him, vibrations weaving through Charles's legs and into his chest. He turns toward the door.

Hannah has on a gray pea coat and tall black boots, her face radiating pleasure. "I've found you!"

Charles is filled with a sense of dislocation. "What on earth are you doing here?" he stammers.

"We're neighbors! How about that?" she says, trying to snuff out a smile. "I'm staying just a few doors down, though your cabin is minuscule by comparison. I splurged for a double for myself and my non-existent brother in case the ticket agent decided to give me a hard time for traveling alone."

"How did you know . . . ?" His pulse quickens. Because he's been discovered. Because it's Hannah who has found him.

"After we spoke yesterday, I knew I couldn't stay any longer. Harvard isn't safe anymore. America isn't. Not for me anyway. Then I found your note. And your adorable little bird. Don't worry—my roommate is taking good care of him. I ran to your office to try to stop you. There was a newspaper on your desk. You'd circled the ad for this ship. I'm pretty good at putting two and two together. You'd spoken so highly of South Africa, I figured I should probably see it for myself. And also . . ." Her green eyes turn serious. "You didn't say goodbye."

He glances at the porthole as the night swallows the shore. "I didn't want to leave that way. That's not who I am. The university is trying to press me into service for something horrible. I didn't have a choice."

"The more I get to know you, the more I think we're not so different," she says. "I also want to live in a place where I don't have to pretend to be someone I'm not." There's a flicker in her eyes. "Fate sure is funny. Who would have guessed just a few months ago that you and I would be traveling to South Africa together?"

She surveys him, waiting for his reply. Slowly, her smile begins to fade. "I assumed you'd be glad to see me."

"I am . . . surprised to see you."

She looks hurt. "You kissed me yesterday."

The ship jerks abruptly. The tugs detach from the stern. They are unmoored.

Did he mislead her? It was only a kiss on the cheek. But he can't pretend that he hasn't imagined what it would feel like to run his fingers along her body, to feel her hands running over his.

"I owe you an apology," he says. "I shouldn't have—."

"We're no longer at Harvard, Professor. And I didn't take offense while we were."

"Hannah, the thing is, I can't have a . . . travel companion right now. Not even you."

Her eyes darken a shade. "You know what—let's just drop it."

He's sinking under the weight of so much change. He's left Harvard. He's forfeited tenure. All to find Marais. That is his singular purpose. He has nothing to give her right now.

"I won't bother you," she says curtly. "I'm a quiet person. I want to reach South Africa just as much as you do. We can keep things on the level of business."

"It's not a matter of noise. Or business. I can't have you with me."

She peers curiously at him. "You're married?"

"Of course not!" His throat is raw. "Hannah, listen to me." He doesn't want to turn her away. But this is not part of the plan. "I know you've paid for a ticket. But we're not traveling together. Even if we're both on the same ship. Even if you ultimately head to the same destination. You're free to travel where you wish. But not with me. I have things I need to take care of."

She pulls her coat tightly around her chest. "I get it. No problem then. You don't need to say another word." She turns abruptly, letting the cabin door slam shut behind her.

Along the main deck, couples in tuxedos and evening gowns hunker down with steamer blankets and martinis. A seven-piece band pounds out a ferocious beat. Women have wrapped themselves with sequins and boas and flowers. There's an air of pure festivity. The place is crawling with dancers.

Charles feels himself unraveling. They've barely left Boston Harbor, and the trip has already been turned on its head. How can he possibly take on responsibility for Hannah?

A shimmering frost coats the upper deck. He pulls his cap over the tops of his ears. The salty spray that fills the air is so cold it burns his skin.

The ship plows through the choppy sea. The sky pales with the coming morning. Charles loses himself in his thoughts. Nearly an hour has passed when he notices her, gripping the railing a dozen yards away. She's wearing the same peacoat that she had on earlier. Underneath she has changed into an evening dress. Silver hoops dangle from her ears and swing wildly in the wind.

"Look, I feel terrible," she says as she approaches. "I shouldn't have come without asking you."

A small seabird hovers off the side of the ship directly across from him. It rides a gust with barely a shake of its wings. Charles scans the sky for a mate—the bird seems to be flying alone. Images of Tonto besiege him. He left his pet with a woman he barely knows who gave it, in turn, to a stranger. He'll ask Hannah to telegram her roommate as soon as they reach land. He'll provide detailed instructions for Tonto's care. He needs to know the bird is safe.

"It seemed like a good idea at the time," says Hannah. "I guess that's the thing about ideas. They often do. Even when they're not. You're giving up so much. You emboldened me too. I figured if South Africa will accept me as I am, as a Jewish woman—as you said it would—then I'm ready to travel to the other side of the world. But I never intended to spoil your trip."

She gazes out at the briny water, her cheeks pink with cold. Charles is floored by her intrepidness. By the risks she's willing to take. Does she put this much faith in him? Where did she even get the money for such a voyage?

"What will your poor parents say when they find out where you are?"

"They won't say a thing."

"Of course they will. Any parent would be worried sick at the thought of their daughter taking off alone to a distant part of the globe."

She turns to face him. "My parents are dead, Professor."

He completely forgot. She told him early in the semester. It was this fact—that she too was orphaned—that first tethered the two of them.

"I'm the only child of two only children," she says. "The three of us couldn't have been any closer. But just like that, I'm a party of one now."

The bird still hovers parallel to Charles, a dozen yards from deck, carried along by the thrust of the wind and the drag of the hull. Why would an animal journey alone this far over the ocean? As if asking itself the same question, the bird veers off to the west and disappears from view.

"They were driving to Manhattan," says Hannah, "on their way to a Broadway show. My mother was so excited. She loved musicals. It didn't matter how silly they were. The moment a character burst into song, she'd get teary. They were stopped at a light. Half a dozen men surrounded their car. They overturned it, attacked my parents with knives and clubs. The papers said the violence was indiscriminate. 'A random act of barbarity.' But is barbarity ever really random? The detail I come back to again and again is that they had a Jewish star hanging from their rearview mirror. How could I forgive the world after that?"

He pulls his collar tight around his neck. He thinks he knows what she means. The death of his mother, Marais's disappearance, the camps—he still hasn't forgiven the world for everything he's endured. "I'm so sorry," he says.

"I don't know why, but I never pictured myself living very long," she says. "My parents, though—I always expected them to be around forever. And then, just like that, one day they were gone. I have plenty of money now, between the inheritance and the insurance. There's just nothing I want to spend it on." She laughs bitterly, wipes her eyes with her wrist. "What I want is my family back. It's the only thing I want, and the one thing I can't have."

Charles has spent an entire semester with this girl, confined to the same small classroom for hours each week, oblivious to her tragedy. "I lost my parents too," he says before he can stop himself. "Shortly after I was born." There it is. He's told her. The story that has become so entangled in his heart. That he was orphaned, though Marais, of course, still lives. There's a tightness in his gut, a sharp pang of guilt as he lies to her.

"Well, here we are, Professor," says Hannah. "Two orphans together on the high seas."

For a moment, he thinks maybe they *can* travel to South Africa together. But he swats away the idea. He has to stay focused on finding Marais. He doesn't have time for distractions. There's not enough of him to take care of Hannah too.

Still, it's only a week. Once they arrive in England, she'll have second thoughts. Europe is magnetic with its endless attractions. She'll choose to stay on there—and he can continue alone to Cape Town. "We can travel together until Southampton," he says. "Once we dock, I need to part ways."

"If that's how you want it," she says.

"That's how it needs to be." He folds his arms loosely across his chest, relieved to have reached agreement. "You're not a bad sleuth, you know."

Her eyes crease when she smiles. "You'd be hard pressed to find a better one."

She reaches into her purse and digs out a small camera, a 35mm Contax that he's seen advertised in the papers. "If we only have a week together, I plan to remember it," she says. She trains the camera on him. She twists the lens to focus. "Say *cheese*." The button snaps, the shutter fires.

* * *

Supper the next night is smoked eel, calf's tongue, fried celery, and cheap red wine. Charles sits alone in the far corner of the dining room scouring through yesterday's copy of the *Boston Post.* His arrangement with Hannah is working out fine. The ship has enough space for them after all. Eventually, the room starts clearing out. His eyelids grow heavy. He trudges downstairs and jiggles the key in the lock. He takes off his shoes, reclines still clothed in his bunk.

Sometime in the middle of the night, the skies break open. Hailstones lash the ship. The sea churns and writhes. Chunks of ice pound at the porthole with the explosiveness of artillery. His cabin groans like a waking animal.

Charles has never been prone to seasickness, but this is different. It feels as if he's falling through space. He grabs onto the mattress as the ship heaves to starboard. His hip and head are driven into the wall. The floorboards creak so violently he worries they'll snap. What rattles him most is not the rising nausea, but this one recurring thought: nothing lies between the ship and the sea floor. For ten thousand feet below, there's nothing solid. He tries to banish from his mind the two names that the Cunard and White Star lines made infamous—*Lusitania,* and that other one, the T-word, which every passenger knows never to speak aloud during a crossing.

Outside, the wind howls with rage. Water smashes so hard against the porthole that the glass pane feels on the verge of blasting inward. On the next roll, he is nearly flung from the bunk to the floor. A woman in the adjacent cabin screams.

With a jolt he remembers Hannah. He gets to his feet, knocks around in the darkness. He flicks the light switch, but nothing happens. When he opens the door, he nearly lurches from his cabin. He feels blindly along the dark hall, counts rooms until he reaches the seventh.

He knocks against the wood, whispers as loudly as he can. "Are you all right in there?"

Moments later her door swings open. "Thank God you're here." Her voice is hoarse in the darkness. "It's worse than I'd imagined."

She shouldn't face this storm alone. Until they reach England, he's responsible for her. "If you'd like company, I'll stay till it blows over."

"Bless you," she says. "Yes, please. You can have the top bunk, Professor."

He waits until the next lull, then gingerly scales the ladder. He pulls back the woolen blanket, tucks himself in. "You don't need to call me 'Professor' by the way—we're not at Harvard anymore."

"I appreciate that," she says. "Thank you, Doctor." The bunk creaks when she rolls to her side. "Just joking. Goodnight, Charles Marais."

In the darkness, he smiles. "Goodnight, Hannah Tauber."

In silence, he listens to the wind, counts each time it rips against the window.

Gradually, the sea exhausts its anger. The waves calm and settle. Charles lets himself sink, half-conscious and grateful, into the mattress. Before the rocking has completely stopped, Hannah's breathing slows and deepens. Each breath ebbs like the tide. He lies just four feet above, so close he is nearly beside her.

He wakes at five in the morning, night still clinging to the sky, and climbs quietly down. Hannah lies thick in sleep. In the brightening darkness he can make out the slight flutter of her lashes, the delicate ridge of her nose. A bare shoulder peeks out from her nightgown. Even asleep, she is a vessel of elegance.

On the damp lower deck, he exercises—push-ups and sit-ups, handstands and side-bends—with no companions but the sea, a passing steward, and an occasional dolphin breaching in the bow wave.

For the next few days, he barely sees her. He doesn't set foot in her cabin again. During meals, he eats alone: chops and kidney, rarebit and ham, and unnaturally sweet, tinned fruit. He didn't expect her to keep to herself like this. She must be preparing mentally for their separation when the ship finally docks. Left to himself, he cadges a copy of *Moby Dick* from the first officer's private collection and spends hours relearning the more spectacular terms from Melville's nautical lexicon: like *quoin* and *gam* and *cuntline.*

At one point, he and Hannah pass each other during his shipwide perambulations.

"Only sixteen hours until we reach England!" she says. Her legs are springy, nearly electrified. "How does it feel to be returning after so long?"

"A little mind-blowing to be honest." Mind-blowing is an understatement for what he feels now, on the verge of returning to London, the city where he came of age.

"I bet," she says, touching his arm. "It's good to be traveling with you, Charles. Even if we're not technically traveling together. It's the first time in a year that I haven't felt alone." He knows exactly what she means.

Just before midnight on New Year's Eve, the crew in the crow's nest spots the lighthouse at Bishop's Rock, the westernmost point of the Isles of Scilly. Charles squeezes onto the promenade deck among hundreds of couples celebrating the arrival of 1936. England's south coast is a glimmer on the horizon. A great cheer goes up. It has been a week since he last saw land. He feels euphoric.

The Channel is unusually gentle. The ship cruises northward from Cherbourg to Southampton, propelled along by the cold ocean winds. After breakfast, Charles returns to his cabin to pack. For the first time since they left Boston, he lets himself loiter. Sun sluices through the porthole and stains the floorboards gold. He empties his drawers and armoire. He reloads his bag, secures his passport inside. Everything *has* worked out.

From the main deck he watches as the ship swings to the west of the Brambles—Southampton's sprawling shoal. They shoot past Calshot Castle, then inch up past Netley. Tugs wedge them into port in Southampton and prod them to berth.

He still hasn't seen Hannah. She must have disembarked in the first line. He is swayed by an unexpected tide of regret, a loamy sadness, at having been left by her. This type of goodbye, though, is easier than the alternative. He'll make the two-hour train ride to Waterloo Station without her. From London, he'll be free to sail to Cape Town alone. She knew they couldn't continue on together. This is all for the best. If she were still with him, he's not sure how he would have said goodbye.

Cranes roar. Tugboats whistle. Charles grabs his duffle and takes off down the gangway, his feet rejoicing at the touch of solid ground. He follows the strip of pier through immigration and across to the boat train. Electric light floods the carriage. At the rear of the car is an empty set of seats with plush leather cushions. He stows his bag on the rack above. He rests his head against the window.

The train lurches forward. Wheels shriek against tracks. He lets his eyes close as wisps of black smoke peel off to the west. In two hours, he'll be back in London, his former home. Harvard is a lifetime away. For a brief moment, the specter of Conant and his wire-rimmed spectacles burns away the calm, but he inhales and lets it all dissolve.

When his eyes flicker back open, London's skyline is peeking above the horizon.

"I was just getting ready to wake you." Hannah's shoulder presses warmly against his. She has on a blue crepe dress that makes her look cosmopolitan in a European sort of way. "Just thirty minutes to go."

Charles rubs his eyes. "I thought I'd lost you."

"I don't get lost that easily."

He catches the floral scent of her shampoo. He is filled, unexpectedly, with relief. They can say a proper goodbye after all.

The train plows through what remains of the countryside. A food cart wheels down the aisle with tea and cherry cakes. It feels like days since their last meal. He's ravenous all of a sudden.

"My treat," he says. "You can't face London on an empty stomach."

The steward pours the tea. He slices the cake. He sets plates and cups and saucers on the table by the window.

Charles reaches into the breast pocket of his coat for his wallet but fails to find it. He checks his other pockets. No luck. He clambers to his feet, reaches into his trousers. He pats himself down, hits every pocket in his shirt and coat. The steward glances at his watch.

"I can get this," says Hannah. She pays for both of them. The man looks relieved to be moving on with his cart.

"I don't know where I put it," Charles says.

"What does it look like?"

"Like a wallet. Like your regular, run-of-the-mill, brown leather wallet."

"But were there distinguishing features?"

"It contained all of my savings."

Hannah's eyes widen. "Well, it's got to be around here somewhere. Don't worry—we'll find it."

Charles tears down his bag. He rifles through the contents. Hannah hunts beneath cushions and seats. Every article of clothing that he brought with him he heaps into the aisle. He remembers emptying the cabin. He triple-checked the room. He doesn't make these sorts of mistakes.

For a moment, suspicion flares in his mind. Has she robbed him? He shakes off the ridiculous thought. Hannah doesn't need his money.

"I can't get to Cape Town without that wallet."

"I am so sorry," she says. "Here's an idea. It's just one possibility, and of course you can say no. I have plenty of cash—I'd be happy to purchase a ticket for you."

"There's no way you're buying me a ticket to South Africa."

"It would just be a loan. You can have the money wired to me later."

Charles sets aside his cake. His appetite has vanished as quickly as it came. How could his wallet have just disappeared? He considers his rapidly dwindling options. Maybe she has a point. It could be a simple loan. He could repay her with interest. "I could wire it to your bank in Boston within a couple of months."

"I already sent a letter to close that account. You can have it wired to me in South Africa."

He lowers himself onto the mountain of clothes. "We're parting ways in England. We discussed this. We had an agreement."

"But how will you get to Cape Town then? That's the important thing, isn't it?"

If only he had an answer. He stares out the window as a hundred tracks converge. The train pulls into Waterloo Station amid clouds of smoke and soot.

Before the coach even jerks to a stop, the other passengers snap to their feet and swarm the exit. Outside, boxy black cabs queue in the rain. Men whistle and flag down taxis. They usher wives and children inside. Could she have taken his wallet to keep him traveling with her? Again, he lets suspicion melt away. She's never been anything but honest with him.

Hannah touches his arm. The coach is empty now, except for the two of them. "It's time to go," she says quietly.

Charles rises reluctantly from his seat. He stuffs his belongings back into the bag. The zipper growls as he pulls it closed. "We're going to have separate cabins again," he calls as he follows Hannah out the door. "That is not up for discussion."

"Of course we are," she calls back. And although he can see only the back of her head, he can tell that she is smiling.

Thus have I heard.

January 1906, Waterberg, Transvaal Colony, British Empire

Marais waded into a knee-deep section of the Doornhoek creek where the water chirped and sang. He dunked his pan below the surface and trolled along the gravelly bottom. The air was blue and crisp, and the verdant woods that encircled him crawled with fauna: insects, rodents, water fowl, rhino, buffalo, elephants, even big cats. Waterberg was already more than he could have hoped for. Every waking moment in Doornhoek—in this giant pulsing place—was a reminder of how small he was. The wildness suffused him with relief that even morphine couldn't provide. In fact, since he'd arrived in Waterberg, he hadn't touched his supply. Withdrawing had been ugly—for days he'd been wracked with fever and nausea and nightmares. But now he was free. And he was finally fulfilling Lettie's request—never again would he shoot the drug into his veins.

A hundred feet upstream, his claim mate Alec Austin labored in the water, grunting and splashing with his back to Marais. During working hours, the prospectors kept a distance from one another to avoid giving away proprietary "techniques."

Marais had always been deft with a tool, and he relished a good challenge. As a young man, he'd been fascinated by the gold mining operations around Jo'burg. But he had never prospected for metals himself, and since arriving at Doornhoek weeks ago, he hadn't unearthed anything of value. He knew nothing about panning for stream tin, but admitting that he knew nothing about something was even harder than not knowing. He didn't know how to sniff out which segment of a creek bed was most likely to yield paydirt. He didn't know how to agitate a pan without losing the sift to the water's quick current, nor did he understand the finer points of handling a sluice box. And even when, in spite of his missteps, he ended up with a few slivers of metal in his pan, he couldn't distinguish the precious cassiterite from the worthless wolframite.

He stabbed once again with his spade into the sandy bed, loosened the gravel around his feet, and scraped the rock into his pan. As he lifted it from the water this time, he felt a twinge in his hands, like the shock that comes from the first strike on a fishing line. The pan was substantially heavier now. All around the riffled edge, a rainbow of minerals—amber, cobalt, and maroon—sparkled in the sunlight. It had to be tin. This was how fortune functioned, he thought—suddenly and without warning. He'd finally tapped a mineral vein. It could be the beginning of a trove.

He spun the pan clockwise and dug through his haul. He fingered hungrily through the contents, discarding the waste as he went. But by the time he finished, he'd come away with only crumbs of granite and cloudy hunks of quartz. There was nothing at all of value.

He tossed the rocks onto the bank, dipped again into the stream, and hummed to himself. With his toes dug deep in muck and his rolled-up trousers sodden to the crotch, he couldn't recall ever feeling so hopeful. It wasn't the prospecting that had dispelled the dark mood. It was the chacmas.

Two weeks earlier, he'd taken a pony and cart down the mountain. A baker in Naboomspruit sold him a dozen burlap sacks stuffed tight as pork casings with mealies. With some coaxing, the little horse hauled the coarse maize back up the washed-out road to Marais's hut at the foot of the kloof. Every afternoon since, he'd enlisted Austin to help bribe the chacmas with food. They were acclimating the baboons to their presence. All the while, Marais knelt beside the stream and recorded what he observed. Their movements, the troop's structural hierarchies, their observable attractions and fears, their turns of mood at different times of day. His field notebook read:

> *My plan has worked. Twelve chacmas, ranging from one to perhaps thirty years old, now visit me late each afternoon. As I've come to distinguish one from another and to understand their individual personalities, I've numbered and named them: Peter, Andrew, James, John, Philip, Bartholomew, Matthew, Thomas, Lady James, Thaddeus, Lady Simon, and Judas.*
>
> *Peter is the senior member of the sub-troop and, based on their rivalry, an elder brother to Andrew. Peter is the first to rendezvous at the creek in the afternoons and the last to leave. In truth, it seems that I am as much an object of interest to him as he is to me.*
>
> *Thomas is the baby of the troop, a rust-colored one-year-old who insists on manhandling (and when given the opportunity, appropriating) everything my assistant and I leave on the ground for more than a few seconds. I attribute the*

disappearance of a pocket watch, two gloves, my best spade, three pairs of underwear, and a belt of giraffe leather all to this one small thief. Still, I have a particular fondness for Thomas—the young chacma reminds me of a chimp that I raised in London . . .

London! How strange to think of it. At this very moment, the city would be heaving under its early-morning bustle, while Marais was digging for stream tin in the middle of the African forest. It occurred to him that the boy must have reached London by now. He must be settled into his new school. He could picture Charles tucked into his dormitory bed, cradling the magnifying glass that Marais had given him. *Is he frightened being so far from home? Marais wondered. Does he miss his family? Does he ever think of me, his father?*

He gripped his pen, unable to stomach the seeds of regret that began swirling inside him, and continued with his notes:

The two female chacmas are smaller than the rest. They take their food last to avoid confrontation, but any crumb that their male counterparts overlook they will devour.

Judas is different from the rest, a solitary ten-year-old who will accept bread and maize one moment, then snarl and lurch at us viciously the next, as if he's never seen us before. It's on account of Judas that I keep the Mauser loaded whenever I approach the troop.

Judas differs by more than temperament. The skulls of the other chacmas are decidedly anthropoidal in shape, whereas Judas's is cynocephalic with prominent orbital ridges. The more I've observed the troop, the more I'm convinced that the two differently shaped skulls signal two distinct mental variations.

During my stints with the chacmas, I've begun to feel something I can't remember experiencing since I was a child, something akin to joy. In truth, I enjoy them more than people. With the chacmas, there is no pretension. There are no quarrels, no disagreements. The chacmas and I are two different species, but there is something familiar about them—something, dare I say, familial.

Marais descended once again into the creek. He felt the sandy grit under the soles of his bare feet. The metal pan chilled his hands.

He had made promises to Austin, promises that he was not exactly keeping. For example, he'd promised that their mornings would remain dedicated to prospecting. But the chacmas were approaching them earlier each day, and he couldn't realistically abandon them when they were actively seeking him out. He'd promised Austin that his research would not keep them from amassing the fortune for which they'd both journeyed to Waterberg in the first place. But Marais had earned nothing since he arrived. Already they owed Dolf Erasmus next month's dues for their claim.

Marais plunged the pan back into the creek. He dug the lip blindly into the bed, trawling his way through the sand. Water coursed up to his elbows. It splashed over his shirtsleeves.

"May I ask what it is yer hunting for down there?" Austin called from upstream.

Marais turned to face him. Austin's head was all hat in the wide-brimmed Boer-style.

"I'll bet you could answer that yourself," Marais called.

"Let me guess . . . is it trout?"

"No."

"Bass then? If it's not trout, it's got to be bass."

Marais hurled a chunk of quartz at his claim mate—it landed with a splash by Austin's knees and sprayed his beard. "You know very well that I'm prospecting for tin, not fish!"

Austin feigned surprise. "Ah! I'd never 'ave guessed. It's an interesting approach yer got. Seeing as there's no 'effin tin over there where yer been pissing about all day. That's just sand and rubbish rock."

"Well, if you'd be willing to part with a few words of wisdom from your vast storehouse of knowledge, perhaps I could locate some cassiterite."

"Yer on. Tip number one: stop daydreaming. Tip number two: if it's the metallic stuff yer aiming for, stick to the places where the waters pool. Yer welcome to join me up 'ere if yer like."

Marais pitched his tools on the rocks. He clambered onto the bank and hiked upstream to where his claim mate was kneeling in the creek. Austin slid a pack of Ogden's from his pocket. He removed a cigarette and tucked it between his teeth, then tossed the pack in the air.

Marais caught it with one hand and slid out a cigarette for himself. "How did you manage to find Ogden's all the way up here?"

"I didn't 'find' them exactly," Austin said, twinkling. "I scarfed 'em—from the pocket of a British officer in Jo'burg when 'is back was turned. Now watch and listen so yer can learn to pan properly, instead of splashing around like a giraffe hopped up on whiskey."

"Just go ahead and show me—I'll decide if it's useful."

"The counsel's free. If yer embarrassed to be taught by a Boer who has never earned a legal degree, medical degree, or doctorate in the science of speaking out one's arse, yer welcome to tell Dolf yer figured it out for yerself. But either we make a real tin strike soon or I can't continue to assist in your monkey business—"

"Just show me the damned technique already."

Austin raised an eyebrow. The tip of his cigarette glowed red. "Since yer asked so nicely." He bent from his waist and dunked his hands into the water by his knees. He whisked the pan slowly, ushering it through the creek with a series of quiet grunts.

The breeze picked up. Leaves rustled and danced.

Austin raised his pan just below the water line and tipped it ten degrees sideways. He began sifting off the lighter sand. "This is the trick, see—yer got to do the sifting *under* the water." He rotated the pan, shaking it just enough to urge the lighter matter over the riffled edge. When he raised the pan from the creek, what remained was a concentrate of dark metallic minerals and rich black sand.

Austin climbed onto the bank and shook his rump from side to side, the way a dog dries himself. He trotted the pan over to a small wood fire that he'd left smoldering in a pit and looked up to make sure Marais was still watching.

"Step number two: dry out yer haul. It's got to be fully dry before yer continue. Still with me?"

"Very much so. I just never noticed how handsome you are, Alec."

"Feck off." With a rag, Austin jiggled the pan over the burning sticks, letting the flame lick the bottom. The water gradually steamed off. The larger pieces dried and brightened. When steam stopped rising, he steadied the pan on a large flat rock, squatted in front of it, and eyed the fruits of his haul. He took a small horseshoe-shaped magnet from his pocket and held it against each of the larger black rocks. One by one, he extracted them from the pan.

"This 'ere is all iron. Worthless." He tossed the rocks into the bushes.

The black sand, Austin concluded, was also no good. He scraped the filings from the magnet and let them fall to the ground and sink into the mud. When he'd fished all the iron from the pan, what remained were three small black specimens. With the side of the magnet, he rolled them over—no sign of magnetism. He poked them with his little finger.

"'Ere we are then. Place yer bets, Marais. What is it we've got? Wolframite? Or stream tin?"

Marais lifted Austin's specimens with his own tweezers. He examined them all, the metallic grain flashing in the sunlight. The three pieces were identical. Marais didn't have the slightest clue as to whether they were tin or wolframite. "Whatever they are, all three are the same."

"Maybe, Doc." Austin took a small quartz crystal from his pocket and glanced at Marais with one eye. "And maybe not."

He tweezered the first piece and scratched against it with the quartz. A sharp white line trailed along the rock's surface where the crystal touched it. "Wolframite," he spat. He tossed the specimen into the trees. The second piece also scuffed. He pitched this one into the woods as well. The third specimen, however, didn't scratch. No matter how hard he scraped, the crystal left no trace of abrasion.

Austin flicked the stub of his cigarette into the tall grass. He held up the small black rock. "Here, Marais, is yer 'effin stream tin."

Marais's heart soared. It was that simple then. Now that he knew how to pan for tin, funding for his chacma research would be limitless.

Austin scooped up the specimen of tin he'd panned. He turned it over, examined it, then tossed it into the sicklebrush.

Marais couldn't believe his eyes. "You're a rich man all of a sudden? Throwing away good tin?"

Austin unhooked a small glass vial from his belt and held it up to the sunlight. "This 'ere's everything I've panned in one month's time. Take a look. Amounts to less than an ounce. There's no point in continuing at this pace."

Two warthogs scuttled from the bushes. They sneered, spun around, and padded through a wall of leaves.

Hasn't panned a single ounce? How would they pay Dolf? Then there was the pound-a-day wage that Marais had promised Austin for research assistance.

"When I first arrived," Austin said, "the tin came out at a good clip. But I'm starting to think we've exhausted the claim already. No way it should 'ave happened so fast. Makes no sense. Dolf says 'e pulled ten pounds from 'is own claim just this week. And 'ere we are pulling nothing and paying for it out the effin arse!"

He spat in the creek. The yellow gob floated on the surface like a bug.

"It's not just *our* claim that's barren neither. The rest of the prospectors are grumbling that ole' Dolf's buggered them real good too. We're all meeting at the 'otel tomorrow night to decide what to do next. I don't like to say it, but another week of this and I'm abandoning this whole monkey-infested ship."

Marais's breath caught in his throat. "You'd leave Doornhoek?"

"I certainly would, Doc. I've got no effin money left to pay Erasmus for this bloody claim. Better off trying my luck elsewhere."

Even if he could manage for some time without a research assistant, Marais wouldn't be able to cover the cost of the claim himself, not even for a month. He'd have to forgo the entire enterprise. He'd have to give up on the chacmas. And return to where? To what? This was happening so quickly. "Two pounds then!" Marais shouted.

"What?"

"I'll double your daily wage." He didn't have anywhere near this kind of money. But what choice did he have? "You're a good assistant. You're a good friend. You need the money. We'll make this work."

Austin narrowed his eyes. He sucked a column of air through his nose. "And yer going to pay for this 'ow?"

Marais forced a smile. "With the hoard of effin tin that we're about to pull from this mountain."

Marais sat cross-legged at the edge of the creek, putting the finishing touches on his notes. He was tired after the day's observations. He thought he'd play with the chacmas a bit before they returned to their cave high above them at the top of the kloof.

On a whim, he took a flask from his pocket and filled it with mealies.

Thirty feet away the chacmas peered at him. They licked and smacked their lips.

When the flask was full, he stuffed the rubber stopper back into its mouth.

The chacmas snorted at the sight of food. They pulled at the skin on their faces.

Marais tested the stopper to be sure it was tight. Then he pitched the bottle at the group. The flask soared through the air and landed with a thump on the bank. The chacmas shrieked and scattered, barking until they realized they were not being attacked after all. It was just a game, a good-natured bit of teasing.

Peter approached the flask first. He kicked the bottle with a hairy toe.

James grabbed the flask from him with both hands and hammered it against a rock.

Judas leaped maniacally into the air.

The others hooted. They cried. They pounded their chests.

Ten minutes passed. They hadn't managed to open the flask. Nothing they tried would work.

The day burned on. It was almost dinner time already. Marais yawned and stuck out his hand. "All right, let me have it. I'll open it for you."

James eyed him skeptically, unsure whether to accept the gamble and return the prize. He waggled his head. He gnashed his teeth. Then he dropped the flask in the mud and backed slowly away.

Marais scooped it up. "Now watch carefully," he told the chacmas. He held out the flask where the entire troop could see it. "The trick is to pull and twist simultaneously." Marais demonstrated, tugging while twisting counter-clockwise for three full turns. At the end of the last turn, the cork popped out. The sound echoed along the cliff.

The chacmas bellowed with delight.

Bartholomew spun like a dervish.

"See, fellows? It's not that difficult." Marais stuck the stopper back into the flask, banged it tight with his fist, and tossed the bottle back at the group.

Ten male chacmas pounced on the flask. There was no way they'd ever open it, of course. The task was too complex. But Marais was enjoying the game. He figured he'd tease them a little longer before returning to his hut.

There was a roaring now, sudden and thunderous. Out of nowhere, Peter stampeded into the fray with his chest puffed out and slapped away the others. He seized the flask, snarling until the remaining chacmas retreated, then turned over the bottle in his strong woolly hands. He pulled at the stopper until his knuckles whitened. He started to twist. The stopper turned slowly in place, but it remained stuck in the mouth of the flask. Livid, he hurled the bottle into a ditch. Then, for good effect, he stomped it with his foot.

Lady Simon, aware that Peter's billowing anger would lead to no good for the rest of the troop, crawled to his side. She cooed softly, a baboon's sweet nothings, and rubbed her dark haunches against his leg. Peter kicked her hard in the chest. She cried out and limped away.

Peter collected the flask once again. He joggled it in frustration. Then his expression changed.

Marais met his eyes, and the look he saw there was, strangely, *human*. There was no other way to describe it. "Go ahead," Marais said quietly.

As if remembering how he'd seen Marais do it, Peter began pulling and turning the stopper at the same time. Marais watched with fascination. He couldn't take his eyes from the chacma.

The top of the stopper began to stretch away from the bottle's mouth. Peter's own eyes widened. He pulled even harder as he twisted. The sound that came from his chest was like a deep orgasmic growl. And then, all at once, there was a tinny *pop*.

The shock on Peter's face mirrored the thrill in Marais's chest. The chacma had remembered Marais's lesson. He'd learned to master a complex task through observation.

While Peter stood marveling at the open bottle in his hand, the rest of the troop flew at the flask. He pivoted just in time, escaping before the others could pile onto him. Marais watched the group bound back up the kloof with a chorus of howls.

It took a moment before he realized that his flask was gone for good. He'd just forfeited another possession to the chacmas. But the losses were now in the name of science. His plans were suddenly grander than anything he'd let on to Austin. He recorded in his notebook:

> *I'm increasingly certain that the chacmas have attained an intermediate state of psychic evolution between the lower animals' "phyletic memory" (the instincts passed on to all members of a species) and humans' fully formed "causal memory" (the ability to acquire individual memories in the course of a lifetime).*
>
> *Phyletic memories are transmitted hereditarily from one generation of a species to the next. It's what enables one's descendants to survive in their native environment. But causal memories can't be inherited. In fact, they must not be. If they were, they'd chain the next generation to their environment and defeat their evolutionary purpose: to enable highly evolved mammals to adapt to rapidly changing conditions, and to relocate when necessary.*
>
> *With natural selection, Darwin explained the origin of species and the process of evolution. I shall go one step further. With the chacmas' help, I intend to prove the evolutionary origins of the psyche. And not just the primate psyche. That is*

> *only a means to an end. It is the human psyche whose depths I intend to plumb. Apart from a few lingering survival instincts that have remained intact in humans—the knowledge at birth of how to nurse from our mother's breast, certain startle reflexes that disappear after a few months—we humans have lost access to nearly all our ancestors' phyletic memories. It's why it takes years after birth before a human can care for itself, while insects are self-sufficient the moment they hatch.*
>
> *The recent rise of causal memory in humans has enabled us to construct languages. Which has enabled us to construct tools and ships and guns. Which, for better or worse, has enabled us to construct empires.*

Marais stayed up all night, the gears of his mind grinding so hard that at times he thought he could hear his own thinking. What if we could re-awaken instinct within ourselves, and by doing so, weaken the terrorizing grip of the memory faculty? *Before you can conquer your enemy, you must first know him.* Here was his chance. He had the perfect research subjects, an unlimited pool of time, and an able assistant.

* * *

The Doornhoek hotel was a two-story, eight-room, ramshackle affair built right into the belly of the mountain to provide temporary accommodation for new white arrivals and those passing through. Somehow there was just enough through-traffic that the proprietor of the hotel managed to keep himself in business. It helped that the hotel's saloon was the only place for miles where you could get a real steak. And that every pint of beer came with a guarantee that it would not cause diarrhea. As Marais learned on his first visit, the same guarantee did not come with the steak.

The whole area was thoroughly segregated, of course. Inhabiting the periphery of the Waterberg were large pockets of native Africans, a handful of whom worked at local businesses or on Boer farms, and all of whom were poorer than poor. Marais also knew of a clan of thirty bushmen, Vaalpens pygmies, living on the veld northeast of Doornhoek near the Mogalakwena River. There were barely a couple hundred white men in the entire region, and they owned everything of value.

By the time Marais and Austin finished with the chacmas for the day, changed into their least foul-smelling shirts, hiked to the bottom of the mountain, and stepped into the hotel, every man in Doornhoek, minus Dolf Erasmus, who'd not been informed of the meeting, had already arrived and knocked back several pints. Boers and Welsh, Scots and French Canadians, Australians and Irish all sat on high stools set around large wooden barrels. It was Saturday night, and every man knew that there'd be no liquor for purchase the next day in all of Waterberg. The saloon smelled of sweat and sex, liquor and meat. Inside the doorway, the owner's twelve-year-old son balanced on his one leg, struggling to urge an old Boer dance tune from a rickety concertina. Seated on top of the bar with their knees spread were the proprietors' only regular employees: two Boer girls with low-cut blouses, high-cut skirts, and faint mustaches, and an even younger Black girl with red stains on her bodice and a tired, expressionless face. All three had tried to capture Marais's attention when he first arrived in Waterberg months earlier, and though he sometimes touched their noses and kissed their cheeks when he visited the hotel, he'd made it clear that they were too young for him. Now they addressed him as "Oom Eugene," just like Charles had. The rest of the men paid the girls no attention tonight. There was rage in the air.

"I need a show of hands," one prospector called above the din of voices, the smash of glasses, and the death-throes of the concertina.

Marais signaled to Austin. The two of them squeezed through the crowd toward a couple empty seats at a barrel table in the back of the room.

"Who's struck any real tin in the last month?" the prospector demanded.

Five hands out of forty shot up.

"Lucky bastards," one of the Canadians mumbled.

"But slivers only," said one of the men.

"Nothing worth keeping."

"Won't pay for even a quarter of the cost of my claim."

"I can't afford my claim no more," said a young Welshman with tiny yellow teeth. "I'm completely cooked."

An old Boer in a heavy flannel coat leaned over and patted him hard on the shoulder. "Keep your head up, son. We're all in this together."

"Not all the claims are barren," another called. "I ran into Dolf this morning. Says he struck platinum yesterday."

"Platinum!" shouted the Irish. "No sir, he did not."

"He showed me the rock. It was the size of my fist."

"How do we know it came from Doornhoek? I say he's just snookering us into staying on and paying him."

Ever since the discussion with Austin earlier in the afternoon, the same question had begun to gnaw at Marais. Had he been duped by his old friend? Had they all? With the monthly rent from twenty prospectors, Dolf would be rich by now even if he'd struck nothing at all.

The first man scrabbled onto a barrel and folded his arms across his chest. His grizzled beard reached nearly to his navel. "So what are we saying?"

"That the claims Erasmus rented us are worthless!"

"Has he known all along?"

A hailstorm of voices.

"Course he's known all along."

"Erasmus is a bloody squirrel!"

A chair sailed over Marais's head. He ducked just in time. It splintered against the wall. One of the white girls on the bar laid her head in the other's lap and closed her eyes.

"Not all at once!" the first prospector called. He stomped on the barrel top with the sole of his boot. "Quiet down now. So we agree we've been buggered by Erasmus. The question is what are we going to do about it?"

"Demand he return what we've paid him!"

"All of it!"

"But is that enough?" the man on the barrel said, emboldened by the others. "Think of everything you've spent to get here, to stay on all these months. Add to that what you've lost by not working elsewhere."

"He'll never repay that much," the Canadian said.

"Then there's only one choice left!" blurted an Australian. The man had a pocked, grizzled chin. "We'll slit the bastard's throat!"

Silence settled over the room. The Australian glanced at the other prospectors for approval. "Who's with me?" he called, trying to remain firm. There was a tremor in his voice now. The initial flame in his blue eyes dimmed.

The flannel-coated Boer got to his feet. "I am," he growled.

The proprietor's son glanced anxiously at the Boer, lowered his concertina, and hopped into the back room.

"And I," said another.

"Me too."

Hands fired up. Fists pumped the air.

From behind the bar, the proprietor shot Marais a fearful look. Dolf's murder would mean the end of their work at Doornhoek. British authorities would descend on the town and shut down the claims. Their arrival would mean the end of the hotel's ability to evade British taxes. Without a means to support himself, Marais's work with the chacmas would be finished. He had to act quickly.

He rose, straightened his coat, and clapped his hands. "Gentlemen, may I have your attention?" All eyes turned. The noise gradually simmered.

"This discussion is important, and I couldn't agree more with the general sentiment. But friends, we have advanced too far and in an ill direction. At best, violence would bring imprisonment for the perpetrators and lost opportunity for the rest of us. It could bring capital punishment, or worse, forced return to the places from which each of you has come."

At this last bit, a hint of a smile passed over the Black girl's face. She didn't seem particularly upset at the prospect of losing these clients.

"Vengeance would do nothing to right the wrongs of which Erasmus has been accused," Marais continued. "And these, we must remember, have not yet been substantiated."

"Are you defending the maggot?" called the Australian. His face glowed red.

The men shuffled in their seats. A low murmur of voices reverberated against the floorboards. Marais was a newcomer and an advocate. Would they trust him any more than they trusted Dolf? He needed to prove himself partial to their cause. "Here's another idea," he continued. "Let's demand a waiver of rent on all claims for the next nine months. Any man who makes a significant strike during this time can easily pay his back rent to Erasmus with interest. Those of us who aren't as fortunate would be free to leave without further payment to him. It's a fair deal and an arrangement that could realistically be negotiated. If we can agree on the approach, I will obtain agreement from Erasmus. Let's put it to a vote. Those in favor, say 'aye.'"

The prospectors glanced tentatively around the saloon, gauging the others' reaction to the new proposal. Marais needed a quick show of support. Under the table, he kicked Austin hard in the leg.

"Ow!" Austin cursed under his breath. He stumbled to his feet and cleared his throat. "I mean aye," he called. "Aye it is for me."

The Scots shuffled in their seats. The Welshman hacked up a cough.

"Aye as well," said the man on the table.

The Welshman wiped his nose with his sleeve. "Aye for me," he called. The proprietor winked at Marais.

One after another, the rest of the men called "aye." Even the Australian voted in favor.

"We're in agreement then," Marais said. "We have a way forward." He turned to the proprietor. "Another round for our good friends! This one's on the house, I believe?"

The proprietor grimaced but began dispensing.

When Marais looked up, Dolf was hovering in the doorway. His bald head shone in the lamplight. Marais darted for him, forcing his way through the barrels. He had to get Dolf out now. The prospectors were liable to attack if they saw him.

"Sorry to disturb you gentlemen on a Saturday night," shouted Dolf. "But it seems we have a problem." Marais jerked to a stop. He was too late.

The room quieted. At the corner table, one of the prospectors spit out a wet belch.

"Yesterday," said Dolf, "a man broke into my place while I was out working my claim. Punched a hole in the window and helped himself to my belongings."

"Not the collection of French . . . photography, I hope," the Welshman whispered. Laughter shot across the saloon. Fists pounded on barrels. The Welshman snickered.

A blue vein throbbed in Dolf's neck. "There's five hundred pounds missing from my fecking cabin!"

The men shifted in their chairs. All smiles vanished. The proprietor looked on the verge of a stroke.

"All of Doornhoek is here. So I know the thief's in this room. And because I know how much you all want to continue renting the rights to your claims, I know you're going to tell me which one of you did it. Come clean with me, boys. The Lord has mercy for the sinner who repents."

Who had the gall to swipe that sort of money from Dolf's cabin? Marais scanned the faces in the saloon: rough, reddened, rounded faces. Peel away the exterior distractions—the shoes and hats and coats—deafen yourself to the various languages, and it wasn't difficult to see the primate in the men. The puffed-out chests, the bravado, the base urges, troop formation, the inclination to protect or fight, the inclination to steal and to avenge. The urge to violence. He could see, suddenly, the animal in each of them. Even in himself.

"No takers, eh?" said Dolf. "Then we'll up the ante. One hundred pounds to the man who's brave enough to turn in his wicked brother."

The men's eyes hardened. Beneath tables, hands groped for knives.

As a child, Marais had watched as Dolf unleashed a sharp right hook to the cheek of one of their classmates, a mangy boy who'd accidentally switched lunches with him. The boy's knees had buckled under the punch. Marais expected Dolf to leave him on the ground and walk away. But instead, Dolf walked over and drove his boot into the boy's ribs. Then he took the boy's face and pressed it mouth-first into the mud.

If Dolf lashed out tonight, he would incite the prospectors' rage. The silence in the room rang so loudly that Marais's ears began to ache. Who did it? He scanned the stubbled faces. The Australian? After all, didn't every Australian issue from criminal stock? Or the Irish fellows, who for no particular reason had always seemed to him rather suspect? What about the Canadians? The Welsh? As Marais considered the men one by one, his gaze fell upon his claim mate.

Austin was staring into his empty lap. Marais tried to catch his attention, but he wouldn't look up. His lips had turned bone-white.

Marais recalled what Dolf had told him the day he arrived at Doornhoek—Austin had a warrant out for his arrest. Dolf said that the charges were unfounded, but because of the warrant, Austin couldn't risk returning south. He needed money. The more Marais observed his claim mate, the more he became convinced. Austin was the thief.

"No one's brave enough to rat out the perpetrator, eh?" Dolf spat. "Then prepare yourselves. I'll be interrogating each of you individually. And so help me God, I shall bring the goddamned thief to a very unpleasant justice."

Dolf shouldered his way through the tables. The double doors swung behind him long after he was gone. When Austin finally exhaled, Marais heard fear vibrating in his breath.

* * *

Later that night Marais stretched out along the bedroll on the mud floor of his hut, smelling the forest in the walls. Dolf's wrath would soften with time—he wouldn't risk losing the income from the prospectors. Until then, Marais would have to keep Austin inconspicuous.

The paraffin lamp flickered over his shoulder as he opened his notebook and got to work. What was it exactly that marked Judas as different from the others? he asked himself again. For one thing, the young baboon didn't have the same causal memory capacity as the others. He seemed incapable of remembering what transpired from one second to the next. At times, he appeared amnestic. But his instincts were clearly intact: he remembered how to procure food, he knew his way perfectly around the forest. He always managed to find his way home . . .

A line of swollen-headed ants snaked along the floor. From the doorway near Marais's head to the window two yards past his feet. Each ant was grasping a crumb in its mandibles. They were headed home.

Was this it? He wet his pen.

Hypothesis: if it's true that the instinctive memory of a species becomes submerged with the rise of causal memory, and if it's true that Judas's causal memory has not evolved like the other chacmas in the troop, then conversely, the homing instinct would be stronger in him than in his more psychically evolved companions. This hypothesis must be tested. It must be verified.

Marais knelt by the window and gazed out at the billions of lights kindled high above the fig trees. An image of his mother rushed toward him, short and stern in her powder-blue dress, her neck ringed with pearls. She'd died more than a decade ago, but he could still conjure her clearly. He thought, too, of her mother and father—his grandparents—and of their parents in turn. Marais had never met his great grandparents. He'd never seen a photograph. They'd come from France and Holland, but he knew little else of their origins. Now he found himself wondering what he had inherited from them. The gray tint of his eyes, the swing of his gait, his wayward moods? His mind reached backwards through history. He tried to imagine the generations of humans before him who had battled against nature, struggling to survive long enough to reproduce. Their physical and psychic traits had fought and mixed and finally culminated, through an elaborate chain of Mendelian processes, in his standing right here at this very moment gazing at the sky and struggling to understand the mystery of the past. Somewhere in the evolutionary history of his ancient animal ancestors—snouted, hirsute jungle-dwellers—causal memory had begun to arise and instinct to disappear.

An itch arose, a fiendishly pleasurable itch that burned in his chest. Morning was not far off. *Tomorrow*, he thought, *I shall begin to find the answer.*

The first capture went more smoothly than he had predicted. Thomas was trusting, and it didn't take long to lure him from the kloof to the far side of the hut. Marais felt a pang of guilt as he turned his back to the young chacma, slid the burlap sack from his coat, then spun around with the opening held high. Thomas didn't suspect a thing until the moment the bag was thrust over his head. He screamed then from fear and betrayal. But once Marais secured the knot at the top of the bag and he could no longer see the young chacma's face, his own guilt ebbed.

Judas's capture was not as simple. The older chacma was innately distrustful and loathe to separate from the rest of the troop. When he finally strayed to the creek in search of a drink, Austin jumped him. He wrestled the chacma to the ground while Marais grabbed a rag that he'd soaked in chloroform and clapped it over Judas's nose and mouth.

Judas kicked and scratched at them, as a rumble started up amid the trees. Marais turned in time to catch Peter and three other males stampeding toward them with bared teeth. The whole kloof shook beneath their feet.

"They're going to kill us!" Austin shouted. He yanked Judas's claw from his throat.

The males were nearly upon them now, preparing to tear them apart. Marais pulled the Mauser over his shoulder. He aimed just above their heads. He squeezed the trigger and fired. The crack of his shot echoed over the mountain.

The elder chacmas stopped abruptly. They turned on their heels and galloped back onto the rocks. Judas's entire frame had already gone limp.

The experiment was straightforward: they would assess the extent to which the homing instinct was present in each baboon.

Marais and Austin rode their subjects to two different designated points, each fifty miles from Doornhoek. At precisely three in the afternoon, they untied the bags. Marais tracked Thomas. Austin tailed Judas. They recorded the exact routes that the chacmas took, the number of missteps, the time between rests.

For three days Thomas wandered in circles. Marais followed the young chacma across the arid veld, past eucalyptus-studded koppies, a string of jagged krantzes, and back along the windswept plains. In the middle of the second night, Marais lost sight of him. When he found Thomas the next morning, the young chacma was face-down, wheezing in a foul-smelling puddle and twitching from dehydration.

Marais had nearly killed the poor creature. He jumped from his horse and hand-fed Thomas maize and water until the young chacma could lift his head again. Then he secured him gently to the front of the saddle and rode them both back to Doornhoek.

It was midday when they arrived, the air searing white under an oyster sky.

Austin was lying on the bank next to the creek without a shirt, his hat laid across his face.

Marais lowered Thomas carefully to the ground. The young chacma's condition was improved. He ran gingerly into the kloof, then bouldered up to the cave on the plateau.

Austin swatted off his hat. He sat up and rubbed his eyes. "I figured yer'd been eaten by leopards, yer'd been gone so long. So I 'elped myself to yer whiskey. Didn't make sense to let it go to waste. Good stuff by the way—yer'd been 'olding out on me." He cleared whiskey phlegm from his throat. "I've been back more than twenty-four hours. That crazy Judas somehow found a direct line 'ome, didn't stop galloping till 'e reached the kloof. The speed was unbelievable. I could barely keep up on the pony."

A direct line home? From fifty miles away? And the chacma had been blindfolded when they transported him. The homing instinct in Judas was as strong as it was in the lower orders of animals. Yet, in Thomas, it had degenerated to the point where it barely functioned.

Marais glanced up at the plateau. Judas was pacing along the edge, regarding them suspiciously. Something spectacular was happening in Marais's body. He felt sharp and alive. "What if we still have the same instincts, Austin? Maybe we just lost access when causal memory eclipsed them?"

"Maybe I'm the prince of effin' Wales."

"I believe I'm right. And *if* I'm right, then these instincts would still be intact in primitive peoples."

"Who cares? Yer could never prove it."

Marais stared at him. He hadn't even dismounted from his horse yet, but ideas were firing nonstop. "On the contrary. We *can* prove it. We can remove one, just as we removed the chacmas."

"Beg pudding?"

"We're going to run the same experiment. But this time with a bush boy."

Austin's lower jaw fell nearly to his navel. "You're talking about . . . kidnapping?"

"That's not a term I would use. You're speaking about rules laid out by a manufactured God. I'm speaking of science and the improvement of mankind."

Austin waved him off. "Yer a great talker, Marais. Go talk yerself into whatever mischief yer like."

"I need your help if I'm going to capture one," he said.

"Yer want *me* to 'elp with this craziness? This is *little* ones we're talking about. It's people now, not monkeys! I ain't napping no kid."

Marais reached casually into his back pocket.

"Don't yer even *think* about trying to buy me off," Austin scowled before Marais could find his wallet. "This is yer own business. It's wicked, and I'll 'ave no part in it." He shook his head disdainfully. "What the 'ell is it yer running from with all this 'research' of yours anyway?"

The creek gurgled grotesquely. "I don't know what you're talking about."

Austin spat on the bank. "I think you do." He spun around and stormed into his hut.

Over the next few days, Marais tried everything he could think of to convert his claim mate. He purchased chocolates in Naboomspruit and left them on his porch. He penned letters of entreaty and comradeship that were so friendly he began to worry they might be misconstrued. But Austin wouldn't even tell him to "feck off" anymore.

Marais spent an entire afternoon in his hut trying not to look at the black bag tucked away in the corner. He flipped open his canteen and sucked down draughts of water. He tried scratching away the frustration that was infecting his arms and chest. Since arriving at Doornhoek, he hadn't touched his morphine. He'd barely thought of it. But now the bag beckoned with the deliciously sweet voice of a Siren. *You know you miss me. Why not have just a little?*

The bag had a point. All Marais needed was a small shot to calm him and relieve the rumblings in his head.

He dug out his tablets and melted them over his paraffin lamp. The milky liquid sloshed over the edges of the spoon. The odor that wafted through the hut reminded him of Christmas dinners as a child; it smelled like home. He drew the liquid into his syringe, and with a firm push on the plunger, shot it into his arm.

A fire ripped through him. A million pins pricked at his skin. He melted another tablet and injected it. His thoughts were so clear he could touch them. He could hear people speaking miles away. He could actually see through the walls—so clearly that for several nights he just lay there, observing the packs of nocturnal creatures that slinked through the woods.

During one of these nights, he heard the earth explode. A hole opened above him and a colossal creature plowed into his hut. He saw the legs first, massive trunks that led up to a torso twice as thick.

"Bloody 'ell!" a voice said.

Marais tried to bow to the monster, to show obeisance. But he couldn't find his own body. "Who are you? What do you want with me?" he stammered. Death, he knew, was near. The giant clomped into the hut and began to claw Marais apart. It tried to drown him in liquid. Marais struggled to ward off the assault, but he couldn't focus enough to land a punch.

"For Christsake, Marais, let me 'elp yer. Drink this already."

Cool bands of liquid cascaded down Marais's throat. He couldn't stop gulping. The water was so bracing and wet that it jolted him awake. How long had it been since he'd had anything to drink or eat?

A face gradually crystallized from the matted blur in front of him. "Austin?"

"What did yer do to yerself?"

Marais looked down and saw that he was naked, curled up on the floor of the hut. He glanced at his hand. His skin looked luminous in the moonlight. "How long have I been here?"

"Five days at least."

His temple throbbed. He was stung with embarrassment, assaulted by the tang of excrement still steaming in the corner.

"I kept expecting yer to come out, but yer never did. Finally figured I better check. Damn lucky it was."

Marais managed to pull himself to his knees. His head was pounding. He tried refocusing his eyes as they scanned his own naked body. The nails of these hands were once claws for climbing trees. The bone at the bottom of this spine extended to a tail that his ancestors used to swing through their arboreal habitat. This hair on the chest and legs, the head and face, protected them from the elements. Every feature had a purpose.

He suddenly remembered the experiment for which he'd failed to enlist Austin's assistance. Five days he'd lost. "I still need your help."

Austin rolled his eyes. "Not that again. I couldn't 'ave been any clearer. No kidnapping for me."

"You think I'd harm a child? I'll promise you right now: no one is going to get hurt."

"I just saved yer life and already yer 'arping on the crazy stuff? Is it the *n* yer not understanding, or the *o*?"

Marais's wits returned with a fury. He remembered the theft from Dolf's cabin. What he felt now was an unflinching one-pointedness and the complete dissolution of patience. "I don't like to have to say this. You're a good friend, Austin. Always have been. But if you can't bring yourself to help me, I'll need to inform Dolf."

"Dolf doesn't give a boar's testicle if I 'elp yer or not."

"I'll have to tell him about the money, I mean." He gave Austin a significant look. "You and I both know who took the five hundred pounds."

Somewhere outside, a lion yelped for his mate. Austin shifted his weight to his other foot. His eyes narrowed. "If yer accusing me, the charge is unfounded."

Marais brought his face within inches of Austin's nose. "Then why have your cheeks colored, man?" He slid his forefinger along the bristle of Austin's upper lip and showed him the glistening liquid. "Why the perspiration?"

"Because . . . " Austin gritted his teeth. "Because . . . these sorts of accusations make me nervous. I've got a reputation to protect."

"That's exactly what I intend to help you accomplish. We'll begin the experiment first thing in the morning."

Austin's lips parted. He looked as if he'd been struck. "I'd never 'ave thought . . ." He lowered his voice to a growl. "Yer . . . effin' bastard."

They started at daybreak for the bush clan. In reality, the Vaalpens pygmies were mixed descendants of the full-blood Vaalpens who used to inhabit the area, but they still subsisted under the same primitive conditions in rock huts or holes dug straight into the ground. They had no trade apart from hunting and trapping game. No one had ever deciphered their native language or traced it to any known linguistic family.

The boy was playing alone with a pair of melon-sized rocks half a mile from the clan. He was at most fourteen years old, less than four feet tall, with sinewy arms and skin the color of obsidian. He was pitching the rocks high into the air, one after the other, and trying to catch them. Each time he missed and a rock fell to the ground, he clicked his tongue and slapped himself in the forehead.

Marais and Austin hid in the bush. When the time was right, they jumped the boy from opposite sides. They bagged him just as they'd captured the two chacmas. Marais lashed the bag to the front of his saddle, then mounted his horse. The lump inside writhed and floundered but made no sound. Marais hadn't noticed the rush of his own heart until they galloped off. Now, as he settled in to the beating of hooves, elation overtook him. No one, as far as he knew, had ever attempted such an investigation with a human. He would be the first.

He and Austin, his lips tightly clamped, rode side-by-side along an old, rutted road that cut straight through the veld. The sun blanched the center of the sky. Soon they arrived at the outskirts of a small village. Marais was wary of continuing in this direction in case they should run into someone and have to explain the wriggling contents of the bag. He veered off the road with his horse and led Austin eastward through land half-cultivated and half-wild. They stole through ranging apple and almond orchards and fields teeming with brightly colored weeds and lettuces.

"I'm getting dizzy following yer," Austin called from behind. "Let's get back on the road. I agreed to 'elp. At least give my arse a break."

"No point in testing his homing instinct if we make it easy for him to find his way back."

For hours, they spiraled through the broiling heat, trotting at a brisk clip through the green-brown scrub. They looped past lanky Marulas and fever trees and monstrously craggy baobabs. They stopped twice to water the horses and once to remove a quarter-inch-thick thorn that had become so embedded in the hoof of Marais's pony that she lay down and refused to continue.

The sun beat down on the Hanglip range, turning the mountains white and nearly translucent. The rocky outcropping at the far end of the escarpment loomed sphinxlike over the veld. A family of elephants swayed in the heat. A pair of shriveled black rhinos eyed them suspiciously and snorted, then returned to grazing. The horses churned the soil beneath them, kicking up hot red sand. Marais tasted grit and dust in his mouth.

It was late afternoon when he finally pulled on the reins. His horse whinnied and slowed to a stop. They'd traveled with the boy for nearly seventy-five miles, circling and retracing their steps to increase his disorientation.

Marais drew on his canteen and wiped his mouth. "Once we release him, we'll need to track him tirelessly. Follow his exact route."

Marais dismounted. He roped his horse to a sugarbush and got to work untying the clump of knots that cinched the bag shut. The contents inside kicked wildly. "I can't do this alone. Hold it for me."

Austin stepped down and secured his own horse. While Marais unknotted the rope, Austin grasped the bag with both hands, careful to keep his head out of kicking range.

When the last knot gave way, Marais glanced at his claim mate.

Slowly, he parted the sides.

Like a shot the boy leapt straight from the bag. He flew two yards before his bony feet even touched the ground.

"Follow him!" Marais cried.

They freed the horses and saddled back up. The boy was already a hundred yards ahead.

They whipped at the horses, pushed them as hard as they could go. But the boy was infinitely more nimble in the bush. His raw speed was shocking. He could dodge cacti, shrub, and craters without slowing, while the horses had to turn with every obstacle. The wind cut at Marais's eyes. He could see nothing alongside him, just the shaking ground directly in front and the figure of the boy pounding toward the horizon. Over and over, he repeated: *I must not lose the subject.*

They rode through the night barely pausing to water the horses or to eat or relieve themselves. Fortunately, the moon was near-full, and each time they lost sight of him, the small shadow of a figure would re-emerge in mid-air, vaulting like a steenbok over a thicket of northern hedge or dodging a cypress stand. Whenever the boy glanced back, there was terror in his eyes—as if he were being hunted. Then he'd turn again and accelerate even faster. Apart from his rhythmic panting, he was silent.

At some point, Marais noticed the first light of morning yellowing the air. He recognized their surroundings. They'd reached the same barren stretch of veld where they'd captured the boy, a day earlier than anticipated. He was so awed by the boy's homing ability that he was already drafting a paper in his head, documenting his incredible discovery.

Several dozen large birds—terns and kites—were clustered in flocks directly above them, cawing hysterically. The boy, still several hundred yards ahead, re-entered the area on the opposite side from which they'd originally found him.

Marais's horse was so tired that it stumbled twice over the scrub and nearly brought them both to the ground. "Don't lose him now!" Marais shouted.

Austin charged ahead. Marais had instructed him to note the exact time the boy reached his home.

When his horse regained its footing, Marais rounded the final cluster of trees between him and the Vaalpens' rock huts. He expected the boy to stop and disappear into one of the ramshackle structures, but as Austin pursued him, the boy sprinted onward.

Then something emerged from the ground. At first, Marais took it for an animal. But it wasn't an animal at all. It was a hand, a dark hand that jutted up from a crack in the ground and grabbed hold of the front left leg of Austin's horse.

The horse tumbled into a rock pile, a tangle of hair and muscle and bone. Austin crashed onto the beast with a terrible grunt. The owner of the arm squeezed up from his subterranean lair. He was barely four feet tall, cloaked in a zebra skin with a headdress of ostrich feathers, and blinking as if shocked by the daylight. He threw himself on top of Austin and struck him viciously in the thigh.

"Goddamn it!" Austin rolled onto his back and grasped his leg in his arms.

When the man stood up, Austin's leg was spurting blood.

The boy stopped by a rock pile fifty feet ahead and waved his hands manically in the air. At the top of the pile, an old woman with an animal skin wrapped around her hips stood clicking her tongue in short, syncopated spurts. Marais was within twenty feet of Austin now. He pulled hard on the reins, scattering up a cloud of dust.

The man raised the knife again, the blade flashing in the sunlight. He plunged his hand sharply into Austin's side. Austin screamed and choked.

Marais felt the wind knocked from his lungs. They'd executed the experiment perfectly. Now it was all unraveling before his eyes. The man raised the knife once more, this time above Austin's chest. Austin held up a dusty hand. He clenched his eyes shut.

Marais couldn't lose him now. There was too much still to do. He pulled the Mauser from his shoulder and aimed at the Vaalpens's calf. He'd wound the man and knock him off Austin.

But as Marais squeezed the trigger, Austin freed a leg, which he jabbed hard into his assailant's stomach. The Vaalpens fell backward.

The bullet entered the man's left temple and exited his right ear, as if passing through soft cheese. He pirouetted on his bare feet, his shoulders slumping forward. The man gazed at the boy and at the woman, a scallop of flesh dangling from his ear. Six times his tongue clicked. On the seventh click, his legs buckled.

Austin lay shaking in a heap. His shirt and trousers were soaked with blood. Marais jumped from his horse and poured water over the wounds. "I've seen you looking better."

"Just get me 'ome," Austin coughed.

The woman and the boy were already running toward them. Other Vaalpens had to be nearby. Marais thought he heard galloping ahead of them in the bush. Austin's horse was dead. Marais heaved Austin into his arms, laid him across the front of his saddle, and climbed up behind him. He snapped the reins and kicked his horse hard in the hindquarter.

As they wheeled around, Marais glanced back. The boy and the woman were kneeling on either side of the man, holding his head and stroking his chest, which was covered in a rainbow of tattoos.

No one was to get hurt. That's what Marais had promised. Instead, he had left a woman widowed, a child fatherless. The man was only trying to protect his son. He was doing what any father would do.

The boy looked from the man's body to Marais. At first it seemed the boy was smiling. But the boy's cheeks, Marais saw, were streaked with tears, and he began to choke now with a terrible ululating wail that made Marais's spine tremble. It was the first sound the boy had made that Marais understood.

January 1936, London, England

Waterloo station drones in Charles's ears with the cries of newspapermen and the tromp of British troops and the swish and scratch of shoeshine brushes. Mustard-colored light floods through the peaked glass roof high above them. Dust motes tumble and twirl like snow flurries.

Charles dodges the swarm and hurries with their bags, struggling to keep Hannah's blue coat in view. It would be easy to fall prey to a pickpocket in this crowd. To lose a purse or wallet. Again, he tries to deduce where he could have lost his. He nearly careens into a pair of nuns, then knocks into a boy pushing a barrow full of baggage.

"'Ey!" the boy shouts. His bags have tumbled to the ground. "You blind, Mister?"

"Sorry about that," Charles says. He drops his own bags and, without taking his eyes from Hannah, helps the boy reload.

Outside the station, London's steady drizzle patters the streets. Buses clang over pot-holed puddles. Half a dozen schoolboys sprint past, tenting newspapers over their heads and laughing. Across the river, the towers of Westminster and Big Ben loom skyward. Water churns with dirt and rubbish and flows in brown, sedimented rivulets along the pavements and over Charles's shoes. Despite the cold and the rain, despite the city's roar and bustle, he is glad to be back in London. Twenty-five winters he spent in this city. As he stands umbrella-less on the corner of Waterloo and Stamford in his sodden coat, waving for a cab, the city's smells—pastries and curry, smoke and sewage—mingle with rising memories from a previous life. A quarter century in London comes rushing through him: carvings gouged into classroom desks, sagging dormitory beds, endless cricket games, girls he kissed.

As Charles hunts for a cab, another thought arises, one that he never considered during all those previous years in London. This was Marais's city too, before Charles ever laid eyes on it. Marais abandoned Charles to study law here. How often did Marais stand in the rain on this exact patch of ground outside Waterloo station, waving his arm for a ride?

He drags his foot through a puddle. He slides it across the gravel that has sunk into the mud. *Is it possible,* he wonders, *that some small part of ourselves gets left behind on each bit of earth we touch?* Molecules? Atoms? Maybe some vestige of Marais is still here, a fleck of skin, a strand of hair.

Hannah waves him back over. A taxi has veered to the curb. Charles tosses their bags in the boot, and they climb in. "We're off!" she says, patting his knee.

The car lurches forward. The driver propels them down cobbled streets, past throngs of bicycles, and buses, and trolleys, through the ventricles of Charles's old city. "That shop with the blue awning was there when I was a kid," he says, gesturing through Hannah's window. "That's my old pub with the sculpture of the dancing bear. And my old bus stop. It's as if nothing has changed." But it feels as if he's lost more than his wallet, as if he is observing the city from a great, unbridgeable distance.

"Maybe we should stay for a while," Hannah suggests. Rain still clings to her lashes. "To break up the trip. I've always wanted to see London."

"I wish I could." He truly does. But Marais wrote that he was incapacitated. For all Charles knows, he may be near death. He needs to find his father, while there's still time. "The thing is I've got family business to—" He cuts himself off.

Hannah peers at him curiously. "Family business?"

It's too late to disclose the truth. He told her that he *has* no father. He's tangled himself up with lies and secrets. "Yes, to take care of in South Africa."

"Such as?"

"Just personal stuff."

"Oh." Hannah straightens her back. "I see." She's upset that he won't confide in her.

"Look," he says, "I'm not asking you to tell me all your private business. I'm on my way to find someone. Please—let's leave it at that for now."

To his relief she does, but not before scooting herself a foot away from him. "Driver, it looks like we're heading to southern Africa."

The man behind the wheel glances in the mirror. "This car don't swim, ma'am. East India Docks is as far as I can take you."

The car splishes over Waterloo Bridge, then tracks the north side of the Thames, skirting St. Paul's swollen dome.

"That's the Tower of London. I'd recognize it anywhere." Hannah roots around in her purse and pulls out her camera. She presses the lens against the windowpane and snaps the shutter.

Charles lets himself sink into the seat and watches her shoot the crowds that cram the bridges, buses packed with commuters, flustered nannies with covered prams. Businessmen with giant umbrellas fan over the sidewalks. Bands of children in mud-stained clothes drop stones from London Bridge on passing boats.

"At this rate, you'll be out of film before you reach Cape Town."

"Not a chance. I brought a hundred cassettes with me. You can check my valise. I've packed almost nothing but film."

The taxi pulls a hard right. His shoulder knocks against hers. *Who is going to look at so many photos?*

"They're just for me," she says before he's even asked the question. She crosses one knee over the other, scans the streets for her next target. "I never cared much about taking pictures until I lost my parents." Her eye is glued to the viewfinder. "In the first days after the funeral, I searched everywhere for photographs. Their basement had flooded earlier that winter. Water had destroyed everything. I wanted to know that I'd be able to remember them. But nothing was left. Not a single photograph. The death of my parents broke something in my heart. But losing those photos—all those memories—was nearly as bad. So now I'm taking as many pictures as I can."

Charles recalls the one photo stowed in his bag. Never before has he thought himself lucky to have a single photograph of his mother. But that one picture is infinitely more than nothing. The last time he unwrapped it and scanned her face, he felt certain that he remembered her voice—not words, but tones, inflections. He felt as if he were being held.

A hearse veers suddenly in front of the car. Their driver brakes with a screech. On instinct, Charles throws his arm across Hannah to protect her, to keep her from flying forward.

A dozen cars in funeral procession snake along the intersection.

Hannah leans over his arm to get a better view, ignoring the pressure of her body against his. He can feel her ribs, and the rise and fall of her breasts. She focuses her lens. All motion stops. He doesn't move his arm. She doesn't ask him to. She snaps the shutter. She's so close he can count the freckles on her cheekbones.

* * *

The clerk in the ticket office flips through his Departures book. "Well, I have good news and bad news," he tells them. He's an impish man with round wire glasses and a waxed mustache. "Good news is there's a steamer leaving for Cape Town tomorrow. Bad news is there's not a cabin left on the ship. In fact," he says, shutting the book, "it seems every ship for the next month is booked."

For the next month? Marais could be dead by then for all Charles knows.

"What about non-Castle liners?" Hannah asks.

"This is *the* Book. Lists every regular ship on every line. Only thing it doesn't list is charters. They keep their own schedules. But those are private concerns. It's not as if you can just board someone else's charter when the scheduled ships are booked."

Something about the man's tone gives Charles an idea. He catches Hannah's eye, rubs his fingers lightly together. She seems to understand. Casually, she extracts a one-pound note from her purse. She places it on the counter and smiles at the clerk.

The man's hackles rise. "You mistake me for someone else, Madam," he says, pushing the note back at her. "I take offense at the suggestion that I could be purchased so easily, and in public no less." He gives them a weighty look but doesn't ask them to leave.

Charles knows how this works. He folds a sheet of paper in half. He borrows two more pounds from Hannah, slips all three bills into the fold, and slides the paper across the counter.

The clerk glances behind him. The office is empty. "Well, if you're really feeling adventurous, we could try to get you on *that* charter."

Charles follows the man's finger to the window. A ship is materializing from the fog, six stories high with the colors of the North German Lloyd line—red keel, ebony hull, crisp white decks. A pair of buff funnels spit smoke into the clouds.

"I hear she's carrying Jewish refugees from Bremerhaven to South Africa," says the clerk. "Just docking here briefly before heading to Cape Town. It's possible they may have a few empty cabins I suppose. But they'd be intended for Jews."

"I *am* Jewish," Hannah blurts excitedly. She glances at Charles. "And so is my . . . brother here."

Charles stares at her.

"What do you know?" says the clerk before Charles can interject. "Perhaps we *can* make it work. If anyone asks, we'll tell them you're Austrian."

The skin around Hannah's eyes creases like wings. "*Vielen dank*," she says, shaking the man's hand. "We'd like two cabins please."

* * *

"We can't travel on that ship," Charles says, once they're outside. "You know I'm not Jewish. I'd be taking space from someone whose life may depend on it."

Fog hangs in dense ribbons. The sky has flattened into a dull marbled haze.

"It's a white lie. The cabins will go empty if we don't take them. Fortunately, my German's pretty good. Charles, this may be my one chance to make it out of America, and Europe, unscathed. Surely you can sense the violence that's coming. Plus, we shouldn't miss this opportunity to get you to your . . . business. Let's go now."

She grabs her valise and hurries along the pier toward the wooden gangway.

This plan is wrong for so many reasons. For one thing, Charles wants to shout to her, he'll never pass as Austrian. He hasn't spoken German in years. But Hannah is already boarding the ship. She disappears into its iron skeleton with one, quick glance back at him.

From the main deck, Charles watches as a handful of gray tugs swarm around the steamer and push them out to sea. There's no turning back now.

He stashes his bag in his cabin on top of a small dresser wedged next to the bed. He runs a hand along the nightstand, the blankets, the pillow. This is the last room he'll stay in before setting foot on the continent where he was born. He is truly returning to South Africa. For as long as he can remember, there's been a pulling inside him—a feeling that has occupied his whole being, leaving room for nothing else, not even love. It's as if he's been tethered to the memory that Marais chose to give him up, and no matter how hard he's tried to forget that story, to unburden himself, the thought that he was unwanted from the moment he entered the world has stuck to him ruthlessly across continents. Now he's returning. One way or another, he will track down Marais.

Back up the stairwell to the rear deck, he stakes out a space by the railing and watches the tugs turn back and the skyline shrink and fade into a single point in the gray distance. London, his old home, the rock of his adolescence, disappears as quickly as it arrived, without fanfare or promises. A fleeting sadness passes over him. This feeling of leaving has become as familiar as breathing is.

His thoughts turn to Harvard and to his other students—to William, Harry, and Dennis. What will they think when they hear of his departure? What would explain his sudden disappearance? Job transfer, car accident, kidnapping? There was so much more he'd been planning to teach them—the nuances of Indic syntax, the subtleties of Pāli grammar. He wanted them to learn to love the language as much as he does. He feels the remnants of that hope slip like sand through his fingers. Who will stand up to the Sizemores of Harvard now that he's gone?

Turbines crescendo. The ship picks up speed. It punctures the mouth of the Channel and spills into the deep waters of the Atlantic. Charles heads inside to mingle on the promenade deck, away from the chill and spray. It dawns on him that he's the only male passenger whose coat is not unraveling at the seams.

At the corner of the deck, Hannah is kneeling on the floor, snapping photos of a young boy who poses for her with outlandish monster faces. Charles walks over and squats next to them.

"Meet my new little friend," she says, squeezing Charles's hand.

The boy pulls back the corners of his lips with his forefingers and lets his tongue spill through his teeth. Bits of blue lining peek through the patches on his coat. The boy leaps, laughing, into the arms of the woman seated behind him. The man in the chair to her left is wearing an old felt hat and poring over a book. The skin on his hands is rough, the nails worked down. The boy burrows his head in his mother's lap.

"He's so sweet," Hannah says in German.

"Yes. And he knows how to make his parents completely *meshuga*," says the woman, mussing up his hair. "But he's a good boy. It's a relief to know he'll be safe in South Africa. And that Leo will be able to earn enough to feed our family again. The boy is growing. Leo is a pediatric surgeon. A very talented man, my poor husband. How many German children did you operate on during all those years at the state hospital, Leo?"

The man folds his book in his lap and looks up. His beard is cut close, chocolate-brown with flecks of gray. His eyes are bright but tired. "Too many to count. Five thousand maybe."

"Five thousand children?" Hannah says.

"He worked at that hospital for fifteen years," says the woman. "Gave everything of himself. And the day after Germany passes its racial laws, what do they do? They fire him."

"After you'd worked so hard for fifteen years?"

"It's been all right actually," says Leo. He casts his wife a look that says *do not speak of this in front of our guests*. "We've made do. Look at this boy. You can't say he's not healthy." He whisks the child into his arms, hikes up his coat, and buzzes his lips noisily against the child's bare belly. The boy shrieks with delight.

"My doctor husband has been working as a cobbler," the woman says.

"Cobble!" says the boy, laughing hysterically. "Cobble cobble, bobble bobble!"

Leo sets down his son, who scoots along the deck to the next set of chairs. The boy's coat brushes against Charles's arm as he passes.

"It was clear no hospital was going to hire a Jewish doctor. Leo, I thought, you're a smart man, a resilient man. Everyone wears shoes, right? Young, old, Jew, Gentile. Everyone must need their shoes repaired. It would be steady work. Fresh air. It would be a sociable job. I've always been good with my hands. So I taught myself to repair shoes."

"He was working outside on the street corner twelve hours a day in the middle of winter, earning barely enough for our food. Nearly lost two fingers to frostbite."

"Hush, Sarah." He waves her off. "It turns out," he says to Hannah and Charles, "it's difficult to do precision shoe work when one's hands are encumbered with gloves. I kept losing nails in the street. I'd drop my tools and they'd disappear in the snow. I needed to work bare-handed."

"All day he'd toil in the freezing cold," Sarah says. "He worked so hard he didn't even notice. Work always has to be perfect with this one, always his best effort, even if it's just polishing the beaten-up boots of some thankless goyim. One night he walked through the kitchen, gritting his teeth. I asked him what happened. He said he'd hurt himself. He winced like he'd been stabbed. 'Show me,' I demanded. I nearly fainted when I saw that hand. His ring and middle fingers were the color of sapphires. Can you imagine? They wouldn't bend. Brittle like sticks, I'm telling you! 'What's a cobbler going to do without his hands!' I cried. We had no hot water. So I took them in my mouth. It was the only thing I could think of. For two hours I sucked on his fingers. He's my husband—I'd do anything for that man. I didn't stop until his fingers turned pink again."

"My God!" Hannah says. "How terrifying."

Sarah wipes her eyes. "This boy has no idea how much his father has done for him. No idea at all."

"That's a bit of an embellishment," Leo remarks.

"Embellishment! Don't you say that in front of the wife who saved your fingers."

"The misstep I made in choosing this line of work," Leo says, "is that most German Jews can no longer afford to hire professionals to repair their shoes. So I had to rely on Gentile customers. Some didn't ask questions. They'd just say, 'I need a new sole,' or a better heel, or double stitching. But some did ask. Because that's how Germany is these days. They'd stand there as I wrestled off their old leather soles with my pliers, and I'd feel them studying me. 'Are you German?' they'd ask. 'What do you think? Of course I'm German,' I'd say. I've never *met* a man who speaks better German than I do. So, an answer like that was often enough to satisfy them. But once in a while, they'd lower their eyes at me. 'What I mean is, are you a Jew?' That's when the trouble would start. If I lied and was discovered, I'd go to prison. So I did my best to evade the question. 'I'm a doctor,' I said once. The fellow was dressed head to heel like a top-tier businessman—like one of those robber barons in America—with the most expensive boots you've ever seen. 'I asked if you're Jewish,' he said. I couldn't stomach his tone. I dropped his boots in the snow and stood up to meet him face to face. 'Don't you understand German?' I asked the gaudy schmuck. 'I'm a doctor! For fifteen years I worked as a pediatric surgeon. I may have saved your kid's life. I can't have that job now. So here I am, a surgeon repairing your shoes. I'll give you the highest quality shoe work you've seen anywhere. But don't you dare ask me another ugly question like that!' For a moment, the man shrank back, but then something changed in his expression—his eyes hardened, lips curled—and do you know what he did then, the German pig? He spat at me. He spat right in my face. 'You're a lucky sonofabitch,' he said. 'I'm in a good mood today. And it doesn't matter anyway. Soon enough, you'll all be exterminated.' He grabbed his boots from the ground and tromped off through the snow. That day I knew our life in Germany was over."

When Hannah glances at Charles, the look in her eyes nearly breaks his heart. He's read about German attacks on Jews, but glancingly, the way one does with any distant, tragic event: tornados in Oklahoma, earthquakes in India, tsunamis in Japan. Sizemore's predictions about increasing German persecution of Jews, he realizes, are already coming true.

Memories of the British concentration camp come flooding back—the hot stink of sewage, storm clouds of flies, bodies heaped like wheat sacks. Ten percent of his people completely wiped out. Extermination, he thinks, is a fate that you exact on rodents. Or termites.

"So proud, this husband of mine," says Sarah. "Always with the pride."

"I'm hungry, Mama," the boy whispers. Sarah leans down and pulls a fat slab of black bread from her bag. The boy scoots onto her lap and sinks his teeth into the doughy slice.

"I'm not a pessimistic man," Leo says. "I see a glass with a few drops of water and I think it's overflowing. That's how I'd always been. But I couldn't envision a life for our family in Germany. Then we heard about this charter. A former colleague at the state hospital said a group of Jewish benefactors in London was chartering a ship from Bremen to Cape Town—they plan to evacuate a hundred thousand Jews from Germany, God bless them. The rest, as they say, is history."

"How crazy to think of South Africa as the new promised land," Hannah says. "Our modern-day Canaan."

"Perhaps," says Leo. "God-willing, we'll reach the Cape before South Africa's own Nuremberg Laws go into effect."

"What do you mean?" Hannah asks.

"You haven't heard? If the rumors are true, South Africa is on the verge of banning Jewish immigration all together." Leo lifts his water glass. "Here's to making good time, and to earning a decent livelihood once we arrive."

Hannah looks as if she's been turned upside down and shaken. "I need to get some air," she says, rising to her feet.

"I'll come with you," says Charles.

"Please don't," she begs. "I'll be fine."

Charles is the one who gave her the idea of immigrating to South Africa in the first place. They're tangled up in this together now. She deserves a chance. *Faster*, he thinks, willing the ship forward.

"I'll see you later," she says to the boy, rubbing the side of head. "Take care of your parents. They love you so much."

Charles finds Hannah alone on the rear deck, gazing northward over the water. The trailing sea shines glassy in the ship's black wake. Wisps of hair have come loose and fallen across her cheek.

"Do you think it's true?" she asks. "Maybe Leo is mistaken."

Charles hasn't heard anything about impending limits on Jewish immigration, but he never thought to ask, until now. "Honestly, I don't know."

"'South Africa couldn't be safer.' That's what you told me, Charles. Those were *your* words."

"I haven't set foot there since I was a child. It was a different world back then."

"Then why would you say that to me?"

His mind circles back over their last meetings at his office. He wanted to impress her, to smooth over his homeland's dirtier complexities. "I didn't expect that you'd be jumping on the next ship to Cape Town with me."

He gazes down at the soapy churn where the keel cuts through the spume. He can't remember ever feeling this much concern for another person. "Please don't worry," he says. "I'm going with you. If they want to send you back, they'll have to send me back too."

The wind gusts and shrieks.

Hannah leans over the side railing. The cold spray moistens her face. Her skin is the color of plums. "It's a long way down," she says to no one. She lifts one foot and rises slightly off the deck. She leans herself overboard.

She wouldn't. Would she? He's not going to take any chances. He reaches for her shoulders, pulls her from the edge, takes her in his arms.

Clouds collide above the dying sun.

He searches her face. A strange look passes over her, then blooms into a smile. "Charles? You didn't think I was going to—"

"No, of course not," he lies.

"I think you did! I'm not going anywhere, you know. I'm much stronger than that. I'm touched, though. I believe you wanted to save me."

The next day is stormy from the start. A steady rain bursts from drizzle to torrent. Off to port, the Spanish coast looms ghost-like. The ship is large, thirteen thousand tons and only five hundred passengers, and it isn't difficult for Charles to find space of his own. He passes the hours alternately reading in his cabin and walking the lower decks in his green mac. He tries to imagine how it will feel when they finally reach the Cape, when he catches his first glimpse of Table Mountain.

Late afternoon. Darkness has fallen. Charles abandons the deck's brackish air. He returns to midships, takes the stairs down to his cabin.

Someone has slid a small square envelope under his door. He hangs up his coat, drops onto the bed, kicks off his shoes. He turns over the envelope. He knows this writing, but it can't be. Marais? Here? He has tracked down Charles on a chartered German steamer in the middle of the Atlantic. The man is a magician.

He bolts the door behind him. He tears open the envelope. The note inside is handwritten in a rolling cursive:

Join me for dinner on the deck at 7? H.

A blue-green wave splashes against the porthole.

Of course it's not from Marais. Charles feels ridiculous for having had the thought, then more ridiculous for feeling disappointed that Marais *hasn't* found him.

But this simple card from Hannah—not even twenty letters—stirs something else inside him. She has invited him to dinner. He needs time to get his head straightened on. He showers and shaves and attempts to de-wrinkle his only dinner jacket with an old iron that he borrows from the chief steward.

At 6:59 he arrives in the dining room. He finds a table for two in the near corner under a twelve-foot crystal chandelier. And waits for her.

By seven thirty, he has knocked back a sidecar. By seven forty-five, he's knocked back two more.

Waiters fly past, trays clatter, glasses ring like bells. His head starts to swim.

At the table to his left, a father of three young children hands his wife four slices of white bread. When she thinks no one is looking, she folds the bread in a cloth napkin and stows it in her purse.

Leo, Charles notices only now, is waving at him from a table across the room. Their boy is curled up asleep in Sarah's lap. Leo turns over his hand as if to ask, *where's your sister?*

No idea, Charles mouths back.

It dawns on him now that she's not coming. Maybe she's ill. Or injured. He hurries from the dining room to find her, hikes up the stairs, blows through the door to the deck. Thick drops of rain pour from the dark sky above. He buttons his coat, flips up his collar. Icy water pounds against his face. In the dark like this, in the storm, he feels strangely liberated.

"You're getting drenched, Charles. Come over here already."

Lights flicker to his left. He squints through the darkness but can't make out forms. He walks dizzily through the fog, shears his way toward the flash of lights.

A canopy of umbrellas emerges from the darkness. Beneath them is a small, white-clothed table with three candles, flames dancing in jars. Hannah sits at the far side of the table, twirling the stem of a wine glass in her fingers. Her eyelashes glitter with raindrops.

"You're not even close to on time," she says.

"Well, I was thinking we'd be dining, you know, in the dining room." He slides out the other chair and pours wine into the empty glass. It's only now that he really sees her. "God, you look beautiful."

She beams with delight. "You noticed."

A waiter materializes. They order steak and potatoes, the only options still available from the kitchen. The liquor has insulated Charles's insides. He can't feel the cold anymore.

"You do realize it's pouring out here?" he says.

"Pouring, schmouring. I'm not going to be scared off by a little rain. Let the others hide out in the dreary dining room. I wanted to do something special tonight."

"For what?"

"You really can be a bit thick sometimes," she says. "For *you*."

The frustrations of the past week—his wallet, leaving London so soon, the rush for this ship—are melting into something more fluid and gentler. Every day this woman amazes him. "Well then. To me." He clinks his glass against hers.

"I found myself thinking about my father today," she says. "He was the most generous man I've ever known, a better person than I could ever hope to be. If he found a sick animal on the streets of Manhattan, he'd take it home and bring it back to health. When neighbors needed help—money, advice, support during a difficult time—they came to him. And somehow, when I was a child, he still found time for me each day. Every night we played a game of chess. Half the time he'd win, half the time he'd let me. 'Hannah,' he said one night after our game, just before he shut off the lights, 'do you know why I do all the things I do?' I'd never stopped to wonder. It just seemed to be who he was. 'It's because I'm human,' he said. 'I am so lucky. And so grateful.'"

The waiter arranges two salads in front of them. He mills pepper over the leaves.

"He must have driven your mother crazy," says Charles. "How do you live with someone that good? You could never measure up."

Hannah laughs. "I don't know. Maybe it worked because her world was smaller. I was always at its center. When I was a teenager, this enraged me sometimes. I was the luckiest child in the world and completely ungrateful. Imagine wanting a parent to love you *less*."

The idea pierces him. He can't imagine this, no matter how hard he tries.

"Sometimes I find myself grasping at images of them," she says. "I want to remember my mother's gestures, the sound of my father's voice. I want to remember everything. But my memories are already fading. It hurts so much, battling against time like this."

Memories of Charles's own past rise up. He struggles to drive them away. He wants to keep watching her, to be here with her right now.

"What about *your* parents?" she asks.

The question sobers him. "That's a complicated topic."

The waiter arrives with the entrees. He arranges the dishes ceremoniously on the table.

Hannah studies Charles patiently. She is a skilled archeologist, preparing to dig.

"You said you were orphaned as a baby, but you never told me how your father died . . ."

Charles feels the wine sloshing around inside him. He needs to come clean with her—she's told him everything—but he doesn't know how. "I'm sorry. I don't talk about him. I don't even like to think about him." He's nearly shouting all of a sudden.

Hannah blows on her hands to warm them. He feels her back off a step. "Maybe you'd be willing at least to tell me why an orphaned South African would devote his life to studying a dead language spoken thousands of years ago by the Buddha."

Charles looks at the spread of food and the canopy and Hannah, glowing in candlelight. For a split second, they're an old couple, happily married, decades of history built up between them, traveling the world. For a split second, everything vanishes but her.

"The Buddha never spoke Pāli," he says.

"Of course he did. You taught us that yourself."

He thinks back to that first class and realizes he's lied to her more than once. "The Pāli we know today was never a living language. That's what I've come to believe anyway. It was synthetic, fabricated. Centuries after the Buddha's death, a group of Ceylonese Buddhist monks began standardizing the texts with a hybrid language they hoped could compete with the northern Buddhists' Sanskrit—the language of brahmins and kings. They claimed Pāli as the Buddha's own tongue, and it spread quickly across the monasteries of South and Southeast Asia. But I don't think anyone in history, including the Buddha, ever spoke it the way the textbooks would have you believe, not as a first language."

Hannah looks incredulous, then confused, then furious. "But it's the reason I stayed in your class. To read the teachings the way he spoke them."

"You're not alone. The entire field is invested in the idea that the Pāli canon contains the Buddha's actual words."

"And you perpetuated the lie."

"No one wants to be told that a core part of their belief system is untrue, least of all from an outsider like me. I'd be as treasonous as Galileo, though admittedly on a smaller scale. Harvard wants to see innovation. Incremental innovation. Not revolution. Nothing that would overturn the ideas of the men who have run the university for centuries. And what difference does it make if the Buddha didn't speak Pāli? There's still value to reading the teachings as stories."

"If I were interested in stories—in reading about romance and falling in love—I would have enrolled in a literature class."

Wind snaps at the canopy above them. Rain pounds the deck.

"That would have been a better choice. No love letter was ever written in Pāli."

She cocks her head. "Not a single letter?"

"No."

"In tens of thousands of pages? How can that be?"

They're inching back into dangerous territory. He should change the subject. He should return to his cabin and close the door on this night. They can start again in the morning. But he can't help himself. "Because as much as Pāli masqueraded as a language spoken by actual people, it was used to create a vision of the world that isn't local or individual. At their core, Pāli texts are completely impersonal. Remember how easy it was for Vessantara to turn away, to forget his own family—"

The ship rolls to port. Charles grabs for the table.

Hannah looks as though she's stumbled upon the answer to a riddle. "Is that it then? Is that why you entered the field? So you could lose yourself in a language where no one has to think about family or love or the terrible things that happened to them as children? That's crazy—you can't just will yourself to forget the past."

She doesn't know any of this. She's only speculating. "I could will myself to forget *everything*. The sun, the moon, the planets. I could will the Himalayas flattened if I had to."

"Without the past, we have nothing, Charles. Our memory of the past is *all* we have. It's the one thing that's settled. The only thing amid all this chaotic change that we have to hold onto."

His face is hot, his hand trembles. He reaches for his wine but misses and knocks over the glass. It hangs in the air for a moment, then tumbles, shattering silently around their feet. He moves to clean it up, but the waiters have already arrived to sweep up the shards, to clean up Charles's jagged mess with their bare hands.

Hannah reaches across the table and touches his arm. "It's all right," she says. "You don't have to tell me. Whatever happened to you, it's over."

But she's wrong—it's not even close to over. He bites hard on his lip. He stares at his lap so Hannah won't see his eyes filling up.

"I've often thought about my life," she says, "and how meaninglessness it would seem if I were to plot it point by point on one of those graphs you learn to draw in grade school. If you were to look at my jumble of dots, my tragedies would seem completely arbitrary, orderless. We draw these lines, though, to try and make sense of them, to create order where there is none. It makes me so sad thinking that way—that all the terrible things that happened in our past have to mean something. As if we somehow deserved them. How much worse than if it were all just bad luck." She tucks a strand of hair behind her ear. "But this past week, I found myself imagining what my life might look like thirty years from now if all my dots were plotted on cellophane and yours were layered on top of mine, and I could see my life refracted through yours. And for the first time in a long time, I just felt—" Her eyes are glossy with wine and something else. "I don't know exactly what that feeling was. But I liked it."

Eugene Charles Gerard Marais's near-fatal flaw, he thinks, has always been the same—from the day he was first thrust into the world until this moment—he's wanted love too much and taken it too little. He's tried so hard to forget the past that he's nearly forgotten the present.

He pushes back his chair. He rises to his feet. "Hey, come over here."

She takes his hand, and he leads her across the deck. The waiters chase after them, struggling to keep the umbrellas over their heads. "Please," he says waving them away, "we're fine."

Water streams down Hannah's face. He places his right hand on her hip. His left she cups in her right, and here, at the edge of the ship, they're suddenly dancing with only waves and rain as their music.

"I'm not making the first move," she says under her breath. "I'm old-fashioned that way. You know Radcliffe girls."

"You already made the first move. And the second, the third, the fourth . . ."

He draws her against his body. He can feel the pounding in her chest, and the heat of her breath, and the wedge where her thighs give way when his leg presses into them. Then he kisses her.

On the bed in his cabin, he peels off her coat and her blouse. She wraps her bare arms around his shoulders. Her legs enshroud his hips. He buries his head in her neck and inhales her. Tonight he wills himself to remember every detail.

Thus have I heard.

November 1906, Waterberg, Transvaal Colony, British Empire

Marais knelt on the loamy ground and took the scat in his hand. He rolled it between his fingers and inhaled the pungent tang. The scat was fresh, half a dozen rust-colored piles strewn among the fig trees behind the huts. The chacmas had returned.

The chacma troop had severed all ties after Marais's experiment with the two males, Thomas and Judas. They'd stopped approaching in the afternoon. Instead, they'd stationed multiple guards along the lip of the escarpment to keep an eye on Marais. For weeks, he'd waited at the edge of the kloof in the dwindling sunlight, armed with pails of ripe pears and boiled maize, attempting to coax them down. If he didn't win back their trust, his experiments were finished.

But the scat was a sign. The chacmas were returning.

Which was more than he could say for his claim mate. Since the incident with the Vaalpens boy, Austin had refused to speak to him, despite Marais's repeated apologies, despite his insistence on compensating Austin for the loss of his horse. It had been several weeks since he'd fully recovered from the stab wound, but even now, Austin would engage with him only when prospecting necessitated it. The rest of the time, Austin confined himself to his hut, which was separated from Marais's by a six-foot-wide stretch of viscous mud. As Marais hunched on the straw bedroll in his own hut, poring over his books and recording his notes, he could hear Austin's raspy breath. He could hear him counting the small tin specimens he'd exhumed from the stream bed, the bright plunk of nuggets as he dropped them into his pan.

At dusk, the door to Austin's hut would creak open and bang shut, and he'd leave without a word. Marais could hear the shuffle of damp steps through the fallen leaves, which would trail off as Austin made his way along the winding footpath that paralleled the creek and down the steep slope of the mountain to the saloon.

Something had changed in Marais after the experiment with the Vaalpens boy. There wasn't a threat of retribution—the Vaalpens would never approach an enclave of white settlers to exact vengeance. They had no legal recourse. But Marais couldn't stop thinking about what he'd done. The destruction he'd caused. He'd removed a human life from the planet. Even as he tried to convince himself that a child of primitive intellect must also remember less, and thus *feel* less—indeed, hurt less—than a modern child, the weight of his actions stuck like a knife in his side. He'd left a boy fatherless, a child nearly the same age as Charles.

Austin spent mornings knee-deep in the stream with his woven straw hat and rubber boots. He'd gesture brusquely to indicate where he wanted Marais to station himself, when to chisel more deeply, when to concentrate on the looser sediment at the gravely surface, when to filter with the pan and when the size of his haul warranted use of the sluice box. Only if Marais failed to follow a directive did Austin resort to speech, which consisted almost entirely of profanities.

Marais obeyed without protest. Austin had reason to be upset. *Blackmail*, Austin's term, seemed a bit overstated, but Marais *had* pressured him. There was no denying this. He'd accused Austin of stealing from Dolf. He'd coerced Austin into kidnapping a child. But the magnitude of the disaster, all the ways that it had gone so terribly wrong, heightened the importance of what Marais did accomplish. He'd confirmed the existence of the homing instinct in primitive man, and in doing so, he'd taken one giant step toward confirming the origins of the human psyche, the source of our deepest pain, and just possibly, a way out of it.

What Austin needed now was time. He needed the incident to settle and fade.

Which it did. For one thing, the claim unexpectedly began to yield tin. There were no stunning strikes, but they began earning enough to cover the costs of the claim and food and whiskey, plus an extra pound or two a week for pocket money. And a small strike invariably dangled the promise of a greater one. It stoked desire. Like the nightly card games at the Doornhoek saloon, each win strengthened the argument to continue the gamble.

For another thing, the possibility that Dolf would identify Austin as the man who'd burgled his cabin grew dimmer each day. Shortly after the theft, Dolf had confronted every prospector at Doornhoek, trying out a number of techniques for forcing a confession—veiled accusations, outright bribery, verbal acrobatics aimed at teasing out a guilty conscience. The day he showed up to interview Austin, Marais got wind of the visit ahead of time and arranged for his claim mate to be wretchedly sick and visiting the apothecary in Nylstroom. Dolf hadn't returned to their section of the mountain since. With this threat abating, Marais sensed that his claim mate was beginning to soften, and this kindled in him a brazen sort of hope.

It was midday on Sunday. The heat had quieted the forest floor. The only sounds in the kloof were pops and cracks as the sun toasted the fig trees' moss-covered branches. Marais emerged from his hut and found Austin bathing in the creek. His torso was pasty white from his chest to his knees, his neck and calves browned like a roast. He didn't hear Marais slip down to the creek and seat himself on the edge of the bank.

Austin was humming aloud, his slab of back turned to Marais, and scrubbing with a rag between his legs. He lathered his hair with a bar of tallow soap, then bent over and doused his head in the creek, scratching the flakes from his scalp.

"The chacmas will return today," Marais called. "I've been watching them."

Austin leaned to one side and pounded on his head to loosen the water from his ear. "It's funny," he said to no one. "For a second, I imagined I 'eard talking. About *baboons*, no less. But of course that couldn't be. The mind plays sly tricks in the forest."

"I know things didn't go as we'd hoped—"

"It must be the wind. Let's 'ope it blows on soon and carries away those terrible vapors with it."

"We still have more work to do, Austin. Accept my apology already and for Christsake, let's move on."

"I only ever knowed one man interested in the effing baboons and 'e'd sooner squeeze one up 'is fig 'ole than convince me to 'ave anything else to do with 'im."

"We've established the presence of causal memory in these animals. Do you understand what this means?" Marais had acquired an indirect view into the nature of the human mind.

Into the source of human pain. What they hadn't yet established was what happened to instinct as causal memory evolved. Did it disappear entirely? Or was it still lurking somewhere deep inside the evolved primate, inside each of us, ready to be resuscitated? "I know I can find the answer. But not without a good assistant."

"Actually, now that I think of it, I *do* 'ave one thought on the subject of those monkeys."

Austin dried his face. He bent over, lifted one leg in the air, and let out a fart of elephantine proportions. "And that's the 'ole of it."

Marais remained on the bank long after Austin tromped back to his hut and shut himself inside. He leaned back and gazed at the plateau on top of the kloof.

A couple dozen chacmas were squatting at the edge of the shelf, picking lice from each other's fur and watching him. "What do you think," Marais said quietly, "about these ridiculous bickering white men who chose to build their homes in the place where you like to shit?"

The sun was hot and he let his eyes fold shut against the glare. Wind rustled through the stand of lilac trees behind him. Warblers called from the bushes in staccato shrieks. At some point, sleep whisked him away. It seemed that a woman was speaking to him. It had been more than twelve years since he'd last heard Lettie's voice, but he recognized her at once, and even in his sleep, his heart ticked faster. He struggled to pry open his eyes. All he wanted was to catch a glimpse of his wife's face. He'd give anything to speak with her. But it was no use—he could only listen. The forest was lovely, she told him. She understood why he was here. The chacmas would return soon—she knew how important they were to him. But also, he'd made her a promise.

"Above all else," she reminded him, "I wanted you to love our little boy."

He recalled the words instantly, the same words she'd spoken just before she died. But this time, they were drenched with accusation. He had failed to do the one thing that Lettie had asked of him.

But now that he thought of it, hadn't the boy been taken from *him*? That's how he recalled it today. Sophie had insisted that it would be better for everyone if she raised Charles herself. Marais must have argued with her. Surely, he hadn't wanted to give Charles away. The boy had been so small. He had only one remaining parent in the world. But Sophie was older. She was a woman. She'd raised children of her own. Marais must have acquiesced against his better judgment. No father would have willingly handed over his child under such circumstances. He needed to tell Lettie that he'd *intended* to love the boy.

When he opened his eyes again, he was lying on the spongy bank, one cheek propped on a patch of wild fungus as the sun baked the other. The creek gurgled and spat. Directly in front of him, a mirage of Thomas lay curled on his side in a patch of dappled sunlight. He was mimicking Marais's posture, his dark snout inches from Marais's nose. In the chacma's hand was a familiar-looking leather shoe on which he was chewing and salivating effusively. Marais glanced down. One of his own feet was bare. He was still dreaming.

Thomas bit into the sole. He came away with a chunk of leather between his teeth.

Marais blinked to rouse himself.

Thomas was still there, gnawing on the soggy sole.

"You're back!" cried Marais.

He grabbed the young chacma in his arms, clutched him to his chest. The two rolled in the damp dirt and the high grass until, he thought, they were nearly indistinguishable.

With the chacmas' return, his experiments resumed, but on a smaller, less hazardous scale. There were feeding habits to uncover, mating practices to decipher, child-rearing patterns to decode. He filled a dozen leather-bound notebooks with his observations: who was mating with whom, how long grudges were held, how quickly the troop recognized and accepted a member who'd left and returned. When he ran out of paper temporarily, he scrawled along the wooden beams inside his hut. He couldn't risk losing a single idea.

Every conclusion he formulated raised at least three more questions that demanded further investigation. At what times of day was the chacmas' depressive tendency strongest? How willing were they to ingest narcotics to palliate this depression? How susceptible were the creatures to addiction?

Marais longed to discuss his ideas with another man. He pined for his days as a law student in London, when he and his colleagues had tossed opinions about like rugby balls, blocking opponents' attempts to pass, staking out ground, defending positions. He missed the debate, the thrill and vigor of intellectual discourse. One night, when he could no longer bear the silence, he penned a letter to his old friend and editor, Gustav Preller.

> *I trust that this finds you well and that you've not yet tired of city life. I persist in this whole messy prospecting business, though the extent of my skill is evidenced by the fact that I am significantly poorer now than I was when I arrived in Waterberg. That's of no consequence though. My attention*

has been captured by other pursuits—pursuits that would tantalize you in equal measure. My friend, I am in the midst of a most incredible discovery.

Over dozens of pages Marais scrawled the record of his observations to date. When one candle melted down and expired, he dug out another from the wooden box that he'd carved to house his supply.

I'm convinced that the mental faculties of a species evolve according to the same laws of natural selection as its physical traits, and that the apex of mental evolution in the animal kingdom is individual memory. With this faculty, more advanced species are equipped to learn and remember in meaningful ways. The only creature with significantly greater capacity for learning than the higher primates is man. We've gained the ability to reason, to write, to remember. But we are plagued by the very faculty of memory that made our learning possible. We've gained the capacity to remember, but in doing so, we have lost the innate ability to forget, to shake off the pain of the past.

Preller, I believe that I've identified the true unconscious. It's comprised of our inborn instincts—those "skills" that enabled our evolutionary ancestors to navigate their world for millennia in blissful ignorance, devoid of lasting psychic suffering. With memory's ascendance, these instincts have become submerged—and we've become unhinged from Nature. Each day I ask myself: was our evolution really worth the cost?

Two weeks later, Marais rode to Naboomspruit. He'd been so embroiled in his studies that he couldn't remember the last time he'd cooked himself a decent meal. He stopped at the butcher's for liver and a wild duckling. Without feathers, the animal's frame was small and bony. Its skin was a washed-out yellow. At the market in the square by the church, he acquired onions and cabbage and a pair of green oranges. With the provisions socked away in his bag, he strode across the street to check his mail.

"Let us publish your findings," Preller's letter said. "I propose that we do so serially. Send me an opening article as soon as you can, and I'll make the arrangements."

Flower boxes hung from the windows of the blue and white houses that ranged along both sides of the dusty street. A brown spotted cow rambled in front of the cart, quickening only when a wheel nicked its hind leg. Two boys in khaki shorts were stacking sections of blue shale into piles and knocking them over with rocks. Naboom ball.

Preller's letter unsettled him. Marais had ended his publishing life years ago—the British had effectively killed his paper as they'd killed his people—and he wasn't yet ready to part with his findings. He needed more time with the chacmas—years perhaps—to shape his theses into more final form. The moment he published his research, his ideas would no longer be his alone. He wasn't ready to relinquish them. He folded up the letter and stashed it in the pocket of his coat. When he snapped the leather sjambok again, the little horse heaved and grunted, and the cart rolled faster.

* * *

Marais awoke to a loud rapping at the door of his hut. Rays of yellow light filtered through the spots in the roof where the thatch had thinned, which meant that it was at least eight o'clock and he'd overslept. *It's Austin*, he thought, *here to scold me for my indolence.*

"Give me a minute, Alec," he called.

The chacmas were back, and he was certain that with the right approach he could sweet-talk his claim mate into assisting him again. He splashed water from his canteen onto his unshaven face. He pulled on a shirt without buttoning it, hopped into his trousers, and threw open the door.

Dolf Erasmus was leaning against a fig tree and puffing on a cigarette. "Morning, sunshine." He was coveralled, thick-necked, bare-headed.

"I was just getting the panning equipment together," said Marais.

"I don't see that claim mate of yours anywhere."

Marais glanced at the creek, which sparkled in the morning light. Austin should be working by now. But the creek and the kloof were empty.

"He's probably pissing behind a rock pile. I'll send him your way as soon as he's back."

"I want to speak with both of you."

Marais needed to think quickly. Dolf must be planning to seize Austin the moment he materialized. "We'll leave him a note then. You and I can hike back to your cabin in the meantime. He can meet us there."

"I'd prefer to wait here until he gets back." Dolf took a knife from his pocket and began whittling the end of a fig branch into a sharp golden blade.

By the time Marais heard the whistling, it was too late. He spotted Austin the same moment that Dolf did. They watched him lumbering up the slope, a lifeless fox lashed to a pair of sticks balanced over his shoulder.

"Got 'im with a slingshot!" Austin announced to Marais. "First time in my life. You wouldn't 'ave believed it. There I was squatting in the bush for my morning relief, which was a bit slow in coming, so I sat and waited, and next thing I know, 'e's scampering right past me, doing 'is foxy stuff with no idea that I'm squatting there, quietly loading my ammo. Probably just a kid too. Never even saw the effing rock coming at 'im. Look at this pelt!" More words than he'd spoken to Marais in months.

Austin's gaze drifted to Dolf. He stopped where he stood on the rugged dirt path and swallowed audibly. "What's this? A party in my honor?"

"Afraid not," said Dolf, gripping the whittled branch between his fingers.

"Marais?" Austin asked, his voice rising.

Marais shook his head slightly. Austin was not a small man. He was thick and solid, nearly as stocky as Dolf. How was Dolf planning to apprehend him?

Austin glanced nervously to the side, assessing the best escape route. "Whatever yer've 'eard, Erasmus, yer can be sure that none of it's true."

Dolf blew his nose, sending a wad of mucous sailing into the grass. "On the contrary. It's all true. I have the proof right here. Time to pack it up."

The blood left Austin's face. He tossed the fox on the bank. "I don't care what kind of proof yer've got! I'm not leaving."

Dolf snorted. "Like it or not, we all are. It's permanent vacation time, boys. Le grand voyage." He pulled a letter from his pocket and unfolded it. "Doornhoek's mining rights have been sold. You're standing on Union Tin land now. The Brits have struck once again. This time with purse strings instead of cannon fire. But we're buggered just the same. Says right here: we are all to vacate Doornhoek effective immediately."

Marais plucked the letter from Dolf and read it over. His heart plunged. The stamp was authentic.

Dolf flicked the butt of his cigarette into the scrub. "No need for all the gloom and doom. Think of it as an opportunity. I, for one, am planning to spend some time by the sea. Fish a little. Lie on the beach. Rest the weary bones awhile. Though a part of me thinks I might just leave it to fate and see where my legs take me." He tucked the letter into his pocket. "Wherever you wind up, I'm sure we'll be seeing each other soon enough. The world is round after all."

* * *

Marais emerged from his hut wearing leggings and riding breeches with his top hat and cane. When the world collapsed—as it had for him again and again—there was only one way to face it, as a man of distinction. What was it that his mother had said? *We soldier on.* He thought he finally understood what she meant. That we're besieged by the forces of nature. Every step, every breath, is an act of resistance in a grand unwinnable war. You soldier on until your lungs finally fail you.

He had stuffed his trunk to bursting, first with his library of notebooks, second with Darwin and Freud and Coleridge, and only then with the few other items that he was able to squeeze in—a wool coat, change of clothes, canteen, hunting knife, strips of cured beef, and springbok biltong. His Mauser he strapped to the top. Everything else—his bedroll, a chair he'd fashioned of yellow wood, tin pans and pots, cook stove, fuel, plates and bowls and glasses, flasks, tins, silverware, and bundles of paraffin candles—he'd arranged neatly inside the hut. Maybe someone else could make use of the supplies one day.

Austin was packed already, seated cross-legged in a patch of shade. He nodded at Marais, and the two of them started down the mountain together in silence. The air was warm and clear, and there was only the smell of the woods and the sounds of their boots grinding in the dirt and of the trunk, which Marais pulled behind him by its wrought-iron handles. Indigo, blue, and flaxen wildflowers had forced their way up through the path's mud and gravel. Having struggled against heat and flash floods and the appetites of herbivorous animals, they were finally beginning to open. Marais sidestepped the flowers to avoid crushing their young petals.

Before the first bend, he glanced back one last time at the hut he'd built. He regarded the timbers he'd cut and notched, the roof he'd laid and thatched. It all seemed so small in the distance. He looked one last time at the creek's green pools, the water where he'd spent countless days wading up to his waist, hoping to strike metal. He shielded his eyes with his hand and peered up toward the cave at the top of the krantz. The sun was hot in the sky, and at first he could see nothing but the ridge and the outline of the two thin trees that bounded it. When his eyes adjusted to the light, he saw two dozen ancient faces peering back at him—like his own reflection, multiplied and mirage-like, shimmering in the heat. His second family. His children. He steeled himself and turned away before he could change his mind.

"Never understood what it is about yer," Austin said. "I look at them baboons, and no matter 'ow I try, or 'ow many drinks I've got in me, all I see is the same goddamn thing—a bunch of dirty monkeys."

Marais realized that Austin was serious and felt a pang of sympathy for him. "When I look at the chacmas," he said, "I don't see primates at all. I see the origins of the human mind, of memory. I see the causes of my own suffering."

Austin screwed up his eyes. "One more lick of proof that yer really are as crazy as yer look."

They followed the path down to the farmstead at the base of the road, where Marais kept his horse and Cape cart. He'd had the cart shipped from Cape Town, via Johannesburg and Pretoria. It had no equal in Waterberg, and he'd polished and cared for it meticulously. The wood siding, the leather seats, the canvas hood, the elegantly spoked wheels all flashed in the sunlight.

Marais watered his horse, harnessed it to the cart, and offered Austin a lift.

"In that chariot? Nah, I'm planning to foot it. Clear the mind, strengthen the old lungs."

"Where will you go?"

Austin considered the question. "I'll make me a plan I guess. That's what Boers do, right? I could head northward, maybe to Bechuanaland. Only place I *can't* go back to is Jo'burg. The police would nab me before I set foot in the city. So for now I suppose I'm destined to wander. Maybe try my luck in the northern mines. See if I can strike some gold. That's where the real money is, always will be. Follow the greed, I say. That's the way of men." He hauled his bag over his shoulder and turned to go.

Marais climbed onto his cart and took the reins. He was abandoning Doornhoek. He was leaving the chacmas forever.

"Hey," Austin called. "Where are yer going yerself?"

Marais couldn't return to the city. What would he do there? Publish? Practice law again? For three years he'd been squatting in the forest. He'd soured on civilization. There was more chacma than urban denizen in his blood now. How would he ever leave Waterberg? "Honestly," he said, "I have no idea."

He turned and snapped his sjambok before Austin could see his face. The horse started up, and the wheels beneath Marais began to spin. "You take care of yourself!" he shouted over his shoulder. There was a fierceness in his voice.

He followed Voortrekker Road for miles, letting the horse amble at its own speed. The wheels ticked through the dirt and buzzed against stray stones. Every hoof-clomp sent a puff of dark soot into the still, hot air. As the cone-like mountain fell away behind him, it struck Marais that no matter how many acquaintances you made in this life, no matter the number of friends and colleagues amassed, in the end you were always alone.

To the left, a cluster of buzzards was pulling the entrails from a dead buck. The animal's chest had been split open, filaments of flesh still clinging to the tips of its ribs. Marais passed rows of fruit trees—quince and walnut, guava and almond. When he first set eyes on Waterberg, he'd been struck by the land's green fertility, by its raw abundance. Now what he noticed were diseased, browning leaves, rotted fruit that had dropped from branches and encircled the trunks in heaps. A rat scampered through a pile of gleanings, disappeared head-first into the debris, and made off like a burglar, clutching a pit in its razored teeth.

For a split second, he thought he saw the Vaalpens boy, bare-chested, rough-skinned, crouching hopelessly over the corpse of his father. Marais stopped the horse and jumped down just in time to be sick between his feet. When he looked again there was nothing but a polygon of shadows tossed from a nearby bush.

His throat was thick with dust. He reached for his canteen and realized that in the rush to leave, he'd neglected to fill it, which left him and the horse without relief on this sun-scorched stretch of dirt.

Further along Voortrekker Road, he noticed an unusual tree off to the right, an Alhambra with a striking gnarled root network that had twisted into a massive tangle above the ground. Dangling from its branches were enormous clusters of grape-like berries bursting with juice.

He stopped the cart to examine the old tree and twist off some fruit for refreshment. That's when he saw the house, a modest structure built of raw brick and set back behind the Alhambra with expansive views overlooking the valley. A wooden sign nailed crookedly to a fence post named the farm: Rietfontein.

The woman who answered the door had a gray, square face, a lazy eye, and a slick of mustache that stretched across her upper lip. As Marais stood on her doorstep with his top hat, his steel-tipped cane and riding breeches, the woman's mouth parted.

"Might I bother you for a drink?" he asked. "The road is hot and I neglected to bring water."

The woman glanced over Marais's shoulder at the Cape cart, and her straight eye opened wider. Her hands brushed out the wrinkles in her calico dress.

"You're not from around here, Mister." She looked him over, from his hat to his breeches to his boots and back up. "I can tell by those clothes."

"You have a keen eye, madam." (He couldn't help himself.) "I'm a Pretorian by birth, but these rags I picked up in London."

"You say you been to London?"

His thirst was debilitating. He had to close his eyes to swallow. She noticed him starting to swoon. "Come in, come in, come in. It's too hot out there today. We have plenty of water. I'll get you a cupful. Mister, you can drink as much as you like. Your horse too."

After they'd watered the animal, the woman led him inside to a spartan sofa fashioned from split yellow logs. The room was tidy, filled with awkwardly carved wooden furniture and completely devoid of cushions or color. Suspended overhead, lodged among the boekenhout rafters, was a coffin the size of a small boat.

She brought him some water and watched in amazement as Marais gulped it down. The water barely slaked his thirst.

"Another?" she offered.

"If you wouldn't mind."

This time she filled the glass to the lip and brought with it a plate of rusks and a dish of prickly pear jam, which Marais devoured.

"Made it myself," she said. "I make *everything* myself."

"You must have help with a farm this big.

"It's hard to find good white labor around these parts, and the Africans can't be left to touch the food, as you know. Because of the syphilis. So I do all the cooking and canning and curing and pickling and salting and cheese-making myself."

Marais had known many such Boers—men and women so blinded by their distaste for the native population that they would throw science out the window to justify their views. But he was tired, and the talk of food leadened his feet and kept him from lecturing her. "It sounds like an exceptional amount of work."

"It's kind of you to notice. Not all men do." She gave him a significant look. "I'd like my husband to meet you. Gys loves travel too. Nylstroom's about as far as he's been himself, of course. But he loves the idea of travel. 'Tamaria,' he tells me, 'one day I'm going to take you to see Pretoria and Durban, Bloemfontein and Cape Town.' His eyes always get big when he says *Cape Town*. 'We'll visit all the great cities,' he tells me. He's always been a dreamer, my Gys."

Likely no accident that his name rhymes with *lice*, thought Marais, as he emptied the second glass. He was beginning to feel a bit more himself.

Gys turned out to be older than his wife, a nearly expressionless man in his mid-fifties with severe eyes and hair that spilled from his nostrils and chin and ranged down into a coarse, gray beard. The moment he entered, an overpowering smell filled the living room. Tamaria noticed the look on Marais's face and apologized. "Gys harbors a weakness for garlic. The snuff was eating away at his nose, so we got him chewing garlic cloves instead. It's worlds better for his health, but the smell takes some getting used to."

Gys was a self-taught smith and wagon builder. He showed Marais through all eight rooms of the house, pointing out every item of furniture he'd fashioned from the lilac and yellow wood trees that spread across the farm. He spoke slowly and deliberately as if considering every word before uttering it.

"You may have noticed the piece I'm most proud of," he said, gesturing at the coffin suspended above them. "Solid tambotie wood. Took me a full year to build and sand and stain. Tamaria doesn't approve of it. 'That's too much time to spend on a coffin,' she tells me."

Tamaria frowned at her husband. "'Much less than I plan to spend *in* it,' Gys says."

They both had a good long laugh.

The air in the room glowed orange as the sun sank into the valley. Marais rose to thank them and take his leave. He needed to find food and sleeping accommodations before he lost the light entirely.

"You can't leave without eating," Tamaria said. "Stay with us for dinner."

She cooked a sheep's head with stewed cabbage ("Gys's favorite") and laid out silver and placemats that she'd woven from dried grass. When the table was set and the candles lit, Tamaria seated herself between the men, though noticeably closer to Marais. So close that the back of her hand brushed against his knuckles on two separate occasions during the meal. Every few minutes she asked if he'd be kind enough to refill her glass. The cracked jug on the table contained house-made Alhambra-berry wine the color of pomegranate skin.

Gys snorted with delight at each bite of sheep. He spoke zealously about the wildlife that abounded on the farm. "We've got beasts of every imaginable size—rooikat, mongoose, duiker, bushpig, buntings, coursers, cobras, skinks . . ." He counted the names on his calloused fingers as he rattled them off. "Fact I challenge you, Mister Marais, to name an animal that we *don't* have at Rietfontein."

The talk of wildlife piqued Marais's interest. "What about chacmas?" he asked.

Gys looked puzzled. "The monkeys?"

"The baboons."

"A miserable nuisance. They strip the bark from the trees and plunder our pears. Until ten years ago, we never saw them around here. During the war, they suddenly appeared—must have been searching for food. When the war ended, they stayed on, hundreds of'em."

Marais leaned intently toward Gys. "Is that right?" Maybe his research wasn't destined to end quite yet. Maybe he could continue right here. If he played his cards correctly.

Talk of the war seemed to have struck a nerve in Gys. He shifted in his seat and peered at Marais. "Do you know how many children we lost in the camps?"

Tamaria flinched. She narrowly missed tipping over her wine glass. "A man like Mister Marais doesn't want to hear about such morbid things, dear. It's not dinner conversation."

"Take a guess," said Gys, ignoring his wife.

"From the entire region you mean?" Marais asked.

Gys's eyes dimmed. "I mean from our family."

Marais put down his fork. "I wouldn't want to guess at a thing like that."

"More sheep's head?" Tamaria shrieked.

"Five," said Gys, taking another forkful of meat. "Five children. Oldest was eight. The youngest—I shouldn't even tell you, but I will—the youngest was eleven months. Wasn't walking yet." Tears sprang into his eyes. "In the beginning, the Brits kept captives unsheltered in the camp up here. Said they didn't have tents for Boers, even women and children. Treated us like slaves. Didn't matter that our skin was as white as theirs. Our children withered under the hot sun. The soldiers wouldn't give them enough water. How much would it have cost to give an extra cup each day? Waterberg is overrun with streams." He lowered his gaze to the table. "Our babies died of dehydration, Mister Marais. All it would have taken to save 'em was a drink."

"I'm incredibly sorry," said Marais.

Tamaria cut her eyes at her husband. She stormed from the table to the kitchen.

Marais had drunk too much wine. The smell of mutton had overtaken the room. He regarded the couple in the pale-green candlelight. No matter how far you traveled, every path, every conversation, ultimately returned to the war. He thought of all the individuals he'd met in his forty-five years, all the singular lives with whom his own life had casually intersected. He thought how much occurred secretly inside each one without anyone else ever knowing. Every person was layers thicker than they seemed. There were lives within lives. Bodies within bodies. People within people.

Gys sucked the last bit of cabbage from his fork and lowered his voice. "She doesn't like me speaking of such things. Thinks they shouldn't be discussed in public. It was six years ago. But the wounds feel fresh. I suspect they always will. There are *somethings*"—he said this as one word—"that you don't ever get over."

Tamaria returned with a steaming berry pie and tackled it with a knife the size of a hatchet. She placed an enormous wedge in front of Marais, nearly half the pie, and served a comparable piece to her husband, then laid the remaining sliver on her own plate.

Marais glanced from square face to square face. Perhaps he could stay here for a short time—a few days, even a couple of weeks. Just long enough to ensure continuity of his research and to locate a more permanent setup. They'd have their noses in his business at all times. That was clear enough. But he had nowhere else to go at present, and they seemed like decent enough people with a tidy home, and a farm, he realized as he looked out the leaded window at the last pink light fading into the horizon, that was expansive and lovely.

"Tell us, Mister Marais, about London," Tamaria said with a look of desperation.

The pie was flaky and cloyingly sweet, and it took Marais several minutes to recover between bites. He used these pauses to tell them about the Thames and its network of ancient bridges, about the Tower's famous beheadings, Westminster Abbey, and the zoo at Regent's Park.

Tamaria was spellbound at his descriptions of London dinner parties, and the opera, and the halls of the Inner Temple. "You mean to say you're an advocate?"

"Yes, though I underwent medical training in London as well."

"Why, the neighbors will insist on meeting you! All of them will." She glanced furtively at Gys. "How shocked they'll be to learn that we know a legal man. And a doctor! Gys, can you even imagine?"

Gys considered this. "It *is* rare that a person of interest comes through town."

"Terribly rare," said Tamaria. "The last time it was a crazed Jewish hobo, and he soon proved rather a nuisance—not that we should compare him with a man of your stature, Mister Marais."

"He was not the sort of 'person of interest' one ideally hopes for," said Gys.

"But an advocate and a doctor . . ." Tamaria said.

Now for the strike, thought Marais. "That's all in the past now, of course. I no longer have a practice. The truth is I don't even know where I'll sleep the night."

"You poor man."

"I've always been self-sufficient. Though in this case, the awful thing is the timing. I was in the middle of a significant research project at Doornhoek. A rather involved study of the chacmas, in fact. If I'd finished the work, I have every reason to believe that it would have been published to scientific acclaim."

"We have those monkeys right here on this farm!" Tamaria exclaimed. "More than we know what to do with."

"I gathered as much from your husband. They can be challenging creatures, but to me they're a blessing. You're very fortunate."

"Fortunate?" said Gys. "They wreak havoc on our orchards and pick our gardens bare."

"Oh, Mister Marais, I just had the most wonderful idea." Tamaria's entire face lit up. "You must stay with us."

There it is. But will her husband agree? "You're terribly generous. My bones will appreciate a rest tonight. I can be on my way before daylight."

"No, no, you misunderstand me!" she said grabbing his arm. "I mean to say you should *stay* with us. For as long as you like. You could live here, in fact, with Gys and me. Legal work would be hard to come by, but medicine is another story. There's no proper doctor for dozens of miles in any direction. You'd have all the patients you could ask for. And you could continue your research at your leisure."

Gys looked confused and then concerned. "But where would we stick him?"

She batted her eyes at her husband and forced a smile. "In the new stoepkamer, dear."

Gys turned to Marais and mimed with his thumb as if he were drinking from a bottle. "She's had too much wine, I'm afraid," he said under his breath. "Sometimes it causes problems. See, we have no stoepkamer, just the stoep itself. Wraps around the far side of the house. But it's not enclosed. Wouldn't be appropriate for a beggar, let alone a man of your refinery."

"Gys van Rooyen!" Tamaria shouted, "I've not had too much to drink! And of course I'm aware that the stoep is not enclosed. I can assure you, though, within two days it will be."

* * *

Tamaria furnished the new room with pieces that Gys had built: a dual-paneled wardrobe, a desk and bookcase of polished beechwood, a bed with thongs of leather for slats, a coir mattress, and a duvet stuffed with soft down from the flocks of geese that reigned on Rietfontein.

Tamaria was a midwife—the principal midwife for a large, sprawling slice of Waterberg. The two interior rooms directly adjacent to Marais's bedroom, the stoepkamer, she used for her deliveries. For some reason, every woman in Waterberg seemed compelled to deliver up her baby between midnight and five in the morning. Barely a week passed when Marais was not an audience to the aching cries of female labor. Tamaria said she'd never lost a patient. Every labor ended in birth. But in the pre-dawn hours, when the cold air outside swirled with silver mist and the jackals began to howl, every birth was a jarring reminder of the one death he had not yet found a way to forget.

He spent these hours tossing in the dark. He remembered his first class in obstetrics at Guy's Hospital in London more than a decade ago. He hadn't enrolled exactly—rather, he'd snuck in. He'd caught the Old Kent bus to Borough High Street and walked right through the hospital until he came across a hundred men in white coats who looked too young and guileless to be doctors. He followed them into a large lecture hall, where a man in a longer coat taught a class on infection. Marais was riveted.

He couldn't stop taking notes. He scrawled so vigorously that his wrist began to ache.

"Some of the most common infections are easily prevented with standard hygiene practices," the doctor said. He was a short man with a large black mole on his neck and green eyes that seemed to dance when he spoke. "Take puerperal fever. There was a time when this was the single greatest cause of maternal deaths—"

Marais raised his hand and stood up in front of his chair. "Sir, I was under the impression that puerperal fever was another name for childbed fever."

"Yes, it's the same condition. Caused by a genital tract sepsis that can develop in the mother after childbirth."

"Then with all due respect, I believe you're mistaken." Marais was electrified at being able to one-up a British doctor on his own turf, though he knew he needed to remain polite to avoid being ejected from a class that he had no earthly right to attend. "There's no way to prevent childbed fever. I know this firsthand. My wife died of the disease."

He felt the eyes of a hundred students turn on him.

The doctor smiled in a way that didn't seem to express pleasure at all, and something about the speed with which his smile faded made Marais suddenly wonder whether he shouldn't have initiated this conversation.

"What's your name, son?" the doctor asked.

"Eugene Nielen Marais."

"Mister Marais, I'm sorry for your loss. It's terrible to lose a wife, especially at your age. Your doctor likely didn't disinfect himself properly."

The mole on the man's neck was hideously large. Marais tried not to swallow. "I don't understand."

"We do still see cases of puerperal fever. But prevention is largely just a matter of ensuring proper hygiene during delivery. If the obstetrician washes his hands in a chlorinated lime solution, it virtually eliminates the possibility of death."

Marais couldn't grasp what the man in front of him was saying. If Doctor Kriel had simply washed his hands before attending to Lettie, she would still be with him now? Surely that's not what he meant—this couldn't have been common medical knowledge back when Lettie was giving birth.

"It sounds like a wonderful new discovery."

The doctor looked apologetic. "It's been standard procedure for forty years," he said quietly.

Marais felt the blood beating behind his eyes. He blinked to stave off the throbbing in his temples. The student to his right shifted in his seat and stared straight ahead. If Marais had left his morphine alone for that one night, he might have thought to order Kriel to clean himself. The entire world would look different. "I had no idea," said Marais. "Forgive me for interrupting." He lowered himself into his chair as carefully as he could. Everything he thought he knew had been blasted apart.

The next day he returned to the class in a white coat. Over the coming months, he didn't miss a single lecture. No one ever asked if he was enrolled, and no one asked him to leave.

* * *

Most days Marais slept until noon in the stoepkamer that Gys had built for him. In bright daylight, the trials of the preceding night would grow hazy and distant. He spent those first afternoons trying to acclimate the Rietfontein chacmas to his presence, but they were less convinced by his offers of maize and stale bread than the Doornhoek troop had been. The chacmas at Rietfontein had more refined palates, having feasted for years on the van Rooyens' tree fruits and planted vegetables. When Marais tried to approach the troop, the elder males spat, growled, and charged at him, stopping only when he discharged his Mauser into the air. Then they'd gallop away into the valley.

When the chacmas abandoned him, Marais would hike through the farm's rolling topography, prowling through fields that turned gold in the late-day heat. He followed the footpath down past the dam, all the way to the Springbok Flats. Between the tall reeds that enshrouded the hot spring, he set a plank across two barrels and created a bathing seat from which he could easily descend into the steaming waters and soak in private for as long as he wished. When his skin puckered and pruned, and he could no longer tolerate the heat, he'd scrabble onto the plank and towel himself off in the sun.

One day tumbled into the next. On his third visit to the spring, there was a rustling in the far reeds.

"Who's there?" Marais called.

The rustle stopped.

On the bank, a red-breasted shrike pecked at the vertebrae of a mouse recently dispatched.

"Who's there? I said."

Soft footsteps glided through the spongy grass. When the reeds parted, a man appeared. He was thin and black, about Marais's age, with sloping shoulders and hair shaved close to his skull. In his arms, he carried a bundle of cut green reeds.

"Didn't realize you were here, sir. I was just collecting these . . . for my sister. She makes them into baskets. Sorry to disturb you." He kept his eyes averted from Marais and hurried to leave.

"Wait. Who are you?"

The man turned slowly around. "Joshua, sir." One of the van Rooyens' farmhands. He looked nervous, as if Marais might turn him over to Tamaria for helping himself to her reeds.

Marais dried his face and chest, and wrapped himself in a towel. "You've worked here a long time?"

"Since I was a boy, sir. The van Rooyens are good people. Very kind. As I've been with them so long, I get one day off each month. I use the time to—" He looked guiltily at the reeds in his arms. "My sister sells her baskets for eggs and meat. She can't walk too far, on account of the gout. So I help when I can."

A loose black cloud buzzed just overhead. A million discrete points seemed to float through the sky at varying speeds. It was like no cloud Marais had ever seen. He was mesmerized.

"They're white ants, sir," Joshua said.

Marais pricked up his ears. The last white ants he'd seen this close were the ones that had colonized his mother's house in Pretoria more than a decade ago. The night that Lettie delivered Charles, Marais had ripped out the wall above the mantle. Thirst engulfed him now, as his mind began to turn. "How big are the colonies?"

"I couldn't say, sir. But some of the mounds are taller than a grown giraffe."

A grown giraffe? Surely he was exaggerating.

"If you like, sir, I could take you to see them."

Marais cinched the towel around his waist. "I would like that."

With his clothes bundled in his arm, he jumped from the plank and waded through the water. He climbed out onto a blanket of lichen and ferns.

Joshua followed ten paces behind.

"Why don't you walk with me?" Marais called back. "It's awkward being followed like this."

Joshua looked uneasy. "The van Rooyens don't like to risk getting touched, so when we're near them, we walk behind."

"Touched?" Marais asked, failing to understand. "Why not?"

"On account of the syphilis."

A bush chicken tumbled out of the grass in front of Marais, changed direction, and darted back into the brush.

"Do you have syphilis, Joshua?"

"No, sir."

"What about the other hands?"

"I've never known a man around here with the syphilis."

"Then why don't you tell them that?"

Joshua considered this. "Mrs. van Rooyen wouldn't believe me. And anyway, I wouldn't want to upset her. Like I said, they're good people."

"Well, you're the one helping me, and I don't like having you way back there. Come walk beside me."

Joshua met his eyes. His stubbled jaw tightened. "If that's how you prefer it, sir." He pulled even with Marais. They pushed past the reeds into a field of tall, fibrous grasses that bowed with the wind.

It looked like a village at first, a village of tall, scattered huts. Spread before them was a sprawling range of giant termitaries, baked into the land like an ancient city. Dozens of rugged cones, some twenty feet high, sprang up from the ground, cragged and peaked. Colonies of millions.

The wind whipped up. Winged insects swarmed overhead, filling the sky. Thousands of hopeful queens and kings sailed through the air. They caught in the hair of Marais's arms and chest, and stuck to his skin. He picked half a dozen from his teeth, their wings still fluttering.

The future unrolled like a carpet. He'd investigated the chacmas at Doornhoek—he'd discovered a window into the evolution of memory and human awakening. A window into the cause of psychic suffering. Here now were the white ants, the social insects, the creatures at the opposite end of the spectrum. Their lives, he'd always suspected, were governed solely by instinct. *What if we could reawaken those ancient animal instincts in ourselves?* It would mean liberation, freedom from the mental faculty that still tortured him. He gazed across this strangely steepled village, a thrill surging through him. He couldn't have hoped for a more perfect laboratory.

February 1936, Cape Town, Union of South Africa

The day begins early and hopeful.

Charles wakes in the ship's dank cabin, listens to Hannah breathing softly beside him. He likes how she smells in the morning—like flour and cinnamon. He likes the warmth of her feet.

When he kisses her cheek, she moans, "Too early" and claps a pillow over her head. He slips out from the starched sheets, throws on trousers, shoes, and a shirt, and plucks his hat and coat from the hook. He'll let her sleep.

Up on the main deck, the salty air is still blue-black. No one else is awake. In the silence, he tests out the word *marriage*—utters it softly, exploring the feel of the syllables on his tongue, laughing it off when he notices where his mind has traveled. He kicks into a handstand and holds himself upside down, legs motionless and skyward. The ship rolls gently from windward to lee side as he counts his breaths. He makes it to twenty-two before his feet tumble back down to the deck.

Under the sliver of moon, with darkness lingering over the sea, the silhouette of Table Mountain rises like a giant carved into the sky. The image is spectral, Olympus-like. Charles rubs his eyes. He squints into the distance. The mountain's sprawling mesa cuts through the foamy clouds. Cape Town harbor is still miles to the southeast, but he feels his heart loosening, breaking into song. After thirty years, he is almost home.

The Cape, concealed somewhere beneath those folds of clouds, wasn't even a part of his country during his childhood in the Transvaal. It wasn't until after he left for London that the four colonies of southern Africa were jigsawed into a new nation, one that he has never laid eyes on before. And yet, he feels connected to this land. An arc of light rises from behind the massive rock, and he nearly applauds—for the impossibility of the mountain's geology, and the raw beauty of the coastline, and the fact that he's returning after so much time to the land where he was born. But one question nags: Will the others be permitted entry when they arrive at the port?

Jewish men, post-prayer, wind onto the deck of the German liner, leather phylacteries still snaked around their biceps and fastened to their foreheads. Their wives follow behind them with white headscarves pinned to their hair. Accessories they couldn't have worn publicly in Germany. Children cling to painted yo-yos and toy animals whose buckwheat stuffing seeps from patched fabric. Eye-rubbing and yawns give way to shouts of excitement at the view to port. The passengers exchange gleeful *Guten Morgens* all around. Amid all this, Charles realizes it's starting to rain. His hat is already damp. Hannah will sleep till eleven if left to her own devices. Any other morning he'd let her. But she shouldn't miss this. Table Mountain is special. It will be her first glimpse of his past.

He sweeps down to his cabin, pulls on the light chain. The bulb buzzes and brightens. "Sorry to do this," he whispers.

The sheets are tangled around her hips and arms. He sits on the edge of the bed and peels the pillow from her head. He touches her lips. She snores in response.

"Hey, lady." He traces her lips with his finger.

Without opening her eyes, she rolls to the far side of the bed.

He reaches under the sheet. His hand travels along her belly to her bare breasts. Hannah is the first woman he's slept with who hasn't felt the need to dress after lovemaking. Charles cups her backside in his palm. He feels his groin stir.

"Just ten more minutes?" she groans. "So tired."

"There's something I want you to see."

She gives him a theatrical snore. Charles fights off the urge to slip back into bed. He decides instead to surprise her and pack them both up. They'll be ready to disembark as soon as they make land.

He slides out the bottom drawer of the dresser and pulls out her blouses and skirts, underthings with frills and ties and lace that he's seen on her but not off. Her belongings have gradually migrated to his room. He folds and stacks them one after another in her valise.

When everything packable is packed, he sets the alarm on her nightstand for five minutes in the future and dashes off a note: *Meet me on the main deck. Last chance for the world-class view. C.*

Now the deck is swarming with passengers. The ship's entire population is on its feet, glued to the railings. The rain quickens, but amid the excitement of their arrival, no one seems to care. Morning has risen. Ribbons of fog have started to lift. The Castle of Good Hope pierces the gray sky. The city unfolds beyond the harbor. Surely, they've made it in time—before the government of South Africa bans Jews altogether.

Charles spots Leo at the prow in a blue hat and vest, trousers, and polished hospital shoes. He has his son on his shoulders. His white-sleeved arm enfolds Sarah's waist. The boy shouts exuberantly at the ships that crowd the waterfront: freighters, tugs, and liners bearing the flags of a dozen different countries. On board the fishing vessels, windswept men take cleavers to tuna, shark, barracuda, sailfish.

When Charles approaches, Leo lowers his son onto the deck. The boy peers through the railings at the fishermen. Charles kisses Sarah's cheek.

"The human mind is a strange machine," Leo says in German. "For the last couple weeks, I thought this trip would never end. But now that we've arrived, it feels as if it's passed in an instant."

"It wouldn't feel like an *instant*," Sarah scolds lightly, "if you'd changed half the nappies I have."

Leo rolls his eyes. "We call this misery poker," he says to Charles. "Her favorite game. I'm the one who got knocked out of bed every night because she insisted we keep the boy between us. 'He won't be able to sleep by himself, Leo. He'll be too scared.' I'm the one with the bruised hips and the head bumps. Do you see me complaining?"

"You see how impossible he is?" she says to Charles. "Blaming a child for his own insomnia?"

"I better stay out of this one," Charles manages to reply in German. "I'm just glad we're here."

Sarah squeezes Leo's hand. "I can't tell you how long I've been dreaming of this day."

Charles gazes across the water as South Africa encroaches. The distance from ship to shore is half what it was ten minutes ago. The old red clock tower in the middle of town blooms into focus. Cambridge feels light years away. Did President Conant really dedicate a plaque to Harvard alumni who fought *against* America? He begins to doubt his own memory. But only for a moment. "You're the reason I'm here, Charles," Hannah told him last night, and as he lay beside her, a thought cycled through his mind: *Maybe this is enough.* They could settle outside Cape Town, he thinks now. Or in the mountains of Stellenbosch. He could learn to farm. Plant grapes and pear trees, raise a small herd of cattle, cultivate chickens and sheep, not too many, just enough to live comfortably. He knows nothing about farming, but he has it in his blood—like every Boer. It would be a simple life. No politics. No ambition. No ethical compromise. No bending to authority ever again.

A pair of orange-beaked pelicans swoops overhead on a return trip to land. They're jostled by the wind, but they ride rather than fight it, never veering off course. Charles watches the birds rise on a column of air, shrink into eyelashes, and meld into the distant hills. He squints, imagining how far he can see, past clustered mountains, waves of burnt desert, serpentine rivers. Marais is out there somewhere. Charles can almost feel him.

But they've been without news since they first left England. What if South Africa denies Hannah entry? No way will Charles leave her behind.

"Now that we're finally here," Leo says, "it's daunting to think of starting over. Leasing an apartment, getting licensed to practice medicine all over again, finding a school for the boy."

"You'll do fine," says Charles, relieved to be distracted from his own thoughts. "You've made it this far. Where would the adventure be if life were all easy?"

Leo shrugs. "All easy I don't need. But a little. I'd take a little in a heartbeat." He re-balances the boy on his shoulders. "By the way, how long do you think it will take Sarah and me to learn the basics of Afrikaans grammar?"

Charles freezes. Why would Leo ask him this? As far as they know, Charles is Hannah's Austrian brother.

Leo slaps Charles on the shoulder. "You didn't realize we're wise to you?" he says in perfect English. "It's not quite the stuff of spy novels—your wife told us the whole story days ago."

My wife?

"Actually, we knew even before she told us. No offense, Charles, but you'd never pass for a native German speaker—absent some mental deficiency. And honestly, even then, it would be difficult to swallow. Maybe you'll give us some Afrikaans lessons once we're all settled? Hannah says you're headed to Pretoria. That's our destination too."

Charles has grown fond of this family, of their perseverance, their humor. "It would be a pleasure," he says in English, though a part of him wonders if he'll ever see them again once the ship docks. He scrawls on a sheet of paper. "This is my aunt's address—if you need help at any point, she can direct you to us."

"Sarah will repay you in kind with the finest kneidlach you've ever had."

"I look forward to that," says Charles. He has no idea what kneidlach is.

A hand touches his back. It's Hannah, her peacoat unbuttoned and flapping in the morning wind.

"You're awake," Charles says.

"Thanks to the alarm you so graciously set," she says, feigning a grimace. She wraps her arms around his waist. "I suppose I do owe you for packing us up though."

"Did you hear that?" Sarah says to Leo. "Her husband even *packs*."

Hannah laughs and hugs her, then Leo, then the boy. As she steps back, she sees the water marks they've left on her blouse. "You do realize that you're all completely soaked?"

"Doesn't it feel wonderful?" Sarah says, laughing. "It's summertime. In February!"

Hannah gazes toward shore and her eyes grow wide. "Your mountains, Charles! We really are here." She raises her camera.

He still remembers the names of the rocky features. He points them out one by one: Signal Hill, Lion's Head, Table Mountain, Devil's Peak. Taken together, they sound like an incantation to ward off evil spirits.

"I don't like scary things," says the boy.

"Actually, before Devil's Peak, it was called Charles Mountain, which personally, I find much more charming."

The boy looks astonished. "They named mountains after you?"

"Only the one I'm afraid."

Hannah punches his shoulder. "No teasing children."

Barely a thousand yards separate them from shore. The ship slows. Turbines sigh and drop an octave. The harbor bustles with brightly-colored vessels.

The boy peers through Leo's binoculars. "Which house is ours, papa?"

"We don't have a house yet," says Leo. "But we will. Don't you worry."

The boy considers this. "That's all right. I'll like wherever we live." Hearing the child try to convince himself, Charles remembers his first glimpse of England as a child, the jumble of excitement and fear that nearly strangled him as he laid eyes on his new land.

"Of course you will," Leo says, ruffling the boy's hair. "Look at this place. What's not to like?"

"The only thing is," the boy says, "I didn't know it would be so crowded."

For the first time, Charles notices the throng of men pulsing on the quays. They wield a mosaic of signs nailed haphazardly to sticks. Dozens of others are running from town to join them.

Leo grabs the binoculars from the boy and trains them on the crowd. When he lowers them to his chest, his face is stiff. "That's not a welcoming committee."

He hands Charles the binoculars. It takes a few seconds for Charles to find the shore through the lenses. He scans the crowd, panning from one man to another. They're all wearing the same gray clothing. Embroidered at the center of every shirt is a spidery black swastika.

"Why the sullen faces?" Hannah straightens Charles's collar. She brushes off his coat.

Charles doesn't know how to tell her. Have they journeyed halfway around the world for this?

"What is it, Charles?"

"There are a thousand men down there. And they're all wearing swastikas."

"They're going to turn us back then? When we've traveled this far?"

"Let's get our bags. We'll need to move quickly."

Hannah pauses at the railing. She raises her camera again and focuses on the mob. The shutter snaps like a gun.

* * *

Four tugs drive the ship into quay number seven. Deckhands lash it to dock posts. They fasten a gangway to the pier. The engines wheeze and cut. The gate opens as if for a horse race.

The passengers whisper to each other. They exchange awkward glances. No one moves to leave the ship. Charles can see the immigration and customs office in the distance, but the protestors have muscled forward to block the passengers from disembarking. The immigration office might as well be an ocean away.

"We can't wait here forever," Leo says. "Let's get going." He takes two bags in each arm and starts down the gangway alone. Sarah hoists the boy onto her hip and hurries after him. He leads his family straight toward the mob.

Charles and Hannah each grab a bag. "Let's stay close to them," he says. He holds her hand as they edge down the gangway. Timbers groan beneath their feet. He can hear hundreds of others trailing just behind them now.

The crowd onshore is twenty rows thick. There's only one path into Cape Town, and it leads directly through the mob. Unused gangways have been erected as barriers. *To contain the mob?* Charles wonders. *Or to contain us?*

At the far end of the waterfront, four policemen linger on horseback. Two of them are trading jokes. A third is chewing on a sandwich.

Rain pelts the bay, drilling holes into the water like machine-gun fire. The mob chants in unison.

"*Gee pad, Jode!*" The first Afrikaans that Charles has heard in decades.

"What are they saying?" Hannah asks.

He can't find his voice.

"Tell me," she demands. "What is it?"

This was to be their promised land. "Jews, go home," Charles whispers.

"So the fascist infestation is no longer confined to Germany," says Leo.

A sun-scorched man in military trousers approaches and blocks Leo's path. The man's hair is yellow and oily, parted and combed to the side. Stitched along the front of his cap is the word *Gryshemde*: Greyshirts.

"Welcome to South Africa." His English is inflected with a sharp, nasal drawl.

"We didn't expect such a warm reception," says Leo.

"Papers," the man replies, ignoring the sarcasm.

Raindrops slide down Leo's shoes and merge into little rivers. "For what purpose?"

"So we can determine if you're eligible to set foot on South African soil."

"I'm sorry," says Leo. "Mister . . . ?"

"Weichardt."

"Mr. Weichardt, we'll be happy to show identification to a government official. Just like in any civilized country."

Over Weichardt's shoulder, beyond the crowd roiling behind him, Charles sees sparkling trolleybuses traversing the main street, chrome flashing in the morning light. Metal poles extend up to a network of electric wires. None of this existed the last time he was here, when he sailed as a child from this very port to England. Men in smart suits stride along cobbled boulevards on their way to work. Sharp black cars slow, windows roll down, white faces peer out to ogle.

"No one proceeds without identification." It's only now that Charles notices the pipe in Weichardt's hands.

"You know damned well who we are and why we're here," says Leo. "We intend to immigrate, like your own ancestors did years ago."

"Leo, don't!" Sarah cries.

"*Ja, ich will!*" he scolds her in German. "We've fled halfway across the globe. Three thousand years of oppression and our people have just kept fleeing. Well, I'm not going to be scared away anymore. I won't have my son growing up frightened to say who he is. Every day of a Jew's life is another Exodus. For Christsake, don't you see, Sarah? They only keep chasing because we keep running."

The chanting behind Weichardt grows louder. A thousand fists pump the air. Charles glances back at the passengers where they huddle, embracing their children and spouses. Why would the arrival of impoverished families make these men so angry?

"I'm not going to ask again," Weichardt shouts. "The boys here are itching to escort you all back onto that ship. Trust me, you don't want their help. It'll make you wish you'd never left Germany in the first place."

Charles is the only Afrikaner among the entire group of five hundred Jews. He has to keep this from escalating further. He has to keep them safe.

"*Hulle is by my,*" he calls to Weichardt. They're with me. "*Ons is op pad na Pretoria.*" We're traveling to Pretoria.

Weichardt glares at him and produces an anemic smile. He couldn't be more than twenty-five. Hannah's age. "We have no more room here for sympathizers than we do for Jews," he replies in Afrikaans.

"Enough of this," Leo says. "We're going through. Follow me, Sarah." Leo marches forward, cutting a careful berth around Weichardt. Sarah's eyes fill with fear, the little boy's with wonder at the noise and energy of the pulsing crowd.

Charles yells to Leo to stop.

When Weichardt raises his muscled arm in the air, the iron pipe he wields shines as if gilded by sunlight. He steadies the pipe above his head, rain coating the rust. Even now, Charles tells himself that it could still turn out all right. Weichardt's gesture is just meant as a warning, like the bluff-run of a rhino. Leo will know now that it's time to stop pushing.

But the moment suddenly gives way. Weichardt whips down his arm. As the pipe strikes Leo's face, there's a steely, sickening *hump* of metal against bone.

The chanting stops. Leo barely sways under the force of the strike, but blood trickles from the corner of his lip. A bruise blooms below his eye. The expression on his face is neither anger nor fear. He looks as if his heart has fractured.

Sarah seizes the boy in her arms. She presses his face to her chest so that he can't see what's happened to his father. "Look what you've done!" she screams at Weichardt. "You should be ashamed!"

The crowd has grown. Charles is forced ten feet back. He elbows his way forward toward Leo, Sarah, and the child, as the mob churns against them. Leo won't desist until he's been knocked unconscious, or worse. Charles has to keep him from getting trampled. He'll wrestle him back to the ship if he has to. There are so many layers of noise that he can't tell who's shouting anymore. He reaches through a blizzard of arms and coats and bags. His fingers graze Leo's sleeve.

The crowd swells with the force of a giant wave. It knocks Charles back onto the gangway, which undulates under so much weight. He's pressed between the protestors ahead and the passengers behind. Amid the tumult, he realizes that he recognizes no one. He reaches back for Hannah's hand. He reaches directly behind him. Hannah is gone.

He stands on his toes. He cranes his neck over the churn of heads. "Hannah!" he shouts.

Terror grips him by the throat. He's lost her. The gangway sags further.

"Charles Marais!"

The next swelling of the crowd knocks him hard against the side of the gangway. His ribs feel like they've been crushed.

"Charles Marais!"

He braces himself against the railing. He hunts for her below.

Beneath the gangway, a long beam juts out. Hannah clings to the wood, legs dangling above the seething ocean. Her face is spotted with blood.

Charles stretches an arm under the railing. He reaches in vain for her hand.

February 1936, Cape Town, Union of South Africa

Joshua shakes his head at the spectacle onshore and rolls up his nets.

Crazy mlungus, he thinks. Beating on each other? Turning back a ship that size? You're the *same* as one another. You're all white.

He dries his hands with a damp rag. The tack of salt on his skin doesn't rub off anymore. The ocean's a part of him now. When he catches his reflection in the mirror below deck he's surprised that he hasn't grown gills. First half of his life he spent toiling on a farm, second half on a boat. That's what he calls amphibious.

He picks the last bits of kelp and seaweed from the netting, cinches the roll with string, and stows it behind his traps, then looks back to shore. What a mess. Can't hear your own thoughts over all that screaming. Gangway's readying to crack in two from so much weight. He doesn't want to see anyone hurt. Not even mlungus. Time to get going anyway. *Stick to your own business, Joshua. There's a boatload of crays to get to market.*

He yanks off a rubber boot, dumps out half a gallon of brackish water, then wraps his hands around the braided rope and winches the anchor over the gunwale.

"Keep out of their sight," Father used to say. "Mlungus see you got a house, you know what they do? They *take* it from you."

There was always that fierceness to his voice. "They see you got an ox? They *take* it. They see you got money? A wife? A baby? They see you got a life, Joshua? You know what they do to you?" Father's eyes bore into him like a shotgun barrel. "Keep yourself invisible, son."

Joshua didn't listen. When he drifted up to Waterberg all those years ago, he took a job as a field hand on a mlungu farm. How else was he going to earn money in the middle of nowhere? He was only a teen back then. What did Father know? The van Rooyens were God-fearing people. They were kind enough to him.

He runs a finger under his nose. He needs to forget all that.

Something pops in the water alongside the boat. A fish, a rock, a bullet. A wild tangle of people is weighing down the gangway. A giant wave of men pulses on the shore. Move this boat now, he thinks. Before they notice you. Before this place explodes.

Rain stirs up the ocean. Water slops against the hull. Joshua cranks the engine and glances warily back toward the ship.

"Marais!" a voice screams distinctly.

The name piques his curiosity. The voice, he sees, belongs to a young woman. She's barely hanging on to a beam that juts out beneath the gangway. Must have got thrown off. Hope the lady can swim. He's sure not going near that mess.

She calls again to a man on the gangway above her. *Marais.* Same name as a man he knew up in Waterberg, a long time ago. Strange fellow—used to wear a silk suit, steel cane, a hat like Sherlock Holmes even deep in farm country. And he was crazy about those white ants. Joshua made the man a promise he didn't keep. Couldn't keep. First time Joshua ever made friends with a mlungu. Last time too. For years now he's tried to box all that up and leave it in the past. Some things are easier said than done.

Marais.

Bet there's a whole mess of mlungus with that name, thinks Joshua. But as he locks onto the man's gray eyes, catches the towering forehead, the arc of mustache, the chiseled chin—he is struck still as a stone.

It's not possible. His mind is playing tricks. The man looks almost exactly as he remembers. Hasn't aged in twenty-five years? It can't be the same man. That would be counter to nature. Men grow old.

Lady screams again. "Charles Marais!"

Joshua blinks. Thoughts fire through his head like shot. He remembers now, in sudden, burnished flashes. Marais told him once: he had a son.

This must be God's work.

Joshua powers the boat through the chop. He aims the prow straight at the woman.

February 1936, Cape Town, Union of South Africa

Charles lowers himself from the gangway toward Hannah. He leans down as far as he can, extends an arm, stretches until it feels like his shoulder will pop from its socket. There's no way to reach her from here.

He spots a small wooden fishing vessel ten yards away at a makeshift pier whose every other plank is missing or rotted through. The fisherman on deck—a Black man, his hair a gray halo—squints back at them for a moment. He waves one hand urgently. With the other, he unhitches his bowline. He pilots the vessel forward until it's centered just below the gangway. He reaches up for Hannah.

"Come quick, Miss," he calls.

Charles watches Hannah grab the stranger's hand. She drops onto the deck of the boat. The fisherman shifts his engine into reverse.

"Wait!" Hannah points up at Charles.

"You'll have to jump!" the man calls.

Charles tosses his duffle over the railing. It lands perfectly in the center of the deck. His eyes search the crowd, shouting and shoving on the gangway. He can't find Hannah's valise. "Where's your bag?"

"I don't know," cries Hannah. "We'll have to leave it!"

"But your camera, your film?"

"I don't need it."

"We have to get out of here." The man cranks the engine again, casts off. The boat aches to accelerate.

"Hurry!" she calls.

Charles scrabbles onto the railing, bodies shoving and pulling behind him. His coat snags and tears at the elbow. He teeters on the narrow beam, ten feet above the little boat. He manages, just barely, to stand up.

"Charles!" Hannah cries.

Spurred by her voice, he leaps across the gap that separates them—right over a line of white geese battling against the spuming tide, right through the black cloud of engine exhaust—and lands one foot on the gunwale.

But the sole of his shoe slips off. He feels himself falling backward. The sky spins above him. His back smacks hard against the water. An icy sensation floods over him as two sets of hands—one black, one white—lock onto his wrists. They tug him, laboriously, onto the boat.

Charles gasps for breath. He lets himself collapse onto the damp wooden boards, wipes his forehead with his sleeve. "Thank you," he coughs.

Hannah drops to her knees and embraces him.

"Are you all right?" he asks.

She flinches when he touches the bridge of her nose. "It's just a bruise. It'll build character."

"Not a bad jump," the man remarks. He's maybe sixty years old, with a kind, weather-worn face. His rubber fishing trousers are suspendered over his broad, sloping shoulders. Charles notices a pair of wooden teeth lodged among two rows of white ones.

"I bet you weren't expecting the welcome you got back there," the man says.

"That's the understatement of the year," says Charles. It all happened so quickly. "You can turn around and drop us by the pier over there. We're headed back to the ship to help our friends."

"There's no question of going back," says the man.

"What are you talking about? Of course we're going back."

The man shakes his head slightly. "Not with this boat."

"We can't leave them there!" Hannah protests.

"Nothing to be done," says the man. "There's more than a thousand Greyshirts by that ship. Got to get out while we still can."

Charles watches in furious frustration as the little boat picks up speed and veers out of the center of the harbor. It's an old trawling vessel, its red paint flaking, its tangle of weighted nets bundled at the stern, with a two-man cabin and barnacles so thickly encrusted that swaths of the hull look like they're fashioned from stone. Soon they're a couple hundred feet from shore. The man turns the prow to the south. They really aren't going back.

"God, please protect that little boy and his parents," Hannah says quietly.

Charles glances back across the boat's wake at quay number seven. A couple dozen armed police have arrived on horseback. They're shouting orders and threatening the mob with batons and the hooves of their steeds. Where the hell were they earlier? He can't see Leo, or Sarah, or the boy, just a pulsating mass of signs and protestors and refugees. He can only hope the police will let the family through safely. Charles's tongue is bleeding—he must have bitten it when he jumped. The taste in his mouth is shame.

"Name's Joshua," says the pilot. He tells them he's been trawling for crayfish—spiny rock lobsters—in the kelp beds along the southwestern coast. His haul has been good the last couple days. He was just heading back to Port Elizabeth when the riot broke out.

"They're a dangerous bunch, those Greyshirts," Joshua says. "I don't mean physically—this was the first time I've seen them armed. The bigger problem is they all vote, even the illiterate ones, and that's dangerous for those of us who can't, Mister Marais."

Charles starts. "Do I know you?"

A shadow passes behind Joshua's eyes. "I must have heard the lady call to you—back at the pier."

Something about his tone troubles Charles. They should get off this boat as soon as they can. "You can drop us anywhere—Kommetjie would be fine, even Simon's Town."

"What would you do all the way down there?"

What Charles is doing is plotting his return to Cape Town to assist Leo and Sarah. But what he says is: "We'll take a car to the nearest station, then catch the train to Pretoria."

"If Pretoria's where you're headed, you can travel with me to Port Elizabeth. We'll dock the morning after tomorrow and you'll be days closer than you'd otherwise be."

Charles glances at the tiny cabin. "We can't impose like that. We'd be taking up too much space."

"I'm expecting a starry night. I'll be sleeping on deck anyway. You two can have the cabin to yourselves. It gets a little humid down there, and the smell of crayfish can be strong at first, but if you can stomach some sea movement while you sleep, you'll be able to make yourselves comfortable."

Hannah gives Charles a pleading stare. "There's nothing else for us to do," she says. "We'd be no match for a thousand men.

And I've seen all of Cape Town that I need to see. There were only white people back there. Some of the angriest white people I've ever come across."

"Plenty of Africans here too," Joshua says. "We've been here forever. It's just not always easy to see us anymore—since we've been relocated."

The rugged headland of the Cape of Good Hope looms ahead to the east. Among the rocky outcroppings, Charles can make out a pair of ostriches plunking along on stick legs and a small herd of zebra queued nose to tail. At the southerly end of the point, a pair of auburn-gray baboons squats together on a flat slab of marbled granite. They rest their elongated snouts on their knees as they watch the boat hum past.

Aren't those . . . ? Charles thinks. He can't recall the name of the species. But he remembers seeing them as a boy. They're the same type Marais wrote that he'd studied. For the first time it fully registers: Marais chose to live with a troop of baboons rather than with his only child.

Joshua cuts a wide turn to avoid the shallow waters around the promontory, then deftly corrects course. They're nearly at the continent's most southerly tip. He aims the boat due east on a trajectory that will take them just south of Cape Point. The sun rises directly overhead and beats down. All trace of the boat's shadow disappears from the water.

Charles is not returning to Cape Town. By now, either Leo and his family have made it through immigration, or the protestors have turned the ship around. If they reach Pretoria, he'll track them down there—as soon as he's completed his business with Marais. He'll make sure they have housing, food, everything they need.

"We're going to pay you for the trip," he says to Joshua.

"There's no charge. Though I wouldn't say no to a tip. And you'd be welcome to cover the cost of food. Actually, we have a special going on right now"—he gestures at the ten crates stacked in the hold—"on crayfish."

Charles reaches for his pocket and remembers his lost wallet. The loss no longer seems as significant though. It was only money. "Hannah here is our treasurer."

"Dinner's on me," she says.

Joshua chuckles while Hannah roots around in the small white handbag that she's kept firmly strapped to her shoulder. The wallet she pulls out bears a striking resemblance to the one that Charles lost.

"Oops. Wrong one," she says, stuffing the wallet back in her purse.

The wind rips like the opening of a zipper.

"Wait a second," says Charles. "That looked like mine."

Hannah's cheeks darken several shades. She slides it back out.

"That *is* my wallet! You mean you've had it all along?"

"Well, sort of." She swallows. "It kind of fell. Accidentally. Just before we reached Southampton."

"Fell where?"

She bites her lip. "Into my handbag?"

"I'd better go check on my nets," Joshua says. He strides quickly toward the stern.

"You mean to say you went digging around in my dresser when I wasn't looking, took my wallet with all of my money, and stashed it in your purse *accidentally*?"

"All right," she says, "it wasn't an accident exactly, but it *was* a mistake. As you may recall, you've made some yourself."

"You're trying to pin this on me?" says Charles. "Let's count up your crimes: breaking and entering. Burglary. Obstructing the truth—"

"I get it. It was a stupid idea. I didn't want you to leave without me. I didn't want to lose you." She threads her fingers through his. "Can you please try to forgive?"

She took it because she wanted to be with me. His anger dims, but it doesn't extinguish. He's not sure he'll be able to trust her after this. "I can try. That's as much as I can promise."

The surface of the ocean blazes with sun, like fire to a mirror. Across the white-tipped chop, he catches a final glimpse of the baboons, a fleeting patch of fur. They're still watching, tracking him. Then the rocks of Cape Point rise up and obscure them for good.

Chacmas, he thinks. That's what they're called.

Dusk blues and fades to night. Joshua lights a paraffin burner and fills a tin pot with sea water. When the lid starts to rattle, he pulls on a thick suede glove, reaches into the crate he was sitting on and pulls out a spiny lobster, negotiating around the serrated claws. Six times he reaches in, dropping crays one by one into the boiling water. He slaps the lid back on and holds it tightly in place.

It's a warm night, and amid the smell of kerosene, the three of them crack their shells with pliers on the gutting station and pick out the meat with fishhooks. Charles is ravenous. He plunders his first lobster and cracks open a second. The shell on the tail peels off like paper. The flesh is white and red-veined, firmer than shrimp and impossibly sweet.

When Hannah has finished her lobster, she tosses the carcass over the side and leans back against the gunwale. Bits of crustaceous shell are stuck to every finger. "Not so kosher," she says. "But amazingly delicious. Surely God will understand?"

"If not," says Joshua, "that god of yours hasn't tried South African crayfish." He takes a bucket and douses the center of the deck. Salt water swirls down the scuppers, washing away the stray fragments.

"I remember eating these as a boy," says Charles. "The crayfish *taste* like Africa."

Hannah rubs his leg and smiles. "Professor Marais here hailed from Pretoria once upon a time," she says.

Joshua turns to Charles. "Ja, I know."

"First time back in thirty years." Charles glances up. "Did you say you know?"

"I hadn't heard that name in a long time," Joshua says. "I knew a Marais up in Waterberg. He was a friend of sorts. An amazing man. Doctor, advocate, scientist, sheriff. His name was Eugene Marais."

Charles gasps. Has Marais put the man up to this? Or is it the gods at work? Regardless, Charles senses with rising unease that he's about to be caught in his own lie.

"Incredible," says Hannah. "Eugene is Charles's given name."

"He mentioned once that he had a boy. When I first saw you back there by the ship, I knew I recognized you. But it wasn't you at all. It was *parts* of you—the forehead, the eyes. Then I heard this woman call your name and I thought, if I had any money, I'd bet it all that you're his son." He grins at them. "You can probably imagine, I don't normally rescue white people from each other."

Hannah looks astonished. "You knew Charles's father?"

"Hannah—" Charles manages.

The lobsterman's face dims. "Well, for a while I did. We didn't part on the best of terms. There was a— an argument." He gets to his feet again and stows the bucket. "That was a quarter century ago."

"Oh, it must be a different Marais then," says Hannah, disappointed. "Charles's father died when he was a baby."

Joshua looks confused for a moment. "No offense, ma'am," he says slowly, "but I don't think that's correct."

"I don't understand." Hannah turns to Charles. "You *were* orphaned, weren't you, Charles? Like me?"

He feels himself start to perspire. He always stressed to his students the importance of integrity. How has he twisted himself up like this?

"*Ja*," Charles says, grasping for a plausible explanation. "My mother died. When I was an infant."

Hannah's features darken. "As I understand the term, losing one parent is not, strictly speaking, what *orphaned* means."

"I probably should have said *abandoned.* For most of my life, it was no different from being orphaned. Marais did reside in the Waterberg when you lived there, Joshua. Later, he returned to Pretoria. The truth is, that's why I'm headed there now. I intend to find him."

"You told me your father was dead!" Hannah insists. "You lied about that too?"

"It's personal. And I said that before we were"—his face is scalded—"you know . . ." He's not doing himself any favors. "Anyway, I'm telling you now. He's been writing me for months. But he's ill. There may not be much time left."

Joshua squats in front of them and wipes with a rag at the salt on the deck. "When I saw your face and heard this lady call your name, I had my suspicions of why you'd returned. The argument I had with your father—it still hangs heavy on my heart, even after all these years. He asked me to do him a favor I never should have agreed to, and I bore the consequence."

This fisherman. This boat. This chance meeting. Charles's history with Marais is more entangled than he realized. There are stories within stories.

"What happened between you?" Hannah asks Joshua. "Sorry, I don't mean to pry. But how awful to have an argument hanging over you for so many years."

"There were words I wished I'd said. But I had to leave quite suddenly. I never saw him again."

An idea flickers behind her eyes. "Joshua, give us a second," she says.

She pulls Charles aside. "Don't for a moment think that I'm not angry with you. But there's a more pressing matter right now. Let's bring Joshua with us."

"Look, I'm not opposed to helping the man. But I can't show up on Marais's doorstep with strangers in tow. Hannah, my whole plan is getting turned on its head."

"Remember that look on Leo's face. We just *left* him there. Here's another chance. Joshua needs our help too, just as your father does. Maybe our good deeds will balance out the bad. Isn't that how karma works?"

But karma is not what persuades Charles. The texts he's translated rarely suggest that doing good in the present will mean reaping benefits in the future. What they emphasize is nearly the opposite: that you are who you are—constrained by your limited choices—because of *past* deeds, long fixed and settled. The best you can do is try to repay your debts. Joshua saved their lives. He needs their help. But this is also not what convinces Charles to invite him along. Joshua knows Marais and the countryside better than Charles does. To reach him in time, they'll need a knowledgeable conspirator.

"We'd like you to join us," Charles says at last. "If you can take some time away from the boat."

Joshua crosses his arms. He smiles with a sort of religious resignation. "It's funny, you know. When this day started fourteen hours ago, I imagined it going a very different way."

* * *

"I'm sorry," says Charles when he and Hannah are alone and bedded down. "I never meant to lie about my father. But once I did, the lie took on a life of its own. I couldn't find a way to reverse it."

Hannah shakes her head just slightly, deep in conversation with herself. She looks up at him. "I suppose I'll get over it. We can call it even. Your not-dead father for my wallet trick."

The little cabin is warm from the heat of their bodies. The night is thick and impenetrable. The objects floating past, he realizes, are shadows from his lashes, projected by the glow of his own eyes.

Until tonight, he's mentioned Marais to no one in his entire adult life. What he feels is a flood of relief now that he's let his father loose to someone else, now that he's confessed the truth to Hannah. He has nothing left to hide from her.

"No more lies then," he says.

"No more lies."

He can feel Hannah's breath, though he can't see her, not even when he rolls over, the sheet tightening beneath them, and touches his hand to her lips. Not even when she kisses his palm in the inky night, when she leans in to wrap herself around him.

Thus have I heard.

February 1915, Waterberg, Union of South Africa

Marais set up a makeshift medical clinic in Gys's outbuilding. He'd managed to quit morphine once again, and while he was convinced that he was less focused without it, he found himself now with more time each day. In a single morning, he could treat several cases of bronchial infection, dress a farmer's bleeding chest wound, mend a child's fractured wrist, drain an abscess, and perform mid-level abdominal surgery on an elderly Boer woman. With no other doctor for dozens of miles, patients were never in short supply. He was earning plenty of money now, though there were few places to spend it in Waterberg. He didn't advertise that he had no medical license, or even a college degree. The sign he'd carved and hung on the fence said simply *Doctor Eugene Nielen Marais*. But the sign was unnecessary. Every Waterberger knew where to find the "miracle doctor."

After lunch, he'd take a notebook, his canteen, and binoculars and set out to check on his experiments: investigations into the tapping beetle's Morse-like code during mating season, the tortoise's impossibly lengthy journey to locate a mate, the extent to which the male kudu's sexual sense was tied to smell.

In the barn, he was running his most ambitious experiment to date. He had raised four generations of yellow weaver birds. He'd kept the birds constantly caged, giving them neither materials for nesting nor worms for feeding their young. Instead, he'd raised them on grain. The eggs of the fourth generation had just hatched, and Marais was nearly beside himself with anticipation.

He unlatched the cage, and with a nudge of his finger, coaxed the adults through the open door. For the first time in their lives, the weavers were free. An incredible thing happened then. The adult birds flew directly to the nearby hay bales. They plucked out strands of dried grass, then returned to their cages and set about constructing the typical plaited globes of a wild weaver's nest as perfectly as if they'd apprenticed all their lives. When their babies opened their tiny beaks, the adults somehow knew to scavenge for worms, the weaver's typical diet, although neither they, their parents, nor their grandparents had ever seen, let alone tasted, a worm themselves. These behaviors weren't improbable—they were miraculous. Marais recorded his findings in amazement:

> *The behavior of my latest generation of weavers cannot in any way be attributed to what we think of as memory. They hold no individual memory of grass or nest or worm, nor did the last three generations of their ancestors. Their actions are directed by pure inborn instinct, a phyletic memory that has been transmitted hereditarily. Even when not exercised over multiple generations, phyletic memory appears to remain fully intact—so fierce is the spark of life that courses through all creatures. Every species is endowed with its own unique set of phyletic memories, designed to maximize its chances of surviving in its native environment. Only the higher*

primates have lost access to theirs. However, I'm increasingly certain that they still lurk inside us.

* * *

Marais's hands were blistered and raw. Joshua tossed his shovel in the dirt and wiped the sweat from his forehead with a handkerchief. Marais had enlisted him to help with his experiments in the late afternoons, after the farmhand had completed his work for Gys van Rooyen.

It was a physically grueling business—digging into dry bedrock under a broiling sun. But Joshua had proven himself an even greater asset to Marais's termite studies than Austin had been to his study of the chacmas. Joshua knew the veld as well as a child knows the creases in his mother's face, and he'd led Marais through remote terrain on horseback and on foot to some of the largest and most pristine termitaries in all of Waterberg. In turn, Marais was teaching him the rudiments of entomology and physiology.

The sun began to drop into the hills, and the birds of Waterberg—buff-streaked chats, sugarbirds, rock-thrush, and blue cranes—were emerging to feed in the grassland.

"Catch your breath and come over here," said Marais. "We're not done yet."

Marais grabbed his knife and bored a gash the diameter of his forearm into the side of one of the giant mounds. He'd never managed to follow the shafts of a termitary all the way to its queen. He'd never glimpsed the fertile mother directly. For years he had imagined her though, swollen to hundreds of times the size of her offspring. The more he dug, the more he failed, but the more he failed, the more he thirsted to find her.

"Watch out, sir!" Joshua called.

Termites began pouring from the wound. Thousands of white ants spread over the ground like fresh snow. Marais nearly tumbled backwards trying to get out of the way. They were scavenging for dirt, hauling individual grains back to repair the rupture. At the same time, a battalion of yellowish, red-horned termites stationed itself around the gash, lances raised. They were so different in appearance from the white ants, they looked like a separate species. The two sets of insects worked together in perfect balance. In minutes, they'd plugged up the hole.

Marais marveled at their work. They must be doing all of this at their queen's bidding. She controlled their behavior without even seeing them. The queen was a mystery for which he'd been searching his whole life, an essential paragraph tucked deep in the heart of a book.

By the time the last of the army insects disappeared inside the termitary, the rupture was sealed up completely. There was no evidence that it had ever existed.

A few feet away at a neighboring mound, a line of workers was returning with food for the colony. Marais crawled through the dirt alongside them. He placed his hand in front of the line and observed. The insects assessed the obstacle. They evaluated their options, then crawled over his fingers. They moved ceaselessly, like the flow of a stream, each insect clutching a white grass seed in its mandibles.

"What kind of thoughts do you think they have, Joshua?"

"These fellows?" He looked curiously at Marais. "No thoughts at all."

"They must at least have some sort of memories though."

Joshua tipped back his head and drew from his canteen. "Not to be disagreeable, but I don't suppose they remember anything."

"Then how do they know their functions within the larger termitarial organism? How do they know how to build or fight or feed their young? How does the queen know how to reproduce? How do they remember their way home despite the obstacles I keep setting in their path? How else if not from memory?"

Joshua leaned against a bush and shrugged. "Insects and I have an agreement. They keep out of my way, I keep out of theirs, and we all get along just fine."

Marais crouched down on his elbows to get a closer look. "The answer, I believe, is that they already know those things before they even hatch. Those behaviors are built into their bodies. They're instincts. What I don't yet know is whether they can also acquire individual memories." Marais glanced up at Joshua. "Perhaps we should find out."

"How would we do that?"

"By experiment. What would you hypothesize happens when one of their own dies? Do they know they've lost a brother?"

Joshua arched an eyebrow. "I wouldn't want to guess."

"Then there's no better time for us to learn."

Marais raised his hand above the line of insects. Sunlight spattered the dirt. With the eye of a god, he scouted for a creature to sacrifice, then brought down his thumb and ground one of the termites into pulp. The hind legs of the flattened insect jerked three times.

Marais held his breath. The other termites paused behind the dead creature. They prodded the body gently with their forelegs. They nudged it with their heads. Not receiving a response, they re-attached themselves to the line, still grasping the seeds in their mandibles, and marched forward as if nothing had happened.

"There's your answer," he said.

"They're not the smartest creatures on the planet."

"It's not a question of intelligence. It's a question of memory. They exhibit no trace of what you and I would call actual memory." His eyes toured over the ground. Another idea occurred to him. "What if they're struck by some greater tragedy? What if a larger segment of their population were completely exterminated?"

"You mean—?"

Before Joshua could finish, Marais squashed the entire rear phalanx with his hand. He smeared eyes and antennae from hundreds of insects into the crisp brown grass.

The termites at the front of the line slowed. They rotated their heads, as if assessing the magnitude of the catastrophe and the risk of danger to themselves. But within seconds they resumed hauling their food toward the termitary. Nothing had changed.

"Look how simple it is for them!" Marais exclaimed. "How unencumbered they are. They have no memory at all."

"Well, we don't know that exactly—"

"I'll tell you something more extraordinary. The termitary is itself a living creature, the insects its component bodily parts, its white and red blood corpuscles, its essential organs. The individuals barely exist independent of their functions within the termitary. All that matters is the continuation of the body. There is only the greater good. The individuals remember nothing. They're immune to love and loss. Tell me then, Joshua, who's more evolved: the white ant or the individual human?"

Marais glanced up through the yellow light. At the side of the path, a bearded goat tongued at its own tuberous scrota.

"I suppose that depends on what you prize more," Joshua said. "Life without pain, or the ability to love."

* * *

The nights went like this.

Tamaria would spend each supper doting over Marais, asking how he enjoyed her cooking and whether he'd had enough to eat. When she was finally satisfied that he admired her at least a fraction of the amount that she did him, she'd clear the plates from the old farm table while the men drank Gys's homemade wine. Gys was known throughout the Waterberg as the man to see if you had grapes that needed squeezing. To Tamaria's chagrin, this had become the source of many a lewd joke.

After the wine, they'd light their pipes while Tamaria stored what remained of the bread and pie and meat. As the room ripened with the smells of vanilla and creosote, Gys would enumerate the latest casualties of the drought in Waterberg. Springs and rivers had once overrun the southeastern slopes of "Water Mountain," but there had been no rain for four summers now.

"Lost another two pear trees today," Gys said one evening. "In the far orchard near the fox hole." With a nail, Gys fished a shred of meat from between his teeth. "Makes four this week alone. A hundred trees since the drought began."

It was a rotten set of circumstances for a farmer. Each time Marais offered to help, Gys had turned him down with a different excuse. But Marais had begun considering other solutions. "We could divert the river for irrigation," he said. "The elevation difference would work to our advantage. With a few weeks of effort, we could draw enough water here to save Rietfontein and the neighboring farms for at least another season."

Gys looked like a man who'd just entered church only to find the preacher screaming profanities. "Heavens no! I could never do that. This drought is the will of God."

"You believe it's God's will to destroy the countryside?"

"I believe we have no place questioning His intentions or trying to avoid His judgment."

It took all of Marais's will to keep from hurling his pipe against the wall. "That sort of thinking is why we lost our country!"

Gys scowled with his small eyes, his features crowding toward the center of his face. The man didn't take well to insults. "That sort of talk is pig-headed blasphemy."

Marais considered this couple his friends. But they represented everything backward about the Afrikaners, everything that had led to their subjugation by the British. "You'd rather lose the farm than engage basic science to—"

"Hush, both of you!" Tamaria swept in from the kitchen. The apron fastened around her waist was stained dark with water. "I won't tolerate that sort of talk during the lighting."

At the side table she lit five white candles arranged from smallest to largest, one for each child she'd lost in the concentration camps. Thirteen years had passed since the end of the war, but every day, she still hand-dipped her candles, and every night, she lit them, closed her eyes, and recited a prayer under her breath so quietly that Marais couldn't make out the words.

For years now, he had watched Tamaria and Gys scuttle about the farm. He'd seen the smallness of their world and their contentment with that smallness. Everyone needed a crutch to help them through this life. They'd chosen the church as theirs, the church and the small god that watched over it. It was a tiny dioramic life they'd fashioned for themselves, but he envied their serenity.

What he missed most these days was London—yes, the same city that had engineered the Transvaal's destruction. But he missed the vast, wild scope of the place, jammed to bursting with every imaginable sort of person, the feeling of sailing aboard the great ship of the world. Only the small raft of his work held him here. There was a hunger inside him that hadn't been sated for a long time now. He needed distance from these people. He needed to come and go as he pleased without being tied to their table each day.

"I'd like to ask a favor, Tamaria," he said when she'd finished with her prayers. "I want to hire an Indian cook. I'm hoping you wouldn't mind if he shared your kitchen from time to time."

Tamaria's good eye settled on him. "You want to put a coolie in my kitchen?"

"Only to cook occasional meals. I developed a taste for curries in London, and I've long missed the heat and spice and smells."

"The smells!" she cried. "You prefer the smell of coolie 'food' over my sheep's head?"

"Not over. As a complement to. It would only be once in a while."

Gys snorted. "All this talk of coolie food is making my bowels buckle." He pushed himself to standing and lumbered out the back door.

Tamaria pursed her lips and shifted her weight to her left leg. "To anyone else, I'd say no. You know that. Just tell this coolie of yours he'll keep my kitchen spotless or endure a fate worse than the wrath of God: the wrath of Tamaria."

Marais rose and kissed her cheek, which was rough and hot against his face, and it struck him that this might be his chance to secure her help with a more important matter while they were speaking of favors. Months earlier, in a moment of resolve, he'd tied his pouch of morphine to a hunk of granite and pitched it into the springs below the farm. A fever had raged for three days after this, and in a sleepless fit, he dragged himself hot and dripping back to the springs to rectify his mistake. He dove for the bottom, again and again, feeling blindly for the tablets amid the muck and sediment. When he finally pulled himself out, dripping with algae, his hands were empty. Days after the fever receded, he stumbled across a second pouch of tablets hidden in the pages of a notebook in his desk. But by then, he'd broken his addiction, and he left the pouch where he found it. He vowed to resist the temptation for the rest of his days. The fact, though, was he no longer trusted himself. Tamaria was a midwife, without formal training but experienced in dispensing medication. For as long as he could remember, he had been orbiting a terrible darkness. He'd come perilously close to the end too many times. Any lull was only temporary. It was just a matter of time before the darkness grew stronger and sucked him back down. Now, while he was free of the addiction, while he could think clearly and plan for the future, he needed to safeguard his supply.

"One other request if I may?"

Tamaria turned back.

The clock's pendulum tocked left.

He told her about the "medicine," though he didn't name it. He didn't need it now, he said, but there was a small chance that one day, sometime in the future, he might. He explained proper dosages, the precise method for dissolving and injecting. He needed her to safeguard and ration his supply for him. If he ever requested his medicine, it was to be one grain per day on average, that is, two tablets. He must never exceed ten grains, even during a period of intense illness. Even if he pleaded with her. Even if he became agitated. Or violent.

As he told her all this, a peculiar look spread across Tamaria's square face. She chewed her lip and reflected in silence. "Course I'll help you," she said at last. "You're family, Mister Marais."

"It's a rather delicate matter though. I suppose I don't need to ask for your discretion?"

Tamaria turned a slight shade of red. "No," she said, waving him away. "You certainly do not."

Marais retired to the stoepkamer, pleased with these developments. In one fell swoop, he'd extracted both favors. He'd no longer be tethered to their dining room or to Tamaria's constant prying. And her agreement to manage his medication was a giant weight lifted.

He lit his lamp and sat down to write his old friend.

Dear Preller,

I am on a most unusual quest, the beginnings of which I described to you previously. My research into the chacmas has given way to a study of the social insects. The two are more closely related than you might think.

I told you of my findings about the rise of causal memory in higher primates. It has endowed us with the ability to learn, the ability to adapt to non-native environments and to thrive. I can scarcely imagine what sort of environmental crisis hundreds of thousands of years ago led to the sudden development of memory. But it has become abundantly clear to me that we've paid a terrible price to acquire the faculty. We've sacrificed our innate instinct, our inherited environmental knowledge. Transplant a modern child to the desert and he'll die there, unable to find his way out. Our homing instinct has vanished, or more accurately, gone dormant.

Of all living species, humans enjoy the greatest protection from natural selection. But without natural selection, there can be no further evolution. The rise of causal memory has rendered us unable to evolve further. We're seeing this already in the rapid increase in mental diseases. Preller, there is no issue more pressing for the human species. No issue more pressing for me. Either we learn to reverse this process, or we won't be around much longer to slaughter each other in battle.

There was a knock next door at Tamaria's delivery chamber. Marais lifted his pen from the page. The door creaked on it hinges. There were muffled voices, soft footfalls, the groan of floorboards. And then, a woman's cries, guttural like an animal's bleating. Not the coughing fits of grief, but cries of deep physical pain. Tamaria's first patient of the night.

Marais needed to keep writing. He wrapped a sweater over his head to dampen the noise and pulled it tightly over his ears. He tried to picture Preller's towering figure, his thin bristled mustache. He tried to picture anything else. But with each scream, the image that came to his mind was of Tamaria's knuckled fingers, probing the folds of a young woman's sex, working to coax out a head, to pull out a pair of gelatinous shoulders, the pliable arms, the fatty knees, the tiny puckered feet. He couldn't stop thinking of the five children Tamaria and Gys had lost. How could she perform these deliveries night after night? Each birth must only rekindle her own terrible heartache.

Or was that it? Maybe she needed to make sure no more babies would be lost.

How reckless his past behavior seemed to him now: how could he have handed his own baby away when so many others had had theirs snatched from them forcibly? Charles must be twenty years old. He must be a man, passing his days somehow. Whole days. Doing what? Thinking what? It was the first time

Marais could remember wondering what was happening within the boy, and not simply *to* him. According to Sophie, Charles was still in London, enrolled now in university, thinking his own thoughts, living through whole days. His son was in London, the city Marais ached for, the seat of the empire that had decimated this country.

Five years earlier, the two Boer republics—the Transvaal and the Free State—had been unionized along with the Cape colony and Natal. But despite unionization, despite the advent of home rule for Afrikaners, this was British land now—a small sliver of the British empire, a tiny fruit dangling precariously on the far side of the massive imperial tree, a fruit that Britain meant to finish squeezing of all its riches. Marais grasped the pen so tightly it nearly cracked in his hand. He continued his letter to Preller.

I am ready to publish my observations on the above and other matters of the natural world. I will need your help, though, to pull this off. Does the offer still stand to assist an old friend?

Yours truly,
Eugene

P.S. You should understand that I intend to publish my findings in Afrikaans only, although my facility with English is, as you know, considerably greater. I will benefit from your deft editorial touch.

Within days, Preller's reply found its way to Marais's hands.

My Dear Eugene,

In Afrikaans only? You must be joking. You'd be shooting yourself straight in the foot.

Confusedly,
Gustav

Marais had anticipated these words.

Dear Gustav,

To publish in English would be to endorse the language of England, and by extension, British imperialism. If it ever comes to the point where I'm compelled to do such a thing, remind me to take up my old rifle and hang up this life. The Brits have made English and Dutch the official languages of this new "union" with no recognition of Afrikaans. Imposing foreign languages on our nation is as abominable as the atrocities they committed during the war. I will not participate in a movement intended to strip us of our heritage. My research will be a contribution to Afrikaner South Africa alone, not to the rest of this wicked world. For me, it will be Afrikaans or nothing.

Resolutely,
Eugene Marais

Dear Marais,

Just because you choose to write in a language the rest of the wicked world can't read does not mean that the rest of the world ceases to exist. It does not mean that the horrors wrought by England on this country never occurred. Your choice of language does nothing to erase the past. This is not a political statement we're talking about. You've conducted good scientific research. Publish in English, and your work could make its way to Oxford, or Harvard for that matter. For God's sake, share it with the world.

Incredulously,
Gustav Preller

Could his research find a place at Harvard? Increasingly, the New World, even more than England, felt like the proper home for his ideas. The thought of academic fame intrigued him. But not enough to overcome the pride he felt in the strength of his own convictions.

Dear Mr. Preller,

Every act of writing is a political statement. You of all people must know this. I'm awaiting, still, confirmation of your offer to assist.

Impatiently,
Eugene Nielen Marais

Marais,

This is madness. Your family, you may recall, does not even issue from true Boer stock—they were Cape French and Dutch, not Transvaaler. From where does this unbending patriotism arise?

No one is a greater proponent of the Afrikaner cause than I am. But publish only in Afrikaans and you'd be electing to consign yourself to provincial obscurity forever. Besides the Boers, the only people in the world who would be able to read your work are the Dutch, and maybe if you're lucky, the Flemish.

Critically,
Gustav Preller

Preller!

The Flemish? The Flemish? There can't be more than a couple of men in all of Flanders who even know how to read, and I can only hope they won't think to seek out my work. And the Dutch, you well know, ceased long ago to have any concern for our people. The Boers may have issued from them, but we are no longer of them.

Surely, you would agree that there is still a place in this world for a man to invoke principle. There are still matters of greater import than ambition, matters that supersede the base desire for riches or fame.

Self-righteously (and aware of the same),
Advocate Eugene Nielen Marais

Marais!

You are a stubborn mule preparing to cut off your nose to spite that ugly face of yours. This will be the last thing I have to say on the matter: you are making one hell of a mistake.

But as to your request for assistance, what do you expect? You're my friend. You taught me how to edit. You taught me the business of publishing. If this is really what you want, I'll do it. We shall arrange to publish your findings serially.

At my wits end,
Gustav

Marais folded up this last letter and leaned back in his chair. This was it then. At last, he was going to make his discoveries public.

He wrote without stopping, long past the time when the muscles in his hand began to spasm. Tamaria interrupted him twice, first to ask why he'd missed breakfast—was he ill or otherwise indisposed?—and three hours later, to ask why he'd missed lunch. Wasn't he hungry? Did he understand how much work went into preparing each meal? Didn't he care for her potbrood and frikadelle, her tamatie bredie and melktert and malva pudding?

He didn't pause even to answer her. He didn't pause until late in the afternoon when he heard a pelting against his window. At first, he took the sound for rain. But it hadn't rained in months. The veld was mired in drought. The land was turning to desert.

The plinks against the glass grew louder. He lowered his pen and yanked open the curtains.

Joshua was standing a hundred feet away, tossing pebbles at his window.

Marais cracked open the lower sash. "What the hell are you doing out there?"

"I'm sorry, sir. I was trying to reach you." Joshua glanced over his shoulder and lowered his voice. "I'm not permitted in the house."

"What's so important that you have to fire rocks at my window while I'm trying to work?"

"I overheard some men in my village talking—about an ant mound."

Marais closed his notebook and sat down on the sill.

"On the Hanglip plateau," Joshua continued. "Not a normal mound, mind you. 'The height of two adult giraffes,' they said. Sorry for the noise, sir, but I was wondering . . . shall I take you to see it? We could go this weekend."

It wasn't possible. A termite colony forty feet high couldn't sustain itself through such a drought. Termitaries needed water just like any living creature. A forty-foot termitary would require the equivalent of a small lake to support its inhabitants, and the lakes above ground had mostly dried up. To reach sufficient water, the insects would have to dig, instinctively, fifty feet down through dry, packed clay.

"Mister Marais, did you hear what I said? Two giraffes is as tall as the government buildings in Pretoria. Hard to fathom how many insects could live inside a structure that big."

Marais looked up. He surveyed Joshua with his denim coveralls and coarsely woven sunhat and forthright gray eyes.

"We'll go at once," Marais said.

"Sorry?"

"This instant. Without delay. Let's pack immediately."

"But it's near supper time already. The Hanglip range is hours away."

"First thing tomorrow morning then."

"Tomorrow's Thursday, sir. My next day off isn't till Sunday."

The fellow dangles a carrot and snatches it right back? "Joshua, I am not a man who waits until Sunday."

"Mister van Rooyen will need me in the fields. I can't leave him without help."

"I'll take care of Mister van Rooyen. I'll arrange to pay him for your time away."

"But sir—"

"Meet me on the road first thing in the morning. Have the horses inspanned and saddled and all necessary equipment readied. And Joshua . . ."

Joshua couldn't hide his distress. His eyes had turned dark and moist.

"Thank you for the reconnaissance."

They departed Rietfontein before dawn. The road was dark, as if saturated with moisture, but it was only a dusting of dew. Within an hour, the entire countryside was scorched once again.

He and Joshua rode side by side while invisible cocks coughed and crowed. Warblers belted out love songs over the steady clapping of hooves. Bush chickens scampered in front of the horses, darting out of the way just in time to avoid a trampling. Today could yield the great discovery he'd been seeking.

He snapped his sjambok. The horse whinnied, whipped its tail, and gathered speed. The rolling farmland was, miraculously, still fertile despite the drought. It struck him that each moment on the land—every unplanned breath, every sunrise, every spontaneous birth—was a miracle that science couldn't quite explain.

A person could understand the behaviors of nearly every species, the fundamental workings of every process in the natural world, and still fail to grasp the meaning of the larger cosmic concert.

Joshua rode up alongside him, the brim of his hat pulled low over his eyes, canteen slung over his shoulder.

"One day, this place will be overrun," Marais said, darkening once again. "The British will come to milk the land. At the first sign of gold or diamonds, they'll descend upon the countryside like the Great Hordes. Their chimneys will obscure the horizon, smoke plumes will belch into the air. The sound of birds will give way to the roar of stamp mills. Waterberg will no longer belong to us."

"To be honest, sir, that doesn't concern me," Joshua said.

"What's that supposed to mean?"

Joshua pushed his hat above his eyes. "Not to be disrespectful, but this land stopped belonging to my people long ago. We fought alongside you in the war. In places, we lost more men than you did. Seventeen thousand black Africans died in concentration camps alone. And what did we get from this country when Britain finally gave Afrikaners home rule? The Natives' Land Act."

Marais pulled his horse to a stop. No Black man had ever spoken with him of politics before.

Joshua stopped his horse too and wiped his brow. "I'm sorry, sir," he said. "I shouldn't be talking with you like this."

"When you have something to say to me, you should go ahead and say it."

Joshua glanced sidelong at him and told him this story. Until two years earlier, Joshua's brother-in-law had been a sharecropper on a farm in northern Limpopo. He grew maize and almonds, cassava and beans—first for his family, then for profit. The land was fertile, he was a hard worker, and he knew how to plant and care for a crop. After five seasons, he earned enough to buy half a dozen oxen. With the oxen, he earned enough to buy a pair of ploughs. With those ploughs, he earned as much as the white farmers around him.

"When the Land Act passed, the farmer who owned the fields my brother worked told him he couldn't farm for himself anymore. The farmer wanted to keep the harvest, and he needed more workers for his fields. If my brother wished, he could stay on as wage labor. But the wage the farmer offered was nothing compared to what my brother was earning by himself. My brother was told his oxen—the ones he'd saved for and bought with his own money—could be used only to serve the farmer. When my brother argued, the farmer gave him an official-looking notice with a signature no one could read. It said if my brother didn't leave, he'd be returned to a reserve—the seven percent of this country where the Act says we, eighty percent of the people, can own any land. My brother was a proud man, Master Marais. He came from a line of warriors. The farm was his life. He wasn't going to move. It was pointless even to ask him.

"When he disappeared, the authorities told his wife, my sister, that he'd been 'removed.' We looked everywhere. In every prison. On every reserve. We still haven't found him. My sisters and nephews are servants now. Everything was taken from them. South Africa's no place to raise a Black child. That's why I never married."

Joshua looked up, anger flashing in his eyes. "If you're Black in South Africa, you're an optimist—because you know that what *could* happen can't be any worse than what *has* happened. So with all due respect: why would I care if the British control this place?"

Joshua snapped his sjambok. His horse took off at a gallop, leaving Marais squinting through the dust.

Marais had always thought of the Afrikaners—of *his* countrymen—as the underdog, oppressed at the hands of an infinitely more powerful people. But the reverse was just as true, he saw now. Much more so in fact. He'd known this on some level since he was a child. He'd seen it in on the faces of the African farmhands who worked the fields and the African servants who worked the houses of wealthy Afrikaners, and more recently, he'd seen it in the squalor of the reserves. Their land—their freedom—had been ripped from them. In truth, he was no different from the English who had devastated his country.

By the time they reached the Hanglip range, it was mid-afternoon and the horses were panting from the heat. Up ahead, the rocky plateau rose straight up from the earth, glowing a ghostly reddish-white. The sun reflected off the sandstone and made the mountains look translucent, as if they were heated and lit from within.

The serpentine path that wound up to the top of the plateau was cut precariously from the rock face. It followed a series of steep krantzes, twisting up at such sharp angles that on several occasions the horses stopped and refused to proceed any further, and the only thing that could coax them forward was a hard thwack to the hindquarters. The stones underfoot were as large as the skulls of lions and loose enough to be lethal. Once, Marais's horse, having lost its footing, nearly plummeted straight over the edge, rider and all.

At the top of the shelf, Marais called to Joshua to pause so that they could water the horses. The termitary shouldn't be far. They outspanned the animals and unloaded the tools. They unpacked shovels and spades, knives and chisels, buckets and boxes, and arranged them by function on the rocky ground.

Moments later, an unmistakable sound started up. *Tick tick tick.* The sound of white ants, only louder. Much louder.

Marais mounted his horse and listened. The clicking was accelerating.

"Follow me," he called back to Joshua.

"But the equipment?"

"We'll get it later. Come on now!"

The sound was coming from the other side of the shelf, directly across from them, only a thousand feet away. Marais kicked his heels into the mare's sides, and the horse took off, bounding over the bronze-green brush. The closer he got, the louder the sound grew. The clicking turned riotous now. It was a call of alarm.

Marais's heart pounded like hammer to anvil. He'd stumbled upon something new, a natural crisis in a massive termite colony.

"Master Marais!" Joshua shouted from behind. "It's not what you think!"

Marais's horse was galloping now. His vision blurred on both sides. He spurred the horse onward, aiming straight for the noise.

"Careful!" Joshua called. "It's thirteen hundred feet down!"

By the time Marais saw the cliff, the earth falling away in front of him, the edge was just fifty feet ahead, and his horse was racing straight toward it.

Marais tugged on the reins. He tugged so hard that the leather straps cut into his fingers. The horse dug its hooves into the loose dirt but kept sliding toward the edge.

"For Christsake, stop!" Marais cried. He leaned his weight all the way back.

The horse skidded with a grunt, landing three feet from the cliff. Its legs were shaking as violently as his were.

Marais lay with his chest against the horse's back, inhaling the chalky smell of its mane. He couldn't tell whether the pulsing between them was coming from his own heart or the mare's.

The clicking had grown wild. Marais swung himself from the horse and dropped to the ground. He peered over the vertiginous edge.

Directly below the precipice, swarming masses of people—women, children, and men—were diving at each other in an enormous circle, which Marais took at first for some sort of battle zone. In truth, they were dancing. At the center of the circle, dozens of drummers pounded out rhythms. The drums rolled, then built to a syncopated crescendo. They defied any musical time he'd ever heard. As they reached a frenzied pitch, which he thought must surely be the end, they exploded still faster.

The dancers were barefoot, clad in strips of animal skin, and as they danced—bodies whirling, arms and hips thrust in every direction—they seemed to be clicking their tongues. They were shouting at the sky, Marais realized, in clicks. He couldn't pull himself away. The movements were so jarring he could only stand and stare.

Joshua ran to his side. "I thought I was going to lose you there."

"What is this?" Marais said.

"They're dancing for the long life of Modjadji, the rain queen. The sound you heard, sir," Joshua said, trying to hide a smile, "was just my people, praying for a little rain."

Marais shook his head. The drought had persisted for four years already. It wasn't going to abate anytime soon. It didn't matter how quickly they danced or clicked. It didn't matter how rapturously they clung to belief in some god-queen.

But as he stood here, he felt electrified. How would it feel to be a part of something so large, to believe in something so fervently that you could force yourself into a trance, throw your limbs at angles that defied physics?

He sensed in himself a violent hunger. He'd witnessed so many deaths—Lettie, his mother, a thousand innocent Afrikaners. He needed to know that his own life would conclude differently, that it would extend beyond the bookends that marked the start and cessation of consciousness. Maybe if the name he forged for himself—the mark he left—were lasting and grand enough, a part of him would persist after death.

Something flashed at the edge of his sight. On the far side of the plain, a bolt of light gilded the sky. It cut a jagged gash through the clouds and exploded like neon. Marais squeezed his eyes shut, then opened them again. Lightning? He felt plinks of water on his arm. It was impossible—and unmistakable. He let the rain soak his head and face, a million drops floating silently down, each no larger than an ant, but together enough to fill a lakebed.

He didn't know how long he and Joshua stood there, gaping. At some point, the lightning stopped. The last streaks of color faded from the sky.

"We should start back for Rietfontein," he said to Joshua.

"But we haven't reached the mound."

Below them, the dancers whirled even faster.

"That's all right. I've seen enough for today."

* * *

As they approached Rietfontein, the sun was blazing through the leaves of the giant Alhambra. Tall grasses bowed under the weight of yesterday's rain. Fat drops of water clung like rows of ladybugs to the undersides of the blades. Marais could still hear the drumbeats. He could still see the dancers' wild spinning.

Not far from the stoep, an old woolen blanket was crumpled in a heap. It wasn't like Tamaria to leave such a thing in front of his room. She was a neat, meticulous woman. As he drew closer, he saw that the lump was, in fact, a man.

"Arvind, sir," the lump said, jumping to his feet. He was small-boned, short, and darkly complected, his hair thick and oily like the pelt of a beaver.

"Why are you sitting here?" Marais asked.

"Waiting for you, sir."

"Waiting for me? Why?"

"The lady of the house says you're needing Indian cook."

The man's cropped hair shone in the sunlight. Behind him, Marais heard Joshua leading the horses to the stable.

"You know of a good Indian cook, Arvind?" Marais asked.

Arvind widened his eyes. "Yes, myself, sir! Best Indian cook in all of Waterberg." Tamaria had preempted him and selected a cook herself.

"How many Indian cooks would you estimate there are in Waterberg?"

Arvind paused. He seemed to be counting to himself. "About one, sir."

"I guess that would give you a leg up. What about your curries—can you make them hot, the way they serve them in London?"

"Sweat will pour from your cheeks and tears from your eyes," said Arvind, beaming. "Perhaps you would like to hire this cook?"

Marais rubbed his hands together and smiled. "Perhaps I would."

As a courtesy to his hosts, Marais waited until Tamaria and Gys had finished their dinner and retired to their room before letting Arvind into the kitchen to unpack his spices: turmeric and cumin seeds, garam masala and curry leaves, cardamom, coriander, asafoetida, chilies.

Marais left Arvind to cook and returned to his room to document the previous day's events. A feeling gnawed at him, a sense that nothing he did in this world would ever be enough to release himself from his past.

Within an hour, the air in his room was redolent with fried onions and garlic. His eyes began to tear from the hot sting. Hopefully Tamaria and Gys were asleep by now.

He peered into the kitchen. Ghee was sizzling in one pan, dark curries bubbling in two others. Arvind pressed his palms together at his forehead, bowed to a small Buddha statue that he'd placed on the table, and chanted:

Evaṃ me sutaṃ. Ekaṃ samayaṃ Bhagavā Sāvatthiyaṃ viharati Jetavane Anāthapiṇḍikassa ārāme. Atha kho aññatarā devatā Abhikkantāya rattiyā abhikkanta vaṇṇā Kevalakappaṃ Jetavanaṃ obhāsetvā yena Bhagavā tenupasaṅkami, upasaṅkamitvā Bhagavantaṃ abhivādetvā ekamantaṃ aṭṭhāsi. Ekamantaṃ ṭhitā kho sā devatā; Bhagavantaṃ gāthāya ajjhabhāsi . . .

There was a dancing rhythm to the words, a lingering on the dentals that gave rise to strangely syncopated phrasing. "That language," Marais said, "is your native tongue from India?"

Arvind looked up with embarrassment and lowered his hands.

"No, sir, it is Pāli language. The language of Lord Buddha."

"But you're a Hindu, aren't you?"

"I was born that way, sir. Last year in Durban, though, I took refuge in Lord Buddha, along with many others."

"You changed your entire religion?"

Arvind looked at him directly. "Do you know what it means, sir, to be Untouchable? To be shunned by your own people? To know that if your shadow ever touched the food of a high caste lady, her food would be uneatable? When I learned of Lord Buddha's teachings, good Indian teachings, I turned my back on Vishnu—not on Vishnu, but on his people, who had enslaved me. My parents back in India don't understand how I could do such a thing to Vishnu. 'Still you cannot work with other Indians,' they say. 'Still you cannot shop at their stores. You cannot pat the heads of their children or prepare their curries. Then what has changed?' they say. They don't understand. But I will tell you, sir. *Everything* has changed." Arvind pushed the hair out of his eyes. "Sir, I no longer believe that I am nothing. In my mind, I am their equal now."

On the stove, curries steamed and bubbled.

"Sing it again, for me," Marais said. "That song you were chanting."

Arvind looked aghast. "I cannot. My voice is no good."

"I don't care about that. I just want to hear the words."

Arvind hesitated, but he closed his eyes again and began to chant. His voice wavered on each note. The tones skipped and bounced across the room.

"What does it mean?" Marais asked when he'd finished.

"That I don't know, sir. Pāli is monks' business. But it's no matter. These are good blessings, taught by Lord Buddha. Buddhist people have been chanting them for two thousand years."

"And that's enough to keep you reciting them—just believing that your Lord Buddha spoke them, without understanding the least of their meaning?"

Arvind stared at Marais as if he were crazy. "Sir, what more would I need? Look at this world. If you're lucky enough to find something good to believe, you must seize it, *with both hands, sir,* and whatever you do, for as long as you live, you mustn't dare let it go." He glanced at Marais's shoulder, and a curious look passed over his face. "Your arm, sir, it's shaking."

Marais hadn't noticed until now. The trembling had returned. He shifted sideways to conceal his arm from view. "I haven't been taking my medicine. Sometimes this causes my arm to shake a bit."

Arvind peered at him. "What type of medicine?"

Marais hesitated. "It's similar to the opium you have in your country."

Arvind dropped some dried leaves into one pan, sprinkled red and yellow powders into another, and stirred thoughtfully. "That's something I can get for you. Only if you need it, of course."

Marais clenched his fist and tried to quell the trembling in his arm. He felt that ache rising again, the hunger gnawing away at him.

"My uncle can pack it in ghee," Arvind continued. "He will ship it to us from India. Very good quality, sir. But not cheap."

Marais thought of Tamaria's hand-dipped candles, the smallness in which she and Gys had enshrouded themselves, and the god that they'd elected to rule over all that smallness. He thought of the dancers who would dance forever if their one small queen would make it rain, and he thought of how he himself had no such support. A creature without troop or tribe or termitary was defenseless against the violence of nature. His one defense, all he'd ever had, were his small white tablets. These were his sacrament. But there were so few remaining, just the one felt pouch that he'd asked Tamaria to secure for him. Everyone needed something to survive. He was no different from the rest of the human species. He had no reason to deprive himself.

"*Ja*," he said. "Go ahead. Place me an order."

February 1936, Port Elizabeth, Union of South Africa

Thirty yards away, the coastline fans out under a sky of lumpen clouds. Cobalt waves lick gently at rows of blue-green stones.

Charles rubs his eyes, adjusting to the daylight. Algoa Bay. On some level, he didn't expect to make it this far. Not after that storm on the Atlantic. Not after the riot in Cape Town. He stretches his arms toward the sky. He drinks in the salty air.

A dozen crested birds circle overhead, scouting for breakfast. In a single coordinated motion, they plunge into the glassy water, then bob to the surface with a catch of sardines. The little fish flash and flop and bow their musculature. Charles wonders if they recognize this as the final moment of their existence—if there's an instant of blinding clarity, as they're squeezed down their captors' beaks, when they think to themselves, "This is it. This is it!" Just before the end, they grow still, as if resigned to their fate, as if nature has shown some unexpected mercy and inoculated them against the pain of that final crush of bone and flesh.

Hannah is dressing in the cabin below. There's a rustle of sheets, the growl of a zipper, the sandpapery sounds of her shoes. She clambers up the rungs of the rickety ladder, pokes her head into daylight, climbs onto the deck. She kisses his cheek. "Where are we?"

"Craziest thing," he says. "It seems we've hit Cape Cod by mistake."

"Don't even joke!"

He points to the coast. "Hannah Tauber, Port Elizabeth. Port Elizabeth, Hannah Tauber."

Her eyes glitter in the yellow light. "So we're here then? Promised land, take two?"

They've moored at the western end of the harbor, not far from the commercial center of Port Elizabeth where fisherman with blood-drenched aprons heave sections of marlin and tuna from deck to dock.

"It almost seems too easy, right?" he says.

"Easy is not exactly the word I'd use."

On the shore in his slicker and rubber boots, Joshua is negotiating with an Indian man who squats on the bumper of a rusted truck, sucking on a cigarette and rubbing his bare belly. Minutes later, Joshua nods decisively. The Indian pulls a wad of bills from his lungi, counts them out one at a time, and hands the stack to Joshua, who counts the bills twice more before pocketing the money and nearly skipping back to the boat.

"Morning you two," he hollers with a smile that shows off his wooden teeth. "I've got good news: I sold my crays *and* got us a ride to Pretoria. It'll take me a few minutes to clear out the crates, but as soon as I'm done, we can be on our way."

On the lip of the shore, lapping waves are tongues softly clicking. Two white herons sand *S*-shaped necks together. *Tomorrow,* Charles thinks, *I'll be back in the village where I was born.*

With a grunt, Joshua hauls a pair of rectangular crates into his arms and starts for the dock.

Charles crouches down and lifts two more crates himself.

"Oh, please, sir," Joshua cries, alarmed at receiving assistance from a white man and a professor to boot. "There's no need to trouble yourself. I can manage just fine."

"It's no trouble," Charles says, waving him away. *You saved our lives,* he thinks. *It's the least I can do.*

Joshua looks gravely concerned, but he doesn't protest. "At least take care of your hands then—keep far away from the gaps in those crates. The cray's pinch is nasty, and I don't want Eugene Marais's son losing a finger."

The crates are heavier than they look. Charles steadies the pair in his arms, sidles carefully over the gunwale, and finds the dock with his foot. Timbers sigh under his sea-weary legs.

Inside the crates, creatures lurch, shells knock, claws snap.

Land lies just ahead, this time without a welcoming mob. North of the sea, past the saline, seaweed stink, Charles thinks he smells home. The thought of Pretoria—of reuniting with Sophie, his aunt and Godmother—melts his fatigue. On his next trip, he loads himself up with four more crates.

The truck coughs and sputters northward along the road to Pretoria. The Indian at the wheel chain-smokes as he maneuvers the vehicle around rocks the size of sheep, cattle napping in the middle of the road, barefoot women with baskets of guavas balanced on their heads.

The ride is long and dusty, but in the afternoon, the sun splinters the cloud cover. Gold light splashes through the windows and across their laps. Further inland, the smells of the ocean yield to piney odors of bush and clay. They stop once to refuel, twice for food, three times for bladder relief, and four to repair punctured tires. After weeks on the water, this isn't a bad way to spend twenty-four hours. The difficult part is the waiting. Charles stifles the urge to ask the driver to go faster.

Pretoria rises out of nowhere. Cranes clang, steam shovels roar and hiss. Glimmering new government buildings sculpt the skyline. The driver motors them through swarms of chauffeured automobiles and exhaust-belching delivery trucks and a thousand zagging bicyclists. The whole city heaves like a waking animal. The church is still here, the old bank, the train station. But this city bears little resemblance to the village that Charles remembers. It's as if he's entered a foreign country.

Something else that's different: nailed to every fifth jacaranda are posters advertising the next meeting of the Pretoria chapter of the Greyshirts—the same group that assaulted their shipmates in Cape Town. Everyone, the signs say, is encouraged to bring a dish to share.

Lovely, thinks Charles. Tea, pastries, and afternoon target practice at South African Jews. For the hundredth time in the past two days, he prays to a god in whom he doesn't believe. *Lord, please let Leo and his family be safe.*

Charles tries diverting Hannah's attention to other sites—the Old Council Chamber, the minareted Kruger Street synagogue, the church that Sophie insisted Charles attend every Sunday of his childhood, although the eighty-year-old minister stank like rotting fish.

The paper in his hand contains Sophie's last-known address. He wields it like a compass. After he left for London, thirty years ago, Sophie sold the home where he and his cousins had grown up and moved further east. As they near her cottage now, he tries to conjure her face—the rigid jawline, waves of brown hair clipped into a taut bun, the fiery blue eyes that told her charges never to *think* of messing with her.

But the picture in his head is three decades old. He hasn't stayed in touch the way he should have. During his first two years in London, he wrote her daily out of a sense of longing and a need to stay connected to the woman who raised him. For the next five, he wrote weekly, detailing his academic accomplishments and exaggerated feats of bravery, secretly hunting for praise. The letters he sent in his late teens grew more distant as his feelings of obligation faded. Over time, the stream of letters petered and fizzled. He aged, graduated, became a man. But his vision of Sophie didn't change with him—it grew more fixed, as if his memories were hewn from stone. How many years has it been since he last wrote or heard from her?

Just past a convent school, the truck makes a hard right. Charles counts the house numbers. Fifteen, twenty-three, thirty-seven. He directs the driver to the seventh house on the left. The man downshifts, revs over a fallen tree branch, and launches them abruptly into the driveway.

A stand of untrimmed cypresses occludes the property. As the truck veers along the path, Charles gradually makes out the profile of a small, two-story structure choking with vines.

Faded blue paint is peeling off the siding in strips. The wooden shutters are worn and cracked. Planter boxes are home to shriveled stalks of dead flowers. A blanket of dried leaves conceals a bench swing and rocker on the sagging, wrap-around stoep. The entire place is marked by neglect.

The Indian flicks a cigarette butt out the window. "Okay to leave you here?" he asks. A two-legged dog blinks at the truck with boredom, then turns and tugs itself toward the street, dragging its rump through the dirt.

When Charles doesn't respond to the driver, Hannah answers for him. "Yes, this will be just fine." She leans across Charles's lap. She punches open the door.

Charles steps down from the truck and slides out their bags. Hannah and Joshua jump down after him. The driver grinds into reverse and begins backing out toward the road.

"Is this definitely the right place?" Joshua asks.

Charles double-checks the address, scans the crumbling property again. Maybe Sophie has died? He doesn't want to follow this line of thought.

"Only one way to know for sure," says Hannah. She takes Charles's hand and brings his palm to her lips. "If she's still in this world, she's going to be so pleased to see you."

"From what your daddy used to say about his siblings," says Joshua, "that might mean greeting us with a knife instead of a shotgun."

"Sophie never cared for surprises," says Charles. Only now does it dawn on him that he should have telegrammed ahead. She might even have a phone by now—he could drive into town and call her, ask when she'd like to receive visitors. Or if.

"I don't care how strict she used to be," says Hannah. "This is one surprise she's not going to mind. You're her son for all practical purposes."

Her son? Sophie never thought of him like that. Not as far as he knew anyway. She housed him because he was dropped on her. Because she had no choice. The memory emboldens him. What does he have to lose? He runs his hands over his wrinkled trousers, straightens his tie and collar. He treads up the leaf-strewn walkway and climbs the rickety stairs.

Fleas feast on a small, brown cat that's curled into a ball in the corner of the stoep.

Charles lifts the wooden door knocker. He lets it clack twice against the stopper.

Wind drags softly over the stoep, rattling the shudders.

No one answers the door. They must have the wrong house after all. He is flooded, unexpectedly, with relief.

As he turns to leave, the top half of the wooden door swings open. An old woman stands there, spine hunched like a parenthesis. White ringlets range down her fissured cheeks. The woman blinks dumbly at Charles. Surely, this can't be her.

"Horses in the stable. Cows in the barn. Thank you very much," she says and moves to close the door.

She thinks he's a farmhand. "Are you Sophie Ueckerman by chance?"

Through the cracked door, the woman's pupils dilate. "I don't know you."

The rattle of the truck's engine trails off to the west and vanishes. Their driver is gone.

Charles tries again, more slowly this time. "We're looking for Mrs. Sophie Ueckerman."

"*Ch!* I said I don't know you. Go on now, get along with the animals."

Charles can't tell whether she's actually heard him. "Can. You. Tell. Me. If. So-phie Ueck-er-man. Lives. In. This. House?"

The cat coils itself around his leg. It purrs in rasping spurts.

"I don't know what you're hoping to achieve here, young man," the woman huffs. "And frankly, your tone is discourteous. If you won't leave by yourself, I'll have to call the lady of the house."

"That would be wonderful. Is she available now?"

The old woman cocks her head, and drop-jawed, gapes back at him. "The lady of the house is too old for such proposals, young man. She'd not make a suitable wife for you or any other man. And you've not even met her in any case, so you're getting very much ahead of yourself."

Behind him, Hannah chokes back a laugh.

"That's not what I meant, of course," Charles says, uncertain now whether she is mad or witty. "We'd just like to speak with her."

"I can't let strangers in. And even if I could, we don't have anything to offer guests. Our girl hasn't brought the shopping. She only comes once a week, which is as much as we can afford these days. The world has grown so dear."

"We'll happily meet her right here on the stoep," Charles suggests.

The woman shakes her head. "We're only going around in circles now." She turns to Hannah and lowers her voice. "Perhaps you could help explain to him?"

Hannah gives Charles a look that says, *Let me try.* "Can you please tell us the name of the lady of the house?"

At this, the old woman brightens. "That is the first sensible question I've heard all day."

Yesterday's rain drips from the eaves and licks at the black dirt.

"Wonderful," says Hannah. They stand there, watching the woman, awaiting the name.

The woman's peach-like smile slowly dissolves. "I think you asked me a question, dear. But I can't seem to remember what it was."

"Maybe we should continue on, sir," Joshua says under his breath.

"You're right," says Charles. There's nothing to be gained by wasting more time here. "Thank you, ma'am," he says. "Sorry to have bothered."

"That makes two of us," the woman replies. She moves to close the door.

"Madam!" a voice calls from behind them. A young African woman scampers frantically up the stairs. "Look at yourself!" She drops a pair of sacks on the stoep. Eggs, coffee beans, potatoes, and cheese tumble onto the grimy floorboards. She takes the hem of the old woman's dress in her hands. "Same clothes you had on a week ago. And no bath either?"

"Don't you fuss over me," the old woman scolds, yanking back her dress. "Not in front of guests!"

The feral cat sniffs the cheese. It swipes a black tongue along the moldy rind.

"We're looking for Sophie Ueckerman," Hannah says.

The young woman, aproned in starch white, turns guardedly. "*You* know Madam Sophie?"

"This is Charles, her nephew," Hannah says.

The young woman looks him over. "Master Charles Marais? Madam Sophie's Charles?"

"I'd be grateful if you could tell us her new address."

"Sir, there's no new address." She gestures toward the doorway. "Don't you recognize your own mother?"

Charles turns back to the old woman. Her dress hangs off a gaunt shoulder, exposing sharp, angular bones. The hem is spattered with brown and yellow grease. Her arms and legs are switch-thin.

"You know this fellow, Annie?" the woman asks the maid.

Charles knows the voice that pours from the old woman's white lips, but there's little resemblance between this tiny woman and the picture etched in his memory. It's as if *his* Sophie has been swallowed up whole.

"Madam Sophie!" the maid says, her astonishment increasing. "Come closer. It's Charles. I know him from your photos. Get a good look now! *Feast* your eyes."

"That can't be, Annie." Charles's aunt squints at him, struggling to make sense of the man in front of her.

A wave of sadness overtakes him. "Hold on a second." He drops to his knees and roots through his bag. It takes a few moments to locate the magnifying glass, the one that Marais gave him thirty years ago before leaving for Waterberg, when Charles was ten years old. Thirty years before that, Sophie had told him when he was a boy, she'd given this same magnifying glass to her little brother, Eugene Nielen Marais, for his insect studies. The initials ENM are still engraved into the beveled handle.

"Do you remember this?" he asks.

Sophie stares at the magnifying glass as if waiting for it to perform a miracle. She takes it from him, rubs her fingers over the scratched surface. She brings the glass to her nose and inhales the wood. The lines in her face soften.

She gazes up at him. Cataracts blur her gray-green eyes. "Charles?"

"It's me, Auntie."

"The same name as my young boy."

A swallow swoops from an unseen roof nest.

Charles turns to Hannah. "I don't think I can do this."

"Hold on," Hannah whispers. "Give her time."

Sophie's knuckled fingers comb nervously through her hair. "Sometimes I wonder if the world is playing tricks on me."

"Please, Auntie. It's me—Charles. I'm the same person."

She looks up at him again. He sees wonder breaking through her cloudy eyes. She reaches for him, pulls him close, embraces him fiercely. Her breath seeps into his shirt. "I didn't expect you back so soon, my sweet baby."

His eyes sting. He feels ribs where her breasts should be. It's been thirty years since he was last home.

"I've been telling her," says Annie, once Charles's aunt has relinquished her grip and gone inside the house, "she needs a live-in girl. Or at least I could help her two, three days a week. She doesn't have enough money to pay me, she says, she's just living on what remains from the boarding house she ran. I've been telling her I don't care about money. I'm not afraid of hard work. 'To live like a queen, you need to work like a slave,' my mother told me. The doctor says her heart is even worse than her head. She's all alone. She's old and sick. It's not right. She *needs* me."

"God, I wish we'd known," Hannah says to Charles. She doesn't mean to accuse him of negligence. She doesn't need to. He's already leveled the charge against himself.

"I'm sorry, Mister Charles," Annie says. "A boy shouldn't have to see his mother like this."

"Sophie's not my mother actually. She's my aunt."

Annie cocks her head. "Truly? That's something. She always says you're her favorite, she's closer to you than the others. She always calls you her son."

Charles doesn't know what to do with this information. For the duration of his childhood, he remembers being little more than Sophie's house guest. He assumed she opened her home to him out of obligation because no one else would. But Annie has no reason to lie. Did he somehow change his aunt into someone she never was? Has his anger at Marais colored the present so richly that he's woven false memories around her?

"Enough talking, all of you. Come inside," Sophie calls from the doorway. She's put on a fresh, coral-pink dress and looks markedly more lucid. The change in his aunt startles Charles as much as her initial appearance did earlier. "We'll get you fed and make up the two bedrooms. You can stay as long as you like."

"That's all right," he says. "We don't want to burden you. We'll find a place nearby."

"Don't be ridiculous. Grab your bag—it's too heavy for an old woman—and come inside this instant."

"I don't want to impose on you, Auntie."

"Nonsense."

It's clear he's not going to be able to turn down the invitation. He glances at Hannah, who nods enthusiastically, then at Joshua, who waits ten paces from the stoep, tracing a figure eight with his shoe in the blue-black dirt. "Do you have space in the house for a third?" Charles asks her. "Joshua will need a bed too."

"I knew your youngest brother, ma'am," Joshua says shyly.

Sophie looks incredulous. "Space for him *inside* the house?"

"Where else would he sleep?" says Charles.

"You *have* been away a long time, dear," she says. "Imagine what the neighbors would say."

"We're traveling together," Charles insists. "We're not turning our friend away."

"We have room in the outbuilding," Annie says. "I'll show him where to put his things."

"Much appreciated," says Joshua.

Charles starts to protest. Joshua holds up his hand. "Things here are as they are—and how they always will be."

* * *

The frayed curtains in Sophie's house are drawn across the windows like bandages. It takes time for Charles's eyes to adjust to the dimness. Dusty artifacts litter a side table—a chessboard, an empty vase, a family of four elephants sculpted from pine and arranged by size from head to tail. Charles runs his fingers along the edges of each object. He's only just arrived, but already he's hunting for clues. Where is Marais?

From the parlor, he can see Sophie hunched over a square table in the kitchen, sifting flour into a squat wooden bowl. She hums to herself as she beats eggs with a fork, then whisks in milk and cider vinegar.

"I need your help," Sophie says to Annie. "We'll cook what we have on hand."

Hannah asks several times for permission to enter the kitchen so she can assist, but her requests are met with increasingly vociferous rejections. The last time Sophie nearly snarls at her. "You are my *guests*! Go away now."

Annie sets a copper pan and cast-iron kettle on the hot stove, then hurries into the room, arms piled high. On the table, she arranges dried rusks with jams, halved pears, and strips of cured biltong. The oil in the pan sizzles and smokes.

Sophie ladles out a syrupy batter and lets the pannekoek form and bubble. She flips the first pancake, then sprinkles sugar and cinnamon over the surface with shamanic intensity. When it's perfect, she rolls the cake into a tube and plates it.

"Pannekoek was Charles's favorite." She arranges the pancake perfectly in front of Hannah.

Charles's stomach rumbles at the sweet, long-forgotten smells. How does she remember this detail when she's forgotten so many others?

"Well, now it's my favorite too," Hannah says.

Sophie's smile swells. She forks a pancake onto Charles's plate and another onto Hannah's. "You wouldn't believe how handsome Charles was as a young man. Smart as sin and so polite."

Charles laughs. "That is completely untrue."

"His only failing is he was painfully shy of girls."

"You don't say?" says Hannah.

Sophie looks at her quizzically. "I'm sorry, dear. I've forgotten what we were talking about."

"How shy Charles was around girls . . ."

"Yes, yes, the year he turned ten—you must remember this, dear—we had a little blond neighbor who was a year or two older than you, but whose top-half was already impressively developed and who had somehow learned to swing her bottom in a manner befitting a twenty-year-old woman on her wedding night. Any time poor Charles saw this girl approach—on his way to school, returning from the market—do you know what he'd do? Dive head-first into the bushes."

"He would not!" Hannah exclaims.

"Oh yes, he would. The unfortunate thing was, at the time, all the bushes for a hundred yards on either side of our home were roses. Do you like roses, dear? I kept the most lovely Spanish roses at that house. As you might imagine, they did not make suitable diving places for shy boys."

"It pains me just listening to this," Charles says.

"Not as much as it pained him *then*. I can't tell you, dear," she says to Hannah, "how many afternoons I spent pulling prickers from this boy's neck and backside. The thing was, I didn't mind any of that trouble." Sophie locks eyes with Charles. "Because you were my *boy*."

He feels blood burning up his cheeks.

"Tell more," Hannah urges. "What didn't he like as a child?"

Sophie considers the question. "Oh, he positively *hated* having to go to bed. From the time he was born until he left for London, he came up with every possible excuse to keep me from snuffing out the light—requesting one last drink of water, saying he needed to relieve himself for the twelfth time, asking charming questions about the origins of the universe. There was only one reliable way that I found to coax him to sleep. Every night, I tucked him in, snuggled up next to him, and sang until his eyes sank closed. I always sang the same song. Maybe you still remember, Charles?" She draws a deep breath and begins to croon:

> *"My Sarie Marais is so ver van my hart,*
> *Maar ek hoop om haar weer te sien.*
> *Sy het in die wyk van die Mooirivier gewoon,*
> *Nog voor die oorlog het begin."*

The second verse reverberates inside the little house, and something begins to unravel inside Charles. By the time she finishes and returns to the first verse, he's a child once again, years before London, decades before Harvard.

"It was popular back then," she says, "though the words changed a bit after the war. You remember, don't you, dear? *Everything* changed in those camps."

The mention of the camps breaks the spell. "We were lucky to make it out alive," he says. "I don't think we would have if it weren't for the fairy godmother we had there."

Sophie cocks her head. "Fairy godmother?"

Didn't she remember? "The woman in the camp. She bribed one of the young guards to give us extra water. Every night she slipped him a few coins—I saw it myself. The next day the soldier would bring us the water, and sometimes even slices of fruit."

Sophie starts to smile. Then she starts to laugh. "That wasn't a fairy, Charles. That was me. Your *actual* godmother."

Charles struggles to revive the memory of the strange woman lurking in the shadows behind their bell tent. Who else would have watched out for him like that? Of course it was Sophie. She *was* his godmother. He embraces her once again. "You saved my life."

"Perhaps."

"And you sang me to sleep every night, before and after?"

"Nearly every one."

"There was one night you didn't, though," he says. "A night Oom Eugene attempted to put me to bed." He didn't intend to broach the subject of Marais so soon. "He was about to leave for Waterberg. It was the only time he'd ever set foot in my bedroom. He didn't know he was supposed to sing to me, I guess, and I was too shy to request it of him. I was scared in the dark, and he didn't know how to comfort me. The one time he tried to act like a father . . ."

Sophie's brow pinches. "Don't talk like that. Do you know what your father did for this country? And for you? I'll tell you one thing: he has made himself utterly sick. I can't even keep track of his whereabouts anymore."

Her face turns suddenly pale. The tendons in her neck tighten and cable. Before Charles can react, she calls, "Annie!"

Annie darts into the room. Her hands are caked with flour. "Are you ready, Madam? *Ja*, you are." She lifts Sophie by the arms. She walks her to the stairs.

Annie turns back to Charles and Hannah. "It's her bedtime now. Been a long day. She needs rest. Don't worry, the morning is always better."

Above them, Annie speaks to his aunt with a soft lyrical cadence. In the kitchen, water drips into the sink precisely every three and a half seconds. Charles touches the frayed stitching in the armchair's upholstery.

"Poor thing," says Hannah.

"If I'd stayed in touch," he says, "I would have known about her condition ages ago. I could have helped before it got so bad."

"Don't start down that road. It won't help anything."

She's right, he thinks. *They're only thoughts—they're barely more than nothing.* And yet, the more he thinks them, the more they spin and swell.

"She's wonderful when she's lucid," Hannah says.

"She's not at all as I remembered her."

A line comes to him from an ancient Buddhist text: Even if you were to carry your parents on your shoulders for a hundred years, even if you were to let them urinate and defecate upon you for all that time, still you would not repay the debt you owe them for taking care of you as a child. Sophie is part of the reason he has returned to South Africa. He didn't fully know it until now. He owes her much more than he realized. There are debts still to pay.

* * *

For the next two weeks, as Marais waits somewhere deep in this country with his own demands, Charles doesn't leave Sophie's side, except when he's sure that she's safely asleep and out of harm's way. In the mornings, he seats her in a pillowed armchair on the stoep, while he sands down layers of peeling paint, or turns the dried soil in her garden beds, or sweeps away the leaves, or mows, or hauls, or hammers.

When he takes her for walks downtown and across the river, with afternoon light streaking through the jacarandas, she clutches to his arm for balance. She holds on tightly as if at any moment the whole world might fall away, taking the roads and trees, flowers and rocks with it. Her heart is weak. The doctor confirmed this. "Your aunt is dying," he said. But the longer Charles stays the more determined he becomes. The more he aches to help her.

Late one night, he visits Hannah in the small bedroom that Sophie assigned her. She lies on a narrow cot in only a night shirt, a book in her hands.

"Are you accepting visitors?" he asks.

Hannah looks up and smiles. She folds the book on her lap. "Only one."

Charles tries to squeeze onto the cot beside her. He shifts his weight to the side but winds up tipping the whole thing over. Hannah can't stop laughing.

"How wonderfully Victorian," she says. "Separate, single beds. And you said the British didn't do anything good for this country."

"Clearly I underestimated British contributions. I mean, what's sexier than being forcibly separated from your lover?"

Hannah looks him squarely in the eye. "Charles Marais, did you just call me what I think you did?"

"British?"

"*Lover*, you wretch!" She pulls Charles on top of her. When her head hits the pillow, it releases a blizzard of down.

"What if I did?" he says, gazing at her.

Her hands unbutton his shirt, trace rings around his navel, cup his nipples. Charles slips under the sheets. He clenches his teeth to keep the mattress from squeaking. "We have to be quiet. Really really quiet," he says. "I'm serious. No noise at all—"

Hannah bites down on the lobe of his ear. "I can't promise that."

Thus have I heard.

January 1916, Waterberg, Union of South Africa

Marais sat at his desk fingering a small brown package postmarked *Krishnagiri, Madras Presidency, India.* It was the sixth shipment he'd received in the past year, and it smelled of newsprint and curry and something more fungal. He unknotted the twine and peeled back the paper. The packaging had retained its shape perfectly during the long trip from southern India to Waterberg. With a swipe of his letter opener, Marais dispatched the leaf in which the goods were wrapped. He observed the acceleration of his heart, the tightening of his scalp, the speed with which liquid pooled in his mouth. Classic Pavlovian responses.

The ghee was a creamy-yellow, thick like butter. Marais carved off three inches all around, scraped away the top layer, and set the ghee aside. Arvind could use it for the evening's meal. What remained was a small black prism that looked like tar and smelled of mushrooms and fennel. Pure opium from the subcontinent. A beautiful specimen. With a set of tweezers, Marais lifted the nugget. He inspected it in the light. *The earth is a maker of miracles. It provides everything a man needs.*

For six months, he hadn't requested any of the medicine that Tamaria had secured in her safe for emergencies. As far as she knew, he wasn't using morphine at all these days. The truth was he'd quadrupled his daily dosage thanks to his guardian angel in India.

There were disadvantages to this arrangement, of course. Marais's savings had nearly run out. His income from doctoring rarely covered the sum he owed Arvind at the beginning of each month, let alone the cost of food, books, and writing supplies. But good fortune ran in multiples. When the sheriff of Waterberg retired, the town council had approached Marais. He was one of the few Boers on the veld with more than a secondary education. Who better to assume the part-time job of sheriff? Marais had needed extra income, and he jumped at the chance.

Afternoon light poured through the curtains now and painted his room a dusky orange. In the kitchen, Tamaria was humming a tune that reminded him of a song his mother used to sing when he was ill as a child and needed cheering.

He dropped the opium nugget into a glass beaker. He measured out the necessary alcohol, and lit a lamp to heat it. When the solution reached the proper temperature, he'd filter it, removing the alcohol from the filtrate, then combine the resulting residue with an aqueous solution extracted through the addition of benzene. A few adjustments to the pH, and voilà. A month's supply of high-grade morphine could be precipitated and recovered in a matter of hours.

He left the opium solution simmering, flipped open his notebook, and took up his pen. He was nearly halfway through the treatise on chacmas that he'd been planning for so many years.

With respect to the origins of the human mind, the acquisition of "causal memory"—the unique capacity to conjure the past in the present and to learn from each preceding moment—is only a recent evolutionary adaptation. Like physiological traits, the fully developed memory faculty has arisen in the highest primates as a protective device, increasing our chances of survival in the face of nature's unceasing violence. Without memory, we could never have produced languages or literatures. We'd never have learned to engineer vehicles or skyscrapers or firearms. We'd never have learned to teach others to take these storehouses of learning and advance them.

But we have paid dearly to acquire this new faculty: "phyletic memory"—our inborn, animal instinct—has been all but buried as a result. Millions of years of our animal past have been submerged into our unconscious.

One can't help but lie sleepless at night thinking of the consequences. We've been liberated from bondage to our environment—now we can adapt to virtually any environmental condition. And yet, causal memory keeps the human psyche chained to recollections of past events, and to the emotional winds and vagaries of the human heart. We pat ourselves on the back, we feast on the illusion of freedom, when we are, at best, prisoners of war in the grand battle of evolution. Here we remain, consigned to squander our mere seventy or eighty years on this planet, dashing in circles, around and around, like dogs roped unwittingly to the fat stump of a tree.

A loud knocking severed his train of thought. Marais glanced at the beaker and then at the door, which fortunately he'd had the good sense to lock.

"I'm indisposed at present," he called. "Leave me alone."

"You have a visitor at the front door, Mister Marais." Tamaria's voice was strained.

"Any visitor to the front door should be able to read the sign I posted there," he called. Here he was constructing his grand oeuvre and trying his damnedest to produce a month's supply of decent quality morphine, and his neighbors couldn't heed a simple sign. "Remind them that I no longer accept unannounced visitors at this or any other time of day."

"Mister Marais, it's—" she paused as if considering her choice of words, "your young girl."

Marais set down his pen.

Jane.

With his thumb and forefinger, he snuffed out the lamp's flame. He pulled the sheet from his bed and threw it over the beakers and burners that were splayed across the table. There was a mortar in the drawer of his desk that he kept filled with mint leaves and fragments of cinnamon stick for such occasions, and he took it out now and ground forcefully at the contents with a wooden pestle to mask the odor wafting through the room.

Tamaria had made it clear without saying as much that she didn't approve of his associating with Jane. She was gracious enough to proffer her aspersions only when Jane was out of earshot, but the sentiment was always the same. "Such a sweet thing, and stupid as a dove," she'd say. "That girl is less than half your age." And then there were the ominously inflected warnings: "Watch how you comport yourself with that bird—people are beginning to talk."

"What do you think I'm doing with her?" he asked Tamaria once.

"I don't want to think about what you're . . . *doing* with her. A woman like me doesn't need to entertain such nasty thoughts."

"Then why don't you stop entertaining them," he'd replied.

He brushed out the wrinkles from his shirt, threw on his coat, and unlocked the door.

Tamaria poked her head into the room. Her mustache had thickened with summer. Her good eye toured over the walls. "What's that smell?"

"A cologne I've been experimenting with. I'm happy to share the recipe if Gys would like to try it."

"Ha! I'm lucky if I can get that man to bathe once a month." Tamaria twisted up her nose. "Speaking of Gys, it's almost noon and I haven't started on his dinner yet." She began treading down the hallway in her wooden shoes, then chided over her shoulder, "I will not have that girl inside my home. Any 'business' the two of you need to attend to will take place outside."

Jane was waiting on the front stoep in a yellow sundress. A wicker basket dangled from her arm. When she saw him, she pushed her hair over her ear and smiled. The air around her smelled sweet like talcum.

"You don't have an appointment today," Marais said.

"Do I always need to arrange in advance just to visit you?"

"You never have before. But today I have a very full day of work. I'll be lucky to get a few hours of sleep."

"Even a man as busy as Eugene Marais needs some spontaneity from time to time. "And I," she pronounced triumphantly, hitching the cloth cover off the basket, "have brought cakes."

Jane was a local girl, the daughter of a widower with a cleft lip who seemed to be in perennial competition with Gys and the rest of the Boers in Waterberg for the title of most frugal farmer. Her mother had been raped and killed while Jane's father was fighting the British. At seven years old, Jane had taken off across the burning veld in search of food. She'd wandered alone for months. After the war, her father returned and rebuilt the farm, but he was never the same. Jane had described in elaborate detail how unexpectedly his mood could change. She had shown Marais the cigar-sized lesions on her forearms. Welts the width of a belt strap decorated her legs and back.

"Why are you here?" he asked her, though he knew the answer already.

When she met his eyes, her cheeks flushed. "I want to be mesmerized, Eugene."

"It's been three times already this week. And it's called hypnotism, what I do. Mesmerism—and all that animal magnetism nonsense—is just pseudoscience." He'd been experimenting with hypnosis, according to instructions documented by Charcot, and Jane had proven herself the perfect subject. She was healthy, willing, neurotic, and susceptible. Not to mention lovely. But four afternoons in one week? The burner was still hot in his room. He thought he could smell the solution all the way out here. He needed to finish precipitating the morphine this morning. If anything happened to that solution before he finished, well, he wasn't sure what he would do.

"I have to get back to work."

"I want to lose myself again. I want to be lost, and I want you to find me, like you always do. I can't bear to be stuck in that dingy farmhouse with an angry old man who will whip me if he finds out that I've been to visit you."

Marais touched her arm. Through her sleeve he felt the subtle flexing of her muscle. He wondered if she'd pull back, if this was too intimate, standing here in broad daylight on Tamaria's stoep with his hand on her arm. But she met his eyes and held his gaze.

"Hypnosis is not a narcotic," he said. "It's not intended to pacify or tranquilize."

"Well, it calms me. And what's so wrong with wanting to forget the world for a bit?"

Jane's lips were the color of raspberries, and Marais had a sudden urge to taste them. More than once, he'd considered asking her to marry him. He'd even allowed himself to think of a ring—it would be small, simple, with a single bright stone, much less elaborate than the first ring he'd purchased many years ago. He thought that he might marry Jane, not because he loved her—he didn't—but in order to jolt himself. After Lettie's death, he'd vowed never to marry again. No woman would ever rival Lettie in wits or beauty, so what would be the point? But it had been twenty years now and Lettie wasn't coming back. Wasn't there something to be said for maturing, for changing one's mind? Today, however, there were more pressing matters than hypnosis or marriage.

Jane moved herself closer until the tips of her shoes touched his. "Surely your work could be postponed for an hour or two." She reached up to adjust his tie, and her fingers lingered on the knot. Her perfume was floral and musky.

The morphine could wait for a little while. He could use the company. "I don't have time for a full session. How about a walk instead?"

She looped her hand over his elbow. "If that's the best offer I'm going to get today, I suppose I'd better take it."

The veld was hot and brittle. They hiked along a rutted path that threaded over the koppies, then descended into sloping fields full of wildflowers and honeybees. In the middle of the path, a black-shelled beetle raced along on its hind legs, proudly rolling a ball of animal dung, as if the small steaming orb were a work of art that it had miraculously stumbled upon.

As they walked, Jane spoke of trails she'd discovered, her favorite streams, childhood hiding places. Marais nodded while making mental notes about the locations of certain duiker and klipspringer herds that he'd been tracking. A hundred yards away, Joshua was preparing one of Gys's fields for planting. He had on boots and overalls but no shirt. As he bent down to turn over a shovel full of dirt, beads of sweat on his chest and back glistened like jewels. He saw Marais and nodded just slightly from beneath his slanted hat. Joshua had always been discreet about Marais's visitors. Jane prattled on without noticing.

The late-afternoon heat blazed. Marais stopped so they could rest in the shade of a yellow wood tree. He offered Jane his canteen. She took a long, slow drink.

"Can I see your badge?" she asked, returning the canteen to him.

Marais fished the bronze medallion from his pocket.

She turned it over in her palm, fingering the coat of arms. "Who would have guessed that one day I'd be hiking through Rietfontein with the sheriff of Waterberg?"

"Or that I'd find myself alone with the prettiest girl in all the Transvaal," said Marais.

"I most certainly am not!" she scolded, but he could see her delight. As she studied the badge in her hand, something changed in her face, the flicker of a new thought. "Have you ever killed a man with that gun of yours, Sheriff?"

The question took him aback. "No," he lied.

"What if a person dear to you were threatened with physical harm? Would you ever take a man's life?"

Did she want to know the truth? Did she want him to reveal the thoughts that circled whenever his dark mood descended, thoughts that were arising these days with increasing frequency? "If I awake one morning sufficiently discontent with the world," he said, "on that day, perhaps I'll take my own."

Jane looked to see if he was jesting with her. When she saw he wasn't, her jaw stiffened and her face turned pale and she said, "I don't like those sorts of jokes, Eugene," and she tramped off along the path.

Only now did it dawn on him that she was talking about her father. How terrified she must be of him. Marais winced at his own blind selfishness. He ran to catch up with her. He reached for her hand.

"You're the smartest man I've ever known," she said, brushing him away. "Which is why I'm always surprised that you can act like such a child."

Did he deserve the charge? Probably. He never should have broached the subject. He hadn't meant to tell her about his dark mood, about the darkness that sometimes completely overtook him, leaving him unable to bathe or eat or sleep. It was at its worst in the evenings—the sadness of twilight, he called it. But he had his medicine and he was fighting it as best he could.

"Our evolutionary ancestors had millions of years to mature. Humans are barely infants by comparison. How can we be expected to act like anything *but* children when that's exactly what we are in the evolutionary order of things. Maybe you could be a little patient today with this particular child?"

Jane rolled her eyes at Marais. "I suppose I can try." She rocked onto her toes and kissed him on the cheek.

By the time he remembered his morphine solution again, the sun had dipped into the horizon and turned the air purple. The sky looked like a fresh bruise. It was too late to send Jane hiking home through the veld and too early to re-enter the house. Tamaria and Gys would be at the dinner table already, and Marais wasn't in the mood to call attention to his companion. Instead, he rolled out a blanket on the grass. He and Jane lay on their backs, shoulder to shoulder, eating cakes and gazing up at the dome of the sky. As the night turned darker, Marais showed her the constellations—Taurus, Perseus, Orion, the Pleiades star cluster, Gemini, Eridanus, Cetus, Canis Major. Jane took his other hand. She held it to her chest.

"To the left of Canis Major," he said, without acknowledging the way her fingers were threading through his own, "is the Queen of England. Follow her scepter down to the wide sweep of her hips and you'll see that she's wearing only her knickers, which is something that no decent South African should ever have to see."

Jane laughed, kicked his leg, and pulled herself closer. The oil in the heat lamp must have burned up hours ago. The morphine would be fine until morning.

Somewhere along the line, he fell asleep.

It was his wedding night again, his first night with Lettie. The guests had finally left, and Marais and his beautiful bride were alone, together, in the little bedroom in Lynnwood House. Lettie snuffed out the paraffin lamp. She lit a pair of candles on the bureau. Her shadow swayed along the wall. Marais untied his shoes. He unbuttoned his shirt. He reclined on the bed with his back against the headboard.

Outside, mosquitoes swarmed and droned.

Lettie shimmied up next to the bed, so close that her hair swept against his arm, and undressed for him. She peeled off one garment at a time—gloves, petticoat, garters, the silk stockings she'd ordered from London just for the occasion. She moved slowly, the way that smoke can spiral and dance. He could barely stand to watch and wait. He reached for her arm, but she gave him a mischievous smile and shook her head. "No touching," she whispered. "Not yet." The more he craved her, the more delighted she seemed.

With all but her undergarments strewn across the floor, she climbed onto the bed. She knelt above him, straddled his waist. Her smell made him wild. She brought her fingers to the top of her corset. One by one, she unfastened the metal hooks without taking her eyes from his. He heard the click as each clasp released. He wanted to taste her. This would be his first time.

As she released the final clasp, though, a strange thought overtook him. This craving in his body, the desire that hardened him and made him salivate, was no different from the newborn's urge to suckle. It was the same evolutionary urge that had kept the world moving forward for billions of years—the urge to make new life. It was not *his* urge at all. Not his desire. He and Lettie were biology's pawns. Nature was working *through* him. They were, it occurred to Marais, just another pair of animals.

But he saw the way she smiled at him. How she looked into him with her astonishing brown eyes. She could have chosen anyone, but she'd selected *him* from among every other man on earth. When he thought about it this way, none of the rest seemed to matter. So what if biology was manipulating them for its own larger purposes? Evolution could wait.

He pulled her onto his chest. Her skin was hot against his own, hotter than he'd imagined. He dug his fingers into her backside. She didn't take her eyes from his. She didn't let them close.

His eyes snapped open. His heart was hammering. It had been twenty years already, and still the memory of Lettie was affixed to him like a cancer.

The first traces of light were bleeding over the eastern horizon. He was spooning Jane. His arm was wrapped over her breast, fingers wedged beneath her shoulder, his knees tucked into the backs of her own, and everything—the grass, the rocks, their hair, skin, and clothing—was blanketed with a light film of dew.

He kissed her eyes. Her lids fluttered open. "We need to get you home."

"Later," she groaned and squeezed her eyes closed again.

"Now. Before your father goes mad with worry."

"It's too late to keep him from going mad. I'm in for a beating the moment I walk through the door."

"Then I'll come with you. He wouldn't dare lift a finger in front of me."

She sat up and shook her head firmly. "I can fight my own battles, thank you."

Marais watched her hurry through the veld toward her father's farm with her basket and wrinkled sundress. As the path turned, a lock of hair came loose. It flashed in the yellow light beneath her wide-brimmed hat. Marais tried to preserve the image. He had a strange feeling that he might not see her again.

His stomach rumbled. In the past twenty-four hours, all he'd had were a few bites of cake. Still, he couldn't recall when he'd last felt this sort of grinding in his belly, the yearning to be filled. He glanced at his watch. Nearly eight o'clock already. Arvind would be putting the final touches on breakfast. These days Arvind was preparing Marais's meals five days a week, which had enabled him to untether himself from Tamaria.

He found Arvind in the kitchen maneuvering around the stove like an eight-armed god. A trio of copper pots bubbled with oil. The counter was heaped with plates of fragrant rice and the treasures of a South Indian feast: idlis, chutneys—tomato, onion, and coconut, vadais dipped in sambar, vadais soaked in curd.

"You're early, sir."

Marais glanced again at his watch. "I'm right on time."

Arvind gestured with an elbow toward the grandfather clock, which Gys had built as a wedding gift to Tamaria. "The clock says I have thirty minutes still before you arrive for breakfast."

"The hands on that clock stopped moving three years ago."

Arvind clicked his tongue twice. "In that case, I am very late. Come: have some tea and ulunda vadai while you wait."

Marais poured himself a cup. He picked out one of the deep-fried pastries and sank his teeth in, unleashing the familiar bite of ground, fermented black lentils. Flavors of chili, cumin, and coriander mingled in his mouth.

Arvind removed the pans from the heat. He wiped the grease from his face with his apron. "We have some bad news, sir."

Marais swallowed the last bite of vadai. "News is rarely all bad."

"This is all bad news, sir."

"Let's not discuss it then." He'd hired Arvind to deal with the cooking. He didn't need to know the details of which farmers were raising prices, which spices were becoming difficult to procure. His hunger surprised him. He hadn't felt this sort of ravenousness in months. He grabbed another vadai, dipped it in the onion chutney, and began mentally walking through the next chapter he'd planned for the book in which he investigated the chacmas' susceptibility to addiction, beginning with grain alcohol.

"My uncle, the one who sends the ghee each month along with your medicine, he is in trouble."

"What sort of trouble is he in?"

"He is in jail, sir."

"He can't be in jail."

"He is very much in jail."

Marais was having trouble stitching these pieces together. The potential implications were manifold. "Then what will we do about my medicine?"

Arvind peered at him. "Sir, my uncle is in jail for helping you. His life may be in danger. He has children who may not see him for a very long time. Tomorrow I leave for India to see if I can help him. I know nothing about your medicine."

The ringing in Marais's ears reminded him of the clatter of Turkish cymbals that he'd heard played by dervishes in London. It took three more vadais and two idlis smothered in chutney for the news to settle: He'd lost both his cook and the supplier of his morphine. This was just a temporary setback, though, he told himself. Arvind would return as soon as the matter with his uncle had been cleared up, perhaps within a couple of weeks. Until then, Marais could cook for himself. He had plenty of morphine left, easily a month's cache from the batch of opium he'd begun distilling yesterday. A month would be enough time to locate another supplier. In the meantime, he'd be busy with his medical practice, his sheriffing, and the book. Nothing was more important than completing that book.

Marais grasped his arm to quell the trembling. He would need a generous dose to reset him for the day.

* * *

As he approached his room, he could tell something was wrong. The bedroom door, which he always left shut and locked securely with the deadbolt, was gaping, propped open with a wooden dowel. A strong breeze struck him in the face as he stepped inside. The windows were all thrown open. The tang of bleach was so strong and disorienting that it took several seconds before he recognized Tamaria crouched on her knees, scouring the floor of his room with a fistful of rags.

"What are you doing in here?" he demanded.

Tamaria wiped her hands with the rags, which were black with dirt. "This room was long overdue for a good scrubbing. You were out so early today, I thought I'd surprise you."

The equipment he'd safeguarded under a sheet had been moved. The table was completely bare. Nearly every item—beakers, burners, flasks, measuring instruments—had been emptied and cleaned and set to dry on a rack in the corner. Water still dripped from the mouths of the beakers. Where was his opium?

Panic set in. It started as a buzzing in his feet, then shot up through his trunk and into his neck, infecting his nose, burning through his eyelids.

"No need to thank me, Mister Marais," said Tamaria. "This is my gift to you. It's what friends do—we appreciate each other."

"What have you done with my experiment?"

"Oh, that horrid potion? It was stinking up the whole house. I discarded it for you. Poured it right into the dirt around my rosebushes. They tend to like that sort of thing."

She shot him a look with her good eye and smiled too broadly, and he knew now that she'd done this on purpose. She was getting back at him, teaching him a lesson for courting a girl who was thirty-five years younger than she was and more beautiful than she'd ever been. She was teaching him a lesson about the consequences of neglect.

"Get out!" he shouted.

"You forget, Mister Marais, this is my house."

"You will leave my room, and you will never enter again without my permission. Do you understand?"

Tamaria shrank back. "That's what I get for my service, is it? Ugly threats? Thanklessness? And I've made myself late for church. From now on, you can clean your own room." She backed herself out the door, watching to make sure he didn't lunge at her. The patch of floor that she'd been scrubbing shone in the morning light. Marais shoved his dresser firmly under the knob. He drew the blinds and barricaded himself inside the room.

He was supposed to have completed the distillation process yesterday. The plan had been carefully crafted to ensure an uninterrupted supply of his medicine. He'd placed the order with plenty of time for the package to be freighted from Krishnagiri across the Indian Ocean, transported through the neck of the Mozambican channel to Durban, then conveyed by train to Pretoria, and by ox wagon from one town to the next until it reached him in Waterberg. He'd received the package several days earlier, exactly as planned, with ample time to distill the new product before his previous month's supply ran out. And then, unexpectedly, Jane had arrived. It was not the plan that had failed. It was the execution.

Jesus, how he needed his plug! Just a single shot of relief.

His eyes ravaged the walls, scanning his maps and skulls and notes. He pounded on the hideous old desk that Gys had built. And then, a thought occurred to him: maybe some of last month's supply still remained.

He yanked the drawers from his desk and dumped them over one by one. He dropped to his knees and clawed his way through rodent traps and monocles, poetry books and yards of rope, tweezers, bird cages, South African maps, stacks of his draft manuscripts, and desiccated specimens from dozens of fruiting trees. He searched blindly for a single white tablet. There were dictionaries, rulers, a pair of steel balances, and thirty oil-stained index cards that he'd swiped more than fifteen years ago from a legal library in London. But there was nothing to blunt the yawing hunger that tore through his body. "For God's sake!" he shouted. "Is there really nothing left?"

A white mouse scurried between the desk legs. It disappeared under the door.

Then he remembered. For months Tamaria had kept his emergency supply stashed in the safe outside her bedroom. He couldn't ask for it himself now, not in light of their argument. But the medicine was his—she'd kept it for him for precisely such an occasion. There was no reason he shouldn't avail himself of his own medication in his time of need. He was not in the business of breaking and entering though. He needed to preserve his reputation. He needed to gain access to his medications while still maintaining his position, unsullied, in this household. Any man in good health whose hands were not trembling could easily procure the tablets for him.

"Joshua!" he shouted, stumbling to his feet. He tore the curtains from his window. Gray, silted light gushed into his eyes. He threw open the sash and jumped out, barefoot. He bolted through the gardens, clods of dirt catching between his toes. "Joshua!"

Joshua was bent over, cutting a trench in the field with a reed hat pulled low over his eyes. His trousers were rolled up to his knees, his lower legs disappearing into the soil. The entire back of his white shirt was stained dark. When he spotted Marais gunning toward him, he rose gingerly and mopped his eyes with his sleeve. He stared at Marais's legs.

"You're bleeding, sir."

Marais looked down and saw the rose thorns stuck in his ankles and the strings of blood running down his feet. "I need your help."

Joshua dropped the hoe. He wiped his hands on his trousers and hurried over to the wooden fence that separated them. His face glistened with sweat. "I have no bandages for your feet, sir, but you're welcome to my shirt."

"Never mind my feet!" said Marais. When he caught his breath, he explained his predicament in the most objective, disinterested terms he could rope together. He was afflicted with a certain illness, he said. He'd run out of medication and needed to procure his supply from Tamaria, who'd been holding it for him.

"She's a fine woman," Joshua said consolingly. "I'm sure she's kept it safe."

"Mrs. van Rooyen bears a grudge against me."

Joshua looked instantly wary. "I'm sure she'll be happy to hand over your medicine."

"I need to get it without her involvement." He stared unblinking at Joshua to make sure the man understood him. "Or knowledge."

Joshua shifted his weight to his left foot and swallowed. "What is it you need from me, sir?"

Marais pulled his hands from his pockets. He held them above the fence post. The day was breezeless, but his hands shook wildly. "I'd do it myself but as you can see, I'm not currently . . . capable. Which is why I require that medicine. I'll pay you of course." He said this calmly. But his heart was hammering like a stamp mill.

Joshua mulled over Marais's words. He wiped again at the sweat cascading down his cheeks. "Mister Marais, the van Rooyens wouldn't take well to a field hand rummaging around inside their house and helping himself to their property."

"It's my property," Marais corrected.

"I don't mean disrespect, sir. But a person like me could get into a mound of trouble."

"I told you already, I will pay for your trouble."

"Sir," Joshua said, avoiding his eyes, "I couldn't accept payment for a job like that."

Marais's temper flared. He'd been a friend to this man since the day they first met, nine years ago. "How many times have I treated your sister's gout without pay?"

Joshua bit down on his lip. "Sir, if the van Rooyens caught me breaking into their safe, they'd have me thrown in jail."

"I'm the sheriff, for Christsake! Do you really think I'd let that happen? This is an easy job. In and out. It's Sunday. They're still at church, which will be followed by church lunch and all the endless tedium that church lunch entails. The van Rooyens will be gone for hours."

"If they lock me away, I couldn't earn money for my mother or sister. They depend on that money for food. Men like me have been known to disappear once in jail."

Marais clutched his hands under the pits of his arms. "Let me be clear. I need your help. This is an urgent medical matter. If you can't bring yourself to assist me at a time like this—" Then what? What would he do? He'd never intended to say such a thing, to direct threats at Joshua, but what choice did he have?

He lowered his voice. "You'll do me this one small favor, or this will be the last day you set foot on this farm."

Joshua looked as if he'd been struck. He lowered his eyes. He stared at the earth he'd been tilling. "May I . . . ?" His voice was lost with the shrieks of olive thrush diving from the nearby trees.

"Speak up!" Marais said impatiently. "I can't hear what you're saying."

Joshua's eyes were moist. His lip barely quivered. He didn't look directly at Marais. "I asked if I can have the key, sir."

"I've gone to elaborate lengths to study that safe. There's a thin layer of sheet metal nailed over a wooden frame with a lock so rudimentary it could be picked by a child. Grab a hairpin from Tamaria's room and you'll pop it open in seconds."

Joshua squinted his eyes. "You want me to steal a pin from Mrs. van Rooyen's bedroom? And then pick her safe to steal her medicine?"

"*My* medicine! *Ja*, and I want you to do it without another word. You'll be rewarded richly in heaven. Now go!"

* * *

Marais uprooted a patch of Tamaria's yellow roses scrabbling back through his open window. He curled up on his bed and pulled the quilt tightly around his neck, unable to stanch the shivering.

The moments grew long. Unbearably long. It felt as if he were chained on his back beneath a leaking spigot, and every few seconds a drop of water would release from the tap, float through the air, and fall between his eyes. What became increasingly unbearable was not the sudden splash or the sharp shots of cold or the gradual erosion of skin, but the gap between the drops, the distended, ticking pause that hovered between each set.

As Marais lay in his bed, his heart thrumming at three times its normal speed, he heard the tromp of horses. The creak of wheels cutting through dirt. Gys's desiccated drawl. Hours earlier than normal. Gys and Tamaria led the most vulgarly routinized lives, lives marked and blotted by each day's mindless sequence of habits. But for this one day, they had changed their routine.

He wanted to warn Joshua. He wanted to tell him to run while he still could. But he couldn't risk shouting. And he couldn't untangle himself from the quilt and wrestle the dresser away from the doorknob in time to alert him to the impending danger.

On the other side of the door, Gys's baritone boomed down the hall. "What's this?"

Marais froze where he lay.

"In our house? Picking our safe?"

"Heavens!" Tamaria cried. "Is he . . . robbing us?"

"It's not what you think, ma'am," Joshua pleaded. "I was only trying to help—"

"Gys, for goodness sake, do something!"

"Oh I *will* do something!" Gys roared.

There was a nauseating sound now. The hump of fist hitting face bone. Once, twice, a third time.

"Mister Marais!" Joshua cried.

"It's always the same with the dark ones," Gys grunted. "There's a reason the Lord painted them black. He was marking them as a warning to the rest of us."

Other sounds followed, more sickening than the first. The thudding of a boot into chest bone. Sharp puffs of lost breath.

Marais pounded his head into his pillow.

"You're lucky it's the Lord's day," Tamaria hissed. "Next time we lay eyes on you, we'll have you hanged."

Marais couldn't hear anything that followed except the roaring in his own head. Saliva leaked down his chin.

"Joshua!" he called. He got to his feet and tried to force the dresser from the wall. He would burst into the hallway and put a stop to this. Joshua was a good man. *He* was a good man. There was a buzzing in the room now, a wicked violent buzzing. He tripped, and as the furniture whirled around him, his head smashed against the floor.

He awoke to dust motes swarming inside cones of blue moonlight that streaked in. His clothing was soaked with sweat. He extracted the cotton plugs from his ears. The only sounds were the screeching of crickets, and down the hallway, Gys's raucous snoring.

Marais tumbled out of bed. He lit the table lamp. The room turned dreamlike in the musty glow. The floor was littered with dung and ash and the detritus of a million experiments that had spilled from the drawers of his desk. The whole room was redolent with the stink of formaldehyde and animal urine. What had he been doing here for the past nine years? What had happened to him? This was, it occurred to him, the room of a madman.

The pill case in his pocket was empty. He thought about the lousy business of rationing and tossed the wretched thing on the floor.

With one hand steadying the other, he took out a pen and paper and wrote the one person he'd never thought to ask for help, his son Charles. The boy would be twenty-one soon. He'd be preparing to graduate from university in England. Marais needed a nurse, now more than ever. He needed a family. Just for a short time, until he could straighten himself out. He would never concede this aloud, but on paper, within the narrow confines of a private epistle, admissions were simpler. He blew on the paper to dry it. He folded it in thirds. He stuffed it in an envelope and tucked it in his shirt. As soon as he found Charles's address in London, he would mail the letter to his son.

As he tried to stand again, his stomach roiled with nausea. He tripped over a jar that housed a six-inch, short-tailed rodent whose genus he couldn't recall now. His legs buckled under a fit of coughing. He'd never make it to morning without another dose. There was no choice. He'd have to get the medicine himself.

Still on his knees, he plucked out a slender screwdriver from the debris of his desk. He shoved his weight against the dresser. Its legs gouged lesions in the floor, but he budged it enough that the door had freedom to swing and he to exit.

The hallway was lightless. He crawled warily, feeling along the baseboard, to avoid tripping and because he knew he couldn't remain on his feet even if he wanted to. The tang of roasted sheep wafted in from the kitchen. Gys's snoring grew louder, more textured.

Halfway down the hall, something cut into his kneecap. A vicious pain erupted, and he clamped a hand over his mouth to keep himself from screaming. With his other hand, he reached down and pried out two small, sharp nuggets—nails that Gys had carelessly dropped on the floor. As he looked more closely, he saw what he actually held: a pair of white teeth. Joshua's. Bits of pink flesh still clung to the long roots. He grasped the wall to steady himself. When his stomach settled, he stowed the teeth in his pocket.

The safe sat like an idol in an alcove at the end of the hallway. Despite the trembling in his fingers, he managed to coax the screwdriver into the lock. He turned it left, then right, then back again. Over and over until something popped. The door clicked open. Was it really this easy in the end? Why in God's name had he demanded that Joshua help him? Had Marais done his own dirty work, Joshua would have remained unharmed. He would have remained *here*.

A pale light washed over the safe.

"Mister Marais!"

His neck turned cold. "Tante Maria," he said, struggling to his feet.

Tamaria held a tallow candle balanced on a saucer. She squinted from Marais to the safe and back again. The flame danced shadows up her neck, over her square chin, along her faint mustache.

"Do you know what time it is?" she asked.

Marais wiped his leaking mouth. He combed his hands through his hair and hid them behind his back. "I was looking for my medicine."

Tamaria's lips parted. "Now, now, you've already had plenty of that for one week. I've been watching. It's too late at night for such silly conversations. Let's get you back to bed."

She reached for his shoulder, but he shook her violently away. "Don't make me beg," he said.

Tamaria's eyes narrowed into slits. "Mister Marais, do I look to you like a woman who breaks her promises? I told you I'd keep that medicine safe from you."

"*For* me! You were supposed to keep it safe *for* me." Bile rose in his throat and burst through his nose, and he erupted again in a fit of coughing.

"Nothing good comes from nighttime arguments," Tamaria said. "Now get some rest and we'll discuss it in the morning." She placed the candle on top of the safe, took a key from a chain on her neck, and started to lock the safe's small door.

Had he been another man, he could have blamed what followed on his own bad fortune, or the alignment of the constellations, on his diet or chance or karma or the devil. The truth was only that it was dark, and shadows made the curl of her lip look sinister, and he was not himself. Nor was it his voice that raged, "That goddamn medicine belongs to me!" Nor were they his knuckles that struck first the candle, knocking it to the floor and extinguishing the flame, and then her cheek, which drove her headfirst across the hallway and into a wall.

"Oh, Mister Marais," she whispered from the floor. In the darkness, her eyes glowed like tiny fires. "Look what you've done."

His hands dug ferociously inside the black hollow of the safe. He felt buttons and earrings, a pair of brooches, a stack of bills. And then, a felt pouch whose mouth he tore open. The medicine was still here, all of it, easily two dozen tablets. He clutched the pouch to his chest and raced past Tamaria, right past her bedroom where Gys's snoring had grown volcanic.

He spilled out into the night where Orion had risen with his arrow drawn, and he footed his way through the garden's wet grass, past the giant Alhambra whose clusters of berries swung heavily in the midnight breeze, until he stumbled onto the dry rutted road. That's when he started to run. Pebbles lacerated the soles of his feet. But he felt only a stinging numbness.

In his pocket, he fingered Joshua's two sharp teeth. Bones severed from the body of his one true friend.

What have I done?

He could never return to Rietfontein. Never again would he lay eyes on the mountains of Waterberg. His life was drenched with loss. It was the morphine. It had darkened him, he could see that now. He'd been deluding himself for decades. All it had done was enable him to heap one great lie onto another, to string one year to the next, and entangle himself in the threads. It was the morphine that had kept him from becoming the man he'd intended to be. It was the morphine that had kept him from becoming the father that Lettie had asked him to become.

Only now did he realize: he'd forgotten the letter to Charles.

March 1936, Pretoria, Union of South Africa

Charles drifts toward the kitchen. If he keeps focused on his feet, he thinks, on the sensations, he'll quiet his mind enough to be able to sleep, at least for a bit. He slides noiselessly from one room to the next. He watches as if from a great distance while each room reveals the outlines of its features. The whole house is asleep. Carpets supine, pillows curled up, kitchen drawers tucked in.

At the far side of the dining room is a plain door made of wooden planks varnished and glued together. Sophie's linen closet. Which she keeps locked. Always. A skeleton key protrudes like an index finger from its door.

Charles steps back. Why would you lock a linen closet? It's odd, even for Sophie.

He twists the key. The deadbolt clicks. The knob whines deafeningly when he turns it.

As his eyes adjust, he finds himself in a cavernous chamber, twice the size of the living room. Floor-to-ceiling shelves are crammed tightly with books. A Persian carpet squares out the center of the floor. A rocking chair rests like an apparition next to a large wooden desk. The surface of the desk is clear except for a table lamp that casts a rusty circular glow when he snaps it on.

Shelves on one side of the room are packed with British poetry—Coleridge and Wordsworth, Keats, Blake, and Shelley, and the odd Italian and Irishman. Volumes of Plato, Aristotle, and the Greek playwrights fill the shelves on the opposite side next to Hegel, Marx, Darwin, and Freud.

Four heavy drawers hang from either end of the desk. One by one, Charles pulls them open. Inside are empty inkwells, glass vials, maps of every region of South Africa, lenses and screws from microscopes, cast-metal sorts for typesetting, sketchbooks, rolled up canvases, and bottle after bottle of what seem to be samples of fur and dried animal feces. He turns one item over in his hands—glass, paper, steel—then moves on to the next.

The final drawer sticks, as if it's been glued shut. Charles yanks hard on the handle. On the second try, the drawer comes loose from its tracks. It lands with a crack on the floor. Loud enough to wake the house. He considers stuffing everything back and making a run for it, slipping out before Sophie discovers that he's trespassed. But the desire to stay is magnetic.

From this last drawer he unearths half a dozen issues of *Die Burger* and *Huisgenoot* advertising groundbreaking research on white ants. He pulls out a dozen leather-bound notebooks and a single sealed envelope. He thumbs his way through the notes. The scrawled writing is outlandish. No margins or white space. The characters are so small, so tightly packed, the pages resemble an Indic manuscript. Words run together in lines. Lines run together in one great spaceless jumble. Charles strains to make sense of the swirls. He decodes certain words and phrases but without any context: *chacma*, *kloof*, *termitary*, *evolution*, *memory*, *unconscious*, *will come to ruin*.

He tears into the envelope. Inside, a single sheet of paper, twice folded. The letter is dated one month ago.

Dear Sister,

Please keep these notes safe as you have kindly done with the rest of my belongings. They represent half a lifetime's work. I am increasingly unable to care properly for anything, including myself.

Fondly,
Eugene

Marais is still alive. At least he was a month ago.

Charles inhales the letter's moist, woody odor. He hasn't mentioned Marais's name since his first day in the house when he criticized the old man and Sophie nearly hit him. He doesn't want to risk upsetting her again. For two weeks, he's waited, patiently tending to her. But barely a moment has passed when he hasn't wondered about Marais. He'll need Marais's help to work through all these notes.

His eyes sweep over the envelope. The return address is in "Pelindaba." In the bottom drawer he locates a map of the Transvaal, which he unrolls and spreads across the desk. He runs his forefinger over the paper, hunting for towns that begin with P: *Potspruit. Potgietersrust. Paardeplaats.* His eyes scan westward. *Pelindaba.* Eighteen miles west of Pretoria. No more than an hour's ride.

The entire world seems compressed into one short radius linking this house with Marais.

He'll pack up tonight. First thing in the morning, he, Hannah, and Joshua will hire a car. Joshua has waited as patiently as Charles has. Each day the lobsterman has taken his meals on the rear stoep, or in the outbuilding when it rains, waiting to track down Marais.

Tomorrow, thinks Charles, *we will.* After so many years and so many miles, all those threads of self-pity and rage that have twisted up inside him into thick, fibrous strands feel as if they're on the verge of snapping. He is going to find his father.

He'll have Marais walk him step by step through these field notes. Assuming Marais has told him the truth, Charles will have his own publisher put Marais's findings in print for the whole world to see. He'll defang Harvard's project once and for all.

He swipes the letter and notebooks, exits the library, shuts the door carefully behind him. The room disappears into unlikelihood. He polishes the door handle with his sleeve, scrubs away all trace of his entry as if he's committed a crime.

The first hints of gray-blue light seep through the curtains. Tomorrow is only hours away.

"So you're the one making all the noise."

Charles spins around. Hannah stands barefoot in a nightgown, her right sole propped on the inside of her left leg, hair tousled into a nest. She rubs an eye with her knuckle.

"I didn't mean to wake you," Charles says.

She yawns extravagantly. "There was a lot of banging. I thought maybe you were making something for me. Like a barn."

"Hannah, I've found him."

"Who?"

"*Him*. Marais."

Her eyes swell. "Where?"

"Less than an hour from here by car."

"How did you ever . . . ? Never mind. I'll take care of your auntie. You and Joshua must go—first thing in the morning!"

Blood beats in his veins. "No, not without you."

"Don't be silly. For the first half of this trip, you did everything you could to *lose* me."

"Not now. I need all the troops I can muster."

Hannah takes his hand in hers. "Then we'll ask Annie to stay. She's already offered. She'll do a wonderful job."

Yes, he thinks, *she will.* Tomorrow he is going to face Marais after all. At the thought of seeing the man, his fight instinct is fully awakened. "It's strange," he says. "A part of me feels like I need to repay him for all the pain he's caused me. It's as if there's a second person inside me, someone who can't stop thinking about revenge."

"He'll be an old man by now," Hannah says in a low voice. "He's ill. He needs your help. Revenge isn't what you want."

"It may not be what *I* want," says Charles. "But this other guy sure seems interested."

Thin shreds of purple light drift through the hallway window.

"Your father wasn't the first person to abandon his child, Charles. Think about Prince Siddhārtha, for god's sake. Have you forgotten his fetter?"

The word hits Charles like a fist. The name Siddhārtha gave his own son: Rāhula. *Fetter*. When his wife gave birth to their little boy, Siddhārtha called the child his fetter. He worried that his tiny, needy newborn would keep him from accomplishing what he needed to do. So he left the baby behind. He abandoned him and moved to the forest in search of an end to suffering. That's what it took, apparently, to fully understand the mind. Was this any different from what Marais did to him?

"Revenge isn't going to magically expel the memory that your father abandoned you," Hannah says. "It would only make the memory stronger. It would only make you think more. It's like a frog caught in the throat of a hawk. It can't be squeezed down. It can't be coughed out. So you've gone on like this for forty years, barely able to breathe. There's only one way to release that sort of memory. You must know that."

When Charles shuts his eyes, he sees tiny flashing spots. "Well, what is it?"

"You need to find your father and *tell* him."

"Tell him what? What should I tell him?"

Her voice breaks into a whisper. "That you forgive him."

Outside, cocks crow like sick coyotes.

"You can't possibly expect me to do that?" he says hoarsely.

Hannah wraps her arms around his waist. She pulls her body close to his. "You'll find a way, my dear Rāhula. I'll be there to help."

He feels his knees buckling. Despite himself, he begins to cry. He doesn't sound like a Harvard professor of ancient Indic languages who almost got tenure. He sounds like a child, and no matter how much she tightens her grip on him, he can't make himself stop weeping.

* * *

Charles waits restlessly at the edge of the stoep, staring at the driveway through bright morning sun. He couldn't have logged more than an hour of sleep, but he doesn't feel tired. Joshua sweeps yesterday's leaves from the walkway. Hannah is putting the finishing touches on the hedges with a set of dull pruning shears. She hums happily to herself.

Annie appears in the front doorway, towel in one hand, watering can in the other. "I called you a car," she says. She's barely able to contain her grin. Charles had worried that she might say no when he asked if she'd move in with Sophie and work full-time in their absence. Instead, she hugged him. "I'm good at my job," she said, beaming.

It's barely nine, and the morning is already alive and brimming with heat. The sun blazes like a fresh yolk. Any moment the car will be here. "I must get your mother dressed before you leave," says Annie. "Your auntie, I mean. She'll kill me if she can't say goodbye."

Guilt caroms fleetingly inside him. *Annie will care for her better than I could,* he tells himself. And he and Hannah will be back soon. Two days at most.

Joshua dabs at his forehead. "Your father's really just eighteen miles from here?"

Charles doesn't want to admit to breaking and entering, even to Joshua. "I think so. I found a letter with his return address."

Joshua takes a seat on his bag. "I can't believe it," he says. "All these years I pictured him still up there in Waterberg. This will sound silly, but sometimes, when I have a big decision in front of me, before I go to sleep, I ask your father for advice. After I left the farm, I wandered for months. Eventually, the road led me to the sea. A fisherman saw how thin I'd grown and took pity on me. He offered me a wage to help on his boat. When he died suddenly without kin, I had a choice to make: return to land or make a life on that boat. Your father was the smartest man I've ever known. 'What would you do, Mr. Marais?' I asked the question in my head and waited for him to answer. And he did. I always pictured him still on the veld way up there at Rietfontein. I suppose because that's the only place I ever knew him." Joshua gives Charles a serious look. "Isn't it strange? The pictures we paint in our minds often barely resemble reality."

Charles shuffles through previous versions of his own mental paintings—of Sophie, of Hannah, of dozens of people he's known who have turned out barely to resemble his original portraits. But in the case of Marais, Charles feels certain that he's drawn the lines correctly. He's filled in Marais's features with photographic accuracy.

The two-legged dog rolls on his back and kicks both feet into the air, as if delighted by the good fortune of having not just one leg but a whole pair.

"There you are!" Sophie calls from the doorway. White hair streams over her shoulders. "Up and about already, I see. Kissing the morning. That's the way to do it."

Charles gets to his feet, wishing they'd left before she found them. "Good morning, Auntie."

Sophie's nightgown is printed all over with daisies that have faded to a dull lemon. Her eyes land on their bags. Her smile vanishes. "What's all this? You're not leaving?"

"I have some business to take care of, Auntie. It's not too far from here. I'll be back in a few days. Annie's going to stay with you in the meantime."

Sophie starts. "No she is not! Not in *my* house. She'll move my jewelry every which way. She'll mix up the cupboards. How am I supposed to find anything in my own home when—"

Charles reaches for her shoulders. "She's going to try very hard. She made me a promise," he lies.

"You don't know what she does when you're not here, Eugene. She's out to get me."

Charles can't remember her ever calling him by his given name. For all his life, he's been Charles.

"Every time you leave it's the same thing!" she cries.

Every time I leave?

"That's how it is with the Black ones. They wait nice and obedient until the master is gone, and then when it's just them and an old lady, they strut around the property like it's theirs. They rule the roost. Mark my words. It will be no different this time."

Charles is appalled, embarrassed for Annie, Joshua, his aunt, himself. "You're exaggerating, Auntie. That's no way to talk."

Sophie furrows her brow. "For as long as I can remember, you've taken their side," she scolds. "You always defended these people. When will you finally grow up, Eugene Nielen, and see the world for what it really is?"

Eugene Nielen. She thinks I'm Marais.

Annie sweeps onto the stoep. She wraps an arm around Sophie's back. "It's all right, Madam Sophie. I won't move a thing. Come see the flowers I picked. Look how pretty. They're right inside." She ushers Sophie into the house, just far enough inside that she's able to shut the door behind them.

A white-roofed taxi wheels into the driveway and grinds to a stop alongside the stoep. The driver climbs out and pops the boot, loads their bags, and locks the lid. He's a young Afrikaner with an uneven mustache and trousers that won't stay on his hips.

"*Goeie môre*," he says, holding open the door.

Hannah inches closer to Charles. "Isn't that the same symbol those men were wearing in Cape Town?"

Embroidered on the man's jacket in thick lettering is the word *Gryshemde*. Greyshirts.

"*Is jy reg om te gaan*?" the driver calls.

Charles hesitates. He's not sure that he *is* ready to go after all.

"Ignore his jacket," Joshua calls to them. He stands to the side by a patch of dahlias. "He'll take you where you need to go. You should get moving along now. I'll meet you there."

"You're not coming with us?" asks Hannah.

"Of course he's coming with us," Charles says. "Joshua, throw your bag in and let's go already." He wants to get away from the house before Sophie sees him again and he changes his mind.

"He's not going to take me," says Joshua.

"What are you talking about?"

"It's not how things work in South Africa," Joshua says.

The young driver leans across the car and taps on the roof impatiently.

"*Hierdie man kom saam met ons*," Charles calls to him.

The driver shakes his head emphatically. "No Kaffir rides in my car," he replies in Afrikaans. "No Kaffir *looks* at my car."

"You two go on," Joshua says coolly. "I'd rather take my time anyway. Look at this beautiful day."

"We're traveling together," Charles says to the driver. His Afrikaans has come flooding back. "We're paying for three. Either he comes too, or we all stay and you've lost the entire fare."

The driver considers this for a moment, then hoists up the waist of his pants and lopes back to the rear of the car. With a twist of his key, he unlocks the boot, throws their bags on the ground, and shuts himself back in the driver's seat. The engine revs. The car spins its wheels. The man tears out of the driveway.

"What a royal asshole," Hannah says when the dust cloud settles.

Charles spent the first ten years of his life in Pretoria. But he doesn't recognize this country. Have these people always been this cruel? Images from his childhood swerve through his mind, flashing like a film reel. It has always been like this, he realizes, dripping with racism. *He* is what has changed. "Let's get out of here."

He grabs his bag and marches down the graveled driveway, past the water pump, past the stand of cypresses, and onto the old dirt road. Behind him, he hears four separate feet crunching against the earth. Joshua stops a few feet away. Hannah sidles up on Charles's left, close enough that her sleeve brushes against his arm. She says nothing. For a while, the three of them stand like this, staring at the road. Charles can't imagine what Hannah must think of this place.

"How will we get there?" she asks.

"We'll find a taxi. We can be there before noon."

"If you're set on traveling all together, I believe we may need a different plan," Joshua says.

"There's no reason three friends shouldn't be able to hire a taxi in the capital of South Africa," says Hannah. "It's a simple enough operation."

The expression that unfolds on Joshua's mouth is not quite a smile. "Well, there is *one* reason, and I'm afraid it has to do with the particular shade of my skin . . ."

A humming starts up somewhere past the trees. It builds to a rumble. A black taxi rolls around the corner, cruises straight for them. *All right then,* thinks Charles. He steps into the street. He waves down the car.

The taxi slows. The engine idles. The driver has on a white cotton coat and tie. He leans over and rolls down the window. Before Charles can tell him their destination, the driver spots Joshua with his bag. He shakes his head and rolls up the window, then pilots past them at a brisk clip.

Hannah sees Charles's face fall. "You came here to find your father," she says. "You've traveled across continents. We're not stopping now. That's all there is to it."

The hours that follow crawl by in similar fashion. A dozen white taxi drivers take off when they realize that the couple seeking a ride is in fact a trio that includes a Black man. The sun becomes a hot white disc, blazing down on them as it begins its descent. A slow beating commences in Charles's temple. He rubs at the side of his head with two fingers. The beating only grows stronger.

"Here's what I think," Joshua calls to him. "It's only eighteen miles from here. I can walk that without a problem. Be there before dawn tomorrow. No reason to hold you both up any longer."

"Don't be ridiculous," Charles says. "Nobody's walking." He's made it halfway around the world. With only eighteen miles to go, he's not going to abandon the man who saved their lives. "We can find a ride. I'm going to take care of you."

Joshua stiffens. "With all due respect, sir, I've been taking care of myself just fine since long before you entered this world."

Charles blushes. "Of course, I know you can take care of yourself. I apologize. That's not what I meant. It's just hot and I'm tired."

"And hungry," Hannah teases. "And frustrated."

"And frustrated," Charles agrees. "Really bloody frustrated."

A beaten-up Ford truck turns the corner. The man at the wheel is middle-aged, Chinese. When he sees them, he pulls over and hops down. He has a straw hat, open-toed sandals, and a barrel-shaped belly. "You need a taxi?" the driver asks in Afrikaans.

"This man will be traveling with us," Charles says, gesturing to Joshua. "Is that a problem for you?" His patience has vanished.

The driver glances at Joshua and shrugs. "Not a problem for you, not a problem for me."

"Well, well," says Joshua. He scrabbles to his feet.

Charles squeezes Hannah's hand. She climbs into the passenger's seat while he and Joshua clamber into the truck bed and squat on top of the luggage.

The truck groans to a start and lurches forward. Soon they're bouncing over potholes and following the path of the sun westward.

Charles notices a smile spreading over Joshua's weather-worn face. He feels the damp wind on his own neck and a subtle bursting inside himself. Eighteen miles is barely a blink.

March 1936, Somewhere Between Pretoria and Pelindaba, Union of South Africa

The old truck lurches over a stone-spangled road. Charles keeps one hand on the side rail and both eyes on Hannah, who sits shoulder-to-shoulder with the driver in the truck's cab ahead.

The air is light and warm, but clouds have gathered overhead and bunched low in the sky. Charles can't tell whether it's mist or a soft rain that cools and wets his face now. How many more miles, he wonders—how many more minutes—until he stands face-to-face with Marais? In his bag he's packed the dozen nearly indecipherable notebooks that he unearthed at Sophie's house. If something in those field notes can undermine Sizemore's work at Harvard, Charles will find it. As he strains to make out forms in the distance, the fluttering in his chest grows as furious as hummingbird wings. This journey, he realizes, is about more than field notes. He needs to find his father. He needs to be healed.

"I wouldn't be surprised if your father chooses not to remember me," Joshua says.

Charles eyes the old man. "What do you mean *chooses* not to?"

"Just that he may prefer not to remember certain events from his past."

"You worked as his research assistant for years. He owes you."

Joshua gazes towards the horizon, his head barely nodding. "*Ja*, I believe he does." He offers a leather pouch full of biltong, but Charles declines. He wouldn't be able to keep food down right now. Joshua picks out a coarse, browned strip for himself. He tears at the meat with his teeth and the two wooden studs in the front of his mouth. He still hasn't told Charles about the argument decades ago that led to the end of his association with Marais. The cause of their discord must have scarred Joshua deeply. Why else would he set aside his work to face Marais after all this time?

"I'll tell you one thing: he'll know *you* the minute he lays eyes on you," says Joshua. "Like it or not, your father is printed all over you. It will be like looking in a mirror and seeing himself, only younger."

Charles laughs uncomfortably. He extends an arm off the side of the truck and lets the wind buffet his hand. They're only a few minutes out of the city, but the thrum of Pretoria feels like yesterday's dream. Apart from the truck's drone, the road is still and quiet.

"Pelindaba," Joshua says. "It's a Zulu name."

On the side of the road, two half-naked boys bite off chunks of what look like the charred remains of a squirrel on a stick. A patch of fur still clings to a limp tail. "Pelindaba," Charles says to himself, fitting his lips around the word.

When he glances at Joshua again, the old man's eyes seem to darken a shade. "Feels like we may be coming to the end," Joshua says.

"How so?"

"The name. It means, 'the matter is settled.' Make of that what you want. My own father used to say there's a reason behind every name."

"I can believe that," says Charles.

"Same here," Joshua says. "And settling matters is how a man like me might finally find justice." Something about the way he lowers his gaze unsettles Charles.

* * *

Marais's eyes click repeatedly like the shutter of a camera, warding off the assault of daylight. How can he still be holed up in this joke of a rondavel on the farm of Gustav Preller, his editor from a lifetime ago? A single rounded room. Old clotted mattress, square dresser, tottering shelves, two stacked crates for a desk. Accommodations unfit for a servant. The curtains are drawn. Still, sticks of light filter through moth holes in the fabric and sting his eyes. He won't look at the mirror that hangs by the window. He's stuck inside an old man's body. Sixty-four years young. So strange, to recall one's age and so little else.

He can't remember how long he has stayed at Pelindaba. After leaving Rietfontein, he drifted through Pretoria's seams, threaded out of the city and back, over and again, entangling himself in his own messy knots along the way. It's not that jobs in Pretoria were scarce. But no box would hold him. As soon as he'd find a place to stay, a temporary source of livelihood, he'd explode again from the inside outward.

The day Marais arrived at their farm unannounced, Preller and his wife Hannie took him in, bathed and shaved him as if he were family, settled him into the empty rondavel. "You stay for as long as you like," Preller whispered to him one night after Hannie had stormed into the kitchen. Marais has stayed quite a bit longer than that. But *how* long? Months? Years? Time has collapsed around him. He's been a decent enough guest though. There's no need for Hannie's bitterness.

The hissing he hears stiffens the hair on his arms. He knows that sound—the shrill warning of a mamba before it strikes. He flips over the mattress. He throws open the drawers, clutching a brick, ready to pound the snake into powder. One bite from a mamba, and you'd be lucky to make it through the next hour. He searches every crack for the nasty viper, every crevice and nook. Gradually, it dawns on him. The sound is coming from his own throat. Each time he exhales, there's the hiss. Look at this old body, this wretched animal shell.

His bladder is on the verge of bursting. He yanks open the zipper of his trousers and roots around for his equipment. He coaxes out the flaccid worm, and with considerable effort, pisses into a bucket in the corner of the room. Long after he's relieved himself, his body continues to leak. He turns over his shriveled sex in his hand. An ancient hooded mummy. To think that once upon a time it was able to produce anything apart from this ceaseless flow of wastewater.

A man's ideas—like his body, these too should be his irrevocable property. Despite Preller's pleading, Marais published his research on the white ants only in Afrikaans, a language virtually no one outside the country can read. What better way to ensure that it would be utilized for the benefit of South Africa alone?

Still, his ideas have been yanked from him, disembodied, disemboweled. By Harvard Fucking University of all places. Nearly every month, Sophie forwards another hand-penned letter from Harvard—from men with names like Conant and

Sizemore—urging Marais to travel to their university to present his research. Of course they'd never have found his work in the first place if he hadn't alerted them to it out of a crass desire for money, and for fame. It was Sophie who told him several years ago that Charles had taken a teaching position at Harvard. Perhaps that connection, she offered during one of his particularly indigent stints, would encourage the university to fund Marais's research. It did nothing of the sort.

He has snipped out the most vile excerpts from Harvard's missives and spliced them into a sprawling collage that occupies the entire wall above his desk. To think that academic prestige was something he ever craved. The Americans are no better than the rest of the colonial powers—British, French, Dutch. They won't content themselves with misappropriating his work. They won't stop until they've taken his whole person, transformed him into a symbol for their shameful racial project.

A banging outside startles him.

"Marais!" Preller's voice drums through the door.

He doesn't stir from his bed.

"I know you're awake," Preller calls. "There are guests here to see you."

Marais picks at the dirt beneath his nails. "Monsieur Marais is currently incapacitated!"

"Makes no difference. These particular guests you'll need to see."

"Not possible. I'm completely indecent."

"You've been indecent for as long as we've known each other. Now open the door or I'll open it for you."

The old door, seared with termite trails, has no lock. Marais has nothing worth safeguarding. He rolls to his side and pulls the frayed blanket over his head. A sharp ache shoots through his shoulder. Tented like this, he can smell his own ripeness.

"Wait here a moment," he hears Preller say. The latch clicks. The door groans on its hinges.

Marais rolls down the blanket to track the movements of his landlord and former friend. Preller stoops to avoid clipping his head on the overhang and swings his lanky frame into the room. His rust-colored hair has thinned and grayed, but the man is as scrawny as he was thirty-five years ago when Marais first hired him to edit his paper. Marais inhales deeply, produces the fiercest growl he can muster.

"Don't you dare, Eugene," Preller warns. "I've promised Hannie: one more misstep on your part, and I have orders to turn you out with the crows."

What in the world was it that froze the heart of Hannie Preller? As a younger woman, she had a sharp, promising mind. Shortly after Marais arrived at Pelindaba, though, Hannie turned against him. Maybe she envied the attention he drew from her husband. She went so far as to take away Marais's Mauser, and then, to pour salt on the wound, posted a sign that read conspicuously: "Guests of the Preller family who keep firearms on this property shall be subject to immediate eviction."

From beneath his blanket, Marais recites his latest ode.

"Out with the crows, the lambs their lows,
No shoes or clothes, and what is worse
I'm cooked because Dame Hannie chose
To stuff me in this wretched hearse.
What ogre, what fiend, what demon, what curse
The heat beneath her skirts hath froze?"

"Ever the brilliant writer," Preller says. "To think how you've evolved: from father of Afrikaans poetry to penner of nasty limericks."

"Maybe if I'd been allowed a small amount of air or light."

"No one has held you here! You have been free to leave—*invited* to leave—for longer than I care to remember."

Preller still has a temper, which Marais enjoys igniting almost as much as he did thirty years ago when it was just the two of them struggling on behalf of a small nation—with nothing but an old printing press—against the yoke of British imperialism.

"I haven't come to mince words," Preller says. "Charles is here. He's brought a couple companions."

The hissing starts up again, only louder this time, more like a mucousy roar.

Preller's eyes flash. He grabs Marais's shoulder roughly. "It's Charles. Eugene Charles Gerard Marais. Your son!"

Has it actually worked? Marais spent the past six months doing everything he could to orchestrate Charles's movement across the ocean. He planned and schemed and drafted until his fingers coiled up in spasms. And somehow he has made Charles come. He summoned the boy, and lo and behold, here he is. The facts are remarkable, and yet, in his heart, Marais never doubted that Charles would find him. But he's not ready. He can't let the boy see him this way.

Preller is staring at him. "Are you all right?"

The rondavel's curved walls squeeze in like a vice. The ceiling starts to collapse. "Five minutes," Marais manages to cough. "Give me five minutes to make myself presentable."

"Five minutes, no more. Maybe you could use some of the time to do something about that . . . " he glances at the chamber pot in the corner, "latrine of yours."

* * *

Charles paces in the garden amid the browning leaves of hydrangeas, the desiccated stalks of agapanthus. Sweat trickles down his neck. Ten thousand miles have led him here. Hannah and Joshua stand at the edge of the field watching Hannie's brother tow a plow behind a pair of oxen.

When Charles glances back at the stone rondavel, he catches a glimpse of a bent, rounded specter looming in the window, peering back at him through the blinds. *Marais?*

"All right," says Preller. "He's had plenty of time. You should go on in."

"You're coming too, of course." Charles feels like a boy all of a sudden, faint at the prospect of facing Oom Eugene.

"I don't want to upset him further." Preller's cheeks flush plum. "What I mean is you should have some time together, without me."

"For God's sake, go say hello already," Hannah urges.

Joshua nods. "You've waited a long time to see one another."

The breeze picks up. Charles's feet feel numb.

"Well, if you're not going in, I'll go meet him myself." Hannah smooths the wrinkles in her blouse, pushes her hair behind her ear, and marches up the three stairs.

She raises her fist to knock.

"Wait!" Charles calls. "I'm going first."

The dim little room houses a dresser, a couple of crates, and a strange collage of clippings pasted on the wall over a disheveled desk. A spider's creamy egg sac stretches like cotton candy over a section of ceiling thatch. There's a familiar odor in the rondavel, dank and fungal and mingled with urine.

Propped against two pillows is a haggard old man. White seersucker suit. Dirt ground into cuffs. Stained silk tie. English safari hat. The ghost he saw through the window.

The man lowers his feet to the floor, wipes his wrist across his mouth. He straightens his shirt, which is pocked with oil stains. He holds out a gnarled hand. "Doctor Marais," the man coughs at Charles. "What a pleasure."

The voice reverberates as if in a dream. Charles gapes at the ghost in front of him. Marais's teeth have grayed. Thick stubble sprouts along his jaw line. His oily hair clings like wet paper to his cheeks. He bears no resemblance to the image in Charles's memory. This Marais is old and skeletal and sick. Charles takes his hand. "It's good to see you again," he manages to say.

* * *

Charles lurks like an ox in his doorway, sun dribbling over his shoulders. He's not a boy at all, and this takes Marais by surprise. Of course, Charles must be thirty-five, forty years old already. A professor, with more formal schooling that he himself has had. Marais can recognize the boy in the man only by the eyes, which are still deep and capacious—Lettie's eyes—though without the fear that rankled them in childhood. Fine wrinkles fan out from cheekbones to temples and lend him an air of gentility. Horrible suit though. The stitches are unraveling at the seams.

The boy can't seem to stop staring at him. *He's surprised*, Marais thinks with amusement. *What did he expect to find?*

"You managed to locate me," Marais says.

"I received your letters."

"All of them?"

"I couldn't say. I lost count somewhere after thirty."

"I trust they weren't too much of a nuisance."

The boy's eyes darken. "I stopped reading them when they became a nuisance."

Ha! Very good. "Then you've come in *spite* of my correspondence. To assist me."

The boy blinks back at him.

Too forward, Marais thinks. This is a delicate matter. Slow down. It will all happen in due time.

The door swings out further. Two others edge into the room—a girl and an older African man—though their entrance is not sufficient to break the spell that keeps the boy staring at him.

"Perhaps you'd care to introduce us?" Marais says.

Charles turns, notices the others. It takes a moment before he thinks to say, "This is Hannah Tauber. My . . . graduate student."

Marais observes the look that she casts Charles. She seems displeased with this introduction.

"My friend, I mean," Charles corrects himself. He glances at Hannah apologetically. "My dear friend."

"It's an honor, Mister Marais," says the girl. She actually looks delighted to meet him. Imagine—in his state. "You're not an easy man to track down," she says. "Steamships, trains, taxis, fishing boats, trucks. We've traveled ten thousand miles—just to find you."

"I must be a very special man."

"You must be," she says, still smiling, "if you're anything like your son."

Sharp as a tack. Charles has done well for himself. Marais's gaze falls on the man hovering near the door. "My God!" Marais says. "Joshua, is that you?"

"Did you forget about me, sir?" Joshua smiles at him with more generosity than he deserves. Two wooden teeth sit like fence posts amid the rows of white ones.

"My old . . . assistant," Marais mutters. His cheeks are burning all of a sudden. "I didn't expect to see you again." He takes a seat on the bed before his knees buckle. "Look at you, Joshua. As strong and steady as you've always been. I guess farm work will do that."

"I'm a lobsterman now."

"You don't say? Your own boss?" Marais asks.

"As I was meant to be."

Suspicion rises like a mamba. Why would Joshua journey all the way to Preller's farm? "You've come to exact a price, no doubt. A pound of flesh. You'd be entitled to ten. Truly, you'd be entitled to anything you could ask for. Unfortunately for you, I'm penniless."

"I don't need your money, Mister Marais."

"Well what do you intend to extract from me?"

Joshua straightens his back. "Nothing of material value."

"Then why are you here? To stir up memories that were put to sleep ages ago?"

"The Lord brought your son and this woman to me. When I learned they were coming to find you, I knew I needed to come too. I wanted to make sure you knew what happened that night at Rietfontein—the last time we saw each other."

Marais hears the rush of air flooding his own lungs.

"I tried to get your medicine for you," Joshua says. "Tried as hard as I could. I know the Ten Commandments forward and back. I know the Lord looks down on stealing. Still, sometimes a man needs help." He steadies himself, exhales audibly. "The thing is, you didn't *ask* for my help. You used me like a tool, and I got caught doing your bidding. That night took a great toll on me—on my mind and my body." He taps a wooden tooth.

A sharp rhythmic thumping starts up around Marais's eyes. "Is this a joke, Joshua? Do you want me to apologize to you now? After twenty years?"

"An apology would hardly suffice," Joshua says.

"Then what is it that you want?"

"I came here to kill you, sir."

Marais laughs uncomfortably. He looks to the others for help.

"I thought that's what I needed anyway. I thought your blood would somehow fix the past. But I'm not a murderer." Joshua's lip quivers. He seems to grow taller, expansive. "You created us—Kaffir, Negro, Black. Before your people even landed on our shores. You all needed someone to step on. So you could lift yourselves higher. Like the Nazis and their Jews. What do I want? I want you to see me. I belong to nobody. I'm a man. Same as you."

ßMarais's head is swimming. A moment ago, things were moving along just fine—step by step just as he planned. He squeezes his palms against his temples. "I can barely remember that night," he lies. "And even if I could, I can't just wave a wand and pretend that the past never happened."

"From where I stand, it looks like that's exactly what you *have* been doing," Joshua says. "You take the time you need. You'll remember. Time's one thing we've got ourselves plenty of today."

Marais forces himself to his feet, searches for an escape. But he is thrust violently back to Waterberg. Here he is ordering Joshua to swipe his morphine, barricading himself inside his room. He hears Gys's boot kicking against bone. He hears Joshua's cries. With his palm, he strikes Tamaria, sending her flying into the wall. Over and over the story replays. He has never left Rietfontein.

He glances up at Charles, the boy who has come to save him. "I need some air," he says, seizing his cane. He moves for the door. "Charles, come with me. Please. There's something I need to show you."

* * *

Charles watches Marais's bent back disappear into a blaze of daylight. He reaches for the door and follows him outside.

Marais charges to the garden on the far side of the main house, overcome by some new source of energy, free for now of Joshua's gaze. "A perfectly fine day!" the old man calls over his shoulder. "No hail, no locusts." When he turns, Charles can see that color has returned to the old man's face. "Raise your voices when you speak. Preller's wife absolutely loves noise."

Charles sweeps alongside him. He hears Hannah and Joshua following closely behind. Is Marais, the unruly guest turned unlikely host, taking them on a tour of the property? Or is he leading Charles to some buried treasure? They pass the Prellers' rose garden and enter an orchard where clusters of oranges still cling to the tips of tired branches and small green pears are beginning to take shape. Charles keeps distance between himself and Marais, but not so much that he couldn't catch the old man if he stumbled.

"It's no Rietfontein, is it, Joshua?" Marais calls back. "Doesn't compare to Waterberg's colors and smells?"

"No place could."

"Well, I think it's lovely here," says Hannah. "Trees, birds, open sky. Not a single other person about. Just us and the earth. I could imagine getting attached to a place like this."

Marais plows ahead with his cane. He leads them into a sloping field where uncut grasses have crisped and browned. A great plateau rises in the distance.

Now Marais begins to talk. For the rest of the afternoon, as they scour the property, he talks—about his youth in Pretoria, about Waterberg, about a kloof near a mine called Doornhoek, about a farm called Rietfontein. He tells them how he lived for three years among a troop of wild chacmas, how he named and numbered and knew each one individually. He tells them about experiments he performed, a child he kidnapped, a man he shot. How he came to discover the communal mind and the nature of the human unconscious. How his research has been ripped from its intended meaning.

Charles finds himself drinking in the details, impressing them to memory. It feels as if Marais is communicating a lifetime. Maybe an explanation for all that Charles has endured is tucked away somewhere in these stories. Maybe it's just a matter of unearthing it.

"I concluded that the termitary functions as one great body, one great hive mind," Marais says. "But I have never suggested trying to eliminate the autonomous thought of segments of the human population. It's true that a number of years ago, in a fit of desperation and self-induced poverty, I wrote your university and asked for funding to continue my research. But I do not now, nor will I ever, support the Nazis."

Late-afternoon shadows bunch east of the path. Charles spots a stout cone of clay rising up from the ground behind a stand of eucalyptus. The cone arches six feet into the air. An ancient memory is set into motion, though Charles can't recall the context. "What is this?"

Marais's eyes catch fire. "Why don't we show them, Joshua—together?"

* * *

Marais lowers his knees into soil the color of aubergines. It's been ages since he attempted a termitarial dissection. He feels flooded with vigor, ready to pounce. It all comes right back. He'll show the boy one of the world's great mysteries. He'll show him how utterly wrong Harvard has been—those men who have disfigured his findings, who have changed his research into something grotesque.

He unclips a knife from his belt. He saws into the mound's thick skin. It takes patience and precision to avoid toppling the structure.

He broaches the shell and reaches in with both hands. He scoops out mounds of earth.

"How can I help?" asks Hannah.

"This is not really women's . . ."

But the girl is already on her knees alongside him, dress hiked up to her thighs, fingers sunk into soil. She watches his movements and copies them, carefully scooping out palms full of dirt with her hands.

Get ready, thinks Marais. He counts heartbeats. *One. Two. Three.*

Red-horned termites pour from the side like blood from a wound. Dozens turn to hundreds turn to thousands. The blind ants arrange themselves in long straight lines, aiming their lances outward to prevent further destruction. Marais hears Charles gasp behind him.

Soon, rows of workers begin filing past. Each termite clamps a single grain of sand in its mandibles to plug up the gash. Marais brushes the insects aside. He cuts through one chamber and then another. The way he rotates his wrist reminds him of surgeries he performed long ago at Rietfontein. Old lives spiral through his mind—editor, poet, advocate, doctor, sheriff, naturalist. How many times did he recreate himself only to fall again?

He penetrates a dozen chambers. The channels converge into larger arteries that intersect in more distant chambers concealed beneath sand and clay. With his pocketknife, Marais slices through these too, through one and then another. The arterial galleries grow fewer and larger. The configuration is unlike any he can remember.

He looks up at Charles, who stands over him, curious, suspicious, perplexed, and then at his old assistant. "Joshua, have a look at this. What do you think?"

Joshua takes his time. He seems pleased to be consulted, to be valued for more than his labor. He leans down and peers into the pit. "They're all moving in the same direction."

"Indeed they are," says Marais. *Are they leading him to her?* Desire flares like a flame inside him. In his heart, he's never given up the hunt.

"Dig around the edges," he tells Hannah. "But carefully. Like an archeologist."

He carves his way further below ground. The channels grow wider still. They disappear behind a wall of mottled granite. *One wrong move*, he thinks, *and we'll lose her.*

"If you need an extra hand—" says Charles.

"Any more hands and we're liable to destroy it." Marais is going to show the boy something incredible. He's going to teach him about the queen and the communal mind. He's going to dump the Nazi interpretation of his work on its head. These are *his* theories, *his* facts. His research on termites has never indicated the existence of a master race.

They shave away layers of sediment. The sun grows bloody and sinks into the horizon. They poke and prod and scrape and pry, and somewhere along the line, as the ground turns gold and the wind settles to a dull breath, it happens: the granite wall comes loose. A chunk the size of a human head settles into Marais's hand. He sets it gently beside him on a dry bed of earth and peers inside the cavity.

"I can't believe it." His voice wavers. "Joshua, I believe we've found her."

Charles sinks to his knees beside his father. They all gaze into the dark hole.

"What is this?" says Hannah.

It's the queen, enthroned in the darkest, wettest, most impenetrable portion of the termitary. Her eyes are dark, bulbous orbs. She's as long as Marais's hand, from fingertips to wrist, and completely immobile in her stone hard cell. Her gray-black skin-sock looks over-inflated, stretched to the point of bursting. And yet she's perfectly alive, surrounded by a moat of mucous that glistens in the early evening light. All around her, workers transport tiny eggs to nurseries in more distant chambers. Dozens of smaller insects clamber over her back. They suck liquid from her fluid sack to feed the babies. To her children, she is mother and meal.

"I didn't know such creatures existed," Charles says.

"She's a miracle," says Marais. "The brain of this whole living organism." He tells them about the queen, how she controls tens of thousands of children, each with its own role within the larger body—so many creatures directed, against their knowledge, to build and feed and transport and defend, to traverse wild veld and mountain top. How they're all part of a single communal mind, one grand group-soul that functions as perfectly as the mechanism inside a Swiss clock. He tells them how he once bisected a termite mound with a large steel plate, separating one half of the insects from the others. In no time, the workers on one side rebuilt it in perfect symmetry with those on the other. There's no predetermined design. It all happens impromptu. The queen orchestrates everything remotely. "She moves them through some force in the ether. Each time they go in search of food, she is what keeps them coming home."

Hannah places her hand gingerly into a hole two chambers away from the queen. A line of workers files over her fingers. "They spend their whole lives like this?" she asks. "Building, feeding, protecting—unaware that none of the decisions they make is their own?"

"A superior being, a god directing drones, the way nature intended. Frankly," says Charles, "it sounds like Harvard may have been right about your work. It sounds like the basis of fascism."

Marais rocks back on his haunches, astounded by the boy's temerity.

"They seem to think," Charles continues, "if they can anesthetize the social groups they consider unpalatable, they can foster this same sort of communal mind—a hive mentality among humans." He gestures at the churning mound. "And that those humans could be made to work willingly for a leader whom they'd otherwise resist. They're so excited by the idea that they asked me to bring you back to speak."

Marais studies his son, this grown boy who was formed from the cells of his own body. "They have perverted my thinking. Never in my life have I suggested anything to that effect. The termite mound is a community. It's not predatory. It doesn't colonize with force. It's thoroughly altruistic, one organism for all, each individual dependent on every other one, bound together through ancient instincts."

"But one being is invested with all the power. Paint some blond hair on it, a pair of blue eyes. You can see how they might have come to their conclusion."

His skepticism irks Marais. Does he think he's dealing with a charlatan? He can substantiate every assertion scientifically. "All that's needed to understand the laws of nature is to take time to observe what's around you. It's not magic. Let me show you. To dissolve this community—countless insects functioning in perfect unison—would require just a single stroke from a knife. The moment the queen dies, the entire organism will collapse."

Marais raises his knife. He lifts it above the fattened queen and angles the blade, barely grazing her neck. Through the steel he can feel a soft rhythmic pulsing. The same pulse that beats through every living creature. The boy will eat his words for dinner. Marais bears down with the knife. *Goodbye, Madam.*

"Stop!" Hannah cries. She shoves herself between Marais and the termitary, shields the mound with her body. "She's given her life to building this place! Imagine squeezing out all those millions of eggs. Who knows how long she's been here? I won't let you destroy a life just to prove a point."

Marais likes this girl. He likes the naïveté of her logic. "Whenever war breaks out or a village is flooded or an earthquake levels a city, we feel shocked," Marais says. "We act horrified. We call these events tragedies, as if they're somehow counter to nature, anomalies in an otherwise orderly universe. The termites know better. They know this is how the world works—the natural order of things *is* tragedy. They know it in the fabric of their being. But unlike us "evolved" humans, they're not shackled by memory. They're free to move about their lives undisturbed by the chaos around them." He chuckles, pleased at her protest. "Still, if it matters so much to you, I'll spare her today."

He rises to his feet, clips the knife back onto his belt. "It wouldn't have been the worst thing in the world, though. We'd have freed her children. Some of them would wander and die without food or water. But thousands of others are waiting for her death." They're waiting, he tells them, for their bodies to mature and the necessary membranes to form. Built right into their makeup is the stuff of kings and queens. They've been growing wings, secretly awaiting the perfect winds. A proto-queen can wait more than a year for the precise air current. Then one day, on instinct, she'll step out, let go, and take flight. The journey might take her a mile away or just yards from home, but for that moment, she'll experience the sensation of flying wind-borne through space. When she lands, she'll unhitch her wings and emit a special scent that's undetectable by humans. He's proved as much experimentally, he says, with the aid of dogs. With this signal, she'll lure a flying male, and the two will burrow together into a damp spot of earth and begin the hard work of kingdom building, the latest in a line of royalty that extends back millions of years.

"Wait," says Charles. "You mean it's not a foregone conclusion which insects become the leaders of a hive?"

He is my child after all, thinks Marais. He knows precisely where to push. "Correct. There is no single, natural-born queen who emerges from the termitary, no one racially superior leader. Tens of *thousands* have that same potential. It's a matter of luck whether or not they become royalty—which day they wind up launching themselves, whether they catch the wind in just the right way, if they're fortunate enough to land in a perfectly damp location. Every one of those creatures is equal to the next when they start out. None is superior to another."

Charles's eyes have caught fire. "And you've documented all of this?"

"Indeed I have." Marais peers up at the pink ribbon of clouds looping across the western sky. He can feel his energy waning. These days it happens like this, bursting and abating. His knees are weak. Either he'll make it back to the rondavel within the hour, or they'll have to carry him. "Time to get going," he says.

Six concerned eyes turn and assess his welfare. He begins pulling himself through the scrub with his cane. The boy will follow.

* * *

Flames lap at a trio of yellow logs angled together in the middle of the rondavel's hearth. Outside, crickets shriek with longing. Charles sits cross-legged on the dank floor between Hannah and Joshua, gazing at the fire and thinking how, even though it's been thirty years since he last laid eyes on Marais, being with him now feels strangely familiar. Every few seconds, he steals a glance at the old man, who sits propped on his elbow at the desk. Marais said he needed half an hour to record his thoughts while they were still fresh in his mind. He revived a bit after their dinner—a simple stew served by a resentfully curious Hannie Preller. But he looks now like he did when Charles first entered the rondavel earlier in the day—pale as the skin of an egg. His wrist strokes are so subtle that at times Charles can't tell whether he's writing or unconscious.

"Should we head back to Sophie's?" Hannah asks.

"It's too dark to travel on those roads," says Charles. "We can sleep on the bedrolls Preller left us."

Joshua gets to his feet. He hauls his small bag over his shoulder. "A very good night to you all."

"There's plenty of space for you right here," Charles says.

Joshua looks at each of them. "I don't think you know what you'd be getting yourself into. If Mister Preller's wife was to find out—"

Marais claps his notebook shut. He turns in his chair to face them. "I don't care about any of that. Joshua, you're my guest. Please stay with us."

Joshua stares slack-jawed at Marais, as if this is the first act of genuine kindness he's ever received from him. "I accept the invitation," he says. He removes his bag from his shoulder. He rolls out a mat on the floor.

"I do have one request," Marais says to Charles. Beads of fevered sweat are collecting above Marais's lip. He scratches a hand through his cloud of hair. "Would you be willing to help publish my field notes? As much as I enjoy a bit of fame, I wouldn't mind if your Harvard colleagues never cite my work again."

Charles has imagined this moment a thousand times since the first letter arrived in Cambridge last September. He's imagined a thousand ways of being asked for help and a thousand ways of denying it. But somewhere along the line, his urge for vengeance lost its stranglehold.

As he persuades himself to say yes, an image arises in his mind of a young Marais handing an infant to Sophie. Charles can't see the child, only the look of shock on Sophie's face. He was too young to remember such a thing. The picture is more a tableau than a baby's eye view. But it feels as real as this room, with its fire-shadows dancing like phantoms along the walls.

"Of course Charles will help," Hannah says. "We both will. We'll hire an army of lawyers if we need to." The look on her face is the one Charles first saw at Harvard that told him she would never capitulate to the world's injustices. It was one of the reasons he fell in love with her.

"It's not that simple . . ." Charles starts. He wants to forgive Marais, just as she suggested. But now the vowels and consonants—dental, labial, palatal—stick in his throat like wax.

Hannah's head tilts leftward. "Why not?"

In the hearth, embers fire like gunshots. The longer he keeps silent, the more urgent her expression grows. He's not ready to agree. He's not ready to forgive.

"Do you have any idea," Charles says without intending to, "what it was like knowing you just handed me off after my mother died? That you willfully gave me away. I've never understood how a father could do that. I know I couldn't."

Marais shifts in his chair. He looks almost at Charles. "'Willfully' is a relative term."

Charles sees that he's caught Marais off-guard, and this propels him forward. "Every day as a child—then as a teenager, and even as an adult—I wondered what I'd done. What harm could I have caused you? When I was 'entrusted' to Aunt Sophie's care,

I couldn't walk, or feed, or toilet myself. I had nothing. You had everything."

Marais's lip starts to tremble. "Had everything? Is that really what you think? 'Everything' had been *cut* from me. I lost the one person I loved. I lost my wife, my impossibly beautiful wife, the only person who understood what I needed to become."

"She was my mother!"

"She was seized from *my* arms! Can you imagine how difficult it was not to think for the rest of my life: 'if only she'd never become pregnant, if only she'd never given birth—'"

Charles can barely believe it. He's known this all along. Marais *did* blame him.

"He was just a baby!" Joshua roars. "He was *your* child. He didn't ask to be born!"

Charles turns around, astonished by Joshua's audacity. The old man looks as startled as he is. Why is this man defending him? Something flickers in Joshua's eyes, the same flash sparking inside him—he's sure of it—as he registers the chain binding the two of them together. The white professor, the Black lobsterman. Marais violated *both* of them. The air in the room is suddenly suffocating.

Before he can respond, Marais erupts in a fit of coughing so violent it sounds as if his lungs could explode. "Water," he says with a voice full of gravel.

Hannah fetches a glass from the shelf and fills it from the spigot outside. Marais gulps down the water. Liquid dribbles from his chin to the floor and sparkles in the firelight.

"I'll get you some more," Hannah says.

"A dose of medicine is what I need. To bring down my temperature." He digs into his pocket and emerges with a small felt pouch. As he releases the strings, a single white tablet clinks onto the desk.

This is the morphine? thinks Charles. This is how he's destroyed himself—with this tiny button?

"Heat it for me please," he says to Charles. "Half a spoon of water, tablet on the spoon, spoon above the fire. It takes just a minute or two."

In his whole life, Charles realizes, he has never had an opportunity to help his father. He collects the tablet before he can reconsider. He takes a bent, flame-ravaged spoon from the desk. He angles the spoon into the glass, scoops out some water, drops the tablet into it, and ferries the spoon to the fire. Ocher flames lick at the steel. The tablet's edges dissolve and sizzle. And there's the same smell of vanilla and pickled meat that he remembers from Sizemore's lab and from his trip to Marais's apartment in Pretoria thirty years before that. How strange that a simple smell can solder the past to the present.

He ushers the spoon back to Marais. The creamy solution rocks against the sides. Two drops veer over the edge and puddle on the floor.

With trembling hands, Marais levels a silver syringe at the spoon. "First time I've had an audience," he says. "Don't worry, admission is free."

It takes a dozen tries, but he finally manages to siphon the liquid into the needle. With his other hand, he wrestles with his sleeve, forcing the cuff up and over his elbow.

Marais's arm is gristle from biceps to wrist, a mass of raised, fleshy scarring. Charles stares at it, his stomach churning. He can't peel his eyes away. "How could you do this to yourself?" he asks.

"*For* myself," Marais corrects. "There's a simple answer. The answer to the world's mysteries is often simple. My life's work has led to a singular conclusion. We are plagued by memory. Infected by the stuff. That's the price, the exorbitant price, of being human. And this," he says, lifting the syringe, "is my one small remedy for the merciless sting of consciousness."

Charles watches the long purple shadow of the syringe. In this light, it looks like a weapon of war.

Hannah shakes her head. "You've got it backwards, Mister Marais," she says. "I lost both of my parents. They were taken from me in a most unnatural way. Memory isn't the *cost* of being human. The cost is having to say goodbye to the people you love. It's missing them so much once they're gone that you can't possibly bear the feeling for one more moment—and yet, still you bear it. Memory is *how* you bear it. It's our gift for being human."

"Why go on then?" Marais demands. "Why would anyone in their right mind choose to continue?"

"Because without pain, there can be no enlightenment. And because life still goes on. Somewhere in the world right now a lobsterman is pulling up his crates. A mother is inhaling her baby's breath. There are children playing marbles, farmers sowing fields, couples making love. It's all happening right now. God-willing, it will *keep* happening." She glances from father to son. "You are two of the luckiest men in the world. You still have one another, don't you see? And yet . . ." she turns the saddest eyes on Charles, "you've convinced yourself that you have nothing."

The air in the rondavel is asphyxiating. A mist fogs Charles's glasses. Marais's coughing erupts again. He stabs at his arm with the needle but comes up short of a vein. He jabs again, then again. Red drops bloom across his arm. The tremors in his hand send the syringe rattling to the floor.

"I'm worse at this than usual tonight," he says.

Joshua sweeps over and retrieves the syringe. "I'll do it for you. Must have seen you inject yourself a hundred times up at Rietfontein. I bet you didn't know I was there, watching you from outside."

Charles stares at Marais—at his red-rimmed eyes, his palsied arms, his soiled coat. Marais always seemed to have everything. That's how Charles remembers him, as a man who had everything and gave him nothing. It dawns on him that all of Marais's years preoccupied with the chacmas' memory, all his years obsessing over the white ants' lack of it, were in the end nothing but distraction and evasion. Here is Marais now, defenseless as a newborn. All of that study has led only to misery.

"I'll help," Charles says to Joshua. "Give us your arm," he orders Marais. He kneels on the floor. He brushes his fingers along Marais's skin, the flesh coarse and thick like animal hide. He runs his hand lightly over the scarring. How many thousands of times has this needle pierced this vein?

On the desk Joshua immobilizes Marais's hand with his own, pins him down. Charles takes a breath. He tightens his grip. Then he plunges the syringe deep into his father's arm.

Marais's torso shivers. "I owe you," he breathes to both of them.

* * *

Marais rubs at his eyes with the back of his hand. He glances at his watch—he's lost hours somewhere. He struggles to sit upright in bed. Through the parted blinds, stars have already filled the sky.

His fever has broken. A cool sweat trickles down the back of his shirt. The room smells of ash.

"I've been addicted to morphine for a long time," he says to Charles. The boy is kneeling next to him, concern imprinted on his face. "Since before you were born, before your mother died, before I met her even. I started using it long before I lost her. It had nothing to do with you."

There, he's said it. Admitted it, and not just to himself, to his son. That's something. He thinks he feels slightly lighter. But then again, what's the point of admitting a problem when there exists no solution to its deeper cause?

Hannah stands alone by the window. She lights a pair of candles. She recites a prayer in a language that he recognizes but doesn't understand.

"Amen," Joshua says.

Marais glances at his old assistant, then at Charles. "She's a Jew?" he whispers.

Charles nods. He returns the whisper. "She doesn't know yet, but I'm going to ask her to marry me."

At this news, Marais brightens. The engine of his mind restarts. Thoughts gather speed, running off in a thousand directions. His own delight surprises him. Maybe, he thinks, because his genetic line isn't destined to die out quite yet. Or maybe simply because Charles, his son, has found a lifelong friend in a woman, as he himself once had.

"You can't settle around Pretoria," says Marais. "It wouldn't be safe for her right now. You must have seen the signs. They say the Greyshirts have plastered them like bark on every tree from here to the capital."

"You should have seen them in Cape Town," says Hannah. She has been listening after all. "I don't know if it's the crispness of the air around here, or the ant hills, or the golden fields, but I do like the countryside. Who needs cities anyway?"

An idea occurs to Marais, a most extraordinary idea. "Last I heard, the Doornhoek mine was defunct," he tells them. "The place was largely uninhabited. But my little hut was still standing in the gorge just as I'd left it. It's a peaceful place, infinitely more so than here. It would need some cleaning, of course. One would want to wash the walls, polish the floors. The roof could probably stand a bit of restoration. But the stove was still there, the pots. Everything a person—or two—would need to live in peace for a long time to come."

March 1936, A Farm Near Pelindaba,
Union of South Africa

The last birch embers snap and sizzle in the hearth. From his bed, Marais gazes at Charles, curled like a fetus on the floor of the rondavel.

Charles is fit, muscular even, though not in a showy sort of way. A good-looking boy, Marais has to admit. Good-looking man. Must be the genes. He watches his son toss about in his sleep—from back to front to back again. He senses a whole world concealed within that head. Does Charles have a phantom of his own? he wonders.

Maybe it isn't the morphine—or the lack of it—that causes Marais's own nightly battles. Maybe it's something about *them*. About the two of them. Marais is aware of Hannah sleeping next to Charles. The girl is lovely and sharp as a razor. Not unlike the brown-haired girl with the huge laughing eyes who has chased Marais night after night for forty years. The one who was lost to both of them.

He's aware of Joshua too, snoring like an engine near the door. He's amazed by Joshua's fortitude.

The Southern Cross rises like a jewel. Marais's lids grow so heavy that he can no longer keep them pried apart. When they finally give way to gravity, a strange thing happens. Even with his eyes closed, he can still see the boy curled up on the floor in front of him. It's truly remarkable. Eyes open or closed, still his son is there.

At some point, Charles stops tossing. The phantom that drove his restlessness abandons him and he settles into his bedroll. It's the first time Marais has observed him like this, utterly still, completely unguarded. The boy's chest inflates of its own accord. His belly and ribs swell with air. And then, all at once, they collapse.

In that moment, it becomes clear that the boy has stopped breathing. He has choked. Or asphyxiated. His son is suddenly gone! It all transpired so quickly. How did Marais let this happen?

But the boy's chest balloons again. It inflates full of vigor. Such a miraculous thing, this human body. Such a miraculous thing, to have a son.

Preller's cocks start crowing at four-thirty, every morning at the same ungodly hour. Sometimes, when Marais is feeling particularly ornery, he'll cackle right back, and the whole thing can degenerate into a verbal cockfight, though this rarely silences them for more than a minute. But today the only person in the world who carries the curious combination of his and Lettie's genes is right here, asleep on his floor. Today, the crowing of Hannie's roosters is symphonic. The room is a tiny palace. It's not the morphine that's intoxicating him, or the lack of sleep, but the crowing itself and the fullness permeating the rondavel. *By God,* he thinks, *I could kiss those roosters.*

Dawn starts up like magic. Blackness melts to indigo. Now fear, like a raccoon, creeps in.

This ecstasy—this full heart—won't stay. Happiness is never permanent. He of all people knows this. And yet, he doesn't want the feeling to end. He doesn't want to end without this feeling. He wants to lash himself to his newfound joy, unmolested by the darker feeling that is sure to return if he continues. *When* he continues, he means. Because that's what one must do, right? Soldier on—as Mother always said—despite the dark feeling. Besides, the dark feeling *was* bearable before, he has to remember this.

But today is different. The chasm between what he's feeling now and the feeling that's bound to return is so great. *Too* great. Which makes him wonder: why would he choose to endure the darkness again?

Joshua yawns sonorously. He rolls to his side.

Marais rotates a thought as if fingering a marble. What if the darkness *doesn't* need to return? What if he were to disappear before it ever has a chance?

He lowers himself to the floor. On instinct, he touches his palm to Charles's soft cheek and kisses his forehead. Look at this boy.

He takes his hat. He adjusts his tie. He trundles quietly out the door of the rondavel.

* * *

Charles is awakened by singing. His eyes flutter open. Orange light is pouring through the window into the little room. There's a chorus of birds.

Hannah sleeps soundly beside him, Joshua on the far side of the rondavel. With the injection he gave Marais last night, it could be noon before the old man rouses himself. That's all right. Let him go on sleeping in his old log bed. As Joshua said, there's plenty of time.

The chorus outside crescendos. Charles rolls onto his shoulder and stares bleary-eyed at the window. Beyond the rondavel is a thin-trunked tree, fifteen feet high, the leaves just starting to color. The tree is swarming with birds, a large flock, maybe a hundred in total, and as they work, they sing.

Yellow weavers! he realizes. Like his old pet. Like Tonto. He can tell what they are from the little globes they're framing out on the tip of each branch. They could be Tonto's distant relations. How did he fail to notice these birds yesterday? Or have they only just arrived this morning?

Charles rubs his eyes, sweeps over to the window, leans halfway out. A hundred nests bulb out and begin to take shape. Behind the tree, a red swath of bougainvillea arcs over the path that winds up to the main house. A pair of hummingbirds dives into a patch of hydrangeas, then bursts into the sky, one pursuing the other. A surge of warmth fills his body. Waves of gratitude unspool within him.

There's a soothing quality to this countryside. He's not returning to the States, or to Europe. That much is clear. He and Hannah will nurse Marais back to health, wean him from the morphine day by day, bit by bit. He's not too far gone. As soon as Marais is healthy again, Charles will help him edit and publish his field notes. He'll salvage his father's name from the science-corrupted bigotry of the world's Sizemores and Conants and Hitlers. At least this one weapon he can strike from their arsenal.

Just like that, the tightness coiled inside him collapses, as if it's been punctured. For as long as he can remember, he has wanted—he has yearned and hungered and longed and ached. But in this moment, he feels himself wanting nothing. Isn't that the central lesson of virtually every Pāli text he's translated over the past fifteen years? True happiness comes from abandoning desire. Of course he knew that. And yet, somehow, he missed the point.

What did Hannah say last night? *No pain, no enlightenment.* He finds himself questioning the story that's at the heart of his whole field of study. What if seeing the four sights—a sick person, an old person, a dead body, and an ascetic—was not actually what led prince Siddhārtha to seek a way out of suffering? As a child, the prince lost his mother—it must have been the deepest hurt imaginable. Just as it was for Charles.

In the back of his mind, he registers the sound of footsteps sliding through wet grass. He turns to wake Marais. He turns to a tangle of sheets. The bed lies empty.

* * *

What a sunrise! Marais really has to hand it to Preller. Preller knew what he was doing when he picked out this farm in the middle of God-knows-where. Marais has been giving the man hell when really it's only Preller's wife who deserves it. Preller's been a good friend. He's watched out for Marais even when Marais has been, well, difficult.

The grass chills his bare feet as he pulls himself—cane, step, cane, step—through the sopping orchard. Trees explode with pears, pecans, peaches, lemons. In places the grass is so deep the blades caress his knees. Dew drops leap and cling to his trousers. Marais could watch that pinkening sun forever, nosing itself up from the horizon.

He exits the orchard through rows of cabbage and kale, then stops in the field where the grass has gone uncut. If he had all the time in the world, he would wait here for the rest of the day watching the pink sun arc through the sky, performing its tricks of color—transposing from yellow to white, orange to umber.

Here is Hannie's brother, working on his ox cart outside his ramshackle house. Marais stops. He asks for a small favor. He asks to borrow a shotgun.

"What do you need the gun *for*?" Hannie's brother doesn't look at him while waiting for an answer. Just keeps on greasing the axle of his cart.

"What do you *think* I need it for?" Marais says. "To deal with a problem."

The man glances up, eyes brushing against him. "What sort of problem is that?"

Marais rubs his hands together. He didn't plan this far in advance. "Snakes. There's a pair outside my place, and they're doing a number on the little birds."

Hannie's brother blinks. Twice. He lumbers over to his outbuilding. The door creaks open and slams shut behind him. When he returns, he is carrying the gun—twelve-bore, double-barreled. He tosses it to Marais. "If you catch yourself an extra snake—more than you can eat—I wouldn't say no."

It does seem a shame to leave on a day like this, with the morning air so cool before the heat descends, and the weavers abuzz, and the sky as clear and blue as it's ever been. But, Marais reminds himself, the darkness will return as it always does. Like his head, or his heart, it will accompany him wherever he goes. It will eclipse everything, even the sun.

Even if he manages to squeeze through the next onslaught, even if he comes out the other side unscathed and still breathing, think of all the time that would still lie ahead. Think of the surfeit of days and hours and minutes, the millions of seconds unfurling before him. Think of how asphyxiating even one moment can be when the dark feeling descends, then think of having to endure and slog through every one of those moments, and it's clear that now is the time. Now is his chance. He will sever the cord in this moment while life is briefly light and golden.

He tilts back his hat, and the sun, now risen, floods through him.

Slowly, he raises the gun. He admires the grain of the wood. The flash of steel in the sunlight. Decent quality craftsmanship, now that he looks closely. He sticks the barrel delicately into his sternum. Easier than expected, turning a gun on oneself. It's as if the bones of his breast were designed to host this exact device.

He slides the gun to the left. Only a matter of inches. Here is where the heart has hidden itself all these days, beating away patiently in its box. *Tick tick tick.*

An itch gnaws at his finger.

We are born into this world with a will to live and a wish to die. When the wish overpowers the will, life comes to an end. The only sensible thing Freud has ever said.

There's the itch again. And that question. Always the same question. *What if?* This time he doesn't need to wonder. The decision, he realizes, is already made. He feels it. He *hears* it. The gate has shut. The bolt slides home. It locks into its cradle.

There's no shame here, he thinks, only courage. To dive fully into this life, to taste from the sea of suffering, to analyze the cause of that suffering, to realize life's inherent unsatisfactoriness, and then to choose—to *choose*—a different course. What could be more courageous?

He's giddy at his decision, at the very decisiveness of it all. He feels like he's drowning in happiness. His toes tap. His legs ache to dance.

God, how his finger itches. See how it trembles on the trigger.

This is it, he thinks.

In the distance, a family of springbok grazes, a farmer tills his field, a pair of birds pins the sky. They are all just soft black spots. The land rolls on forever.

His pulse fireworks through every limb. *Tick tick tick tick tick.*

Easy does it.

He triple-checks his angle. Wipes at the sweat pouring into his eyes. No mistakes. Can't afford that.

Do it now! DO IT NOW!

His heart beats so frantically it could break free of his chest.

This is it This Is It THIS IS IT!

Tick.

* * *

The morning is torn open. Charles jumps up from the window. What was that? An explosion? A *gunshot*?

He is wearing only a wrinkled white shirt and yesterday's underwear as he bursts from the rondavel onto the gravel path that shoots past Preller's house into the fields. He's guided only by the reverberation of that sound. He sprints in the direction of the explosion.

The weavers beat their wings like dragons. They scatter from the tree like shot.

At the far side of the house, he turns the corner and ploughs through the orchard. He slips over fallen red and yellow fruit that squishes beneath his feet, flesh and peel fermenting in piles. When he clears the orchard, he stops suddenly, panting.

Marais stands a hundred yards away in the wet, knee-high grass. His back is turned, Panama hat cocked on his head, silhouetted against the red sky. The sun burns through him. The man—his father—is translucent.

Charles feels disoriented by the light. He tries to catch his breath.

Marais is fine after all. He's perfectly fine. Charles only imagined the shot. The explosion, or whatever it was. How easily the mind deceives itself. His father is still here.

Then why, he thinks, won't my heart stop racing?

* * *

For a moment, Marais is actually relieved. The gun misfired. Piece of junk. The good news is he can still change his mind. If he chooses to. Even if he doesn't, just knowing that he *can* change his mind makes all the difference. It's a relief to have a choice. Heat from the sun spreads through him. His arm was trembling so hard he missed himself entirely. Ha! He never was a very good shot. The good news is that he's fine. Still standing. Free of pain.

He notices blood, trickling through tiny holes in the front of his shirt. Pouring really. And the dozens of tiny holes, he sees, are really one large hole. He thinks he can see his own heart spurting through that one large hole. When he considers all of this, does the basic calculations, it's clear that he can't change his mind after all. There is no choice. This too is a relief.

He turns and there, at the other end of the field, is Charles. Marais waves at him. Charles pauses, then waves back. Funny to be waving at a time like this. There's a look on the boy's face that at first Marais can't make out. When he does, it nearly breaks what remains of his heart. Charles looks genuinely shocked. And that look makes a part of Marais wish that he *could* take it all back. That they could start the morning all over again. Coffee would be nice. He never says no to a hot cup in the morning. And a biscuit or two. Fresh fruit from the orchard.

But his heart is full of holes. There's shot embedded in his chest. At some point soon, his own shock will abate and unfathomable pain is going to set in.

He opens his mouth. He yawns as widely as he can.

Charles starts running toward him, bearing down on him. *What is the boy doing? Nobody runs that fast.*

It turns out the barrel fits even better in his mouth than it did in the sternum. Marais forces his tongue out. Slides it underneath the steel cylinder. Backs the barrel straight into his throat. This time he doesn't delay.

* * *

Marais waves at him across the field, and all at once, Charles knows what has happened. Even from this far away, he can see the blood. He sees the hole ripped through his father's chest. The man has shot himself for Christsake. How could Marais do this to him? Maybe it's the unexpectedness of the whole situation that causes Charles to wave back. He's not waving really. He's pumping his hands, signaling wildly for Marais to wait, because Marais doesn't seem to hear the word *STOP* no matter how urgently Charles shouts.

Then, his father, a hundred yards away, shoves the barrel of a shotgun in his mouth. Charles sprints, prepares to tackle him to the ground. He runs faster than he's ever run, through rows of cabbage and kale, until thunder splits the air.

Charles slides to a stop.

Marais's head jerks backward. He sways slightly to the left, a weathervane buoyed by the breeze. His legs buckle beneath him. His body collapses, the way a doll can drop from a child's hand.

* * *

Marais hears no report. He hears nothing but silence—who knew how loud silence could be?—and he watches from his back as the white sun bakes his face and illuminates the dome of the sky. The sky which is filled with weavers.

He watches from the ground, as if from deep underwater, the slow aqueous movements of shadows. He feels himself lifted, hands curling beneath him. He gives himself over to those hands. Oh, the feeling of being held and rocked!

A face swims above him. It's *his* face, only younger, and Lettie's. He manages to lift his hand just enough to touch that face, Charles's face. For the second time. For the last time.

My boy, he tries to say. *My* son! But something entirely different bubbles out, which sounds like *quock kri lai*. Still, even this is all right. The boy doesn't need Marais to tell him. Charles already knows who he is.

* * *

Charles takes Marais's head in his arms to keep it from getting soiled. He brushes the dust from his hair, smooths out the creases in his shirt.

He wonders why he's not weeping. He should be weeping, he thinks. Instead, he's already starting to construct the framework for how he'll tell this story later today, next week, thirty years from now. He already knows how it will start. How on one particular morning, a vivid bursting morning on a small farm eighteen miles west of Pretoria, the farm of a family friend, he was awakened by weaver birds and the shrill report of a gun.

In Charles's lap, Marais's eyes reflect the open sky. Clouds sail gently through the blue-black blood that pools in the grass alongside Charles's bare legs. He touches the body, inspects the skin, rough and foreign and familiar.

Coarse hair sprouts around the ring on Marais's finger. He still wears his hat, pitched slightly back to reveal his high forehead. His face looks almost normal, clean and shaven. A handsome man, even at this age, even in this state. Charles thinks he can make out certain details of his own face in his father's. It's only when he lifts and examines the back of the head where significant pieces of flesh and skull are missing, a head that has become literally porous, that he sees just how much is out of sorts. Just how permanent a decision can be.

"I've only just arrived," Charles says to him. "I've finally arrived." He tightens a fist, chokes back a sob. "And here you've gone and left me once again."

August 1936, Pretoria Railway Station, Pretoria, Union of South Africa

"Flowers, mister?"

The platform buzzes with hawkers—young Afrikaner boys in frayed wool coats, old women with dark, leathery arms, and every human variation between. Their carts are stuffed with sundries: blistered apples, leafy teas, flaking pastries, sticky sweets, hand-drawn postcards, fraying maps, and heaps of crustless sandwiches.

Charles maneuvers through the crowd with the heavier bags. Hannah strides alongside with the lighter ones, keeping a solid distance between them.

She's annoyed with him. For a full week, they've debated and deliberated. They've embraced and kissed and cried. Admittedly, he's been stubborn. It's an inherited trait. But even here, standing at the station, they still haven't agreed where to go.

Shortly after Marais's death, Sophie told Charles and Hannah that she wanted them to have her house. She wanted them to raise a family there, to have children running over the floorboards for years to come. Four months later, Sophie's heart gave out. Charles isn't ready to settle in Pretoria, packed as it is so tightly with family history.

"Your godmother begged us to stay here," Hannah protested. "And really, where else are we going to go?"

Hannah had a point. They're not returning to Harvard, where Conant still presides, and Europe is out of the question with its rising Nazi furor. They are here in southern Africa now. He needs to see if he can make this place home again.

"We can go to Durban," he replied. "If it doesn't work out there, we'll head further east to Mozambique." Neither of them was particularly persuaded by those options.

Charles buried his father in Heroes' Acre, Pretoria, next to his wife, Charles's mother. It's strange, but with Marais gone, it feels as if some invisible rope that's been towing him along has suddenly snapped. He has been journeying through Marais's field notes with the help of a magnifying glass and a bottomless well of curiosity. He has cut and spliced and reassembled half a dozen volumes into a book-length manuscript on the white ants. The book will reveal to Harvard and to the world who his father truly was. A genius? Perhaps. More importantly, a principled human, a decent man.

"Mister, flowers?"

He didn't want to leave Sophie's place vacant. He tried convincing Joshua to move in to keep the house running in their absence. "I can't do that," Joshua said. "You and I both know your auntie's neighbors wouldn't be too pleased having a man like me living in her house. And anyway, my life is on the sea now. My home *is* that little boat. I don't need anything else. I have every last thing I require."

They were just starting to stow Sophie's dishes when Charles had an idea. Leo and Sarah, their friends from the ship, had said they intended to settle in Pretoria. It didn't take long for Charles and Hannah to track them down through the Pretoria synagogue.

Leo had suffered a bruised jaw and a dislocated shoulder in the Cape Town melee, he told Charles by phone. "But not to worry. The miracle of the human body is that it's designed to heal itself." The next morning, the German family was swinging away on the front porch. The boy ran inside the house before Charles even had a chance to invite them in.

"I could get used to a place like this," said Leo, touring his way around the bookshelves. Charles glanced at Hannah.

"There are Greyshirts all over Pretoria," Hannah reminded them.

"Those guys?" said Leo. "From what we've seen, the fellows up here are small potatoes. At least compared to the Nazis in Germany."

"The truth is, dear," Sarah said, "we're tired of running."

So Charles invited them to stay. The house would be theirs for as long as they wished.

Above the swell of heads Charles tries to catch a glimpse of the train schedule posted on the far side of the platform. Pretoria Station, he thinks, is showing its age. He can almost picture Marais with his cane and hat on this very platform the day the station was inaugurated forty-one years ago. Charles can imagine his father shouting to a crowd of thousands, preparing to lambast President Kruger, to give the old man a schooling about ethics and nation-building and the real meaning of political leadership. He can almost see Marais, at the last minute, swallow a bowl of his own pride, and instead, congratulate Kruger on his accomplishments as he'd been asked to do. When else did Eugene Nielen Marais ever hold his tongue? That day, Charles realizes, he did it for his family. He did it for his wife. And for the child growing inside her.

"Mister, you hard 'a hearing?" A barefoot boy suspendered in ripped khakis is chasing after him with a trio of wilted roses, dirt ground into his fingernails.

"What do you *want*?" Charles says.

The boy lowers his eyes. He can't be more than seven.

"I was only asking if you wanted some flowers," he says shyly. "For the lady?"

"For *whom*?"

"I'm thinking he means me," Hannah says. But the boy is already chasing after the couple ahead of them. "Honestly, Charles, how is yelling at a child going to help our situation?"

"I figured it couldn't hurt to try."

Hannah doesn't crack a smile.

"Look," he says. "I'm sorry. I don't always have all the answers."

Wind tears across the platform. Pages of newspaper whip up and scatter through the crowd.

Hannah edges closer to him. She takes his hand and touches it to her belly, which is already beginning to swell. He's still amazed by her perfect, swollen bump and by the role he's played in its creation. It makes him happy every time he touches her. Which, he realizes with a rush of gratitude, is the reason she wants him touching her now. Sometimes he kneels in front of her and sings right into her abdomen—Afrikaans folk songs, Cole Porter, but also, when he's in just the right mood, Puccini in a stunning falsetto, which never fails to make her laugh.

"I want to name her Aletta," she says, still holding his hand. "In memory of your mother. We can call her Lettie."

Papers drenched in newsprint swirl like birds above their heads. His breath catches in his throat. "How do you know it's a girl?"

"I have a feeling about this. Call it instinct if you like."

A steam train clacks into the station, kicking up dust. Wheels shriek against rails. The train comes to a stop, wheezing through its valves. A few dozen passengers pour out of its two cars into the blustery day.

The conductor paces alongside the train, licks a pencil, scribbles on a notepad. "Nyl . . . *stroom*!" he croons when the train has emptied.

Hannah glances up. "Isn't that the name of the town? The one near the forest where your father said he did his research?"

A small crowd rushes toward the first car and begins to board.

The forest with the chacmas. The hut by the kloof. What did Marais say exactly? That his little hut was still standing—that it had everything they'd need to live comfortably for years? At the time, Charles dismissed it as one more mad scheme of his father's. But here is the train hissing in front of them. In his head, gears begin grinding. Their future is set slowly in motion.

Two young girls in yellow coats are sucking on lollipops with such intensity that they seem to have lost their parents. A man pounces down the steps of the second car and spots them. He shakes his head in amusement. He could only be their father. Without a word, he scoops up a girl under each arm and tromps back up the stairs. They disappear inside the train.

"Nyl . . . *stroom*!" calls the conductor. "Last call for Nylstroom!"

Charles looks at Hannah.

"What do you think?" she asks hesitantly.

When she smiles, there's a touch of sadness in her face, but also hope. He takes her hand, the warmest hand he's ever touched, and together they board the train, bound for Waterberg.

Postscript

November 1937, the Forest at Doornhoek, Waterberg, Union of South Africa

All through the night a chest cold has kept you tossing. I promised your mother I'd watch over you. She needs the rest. It's not easy raising a baby. There are two of us, only one of you, and still we're outnumbered. Your mother sleeps soundly on the other side of our little bed with her familiar snore of reeds and rushes. You're snug and sandwiched between us.

The first spark of light pierces the hut's square window. The sun toasts our one-room home and turns the walls to gold. You roll onto your back and kick your stockinged feet in the air. Your eyes snap open. You belch. You smile. Your diaper stinks. I've never been so in love.

"*Evaṃ me sutaṃ*, little one," I whisper. "'Thus have I heard.' *That* is the story of how you came to be." I tickle your toes, which are wrinkled and colored like apricots. "To know where you're going, you've got to know where you came from." You can't yet understand more than a handful of words, but you're already an expert in voice inflections, which can make you coo or giggle or break into chest-wrenching sobs.

Once there was a man who had everything: fame, family, and all the wealth he required. But when he tasted the depths of suffering, the most brutal sort of pain, he gave it all up. He moved to the forest. He lived like a mendicant. He was intent on understanding the cause of that suffering and the true nature of the mind. I'm not talking about the Buddha. I'm talking about your grandfather. How I wish that you'd been able to meet him. But in a way you already have. He was here. These are *his* walls, fashioned by *his* hands. He knew every inch of this forest, every rock, and tree, and wild creature.

I'll tell you the whole story again when you're older, though the details will inevitably change. Then one day you'll tell it to your own children, and they to theirs. This is how families live on, through scribes like us. With each transmission, the story will be reshaped—from mistakes and embellishments and the raw bits of ourselves that seep into it. Eventually, a story is all that will remain of me and of your mother, and one day, my sweet love, it's all that will remain of you.

I squeeze your fat arms. I tickle your neck. You look up at me with a kind of trust I can't remember ever having myself, until now.

This is not the time to have brought a child into the world. I'm all too aware of this. Europe is combusting with hate. Africa may fall next. But no matter what happens, here's what I want you to remember: The world needs more happy endings.

You crawl across me, your knees digging into my chest, your elbows assaulting my belly, and I gather you up in my arms and change you on the floor. You struggle in vain to peel away your father's hands, *my* hands. You don't like being messed with. With Marais gone, and Sophie too, I can't help but think that I am no longer a child, to anyone. No trace of the child remains in me. I am only a father. I am, entirely, a father.

I zip you back into the green night suit that your mother knitted for you, with its yellow sun and flowering trees and diving birds, and together we gaze out the window into the dense thicket of wild figs.

"Come on, Lettie." I snatch you by the scruff of your suit and tuck you against my chest. "But quietly. None of this noisy stuff. We mustn't wake your mother."

I unlatch the door and pad outside in my bare feet. The ground is moist with silver dew. A glassy stream courses alongside the path that winds up toward the kloof. Mud seeps between and around my toes, and I can hardly tell where the earth begins and I end.

You're radiating heat inside my coat. Your head pokes out just enough that your eyes see everything and fill with the world. The forest is impossibly verdant. It smells like a hundred million years ago. The whole earth is alive and spinning with sounds—squawking, screeching, dying, dancing, buzzing, birthing sounds. It's as if the entire planet is singing for us. "Marais," it sings. "Marais, Marais, Marais!"

"I've been waiting for this," I tell you, and I realize just how much I mean it. "Let's find Grandad's monkeys."

Note from the Author

While *The Farther Shore* is a product of the imagination, many of the characters and events featured in the novel are inspired by the historical record. As a writer of historical fiction, I took the liberty of working both with and around the known facts.

James Bryant Conant (1893–1978), a Harvard-educated chemist, served as president of Harvard University from 1933–53. During his tenure, Conant came to play a key advisory role in the Manhattan Project, which oversaw development of the first atomic bombs. After retirement, he served first as the United States High Commissioner for Germany, overseeing the restoration of German sovereignty after World War II, and then as Ambassador to West Germany.

For details about Conant's and Harvard's antisemitic history, I drew creative inspiration from Professor Stephen H. Norwood's *The Third Reich in the Ivory Tower* (Cambridge University Press, 2009). From Norwood's point of view, "The Harvard University administration during the 1930s, led by President James Conant, ignored numerous opportunities to take a principled stand against the Hitler regime . . . and contributed to Nazi Germany's efforts to improve its image in the West."

According to Norwood, many influential Harvard faculty, students, and alumni shared the administration's lack of concern about rising Nazi antisemitism. The novel's depiction of the faculty's mock trial of Hitler, for example, which Hannah decries, is based on an event that occurred at Harvard in 1934.

That same year, despite protests from Boston's Jewish leaders, Harvard faculty, alumni, and students welcomed the Nazi warship *Karlsruhe* on its visit to Boston, then entertained the ship's officers at a formal ball.

Weeks later, the Harvard administration welcomed alumnus Ernst Hanfstaengl, Hitler's foreign press chief, back to Harvard College for his 25th class reunion. Student editors at the *Harvard Crimson* called on the administration to award Hanfstaengl an honorary degree "as a mark of honor appropriate to his high position in the government of a friendly country." Reunion festivities were interrupted when a prominent rabbi confronted Hanfstaengl in the middle of the Yard, demanding to know what the Nazi official had meant by his recent remark that "everything would soon be settled for the Jews in Germany." The rabbi was trembling visibly. "Does it mean extermination?" he demanded. Hanfstaengl smiled and said that he was not at liberty to discuss work. "I am on vacation. I am with my old friends." He then proceeded to Conant's house for tea.

The novel's opening scene depicts Conant presiding over a ceremony in Memorial Church to honor four alumni who died fighting for Germany in World War I. Details in the novel are taken from Norwood's account of the actual event, which took place in March of 1935. The plaque bearing the names of the four alumni still hangs in the main sanctuary of Memorial Church. The wreath, along with the swastika, was removed long ago.

Paul Kruger (1825–1904), born Stephanus Johannes Paulus Kruger, led the Boer resistance movement following Britain's annexation of the Transvaal in 1877 and was instrumental in winning the Transvaal's independence in the First Boer War. He served as the fifth president of the South African Republic (Transvaal) from 1883–1900. In May 1900, with the Transvaal's mounting losses in the Second Boer War, he exiled himself first to Mozambique and then to Europe to seek assistance for his beleaguered country's last stand against Britain. Kruger never saw the Transvaal again. In 1904, he died in Switzerland. His central role from the early history of the Transvaal through the Second Boer War is meticulously documented by Martin Meredith in *Diamonds, Gold, and War: The British, the Boers, and the Making of South Africa.*

Gustav Preller (1875–1943) was a journalist, writer, historian, and literary critic. After the Boer guerrillas' surrender to the British in 1902, Preller became a leader of the Second Afrikaans Language Movement. Together with Eugène Nielen Marais and others, he paved the way for the nationwide ascendancy of Afrikaans, which ultimately replaced Dutch in legal, religious, and educational matters.

Lord Alfred Milner (1854–1925) was instrumental in Britain's decision to wage war on the Transvaal and the Orange Free State, and later, in administering the newly conquered Boer territories. The meeting in the novel between Marais and Milner is documented by Marais's biographer, Leon Rousseau. Milner left South Africa in 1905 with little to show for his efforts to anglicize the Afrikaners other than a level of anti-British sentiment significantly greater than that which had existed before the war. Over 100,000 Boer civilians had been forcibly relocated into concentration camps, where approximately 26,000—four in five of them children under the age of sixteen—died from malnutrition and disease. Less well-known is that thousands of Black Africans were also interned in separate, racially segregated concentration camps, where as many as 20,000 died. Milner felt betrayed by Britain, which had grown to view the war as a catastrophic and inordinately expensive mistake. Just five years after Britain conquered the two Boer republics, devastating the land and decimating their populations, it handed the Transvaal and Orange River Colony back to Afrikaner leaders.

Alec Austin, Eugene Marais's claim mate and research assistant at Doornhoek, is described only in passing at the beginning of Marais's posthumous landmark work *The Soul of the Ape* as a "young friend and countryman who, under the most disadvantageous circumstances, had attained a remarkable knowledge of the higher African mammalia and their comparative anatomy. An untimely death unfortunately cut short his work." Little else is documented about Austin or the cause of his death.

The S.S. *Stuttgart*, a steamer of the North German Lloyd line, was chartered by the newly formed Council for German Jewry in London to carry 537 Jewish refugees from Bremerhaven to South Africa in October 1936 before a nationwide South African ban on Jewish immigration was to take effect on November 1. On October 26, future South African prime minister H.F. Verwoerd and a number of academics joined forces with the Greyshirts, Cape Town's most notorious fascist organization, to rally against Jewish immigration. That evening more than a thousand protestors convened at the docks, prepared to use violent force to keep the Jewish refugees from entering the country. Fortunately, the Greyshirts' timing was off. The *Stuttgart* didn't arrive until the following morning, beating the immigration ban by just four days. By that time, a steady rain had dampened the protestors' enthusiasm, and the ship's passengers successfully immigrated to South Africa.

LOUIS THEODOR WEICHARDT (1894–1985) was the founder of the South African Gentile National Socialist Movement and its paramilitary unit called the Gryshemde or Greyshirts (modeled on the Nazis' brown-shirted Sturmabteilung). Though Weichardt insisted that his organization was not a puppet of the Nazi party, the Greyshirts' actions proved otherwise. In 1949 the Greyshirts were renamed the White Workers Party. There are a number of interesting parallels between the rise of apartheid in South Africa and the country's history of antisemitism.

DOLF ERASMUS, an old acquaintance of Marais's, was the one who first brought him to Waterberg by arranging for Marais to buy tin prospecting rights from Doornhoek's owner. In his essay "The Road to Waterberg," Marais details in reverential terms his first glimpses of Waterberg while traveling from Nylstroom to Doornhoek with Dolf at the helm of a horse cart.

GYS AND MARIA ("TAMARIA") VAN ROOYEN, the proprietors of the farm Rietfontein in Waterberg, played host to Marais for a number of years after their five youngest children died in British concentration camps. It's unclear whether Marais paid rent to the van Rooyens with any sort of regularity. What is clear is that Marais's relationship with Tamaria was a complicated one—Rousseau, his biographer, suggests that Tamaria exploited Marais's addiction and plied him with opium and chlorodyne at exorbitant rates. According to Rousseau, it was Marais's son, the estranged Eugène Charles Gerard Marais, who, hearing of his father's physical and financial demise at Rietfontein, ultimately traveled to Waterberg, packed him up, and shepherded him back to Pretoria. In 1916, the year after Marais left Rietfontein for good, Tamaria died.

Sophie Ueckerman was one of Eugene Nielen Marais's nine siblings to survive infancy. After his wife's sudden death, Marais left his infant son in the care of Sophie, who raised Eugene Charles, her godson and now foster son, as her own.

Aletta ("Lettie") Marais (1871–1895) died of puerperal fever at the age of twenty-three, eight days after the birth of their child, Eugène Charles Gerard Marais. Her death was entirely preventable.

Eugène Nielen Marais (1871–1936) was a naturalist, poet, editor, diplomat, attorney, sheriff, and a father of the modern Afrikaans language. In 1936, he took his own life on Preller's farm in Pelindaba. He had no family with him when he died.

Marais's naturalist studies were published in book form only posthumously. Of his major works available in English—*My Friends the Baboons*, *The Road to Waterberg and Other Essays*, *The Soul of the Ape*, and *The Soul of the Ant*—only the last is still in print, but they are all very much worth hunting out. The sole biography of Marais, translated into English by the author Leon

Rousseau as *The Dark Stream: The Story of Eugène Marais*, was published in South Africa and has been out of print for decades. Rousseau's work involved a staggering amount of research and has become something of a bible to Marais enthusiasts.

Eugène Charles Gerard Marais (1895–1970s) never studied Pāli, and, as far as I know, never traveled to the United States. Little is documented about this sole heir to Eugène Nielen Marais, other than the fact that he worked as an attorney in the small Transvaal town of Brits and died single and childless. According to a friend of the younger Marais, quoted by Rousseau, Eugène Charles "never begat any children because he did not want any child who might take after his father."

In 2009, I had the good fortune of interviewing one of Eugène Charles's distant cousins in Waterberg. The cousin described Eugène Charles as a lonely, troubled man and recounted an attempt in the 1960s to pay him a visit at his home in Brits. Eugène Charles apparently drove away his cousin at gunpoint.

Two of Marais's books open with brief prefaces written by Eugène Charles that I find strangely haunting. Although he was instrumental in facilitating the posthumous publication of Marais's books, thus ensuring Eugène Nielen's continued modest fame, never does he refer to Marais as his father. His signature in one reads simply "E. Marais"—as if he had no identity of his own. As if he were merely a vessel, or mirror, for his father's thoughts.

Acknowledgments

It takes a sizable village to birth a debut novel, and I'm grateful to numerous people for helping to bring this book into the world:

To Jane von Mehren, who stuck with me until we found the right home, along with Maggie Cooper, Kate Mack, Nayla Delgado, and the rest of the staff at Aevitas Creative Management. To the small and mighty team at Green City Books, including Joe Olshan, Isaac Peterson, and Jessica Hammerman for their vision, flexibility, and support along the way. To Julia Borcherts, David Groff, Grover Gardner, Dennis Kleinman, Brenna Ebner, Fauzia Burke, David Pilip, Sonja Wooley, and Sanda Balaban.

To Ann Patty, who believed in me first, and Brett Hall-Jones and the whole Community of Writers team, who lit a fire and got me started.

To those who met with or accompanied me on various legs of my initial field research in South Africa, including Jack Orsulak, Mauritz Hansen, Clive Walker, Herman van Niekerk, and the owners of the Doornhoek mine. And to those who helped review my Afrikaans and South African history, including Danita Viviers, and especially Dr. Johann Lodewyk Marais of the University of Pretoria.

To Anne Blackburn and Edie Meidav for friendship across continents and decades. To early readers Sylvia Baldwin and Richard Roberts. And to Scott Adler, who egged me on in all the best ways.

To authors Janet Benton, Anna Nordberg, Zeeva Bukai, Bora Lee Reed, Judith Starkston, and Christopher Castellani.

To Jamie Ford, brilliant writer, good friend, and true mensch.

To Professor Donald Swearer, whose passion for Buddhist history and for teaching was infectious. And to Professor Charles Hallisey, who taught me much about the Buddhist world, including the importance of prioritizing ethics and relationships above all else. The character Charles Marais shares his given name and field of study, but there the resemblance ends. All mistakes related to Indic thought and history are entirely my own. My particular gratitude to the students in Professor Hallisey's 2025 Buddhism and Fiction seminar at Harvard Divinity School who read a draft manuscript, penned poems to the protagonists, and prodded me with deeply thoughtful questions.

To Mindela Ruby, my dear writing partner of so many years, without whose camaraderie and fearless editorial insights I might not have completed this book.

To Miles, who, at two years old, had the chutzpah to line up dozens of his matchbox cars across Amy Tan's dining room table, because they clearly belonged there. To Jonah for labeling and stamping a million postcards. To both for their curiosity, humor, and profound goodness.

And to Emily—my partner, dearest reader, and after all these years, still my *kalyāṇa mittā* on shores far and near.

Deep bows to all of you.

Guide for Reading Groups and Book Clubs

Twenty-one years ago, I happened upon an article in *Harper's Magazine* by Duncan Murrell entitled "Swarm" about a termite expert in Louisiana. What captured my attention most in the article, though, was a passing reference to one of the termite expert's predecessors.

Eugène Marais was a South African naturalist and journalist who, at the turn of the twentieth century, devastated by personal loss, abandoned his infant son and absconded to an African forest to study first chacma baboons and then white ants (aka termites). In a number of ways, he was very much the precursor to Jane Goodall, Louis Leakey, and Dian Fossey. Something about Murrell's descriptions led me to tuck the information away for further research.

Years later, I began to dive into Marais's writings and biography, and was astounded to learn how far ahead of his time his research truly was. And his life story was the stuff of fiction. The novel simmering in my mind would need to reconnect Marais and the son he'd abandoned.

Over time, my obsession with Marais grew. After a work trip to South Africa for the World Bank Group, I took a couple weeks and traveled to the forest where Marais had lived. While the area was closed, a series of serendipitous events brought me to the remnants of his hut in the gorge where he studied the baboon troop.

Marais was obsessed with understanding the links between the evolution of memory in humans, our loss of instinct, and our own psychic suffering. Unexpected parallels with Buddhism—a field where I'd done doctoral work years earlier—became apparent, and I decided to make Marais's adult son a professor of the Buddhist Pāli language at Harvard in the 1930s. Soon after, I stumbled upon Professor Stephen Norwood's recently published *The Third Reich in the Ivory Tower*, which details how the Harvard administration was flirting openly with Nazi Germany at exactly the time Charles would have been teaching there.

Startling similarities between the origins of Afrikaans and Pāli, and between the use of concentration camps by the British during the Boer Wars and the Nazis during World War II, along with rising support for authoritarianism in our present day, became rich fodder for the novel. Researching and writing this story with all its historical detail became a core part of my life for over a decade.

Ancient Buddhist literature emphasizes that we must deeply consider our debts to the past. I suppose this book, which brings Marais back to life in completely new ways, is part of my attempt to repay those debts. I'd be delighted to join any book club that selects *The Farther Shore* for a 30-minute virtual Q & A.

—Seth Fleisher

Topics and Questions for Discussion

Select questions from the list of ideas below that most resonate for your group: a choose-your-own-adventure of sorts!

On Fathers and Sons

1. Marais abandons his newborn son after experiencing deep personal tragedy—a choice that reverberates across decades. To what extent does grief alone explain his decision, or does the decision reflect something deeper about his character? Can understanding a parent's reasons for leaving ever fully repair the damage caused by their absence?
2. Charles has built an entire adult identity in the shadow of a father he never knew. When he finally confronts his father's legacy, how does it reshape his understanding of who he is? Is it possible to inherit a parent's brilliance without also inheriting their capacity for destruction?
3. The novel is framed around "fathers and sons," but what about the absent mother—Marais's wife? How does her death set everything else in motion? What role does she play in the story even in her absence?
4. How does the father-son relationship in *The Farther Shore* compare to other literary portrayals of paternal abandonment—e.g., Thomas Stone in *Cutting for Stone* or Nathan Price in *The Poisonwood Bible*? What makes Marais's abandonment of his son distinctive?

On Memory, Science, and Dangerous Ideas

5. Marais's research into memory, addiction, and the hive mind was genuinely ahead of its time. What happens in the novel when those ideas—conceived in one context—are appropriated and weaponized in another?
6. The novel explores Harvard's historical complicity with racial science and its connections to Nazi ideology in the 1930s. How does the novel's portrayal of institutional complicity challenge the way we think about prestigious institutions today?
7. The title—*The Farther Shore*—suggests a destination that may or may not be reachable. What do you think "the farther shore" represents for Marais and for Charles? How does the *Dhammapada* passage quoted at the beginning of the book help illuminate these meanings?

On Buddhism, Judaism, and Spiritual Life

8. Charles is a professor of ancient Buddhist history at Harvard—a field that seems, on its surface, far removed from the political dangers closing in around him. Does his immersion in Buddhist thought offer him any refuge or clarity—or does it complicate his ability to act?
9. What function does the recurring line "Thus have I heard" play in the novel? What is heard, who is doing the hearing, and what are the implications?
10. The novel sits at the intersection of Buddhism, Judaism, Christianity, and indigenous African religions. What

connections or tensions among these traditions does the book surface? How do they inform the characters' understanding of suffering, memory, and obligation?

11. One of Buddhism's central insights is that attachment causes suffering. Marais is a man of extreme attachments—to his research, to his grief, to his solitude. Charles, by contrast, has built a life around detachment. Is there a middle path?
12. The novel offers three different Buddhist models related to the experience of being left behind: Rāhula (the Buddha's son), Ananda (the Buddha's disciple), and the Buddha himself (after the loss of his mother shortly after his birth). Does Charles ultimately identify with one of these models?

On Race, Colonialism, and the Rise of Fascism

11. The novel spans from the British concentration camps of the Boer War to the shadow of the Third Reich. How does the novel draw connections between these two historical moments? What does the book suggest about the continuity between colonial violence and fascist ideology?
12. Marais conducts his field research largely on baboons and termites in the South African bush—work that is later weaponized to support theories of racial hierarchy. How does the novel explore the relationship between the study of animal behavior and the dehumanization of people?
13. The novel is set in the past but was written in and for the present. What resonances did you find between the book's historical period and our own political moment? Did the novel change the way you think about how

institutions—universities, scientific establishments, governments—can become complicit in ideologies they claim to oppose?

14. The novel is told entirely from the perspectives of Marais and Charles with one exception: a short chapter right in the middle of the book told from Joshua's perspective. While Joshua remains a critical character for the remainder of the novel, his point of view never resurfaces. What is the effect of briefly privileging Joshua's point of view and then subordinating it? How does the novel navigate thorny issues of race, gender, and power, particularly in light of the decades of South African apartheid that followed historically?

On Structure, Craft, and the Reading Experience

15. *The Farther Shore* moves between two interlocking timelines—Marais's story in 1890s–1910s South Africa and Charles's story at 1930s Harvard. How did the dual timeline affect your reading experience? What is the effect on you, the reader, when the two timelines suddenly merge toward the end?
16. The novel is.inspired by the true story of Eugène Marais but takes significant fictional liberties. And Charles, as drawn in the book, is largely invented. How did knowing that portions of the novel are rooted in real history affect your reading?
17. Two of the most socially marginalized figures—Hannah and Joshua—play crucial roles in the novel. What does their presence add to the story's exploration of justice?

On the Personal and the Universal

18. The novel explores the vast distances we'll travel to find our way home. What does "home" mean in this novel? Do any of the characters actually arrive?

19. If you could ask the author one question about the novel, what would it be?

Enhance Your Book Club

Learn more about Eugène Marais. The real Eugène Marais (1871–1936) was a South African lawyer, naturalist, poet, and journalist whose work on termites and primate behavior anticipated discoveries that wouldn't be recognized for decades. His books *The Soul of the White Ant* and *The Soul of the Ape* remain extraordinary reads. And Leon Rousseau's *The Dark Stream* remains the definitive biography of Marais.

Explore the historical backdrop. The Boer War concentration camps, in which tens of thousands of Afrikaner and Black civilians died, remain one of the lesser-known atrocities of the British Empire. Emily Hobhouse's contemporary accounts of the camps—in *The Brunt of the War and Where It Fell* and in *Report of a Visit to the Camps of Women and Children in the Cape and Orange River Colonies*—offer a fascinating primary-source companion to the novel's timeline.

Dig into Harvard's complicated history. The novel draws on real history—Harvard's connections to eugenics and racial science in the early twentieth century are well documented. For readers interested in this thread, several recent histories explore American universities' entanglement with scientific racism during this period, in particular, Stephen Norwood's *The Third Reich in the Ivory Tower.*

Listen. If the novel's Buddhist themes resonate, consider pairing your discussion with a short reading from one of the Pāli Canon texts that Charles might have studied, for example, the *Dhammapada* or the *Maṅgala Sutta*. *Tricycle Magazine*'s website offers accessible introductions to ancient Buddhist history and practice.

Cook something South African. Malva pudding is one of South Africa's most beloved desserts—a warm, sticky, toffee-like sponge soaked in a cream sauce. It's simple enough to make with pantry staples, and it pairs well with vanilla ice cream and coffee. Bring it to your book club meeting and you'll be eating from the same world Eugène and Charles Marais inhabited.

Pudding: 1 tbsp butter (room temperature), 1 cup brown sugar, 4 tbsp apricot jam, 1 large egg, 1 cup milk, 2 tbsp vinegar, 2 tsp vanilla essence, 1 cup all-purpose flour, 1 tsp baking soda, ½ tsp salt

Sauce: 2 tbsp butter, 125 ml cream, 4 tbsp brown sugar, 2 tbsp water

Preheat your oven to 350°F. Beat the butter, sugar, jam, and egg together until lightened. Combine the milk, vinegar, and vanilla in a separate bowl. Mix the flour with the baking soda and salt. Alternate adding the wet and dry mixtures into the butter-sugar bowl, stirring as you go. Pour into a greased baking dish and bake for 45 minutes—a knife should come out with spongy crumbs, not wet batter. While the pudding bakes, bring all the sauce ingredients to a boil in a small pot and simmer for three minutes, stirring constantly. When the pudding comes out, poke it all over with a fork and pour the hot sauce slowly over the top. Let it rest for 10-15 minutes to absorb, then serve warm.

Invite the author. Seth Fleisher is available for a free 30-minute virtual Q&A for any book club that selects *The Farther Shore*. To schedule, visit SETHFLEISHER.COM.

Go Deeper: Suggested Further Reading

By Eugène Marais

- *The Soul of the White Ant* (1937)—Marais's groundbreaking study of termite colonies and the organic unity of the termitary, decades ahead of its time. Concepts from his study of the white ants were famously plagiarized by Nobel laureate Maurice Maeterlinck.
- *The Soul of the Ape* (published posthumously, 1969)—his unfinished masterwork on primate behavior, based on years of fieldwork observing chacma baboons in the Waterberg mountains. Introduction by Robert Ardrey.
- *My Friends the Baboons* (English translation of *Burgers van die Berge*, 1975)—a more accessible, narrative account of Marais's years living among baboon troops in the South African bush.
- *The Road to Waterberg and Other Essays* (1972)—collected nonfiction, including some of Marais's journalism and nature writing.

On Marais

- *The Dark Stream: The Story of Eugène N. Marais* by Leon Rousseau—the definitive biography, spanning from early Pretoria in 1871 to three years after Hitler's rise to power, and a deep-dive into South African history in its own right.

On the Boer War, South Africa, and Colonialism

- *Diamonds, Gold, and War: Britain, the Boers, and the Making of South Africa* by Martin Meredith—a sweeping history of the economic and political forces that drove the conflict, from the diamond and gold rushes through the Boer War and the foundations of apartheid.

On Harvard, Eugenics, and the Third Reich

- *The Third Reich in the Ivory Tower: Complicity and Conflict on American Campuses* by Stephen H. Norwood—a meticulously documented account of how America's leading universities, Harvard foremost among them, accommodated and lent legitimacy to Nazi Germany in the 1930s.

Fiction in Conversation with The Farther Shore

- *Middle Passage* by Charles Johnson—National Book Award winner; a philosophical adventure novel about a freed slave aboard a slave ship, blending Buddhism, identity, and the African American experience
- *A Tale for the Time Being* by Ruth Ozeki—Booker Prize finalist; a novel that weaves together Zen Buddhism, quantum physics, and the interconnectedness of lives across the Pacific. Ozeki is also an ordained Zen Buddhist priest
- *A Dry White Season* by André Brink
- *Disgrace* by J.M. Coetzee
- *The Promise* by Damon Galgut

About the Author

Clara Rice

Seth Fleisher is an American author whose work has appeared in the *Bellevue Literary Review*, *Pearl*, the *Journal of Anthropological Research*, and elsewhere. Based in Berkeley, California, he has worked with the World Bank Group and other NGOs in South Africa, India, and more than 40 other countries, and co-founded a U.S.-based democracy initiative to counter the rising tide of authoritarianism. A former Fulbright scholar in Sri Lanka, Seth did Ph.D. work at Harvard in Buddhist social history, a fellowship at Harvard's Center for the Study of World Religions, and a B.A. in literature at Swarthmore, where he and his wife first met in a Chaucer seminar. *The Farther Shore* is his first novel.

sethfleisher

seth.fleisher

Newsletter: sethfleisher.com

www.ingramcontent.com/pod-product-compliance
Lightning Source LLC
LaVergne TN
LVHW091127140926
847902LV00025B/204
9781963101249